"I DON'T KNOW WHERE DAN JENKINS GETS OFF SENDING ME A VULGAR, LOW PIECE OF WORK LIKE THIS ... about football, TV sportscasting, sex, sex, sex, drugs, drugs, and lowlife in Texas and high life in the Jet Set ... I couldn't put it down."
—Liz Smith, *The New York Daily News*

"I LOVED IT! It surpasses *Semi-Tough*. It is laugh-out-loud funny, a hilarious spoof of America, television, football and life its ownself ... Dan Jenkins is a comic genius."
—Don Imus, NBC

"AS HILARIOUS AS *SEMI-TOUGH*—AND MAYBE EVEN RAUNCHIER!"
—*Fort Worth Star Telegram*

"UPROARIOUS HUMOR, superb characterizations, telling observations."
—*Philadelphia Inquirer*

"WONDERFUL! I read it in one sitting and damned near cracked a rib laughing.... My husband is now reading it in bed and keeps waking me up with hoots, howls and fits of guffaws."
—*Cyra McFadden*

"OUTRAGEOUS ... Jenkins will make you gasp and choke and wheeze in laughter."
—*The Arizona Daily Star*

(All this and much more ravin' if ya'll can turn the page ...)

Super Football Books from SIGNET

LIFE ITS OWNSELF

The Semi-Tougher Adventures of
Billy Clyde Puckett and Them

by DAN JENKINS

A SIGNET BOOK

NEW AMERICAN LIBRARY

PUBLISHER'S NOTE

This novel is a work of fiction. Names, characters, places, and incidents either are the product of the author's imagination or are used fictitiously, and any resemblance to actual persons, living or dead, events, or locales is entirely coincidental.

SIGNET, SIGNET CLASSIC, MENTOR, PLUME, MERIDIAN AND NAL BOOKS are published by New American Library, 1633 Broadway, New York, New York 10019

First Signet Printing, September, 1985

1 2 3 4 5 6 7 8 9

PRINTED IN THE UNITED STATES OF AMERICA

This one was always for my ownself.

You win football games with them
horny old boys who want to eat
the crotch out of a end zone.
                    —T. J. LAMBERT

Order us another drink, Billy
Clyde. I'll go ask those girls
what color cars they want.
                    —SHAKE TILLER

There's nothing wrong with my
marriage that a faith healer
can't fix.
                    —BARBARA JANE BOOKMAN

Laughter is the only thing that
cuts trouble down to a size
where you can talk to it.
—BILLY CLYDE PUCKETT

Part One

SEMI-GROWNUPS

ONE

It was never true that I loved my medial collateral ligament more than I loved Barbara Jane Bookman. That was a rumor Barbara Jane started. She started it while I was still active in the National Football League, back in the days when I, me, Billy Clyde Puckett, your basic all-pro immortal, was expected to go out there every Sunday and crack open a 220-pound can of whipass. She also spread it around that I loved Kathy Montgomery more than I loved Barbara Jane Bookman, but, hell, Kathy wasn't my wife. Barbara Jane was. God damn women, anyhow. Sometimes I think T.J. Lambert was right. He always said if women didn't have a pussy, there'd be a bounty on 'em.

As most people know, an injury to the medial collateral cut my pro football career down to an interesting size. All of a sudden, I could sit on a cow chip and swing my legs.

What actually put me out of the game was this thing a speed freak named Dreamer Tatum did to the ligament one Sunday afternoon. What Dreamer did was, he hit me a lick that turned my right knee into a dish of Southern-cooked turnip greens, and when you get a "knee" in pro football, you might as well have a rare strain of incurable, scab-flaking Asi-

15

atic gonorrhea. Here's how they talk about you in the front office:

COACH: Wish we had Billy Clyde Sunday.

OWNER: He's got that knee, you know.

COACH: He'd give us everything he's got.

OWNER: On one knee.

COACH: He's the best we ever had.

OWNER: On two knees.

COACH: Maybe his knee's okay.

OWNER: You can't fix a knee.

COACH: What do you think of our foreign policy in the Middle East?

OWNER: It's fine, except for Billy Clyde's knee.

Fate rolled over on me in the opening game of the season on that Sunday a year ago. Me and the New York Giants were playing Dreamer Tatum and the Washington Redskins. I was in the best condition of my life, ready to start my tenth year with the Giants. In nine seasons as a running back in the NFL, I'd been all-pro six times. Jim Brown's records were safe, but I ranked in your top ten on the all-time rushing list with 9,863 yards. The Giants had been to nearly as many playoffs as the Dallas Cowboys. We had even won a Super Bowl my fifth year when we went out to Los Angeles and whipped the dogass New York Jets.

Not a bad record, some said, for a rascal out of Texas who had come up to Manhattan Island with two pairs of jeans and four dirty shirts and thought veal piccata was a fucked-up chicken-fried steak.

Sorry about the stats. I only recited them because it was my high-gloss reputation as a football hero that made my knee injury seem more important around town than world peace.

If you'd been reading the New York *Daily News*

last autumn, you'd have thought the Commie Chink Iranian Palestinian Nicaraguan Cubans had bombed all the quiche Loraines on Madison Avenue.

GIANTS DON'T HAVE A LEG TO STAND ON!

And other headlines.

The game was on national television that day, so a lot of fans remember the play. They like to bring it up at banquets when I do Q-and-A.

Somebody will say, "Hey, Puckett, tell us about old Dreamer Tatum!" I generally respond with something hilarious, like, "Aw, he still works for the Kremlin."

Maybe it was a Kremlin deal. That injury was the first in a series of preposterous events that not only changed my life but the lives of my friends. It was a year we were going to look back on as the dumbest in the whole history of pro football, and I mean from the flop-eared helmets of the old Canton Bulldogs to the slow-motion instant replay.

All in all, the year was semi-depraved.

My knee turned out to be the least thing anybody had to lose.

The game where I caught the lick wasn't played in Yugoslavia, it just seemed like it. The New York Giants had left Yankee Stadium and moved to New Jersey.

We left New York because our owner, the debonair Burt Danby, got struck with the notion that we would play better football and make more money—mostly the latter—if he took us across the Hudson River and put us down in a landfill for toxic waste.

I hadn't believed we would leave Gotham, even after the New Jersey stadium was under construction.

It wouldn't go unused, I figured. They could always hold gangland rub-outs there. Picnics for turnpike employees.

I had said to the team, "We can't go to New Jersey. What would they call us, the Bridge and Tunnels?"

Nobody was hotter than me about the Giants leaving New York. All of our glory years had been in New York, including the season when Marvin (Shake) Tiller, T.J. Lambert and myself carried us through the playoffs at Yankee Stadium and on into the Super Bowl.

Yankee Stadium was my favorite relic. It reeked with charm and atmosphere. Lacework on the tall bleachers. One end zone along the first-base line, the other out in left-center near the baseball monuments. Ghosts of the past all around you. Urban renewal up there in the sky with the punts and field goals and kickoffs.

There was no sound like the thunder of the crowd in Yankee Stadium. The place had personality. The stadium at the Meadowlands is just the reverse, stark and slick, like walking into the world's biggest skillet.

But Burt Danby is no different from any other owner. They're all in the grueling business of tax avoidance. They all want somebody to give them a modern facility that holds 80,000 people and a wine cellar. If it happens to look more like a Sheraton Hotel than a place for a sports event, so what?

You can dance to this: an owner's taste and sense of history only stretch as far as his greed.

After we moved to New Jersey, nobody in our live-wire publicity office could think of a way to use a hazardous chemical for our helmet logo. The "NY" was simply changed to "GIANTS"—a minor concession to New Jersey's potential ticket buyers. But we continued to be known as the New York Football Giants, thanks to the undying support of our hero-worshiping sportswriters and sell-out broadcasters.

The fans started calling us other things, however.

Comedians, for one. Pricks was popular. Fuckheads caught on.

Back then, T.J. Lambert said, "We just like a little baby what's come out of the womb, Billy Clyde. Little baby can't hurt nobody, and neither can we."

T.J.—nobody ever called him Theodore James— was far more frustrated about the pitiful team we had become than he was about our new area code. He was a lunatic outside linebacker, once a defensive end from Tennessee, who hated the very thought of losing a football game. He'd have an orgasm on every play. From the opening whistle, he'd be as mad as a redneck truckdriver who'd heard a fag come back on his CB.

T.J. truly played football with intensity, which is a word I never heard a coach use but never failed to hear a play-by-play announcer use. T.J. liked to stick his head in there, as they say, which is why he came out of every game with his face looking like a tampon pizza.

T.J. was unique in another way. He was one of those linebackers who didn't need pharmaceuticals to get ready to play.

One day a sportswriter asked him how he always managed to get "up" for the games. T.J. said, "Aw, Coach just comes by and knocks on the door."

T.J. played only one season in the New Jersey stadium. He voluntarily retired after twelve seasons in the league. His career stats were impressive. T.J. accounted for 840 sacks, 84 fumble recoveries, 48 interceptions, 18 permanent injuries, 12 quarterback trades, and 336 limpoffs.

T.J. retired to do what he'd often talked about: become a college coach.

His first coaching job was at Holt-Reams College, a little school out in Kansas that was so rural, the dust bypassed it.

The day he left New York, I went out to LaGuardia to say goodbye to T.J. and his wife, Donna. Donna Lambert was a feisty pine knot of a girl who'd never been as happy living in New York as she was in the days when she twirled a baton in Knoxville.

"We're gonna be fine, Billy Clyde," Donna said at the airport, giving me a hug. "I suppose we'll be on a septic tank, but there won't be no Jews around."

T.J. squeezed my hand and squinted at me. He said, "It's my lifelong ambition come true. Think about it, son. I'm gonna get to mold the minds and bodies of our young pissants."

I thought about it. I hoped the black kids T.J. coached wouldn't mind being called niggers if they fumbled. T.J. would frequently say, "In football, they's niggers and they's blacks. Niggers is what plays for them, blacks is what plays for us." T.J. had drunk with blacks, been laid with blacks, and his roommate on the Giants had been a black guy, Puddin Patterson. Together T.J. and Puddin had wiped out more red-neck honky-tonks than cheap whiskey. But when it came to football, a black better not fumble unless he wanted to be a nigger, just like a white kid better not fumble unless he wanted to be a Polack, a Hunky, a fag, or a Catholic cocksucker. Football players were machinery to T.J. Lambert. Racism was the 220 and the 440.

As a head coach, T.J. amazed all of us who knew him. He quickly turned out two winning teams in Kansas, teams that were loaded with black athletes. Then he upgraded to Southwest Texas State, where his teams went 12–1 and 13–0 and even won the small-college national championship.

I was semi-astonished, if you want the truth. I could just hear him saying to his black quarterback, "One more interception, Leroy, and I'm jerkin' ten pounds of watermelon outta your ass!"

Maybe Joe Paterno wouldn't have been impressed with T.J.'s coaching methods, but I was.

"Fear," T.J. said, explaining his secret to me. "They've took fear out of football, Billy Clyde. Face mask. Quick flags. Can't touch the quarterback, he might get constipated. All I've did is put fear back in the game. Them little fuckers don't win for me, I take away they cars, they dope, they girls, and some I even put in jail. The deputy sheriffs work with me pretty close."

What happened next to T.J.'s career comes under the heading of ironic overload. He moved on again, this time to the head coaching job at TCU, our old school—mine, Shake Tiller's, and Barbara Jane's.

T.J. negotiated himself a five-year contract at Texas Christian University in the bigtime Southwest Conference. The school hired him to restore gridiron greatness to a school which had known it in the days of your Sam Baugh and your Davey O'Brien and your Bob Lilly, not to mention your Puckett and your Tiller.

T.J. went to Fort Worth full of confidence. As he said to the old grads, me included, "We gonna turn this loveboat around. Them Frogs been fartin' upwind."

He had one big problem. It was called recruiting. T.J. soon discovered that the blue-chip athletes coming out of Texas high schools rarely chose to become Horned Frogs. They would enroll at the University of Texas, Oklahoma, Arkansas, SMU, or Texas A&M.

T.J. began to moan about it. He'd call me up and say, "You know what, Billy Clyde? You buy them little shitasses a Trans Am, but if they don't like the way you holler at 'em in practice, they just drive that sumbitch down to A&M and stay there!"

The reality of coaching at a major college sunk in on T.J. his first two years at TCU. The Horned

Frogs lost 18 games and won only 4. T.J. was stunned, but he didn't lose his determination. "Our clock ain't stuck on this two-and-nine shit," he promised the old grads. "We gonna out-work they ass."

I think I can pin down the exact moment the Frogs started on their road to recovery. It was the night I got another phone call from Coach Lambert. In his half-whiskey, half-sleepy voice, he said, "Son, you and Shake Tiller got to help me get that nigger down in Boakum."

Shake Tiller, my oldest and closest friend, didn't like to admit that he cared as much about football as T.J. and me.

Shake's attitude about life in general could be summed up by an expression he often relied on: "It ain't hard to fuck up, it just takes time."

The friendship between Shake Tiller and me—and Barbara Jane, for that matter—dated back to grade school in Fort Worth. Destiny was kind enough to let Shake and me be teammates in high school, then college, and on into the pros. We were as close as you could be without buying each other jewelry.

By close, I mean we were rendered brilliant on countless occasions by the same bottles of young Scotch, we were quite often transformed into Fred Astaire and Noël Coward by the same polio weed, and from our friendly neighborhood druggist we shared the same long-standing prescriptions for preventive fatigue.

Less important to both of us was the fact that we found ourselves in bed with some of the same women, including my wife, the former Barbara Jane Bookman.

For the time being, I'll put aside my recollection of the bulge in Shake's jockstrap, which always brought to mind a boa constrictor. I'll only say that nobody on this planet ever caught footballs the way he did. He had a knack for making the big plays look effortless.

Shake was a pass receiver who ran his routes like a ghost ship. He'd swoop up out of nowhere and hang in the air like a date on a calendar. Then he'd come down with the football on his fingertips, and dart for a touchdown as if the two or three defensive players surrounding him were only out there for set decoration.

One Sunday after he made four leaping catches for touchdowns against the Green Bay Packers, I said to him, "You sumbitch, you're more commercial than water."

He said, "It's not what you've got inside, Billy C., it's how you hand it to the people."

Shake's cavalier approach to life's serious issues almost got me disfigured during a high school game in Fort Worth one night.

Our school was Paschal High. It was south of town, out near TCU, in what was considered to be a "good" area because there were no Mexicans and no trailer camps, your basic tornado targets.

The guys at our school wore clean Levi's with creases in them, golf shirts with little animals on the pockets, and we all had our hair done like Jane Fonda.

On this particular night, we happened to be playing a team from the east side of town, from a school where the guys fancied Mohawk haircuts. They came from a neighborhood where people thought a shopping mall was a self-serve gas station with Ralph's Fill Dirt & Drainage on one side and Wanda's Ceramics and Mill-Outlet Panty Hose on the other.

All through the game, Shake kept getting clipped, speared, arm-hooked, tripped and piled-on by a rather celebrated East Side assassin named Aubrey Williams. My own theory was that Aubrey disliked Shake because he wasn't just a good football player, he was "cute." Aubrey was known to us as someone who liked to puncture tires on cars and hit people with long-handled wrenches. His entire vocabulary consisted of "shit," "piss," "fuck," and "more gravy."

Near the end of the game Shake decided to deal with Aubrey Williams' abuse. He called a time-out and ambled over to Aubrey, removing his helmet and affecting the look of a guy on a peace mission.

But after Shake dug his toe in the ground, the thing he said was, "Uh ... listen, Aubrey. If you don't get off my ass, Billy Clyde's gonna break his hand on your face, and he won't be able to fingerfuck your sister no more."

Aubrey swung instantly, but Shake ducked out of the way, which was more or less how Referee E.L. Burden's jaw got broken. I only lost two teeth and had a bite taken out of my neck in the gangfight that followed.

Shake escaped without a hangnail, naturally. As a matter of fact, in the middle of the brawl, I caught a glimpse of him over on the sideline. He was talking to Lisa Kemp, the only cheerleader we had who didn't make you wear a rubber.

One spring while we were still in Paschal High, Shake performed a series of the greatest athletic feats I've ever witnessed.

It started on the playground during P.E. Some of us on the varsity football squad were playing a game of touch, just jacking around. Our game and a softball game were kind of intruding on each other, and none of us were far from the high-jump pit.

Shake caught a pass in the touch football game and began sidestepping people, me and others. On his way to a touchdown, he scooped up a grounder between second and third in the softball game and threw out the runner at first base, and without breaking stride, he sprinted over to the high-jump pit and cleared the bar at 6-6.

Later that afternoon at Herb's Café, he set a new high-score record on the pinball machine. And that evening when we double-dated in Barbara Jane's family Cadillac, he not only screwed Barbara Jane in the front seat—they were sweethearts then—but he smooth-talked Mary Alice Ramsey into screwing me in the back seat as a personal favor to *him*.

After all this, I never had any doubt about Shake accomplishing whatever he might set out to do in life.

Football came so easy for Shake, he really didn't have much respect for the game. The pros paid him well, which was why he played as long as he did. He was all-pro three years out of his six seasons. But he was always jabbering about wanting to do something more worthwhile, more important, more "meaningful," which is a hard word for me to use without my lip curling up.

A famous book author was what he wanted to be.

There were hints of this illness in college when Shake sought out so many movies with sub-titles, watched so much Public Television, and read so many books.

TCU wasn't Stanford-on-the-Trinity, and Fort Worth wasn't Cambridge, but we did have book-stores and first-run theaters—and a lot more tits. You can't beat Southwest Conference women. Take it from a man who's been in the trenches.

Shake's books were heavier than Godzilla, written by people with slashes and hyphens in their names.

Thick God-damn books. Books that told you why life its ownself was a suit that didn't fit, how your soul was apt to get thrown up on a roof where you couldn't get it down, and how nobody knew a fucking thing except some European with a beard who sat in a dark room and played with himself.

Eventually, Shake decided he knew as much about life as any living American. He said it would be a tragedy not to share his knowledge with mankind. He would become a writer, and why should it be so difficult? All you had to do was sit at a desk and let the Olivetti go down on you.

Frankly, I thought the best reason to become a writer was because of what Shake told me about scholarly women. He said that if he became a famous book author, he could go out on lecture tours and nail a lot of ladies who wore glasses.

Many of those ladies were a hidden minefield of delight, Shake said. Their arrogant expressions intrigued him. Their manner of dress—Terrorist Chic—was deceptive. Underneath the fatigues, the plump ones wouldn't be that plump, and the skinny ones wouldn't be that skinny, and the truth was that when you got behind their icy glares and worked your way down to the goal line with one of them, the thing you would have on your hands was a closet treasure—a squealing, back-clawing, lust-ridden, talk-dirty-to-me, won't-spill-a-drop nympho-acrobat.

"Billy C., we've been severely handicapped all these years because we're nothing but athletes," he explained. "If you'd ever read a novel, you'd know what I mean. What's happened is, you and me have missed out on a whole bunch of literary pussy."

Shake played one more year of football after our Super Bowl season, but I'm not sure you could have called it football.

We spent most of our spare time in bars and honky-tonks, holding our Super Bowl rings up to our lips and speaking into them like they were two-way radios.

The rings were beautiful. They were huge, gold, diamond-encrusted, had a bright blue stone in them, and were fun to talk to.

"Crippled Chick to Mother Hen, come in, Mother Hen," one of us would say to his ring, usually when ordering another young Scotch or Tequila Suicide.

We might be in Runyon's, Clarke's, Melon's, Juanita's, McMullen's, even all the way up to Elaine's, hitting every candy store on Second and Third Avenues in search of Christianity.

Or we might be on the road in a city like Atlanta where they have those after-hours clubs that offer you a little packet of dread with every third drink and don't announce last-call till February.

Wherever we might be, it was inevitable that somebody would holler at his ring, "Mayday, Mayday!"

That would be a signal for everyone to look at the young lady coming into the saloon. If the young lady happened to resemble the third runnerup in the Miss Homewrecker Pageant, you'd hear another battle cry from our table.

"Face mask!"

That would be the ultimate compliment to the young lady from one of our freelance gynecologists.

There were evenings when Barbara Jane went out with us. She, too, would get around to speaking into a Super Bowl ring.

What she most often said was:

"Leaving now. Bored."

Our world-championship team broke up pretty fast after Shake Tiller quit to pursue commas and apostrophes.

The next player to retire was Hose Manning, our laser-vision quarterback. Hose moved back home to Purcell, Oklahoma, to sell front-end-loaders.

Puddin Patterson, my roadgrader, our best offensive lineman, fell in with Dreamer Tatum of the Jets and tried to organize a players' strike. It never got organized, but that's why the Jets traded Dreamer to Washington and Burt Danby traded Puddin to San Francisco.

As Burt Danby put it, those cities were perfect for your "mondo, craze-o, leftist derelicts."

Puddin was pleased about going to the Bay Area. He had always wanted to open a gourmet food store.

Bobby Styles, our reliable free safety, beat the rape charge, but his heart was never in the game after the scandal. He married the fourteen-year-old girl, settled in Baton Rouge, and became a partner in Shirley's Tree & Stump Removal. Shake always said Bobby wore his I.Q. on his jersey. Bobby was No. 20.

Rucker McFarland turned queer. He was the first defensive tackle to make a public announcement about his genes. We were all disturbed to hear about his problem, but at least it cleared up the mystery of why he had kept so many rolls of designer fabric in his locker.

Story Time Mitchell, our all-pro cornerback, was the saddest case. They called it "possession with intent to sell." He was sentenced to fifteen years in a Florida joint.

He handled it like a trooper. Got pardoned after three. Guys from around the league wrote to him regularly and sent him CARE packages—cakes, cookies, video cassettes, beaver magazines—because he refused to name any of his customers. Story Time was a competitor.

These guys were the guts of our team, along with me and T.J., of course, so when they left, there was hardly any reason to wonder why the Giants went downhill.

In the middle of the decline, Shoat Cooper, our coach, dug a deep one out of his ass one day, spit on the floor, and said, "You know what you jokers look

like to me? You look like somebody's done licked all
the red off your lollipop."

Our brain trust, which was Shoat Cooper and Burt
Danby, tried to rebuild the dynasty. The record shows
how good a job they did. Through our portals swag-
gered the grandest collection of scum ever perpe-
trated on a squad room.

When we didn't welcome a sullen, millionaire rookie
who wouldn't learn his plays and traveled with a
business manager, we inherited a malcontent who'd
been with five other clubs and came to us with a
nickname like Dump, Point Spread, or Bail-Out.

It seemed like the harder I played, the more games
we lost. Shake had a good football mind. I asked him
one evening in a tavern what he thought our biggest
problems were.

He looked off from his cocktail for a minute, then
turned back to me with a sigh. "Billy C., I'd rather
try to tell somebody what an oyster tastes like."

Shake was busy on a novel before his last football
season was over. For a time, he flirted with the idea
of giving up his penthouse apartment in the high-
rise at 56th and First Avenue and buying a loft in
SoHo, thinking the artistic environment would stir
his creative juices.

SoHo had become a desirable area of lower Manhattan for reasons that could only be answered by
the friends of dissident poets or rabid sculptors. It
was the newest place to go watch activist groups eat
croissants.

Shake dismissed the idea of moving after Barbara
Jane pointed out to him SoHo had an abundance of
vegetarian restaurants with no-smoking areas.

I wasn't sure what to expect from Shake Tiller the
Writer. Maybe I thought he would take to wearing a
Lenin cap or something, but his lifestyle didn't change.

He did begin to jot things down on napkins, and he grew a short beard, which looked surprisingly good on him.

The title of his novel was *The Grade-B Plot*. I have a confession. Like the vast majority of Americans, I didn't read much past the first paragraph either.

Originally, his first paragraph consisted of three words.

This said Riley:

That was it. New paragraph.

When Shake handed me the manuscript to glance at one night, I said, "You got a semi-colon in there real quick."

"Colon," he corrected.

"Well, colon, semi-colon, what the fuck," I said.

It was the kind of response Shake might have expected from a guy who'd once made an effort to write a book of his own, your typical professional athlete's memoir—why I'm great because I know how to talk to a tape recorder and get a sportswriter to clean up the grammar.

I had failed in my literary attempt, not because it wasn't art like *The Grade-B Plot*, but because I took the trouble to read it and thought it sounded like a joke book that had been put into a blender with *The Sporting News*.

Unlike I would have done it, Shake re-wrote the first paragraph of *The Grade-B Plot* sixty times, but when the novel made its way into the bookstores, the only improvement I saw was in the length. The book began:

The moon was a half-scoop of vanilla that night and Riley had the slab of raw liver strapped to his bare chest when he entered the campus library.

He knew Laura would be in there somewhere, screaming at Proust as usual, or mutilating pages of Dostoyevsky. He figured they might as well go over the edge together. Funny how much she had changed since the Okefenokee Swamp.

Like most first novels, *The Grade-B Plot* sold extremely well in northeastern Kentucky. The publisher, Wanderjahr Books, a subsidiary of Haver & Giles, ordered a first printing of 2,000 copies. Shake's agent, Silvia Mercer, said this was very good, as did his editor, Maureen Pemberton, a good friend of Silvia Mercer's.

Shake said literary pussy was overrated, after all. Maybe the better-known authors in Silvia Mercer's stable could appreciate her 187 pounds of energy, her pigtails, and her smock, but Shake had known pulling guards with straighter teeth and more reverence for the written word.

He was happy to be published, of course, but he wondered how often Thomas Hardy had stooped to "duty fucking."

The reviews of Shake's novel ranged from vicious to—his word—disorienting.

A reviewer in *The New York Times* called it a book for anyone who had "lost faith in the human race."

The reviewer, a professor of English at the University of Arkansas, went on to condemn the publisher for even sending the novel to the printer and binder. "How long," the man asked, "must serious artists go unrewarded while crude athletes, solely on the strength of their names, are allowed to achieve the permanence of hardcover and sit smugly on bookshelves?"

Shake said, "That's interesting. *I* can't find the fucking book anywhere."

Silvia Mercer got excited because *Time* magazine reviewed the book.

"A bad review in *Time* is very important," she said to Shake. "It's better than being ignored."

Shake would rather have been ignored.

The *Time* critic wrote:

In *The Grade-B Plot,* First Novelist Marvin (Shake) Tiller, a former professional football player, devotes 279 pages to the question of inaccessibility. Exactly how far should the writer remove himself from his characters and story? Tiller would have us believe there is no limit.

"What'd I do wrong?" Shake asked his agent.

"You didn't take any risks," Silvia Mercer said. "You didn't stretch yourself."

"I was too busy typing."

The commercial failure of Shake's novel drove him straight into non-fiction. He started to work on *The Art of Taking Heat,* a how-to book designed to help the average person cope with life its ownself, and he took up exposé journalism. He started doing pieces for *Esquire, Playboy, Rolling Stone, New York, Texas Monthly.*

This in itself wasn't so bad. Who among us doesn't like to know that certain leading men in Hollywood are only five feet tall and stuff washrags into their elastic briefs? Or learn that certain United States Congressmen have fathered dozens of illegitimate children in Latin America who will now blow you up with homemade bombs?

I think it's fair to say that Shake's journalistic exploits in no small way added to the confusion in our lives after Dreamer Tatum busted my knee.

*   *   *

About that play.

We were down on Washington's 6-yard line in the third quarter, behind by 14 points. A touchdown could turn the momentum around. Fourth down came up and I expected us to throw the ball, so you can imagine my surprise when our quarterback called Student Body Left.

Student Body Left was a power sweep for me, Old 23. The play had been a moneymaker for us when I had Puddin Patterson to block for me. It was the play I'd scored on in the last four seconds to beat the dogass Jets 31—28 in the only Super Bowl that was ever worth a shit.

The situation wasn't the same, though.

For one thing, Puddin Patterson was no longer around. He was busily selling rabbit pâtés in San Francisco. He had been replaced on the left side of our offensive line by Alvin (Point Spread) Powell. Point Spread Powell's idea of a block was to assume the fetus position about one second after the ball was snapped.

And there was this other thing. Obert (Dreamer) Tatum, The Black Death, was across the line of scrimmage, which was where he had not been in that Super Bowl when we made our game-winning drive.

Any loyal fan of the Jets would be quick to remind you that Dreamer Tatum had sprained his ankle in the fourth quarter of that Super Bowl. Dreamer had been watching from the sideline when we punched it in.

Loyal Jets fans were easy to recognize in my day. You just looked for the little old lady being mugged, and there they were.

Well, Dreamer was not only out there wearing the braid of his five years as an all-pro cornerback, he had something else going for him. I had noticed earlier in the game that Dreamer had fortified himself with a handful of amphetamines.

Dreamer and I had known and respected each other a long time. We had traded enough licks to be married. And nobody knew better than me that you didn't spend a lot of time running the football at him when his eyes had a maniacal gaze and he chewed his gum so fast, the slobber ran down his chin.

Dreamer's condition prompted a minor rebellion in our huddle when the quarterback, Floyd (Dump) McKinney, called the running play.

"Are you crazy?" I said to Dump. "*Dreamer's* over there!"

"We'll hit at their strength. Cross 'em up," he said.

"Who will?"

"Let's go, Billy Clyde. We'll take his ass to the parking lot."

"Have you looked at him lately?" I said. "Put the ball in the air!"

"My hand hurts."

"Your *hand* hurts?" I blurted out. "Did you bet Washington?"

"Fuck, no," Dump said. "They went to ten and a half."

Now, then. I don't happen to be a person who goes through life looking for signs of impending doom. Even so, I hadn't come in contact with a cross-eyed Mexican that morning. I hadn't seen a red-headed spade, or a gray dog shit on the sidewalk, or a lone goose fly across the marsh.

All of which was why I shut up in the huddle and took the handoff from Dump McKinney and ran the ball in my normal way—not fast, not slow, not fancy, but sort of in a threading, weaving, determined fashion.

The blow came while I was in the air.

I was jumping over Point Spread Powell when

Dreamer's shoulder flew into my knee. It wasn't the lick itself that did me in. I landed awkwardly and 2,000 pounds of Redskin stink came down on top of me.

I didn't hear the tear of the medial collateral ligament and everything else that got cross-threaded. Maybe it did sound like somebody opening an envelope, as a newspaper guy wrote. All I knew was, the inside of my knee was on fire. You couldn't have moved my leg with a tractor-pull.

Everybody was untangling when I said, "You can turn me over, Dreamer. I'm done on this side."

"Aw, shit, Clyde, are you hurt bad?" He scrambled to his feet.

"Yeah," I groaned. "I think your pharmacist finally got me.

Dreamer made frantic gestures toward our bench. He was genuinely concerned. He helped the trainers lift me onto a stretcher and he walked all the way to our sideline with me.

The last thing I saw in the stadium was a fat woman wearing an Indian headdress and a buckskin pant suit. She screamed at me like a psychopath as the trainers carried the stretcher into a tunnel.

"We got you, Puckett!" she yelled, waving a tomahawk in the air. She glared down at me over a railing. "We got you good! Does it *hurt*? Oh, I hope it hurts you good! I hope you limp the rest of your life, you slimy bastard!"

Given a choice, I suppose I'd rather have heard the woman sing a chorus of "Hail to the Redskins."

We moved through the tunnel beneath the stands, and one of the trainers looked down at me.

"How'd you like to be married to *that*, Billy Clyde?"

"You'd have one problem," I said. "With all those dirty dishes in the sink, there wouldn't be nowhere to piss."

In the dresing room, the team physician, Dr. Fritz Mahoney, pushed around on my knee.

"Won't know til I see the X-rays, old chum, but I'm afraid you've been Dick Butkused," he said with a hum.

It would have been more accurate if Dr. Fritz Mahoney had said I'd been Gale Sayersed. Sayers had been a running back, Butkus a linebacker. But I got the drift.

Damage to the medial collateral, a vital ligament in the middle of the knee, had prematurely ended the careers of Dick Butkus and Gale Sayers, two of your legendary Chicago Bears. Overnight, they had become famous medial collateralists.

I knew enough about the injury to realize that if I ever did go on a football field again, I'd have to wear a knee brace the size of a Toyota Cressida and play with considerable pain, but even though I understood all this, the competitor in me came out. To the doctor, I said, "This ain't the end of my ass!"

Dr. Fritz Mahoney said, "Spunk helps, Billy Clyde. Never underestimate the value of spunk. We in the medical profession place a great deal of trust in spunk."

"I'll play again—you want to bet on it?"

"Spunk can do wonders," the doctor said. "But I'll be honest. Spunk can't help you this season."

"Next year!" I said. "Football's not through with me till *I* say it is!"

Dr. Fritz Mahoney clasped my upper arm and looked at me proudly.

"I like your style, Billy Clyde."

"Good," I said. "Me and spunk want a corner room at Lenox Hill with a cable-ready color TV."

*   *   *

The most esteemed guests to visit the hospital that evening were Burt Danby; his wife, Veronica; and Shoat Cooper, the old coacher.

"Kiss on the lips, big guy!" Burt said, as he exploded into the room, doing a little dance step. "Hey, I know you're down, right? But are we talking down-down? No way! We're not talking Mondo Endo here. We're talking Johns Hopkins, baby. We're talking Houston Medical. We're talking Zurich!"

I raised myself in the bed slightly. Veronica took a seat, browsed through a magazine. Shoat Cooper dabbed at a tear, his eyes fixed on my right leg. His whole offense lay in my bed.

"Them niggers is gonna pay for this," Shoat said.

Burt Danby kept moving around. "Get this," he said. "Know what I told the media about Twenty-three? I said, Whoa, assholes, my man'll be back next season with a Gucci knee, and it's look out, Super Bowl! Whammo-spermo! Right up the old anal! Listen, you got everything you need here? How's the food? Right in the shitter, huh? Let me order you some Chinese. How 'bout some minced pork with lettuce? Fuck it, I'll call Pearl, she'll bring it over herself!"

Burt Danby was a wiry little man who had never stopped talking like an advertising executive. His old agency, DDDF, had purchased the Giants from the Mara family in the early Seventies. Burt had been named the club's chief operating officer. He had presided over our Super Bowl victory. He had suffered so much throughout the turbulent contest that he had sworn to God he would give up drinking and cheating on his wife if only we could win that one game. I later heard that after I scored the winning touchdown, Burt had jumped to his feet, shook his fist at God, and hoarsely screamed, "Fuck you, Skipper, if you can't make it in Big Town, go to Des Moines!"

A year after the Giants won the Super Bowl, Burt had somehow gained majority control of the franchise in a mysterious stock transaction and left the agency. It was said Burt had a silent partner in the deal. It was also said he might wind up living in Costa Rica if the Justice Department ever took a close look at the stock transaction.

"TV!" Burt said, brightly, feeling the need to cheer me up. "You'll go straight into television when you bust out of here! You got a season to jerk off; why not?"

Burt said the networks were sure to offer me a job as a color announcer. CBS and NBC would get in a bidding war. Billy Clyde Puckett would be the only winner.

"You serious?"

"Does the Pope shit in the woods?"

I laughed at that and Burt pressed on. "You think you make good dough from me? TV is God's way of telling you to rape, steal, and plunder. It's a fucking soufflé! You know what those guys make? Gifford . . . Summerall . . . Madden? Cosell? Meredith? They can buy the Vatican and redecorate!"

Burt went into a crouch. He stared at an imaginary object in front of him. "Here's the network, you're the Canadian sheepdog, okay?."

He humped the thin air.

"Uh . . . uh . . . uh!" he moaned, then straightened up. "Now you scoop the coin; see you later!"

"I wouldn't be any good on television," I said.

Burt looked astounded.

"*Good?* You want to talk good? Good is who wears a blazer and has a microphone. Know how you make it big in TV, Billy Clyde? First, you're an athlete, then you go to makeup. All you gotta be after that is deaf, dumb, and blind!"

Shoat Cooper's eyes were still misty. He said he guessed he'd better shove off.

"Africa," Shoat said, taking another look at my leg. "You can trace the whole blame back to Africa."

Burt's wife, Veronica, comforted me by commenting on how unattractive hospitals were.

Veronica Danby was an ex–"fashion person," a cadaver whose dark brown hair had been styled into a shower cap. She was two-thirds cheekbones and one-third pout. She seemed disappointed that my room wasn't a boutique in which she might pick up a little something from Ungaro for $1,500.

Veronica did ask if Barbara Jane had done anything to her eyes yet.

Not that I was aware of, I said, but what did I know? Barb was out in L.A., working on a pilot for ABC. Anything could have happened.

"She's thirty-four, isn't she?"

"Will be," I said. "Is that the age when your eyes go?"

"One never knows. Wrinkles are so treacherous."

I accepted that piece of information with a nod.

Veronica said, "I'm sure she doesn't use strong cleansers anymore. I've learned to stay strictly with non-alcoholic lotions."

"Oh?" I said.

"They refreshen the pores," said Veronica. "Occasionally, I put on a light cream to soothe the skin and increase circulation, but when I have a facial massage, I make sure I tell the masseuse Do *not* pull the skin! It's the worst thing you can do!"

"Really?"

"Oh, yes," Veronica said. "The idea is to keep the skin taut and firm."

Burt beamed at me as they were leaving.

"Got one for you, big guy," he said. "Pal of mine at Doyle Dane goes with this actress on *The Guiding Light*. He thought they'd done all the sperm capers but he made a hell of a discovery the other night. Eyelashes on the clit. Says he can blink her off in no time."

I had a while to think about that before the phone started ringing.

Dreamer Tatum called. T.J. from Fort Worth. Ex-teammates like Hose Manning and Puddin Patterson. Jim Tom Pinch, an old newspaper buddy. Others. Hang in there, they all said.

Shake Tiller phoned from Houston. He was swinging through the South on a promotional tour for the paperback release of *The Art of Taking Heat*. His book had been a nonfiction best-seller the previous year.

The book had been published in hardcover by Viva Press, a subsidiary of Quillam, Dupe & Strike. Silvia Mercer, Shake's agent, had peddled the idea to an editor friend named Rosemary Compton, arguing that *The Art of Taking Heat* would appeal to that mass of readers in the Advice, How-to, and Miscellaneous category who might be fed up with diets, exercise, and money-managing.

Shake's book sold over 200,000 copies in hardcover, though it never dislodged *Get Rich in 30 Seconds* as the No. 1 best-seller on all of the heavy lists. Still, the book's success had turned Shake Tiller into a semi-known author. This not only meant he'd had to appear on drive-time radio shows and early-morning TV shows around the country, he'd been obligated to fuck Silvia Mercer again, and then Rosemary Compton.

He had once said that Xeroxing was the toughest part of writing, but he had changed his mind.

Paperback tours differed from hardcover tours, Shake had discovered. You didn't sell books or autograph many of them on either tour, but there was drastically less literary pussy on the paperback tour—unless a man had a weakness for the pudgy girls who ran the checkout counters at supermarkets.

On hardcover tours, Shake had spent most of his time apologizing to the cultivated owners of bookstores because his book had been published and theirs hadn't. Occasionally, he would sit and smoke at a table in the store and point out to a browsing customer where the bird books could be found. On the paperback tours, he would mill around the grocery stores, occasionally be recognized as an ex–football star, and be asked to autograph twelve slices of Virginia ham wrapped in butcher's paper.

Now on the phone from Houston, he said, "Hi, gimp. Luckiest thing ever happened to you, B.C. You can go into TV. Rob everybody's ass."

"You're the second person who's told me that tonight."

"You went out perfect, man. A wounded warrior whose career was struck down by tragic fate. Fuck 'em. Football's not the same anymore, anyhow."

"There's still eleven men on a side."

"Not on the Giants," he said. "Go for the slick, B.C. Sit up there in the booth with Summerall. Tell everybody how the quarterack wants to isolate on the linebacker. Hell, you might wind up in a beer commercial."

"I drink Scotch."

"We'll do some of that when I get back."

"How's the book going?"

"Selling like salami."

The conversation with Shake didn't necessarily boost my spirits.

For the next hour, I squirmed in the bed. I was half-rooting for the painkillers to get with it, half-wondering if I would ever play football again.

Was it really possible I'd never climb into another uniform, never trot into another stadium, never blow another one in there for six, never hear the crowds again?

Football was the only thing I'd ever done.

I was in a fairly miserable state of mind, feeling a terrible sense of loss, when the phone rang for the last time that night.

I fumbled for the receiver and greeted the caller with a weak hello.

"Quasimodo, how you doin'? A little trouble up on the bell tower, huh?"

It was the witty voice of my sympathetic wife.

TWO

Somebody once described marriage to me as one year in Heaven and twenty years in the Light Heavyweight Division.

It couldn't have been my Uncle Kenneth who said that. He stored up a backlog of ex-wives for sure, but he never stayed married long enough to know their bathroom habits.

Not that my uncle was ever torn up when the ladies walked out on him, usually in a foaming rage over some domestic misunderstanding.

Uncle Kenneth would just shake his head, light a Winston, and say, "There goes old Connie. God help the world if she'd been born twins."

Having been raised by my uncle in Fort Worth, I was privileged to watch a steady stream of bimbos go in and out of our duplex apartment.

Some of their names were easier to remember than others.

Dorothy was the one who had hair the color of V-8 juice. Ina Fay ran up the department-store bills. Patsy had an epileptic brother we used to imitate. Teresa played the radio loud and jitterbugged around the living room in her shortie nightgown. Bobbi Lynn had trouble with fever blisters.

All of Uncle Kenneth's wives knew how to cook

butter beans. They had jobs. They either answered the phone for optical companies or licked envelopes stuffed with freight invoices.

They looked like funeral wreaths when they dressed up to go somewhere. None of them drove air-conditioned cars.

Connie was the one who could outcuss Uncle Kenneth. She was kind of attractive for a woman whose hair was always in a blonde beehive and whose skirts were too tight, but she wasn't too pretty when she was displeased with my uncle.

If Uncle Kenneth would come home late from a hard day of betting football games at the pool hall, and if he happened to have a can of Budweiser in his hand, and if there was the normal amount of vomit on his tasseled loafers, Connie's lecture would have a little something extra in it.

She would say:

"Fuck you, Kenneth, and everything your light-weight ass stands for! You smell like four kinds of turds in a Goddamn fillin'-station toilet! What whore's ass did you crawl up and die in tonight? You think you're a slick cocksucker, but you ain't no slicker than two snakes fuckin' in a barrel of snot! Don't come near me, you limp-prick motherfucker, unless you want to wear that beer to the emergency room!"

Uncle Kenneth learned not to step up the back-talk with Connie. He would just stroll quietly across the room and stretch out on the pink chenille spread that covered the day bed from Montgomery Ward and turn on TV to watch what he called the "ambulance news."

Once he had responded to one of her tirades with "Connie, are you sayin' my poem don't rhyme?"

That was the night she whapped him on the ear with the metal bar from a Eureka vacuum cleaner.

I used to wonder why Uncle Kenneth kept getting

married. It always turned out the same. One day I put the question to him at the Texas Recreation Parlor.

"Aw, I don't know, Billy," he said, studying a tout sheet, trying to figure out why Purdue came 3½ over Duke. "I think you have to blame it on Wilbur. You can't talk no sense to him."

Wilbur was the name of my uncle's dick.

My momma and daddy split up when I was six years old. As Uncle Kenneth liked to tell it, my dad, Steve, unfolded a Texaco road map one evening and laid it out on the kitchen table. He drew a vertical line down the middle of the United States. He then turned to Dalene—that was my momma's name—and said:

"You take this side and I'll take this side right here."

"Fine," Dalene said. "Are you sure half the country's enough room for you to chase after your little girls with the yellow curls and the merry eyes?"

Steve said, "That's what I'll be looking for, fond as I am of your hair-curlers."

"Butt Hole!" my momma shouted. "If you don't get what you deserve in this life, you can thank God for His kindness!"

Steve said, "What I'll thank him for is that you ain't gonna haunt my heart like a damned old movie star! You won't even be a memory!"

"Is that a fact?" said Dalene. "Well, all I'll remember is your zipper goin' up and down like a window shade!"

Life is a series of choices. I was told I could either go to California and watch Steve sell floor covering, or I could go to Mobile and watch Dalene take care of her sick mother and look for a new husband.

Evidently, what I said to both of them was "I want

to go to Uncle Kenneth's house. He likes sports and he don't holler."

I never saw Dalene again.

She did send me $5 every Christmas until she died when I was fourteen. She had remarried by then and given birth to three other kids. Apparently, the kids jumped up and down on the furniture so much, a headache did her in.

Uncle Kenneth took me to the funeral in Mobile.

It was my first funeral, but I figured out from the seating arrangement in the funeral parlor and at the cemetery that her new husband, Raymond, was the man on the front row in the windbreaker and the Schlitz cap.

Being at the funeral was a strange feeling because I didn't know my momma at all, but the trip wasn't a complete loss. After the funeral, Uncle Kenneth and me drove up to Tuscaloosa for the Alabama—Ole Miss game.

I saw my dad only one time after he moved to California. It was when I was a junior at TCU and we played an intersectional game against USC in Los Angeles.

On the morning of the game, I was standing around in the lobby of the Century Plaza Hotel with Shake and Barbara Jane. We were killing time. Shake and I were waiting to board the team bus to the L.A. Coliseum. We were laughing at all of the TCU fans in their purple blazers and purple leather cowboy boots when this man came toward us, and I couldn't help staring at him because of his outfit. He wore green slacks, a pink Munsingwear shirt, a red-and-yellow-checked linen coat, and white mesh-top shoes. He had an admirable tan. I thought he was just another California nitwit who wanted an autograph from me and Shake, your basic All-Americans. He didn't look anything like Uncle Kenneth, his brother.

"Hello, Billy," the man said, sticking out his hand. "I'm your dad."

Before I could speak, Shake said, "What's your name?"

"Steve." The man looked blankly at Shake. "Steve Puckett."

"What was his mother's name?" Shake gestured.

"Dalene."

"What street did you live on in Fort Worth?" Steve stammered.

"Uh . . . Travis. Then over on Hemphill."

"Could be him."

Barbara Jane folded her arms as she studied Steve. She said, "Sir, I'm sorry, but I've known Billy Clyde's mother and father a long time. They're both named Kenneth."

Out of embarrassment for Steve, I led him aside, seeing no reason to subject him to Shake and Barbara Jane's wisemouth.

We had a brief visit. He said he was proud of me. He said he followed my "dipsy-dos" in the newspapers. He said he had meant to write several times over the past fifteen years, but things had been hectic in the floor-covering business. He said he'd bought a new set of MacGregor irons and they had lowered his handicap to 12.

He glanced around the lobby at my teammates, some of whom were black.

"How you get along with the nigs?"

"Fine," I said. "They're good guys."

"Nigs is?"

"Yeah."

"Don't steal nothin'?"

"No."

"Don't even borrow nothin'?"

"No. I borrow some of their albums."

He said, "Lord, I seen one the other day that

gimme a pause. He was one of your hippie nigs? He stood there on Wilshire Boulevard and took a piss in broad daylight!"

"No fooling?"

"Yep, right there on Wilshire Boulevard. I said to myself, Well, is this the end of civilization as we know it, or is it just another nigger pissin' on Wilshire Boulevard?"

"It's a great country."

My dad apologized for having been semi-halfway responsible for making me the victim of a broken home.

I said he didn't need to apologize for a single thing. Uncle Kenneth had given me everything I'd needed, plus a good many laughs.

He said, "Billy, I was sorry to hear about your mother. I never wanted her to bogey eighteen. I did root for a sore throat from time to time. Damn, she had a temper."

"You got married again, didn't you?"

"Twice," he said, sheepishly. "Learned my lesson. Cora burned my name in the eighteenth green at Rancho Park. Eileen threw a brand-new set of Pings in the ocean—can you believe that?"

My dad was killed two years later. You could make him sound like he was a successful businessman if you said he got killed in a private-plane crash. The fact is, he got killed on the golf course where the private plane crashed.

He hadn't been able to get his Titleist 4 and Wilson wedge out of a sand trap in time to avoid a Cessna that lost power and suddenly dropped out of the smog and made the bunker a little deeper.

Old Steve was no big authority on relationships, but that morning in the Century Plaza lobby, he left me with some words I never forgot.

"Billy, I ain't too smart or I wouldn't be trying to

sell cork tile," he had said. "I know you play a tough sport. You got them big, mean tackles comin' at you. But I'll tell you one thing about life. You ain't took no lumps at all till you've tried marital discord."

Given the mood I was in while I floundered in the hospital bed for a week, you couldn't blame for me for the ludicrous things I thought about.

I spent days watching elderly patients creeping past my room, and I wondered how many of them would be shuffled into a nursing home where they'd live out their days playing dominoes until they swallowed the double-6, believing it to be an Oreo cookie.

I tried to estimate how many patients might be dying of malpractice because of my floor nurse. She continually looked flustered and said things like "This God-damn place is comin' down over my ears!"

But mostly I thought about all of the obstacles life puts in the way of marriage.

There in my room at Lenox Hill—me, my knee, and a mound of magazines and newspapers—I pondered the fact that I was now in my thirties and I only knew two couples who hadn't been divorced or estranged.

One couple was Barbara Jane's parents, Big Ed and Big Barb Bookman. They had exchanged some sharp language, but they would never entertain the idea of divorce for two reasons. First, it would be socially inconvenient, and second, it would take Big Barb and her lawyers the rest of their lives to dig up West Texas and find all of Big Ed's money.

Big Ed once said, "Show me a woman who wants a divorce, and I'll show you a beady-eyed lawyer comin' out of her closet!"

The other couple was T.J. and Donna Lambert. They would never split up because they both liked Stouffer's chicken pot pies.

But almost every guy I'd ever known had been married two, three, and four times, most often to an undiscovered actress or airline stewardess—er, excuse me, flight attendant.

This didn't include Shake Tiller. He had been on record for years as saying he would rather be confined to a Syrian prison than have to discuss furniture ads with a female roommate.

Dump McKinney came to mind with no trouble. I thought of how he might just as easily have fumbled the handoff to me the way he had fumbled all of his marriages, in which case I'd still be playing football. I wouldn't be in a hospital trying to read a story in *People* magazine about a meditative movie actor who recommended tofu with sage as an alternative to a heavy Thanksgiving dinner.

Dump McKinney held one pro football record that would never be touched. He married three flight attendants and two Dallas Cowboys cheerleaders. I learned of his fifth marriage and fifth divorce one evening watching television.

It had come to the attention of *60 Minutes* that the progressive city of Dallas had spawned a flurry of drive-in divorce centers in which lawyers were handling as many as 175 quickie divorces a day. I was watching the program when who should pop onto my screen but a disheartened Dump McKinney and his new ex-wife, Cheryl.

"I can't explain it," Dump said to the camera, his head drooping sadly. "I thought we were the two happiest people in the world."

The TV reporter turned to Cheryl. "How long were you married?"

"Three days."

"Three days?" said the reporter, trying not to laugh. "What can go wrong in only three days?"

Cheryl ran a brush through her long blond hair, and said, "We just didn't have nothin' in common."

Love was brutally outnumbered. That's how I saw it in the hospital that week. Maybe love could hold his own during depressions and wars, but if you gave people a little money and leisure time, love was in deep shit.

I made a list as I lay in the hospital bed. There wasn't much else to do but glower at the cast on my leg or watch vampires make rock music on cable TV.

As I observed it, love was forced to go up against the following enemies:

- The insane cost of living.
- The stranglehold of analysts.
- Male-chauvinist jerks.
- Male-chauvinist feminists.
- Liberated wenches.
- Bizarre sexual demands.
- No sex at all.
- His or her lack of political "awareness."
- Whiskey.
- Recreational drugs.
- Born-again.
- Porsche overhauls.
- Rumors.
- Gossip.
- Confidant fags.
- Overly familiar barmaids.
- People "preoccupied with success."
- Partners "suffocating" for undisclosed reasons.
- Partners who have stomped on all the magic.
- People who change.
- People who refuse to change.
- *Architectural Digest.*
- Pornography.

- Bumper stickers ("Nuke the Fag Whales for Jesus").
- Office flirtations.
- Jogging.
- Business travel.
- Dinner parties.
- Sports on TV.
- No-smoking areas.
- Discos.
- Cold pasta salads.
- Betamax.
- Bloomingdale's.
- Perrier.
- Ingmar Bergman.
- She's too "assertive."
- He's not "supportive" enough.
- Numbing boredom.

And . . .

- "I'm a person, too, you selfish mutant!"

There was a time when Barbara Jane would have agreed with me that none of those things could have affected us. We were too clever. And then some of them *did* affect us—and there we were, as human as everybody else.

Nothing in our history had indicated we would ever become human. If anything, the opposite was true.

Barbara Jane and Shake Tiller and I had known each other since the third grade. It was in the third grade that we had formed our own private club, a society dedicated to laughing at life its ownself.

We began by laughing at the things other kids put in their sandwiches at Daggett Elementary. *Chunky* peanut butter? Then we laughed at everybody's clothes, and everybody's parents. I suppose you could say it got out of hand because everything after that seemed humorous, especially anything serious, except Barbara Jane didn't laugh much about Kathy Montgomery later on.

Growing up, the three of us developed the same outlook on learning, achieving, surviving. We came to share the same beliefs about all the big stuff. Observing grownup behavior, I suspect, had more to do with it than anything.

We agreed you had an obligation to take whatever you were blessed with in life and try to keep a shine on it.

We said you shouldn't live out your favorite songs too seriously.

We took an oath not to hurt anybody on our way up, but we said it was okay to use some lip if you started to slip.

We thought the main thing you had going for you in life was what *you* did.

We considered it dangerous to place our complete trust in anybody who hadn't gone to Paschal High.

We nominated pretension as the gravest sin of all.

And we were willing to argue that a chicken-fried steak and cream gravy at Herb's Café could duke it out with any phony Frenchman who ever wore a chef's hat.

We were armed with these notions when we moved to New York City.

Shake and I had made a pact. We would either play for the same NFL team or go to the Canadian League. We had some bargaining power, having been your sought-after All-Americas. We also had Big Ed Bookman for a "bidness" consultant.

Big Ed talked a lot about bidness. The oil bidness, most often. "The oil bidness is America's bidness," he would say.

The New York Giants went for our deal, probably because Burt Danby got tired of hearing Big Ed drop the names of Lyndon Johnson, John Connally, John Tower, and Gen. William Westmoreland, who hadn't inducted us into the army during Viet Nam because we'd had the wisdom to be born white and our hair didn't hang down below our earlobes.

The Giants selected me in the first round of the NFL draft; then they traded a future No. 1 and some cash to the Cleveland Browns to acquire Shake Tiller.

Barbara Jane moved to New York at the same time we did. Her parents didn't get to vote on it. She was still about half in love with Shake at the time, or thought she was.

We lived at the Westbury Hotel while Barbara Jane hunted for an apartment that would be suitable for the three of us. She came up with a Park Avenue co-op for us to buy. It had four terraces and three wood-burning fireplaces.

Shake and I agreed it was suitable for the three of us. Luxembourg could have slept in the living room.

Barbara Jane had majored in English and minored in journalism at TCU. She had expected to walk into one of the TV networks, pronounce Dien Bien Phu correctly, and get a job as a production assistant, but she never had the opportunity.

Fate kept on happening.

Barb was "discovered" by Burt Danby the first time Big Ed and Big Barb treated us to a night at "21," Big Ed's favorite New York restaurant. We were fresh faces in town. Barbara Jane was still buying Oriental rugs for the apartment. We hadn't even found out what bars not to go in—like "21."

But in we waltzed, and there was Burt at the bar with all the little model airplanes, trucks, cars, baseball caps, and polo mallets dangling over his head.

Burt was swirling in a clump of network biggies when his eyes suddenly feasted on Barb.

"Holy shit," he said, "who put the tits on Lassie?"

Burt sprang into action right away. His introductions set all the machinery in motion that helped turn Barb into a high-rent model.

Few people ever blitzed Big Town quicker than Barbara Jane. She kissed it on the lips and backed up the trucks.

All of a sudden, she was not just in our apartment, she was everywhere. You looked at a magazine ad, and there Barb was, telling you what to smoke or drink. You looked up on a billboard and she showed you how to get a suntan in your bikini. She slinked across your TV screen, advising you to stay in a specific chain of hotels. She saucily tossed her hair at you on TV, daring you not to drive on her steel-belted radials. And she washed her hair on TV, strongly hinting that your own hair would come out by the handfuls if you didn't use her shampoo.

None of this surprised me. One way or another, I had figured Barb would trick New York. She was too good-looking for it not to happen.

Barbara Jane was so heart-stopping pretty, she could raise the blood-pressure on a marble statue. She had flowing hair of streaked butterscotch, skin that tanned easily, and dark brown eyes that seemed to approve of everything you were thinking or saying. Her body was merely perfect—not the kind to set off burglar alarms in a tri-state area, but simply a luscious body with nothing out of proportion.

When she walked down Fifth Avenue in a pair of snug jeans and flashed her pretty smile, guys tripped over street vendors and fell into piles of stolen jewelry. In the summers when she'd walk into a restaurant wearing something white and semi-revealing over that wood-stained figure, forks dropped all over the room.

Barb could have scooted by on looks alone. Most beautiful women do. But she had all of the extras— the ones I admired, at least.

She had spirit, independence, street smart, book knowledge, wit, a quick laugh, and a lethal tongue. Unlike most models, she was alive, energetic, inquisitive.

Being intelligent, Barb never had any respect for the modeling business, even though she earned some disgraceful amounts of money at it. Not respecting the business didn't make her stupid. Like she said:

"Hey, if the agency dopes want to pay me this kind of bread to wear their corsage, I'll go to the prom, okay?"

She playfully described herself as a "prime-time hooker."

Shake liked to tease Barb about modeling. He'd try to get her to confess that she believed her talent was essential.

We were hanging around the apartment one night when he said, "Don't be ashamed, Barb. Models are great for the economy. They create activity in the marketplace. You believe in some of the products you sell, right? I think you're protecting the consumer from inferior merchandise."

Barbara Jane thought this over for a moment, then slowly broke into a smile.

"That dog won't hunt," she said.

Through all the years of Barbara Jane and Shake's on-again, off-again love affair, I was the good friend. I scoured the countryside to find a Barbara Jane of my own, but there was only one.

Barb didn't help my cause. Not once did she ever give her total approval to any girlfriend I had. Oh, sure. She would be nice to the girl if I happened to be in the middle of a romance, but she would never say something like "Gee, Mary Alice Ramsey's a great girl," or "Golly, Rachel Watson's a lot of fun."

What Barbara Jane would be was tolerant. Great word. She would be all-out, full-on, no-holds-barred tolerant.

The days and nights weren't without laughter and frivolity in the days when Barb and Shake and some girl and I would go out on the town together, or stay home together, or even take a trip together. And occasionally there would even be the unique entry— the keeper—that Barb might adopt as a friend. But eventually my relationship with the girl would be ruined—buried, forget it—because Barbara Jane's "review" would come in.

Sometimes I would ask for the review, but even if I didn't, the review would come in. One word. Maybe two. A short review but a killer.

And dead. The poor girl would be a goner. She might be a pile-driving, bone-crunching showstopper, but Barb's review would reduce her to the lame, gnarled, disease-trodden, nuisance-peddling intellectual dwarf I urgently had to get rid of.

Take high school. Mary Alice Ramsey was a prize. She was beautiful, stacked, sweet, generous, kind. But one evening at Herb's Café, as Shake and I and Barbara Jane were sitting around—a major-league sport in Fort Worth—I made a tactical blunder. I elaborated on the virtues of Mary Alice Ramsey.

"Daddy," Barbara Jane said, slipping a word in.

"What?"

I was looking up from a cheeseburger as I reacted to the word.

"Mary Alice talks about her daddy a lot, doesn't she?"

I thought it over. Barb had been right. Scratch Mary Alice Ramsey, that filthy bitch.

After Mary Alice, I had a good run with Mopsy Newsome, a very sexy Junior Favorite whose talent for lap-dancing was far ahead of its time. The affair ended after one word from Barbara Jane.

"Overbite."

Our senior year in high school, I became an item with Rachel Watson. Rachel was a knockout, cool and sophisticated, a girl who stayed ahead of the trends in music and fashion.

"You like Rachel a lot, don't you?" Barb got around to saying.

"She's different," I said.

"She's awfully pretty," said Barb, "but . . ."

"But what?"

Barb held me in suspense.

"*What?*"

Barbara Jane shrugged apologetically.

"Clothes Nazi."

And so it went. On through college. On into New York.

Only a fool would have dropped some of the convivial helpmates I was involved with, but Barbara Jane's reviews knocked them off like 21-point underdogs.

Cissy Walford?

"Hamptons."

Charlene Gaines?

"Gucci."

Becky Taylor?

"Grateful Dead."

Dede Aldwyn?

"Clone."

Sally Anthony?

"Dits."

Melinda Rideout?

"Nose whore."

Tiffany Howell?

"Chunko."

Ginny Beth Martinson?

"Y'all come out to the ranch."

Eileen Brice?

"United."

Cynthia Rogers?

"Sushi bar."

I once made it through two months without a review. It was our third year in Manhattan, the football season I fell in love with Jan Fletcher.

I had first seen Jan Fletcher on television. She had burst onto the screen one night as a reporter for a local independent station.

Jan was intoxicating, a girl with long black hair and eyes as blue as a soap wrapper. I would later discover she didn't have a blemish on her entire miraculous body.

I called Jan up for a date the first week she was on the air. There was something engaging about her delivery. If she looked into the camera and said, "The fire apparently started on the fourth floor of the tenement," it came out as if she had said, "Please fuck me, somebody."

Jan was more than ravishing and sultry. She was good-natured, carefree, quick as Barbara Jane. Shake found nothing wrong with her. I certainly didn't. And neither did Barbara Jane—not for two months, anyhow.

Then I blew it. I as much as challenged Barbara Jane on the subject one evening as we sat at the bar in McMullen's and I rambled on too long, too rapturously about Jan Fletcher's flawless face, body, intellect, and personality.

Barbara Jane interrupted me with two words.

"Piña colada."

The words came out softly, but there was a gleeful look in Barb's eye.

I clung to my drink for a moment, the words

twisting deeper into my heart. I could only stare off into a void, past the other models in the room and all the guys suffering from acute hay fever. I was trying to deal with the undeniable fact that Jan Fletcher drank nothing but piña coladas, and probably because she liked the sound of it.

We didn't break up the next day. Our relationship just gradually decayed, passed into oblivion. Shake observed that I crawled away like a sick rat looking for a drain.

There were those who said Barbara Jane saved me from an enormous amount of torment. It developed that Jan Fletcher was more concerned about her career than anything else.

She hopped into enough beds to get a job as a network correspondent and moved to Washington to cover the merry pranksters in our nation's capital. There, she indulged in a public affair with a married Congressman, then with a married Senator. Her own well-publicized marriage to a New York magazine editor didn't work out. Neither did her second well-publicized marriage to a music company mogul. That marriage led her to Hollywood. The last I heard of Jan, she was feverishly screwing her way up the production ladder at a major studio, one of those Universals, and she seemed to be living happily in the condo she had built in Liz Smith's column.

Not to give myself a greater sense of honor than I deserve, but I would never have had a serious romantic thought about Barbara Jane as long as she and Shake Tiller were in semi-love.

Many's the night I yearned for her. She was the reason I searched so diligently to find a girl with all of her attributes. But it wasn't until she and Shake realized they weren't in a married kind of entanglement that I looked at Barb with my eyebrows raised.

All but close friendship was over between Shake and Barb by the time we were pushing thirty. About a week after the game in the winter of that year we won the Super Bowl, Shake made a big decision. He wanted to explore foreign lands. Alone. He explained to Barbara Jane that he was twenty-eight and three-quarters, he hadn't written *Madame Bovary* yet, and he needed to seek adventures that would enhance his literary talents. Also, he wanted to get laid by a variety of accents.

We were sitting in the back room at Clarke's the night he broke the news to Barb.

"This is something I have to do alone," he said. "I want to see if it's true what they say about French women."

"What, that they're a size five?" said Barb.

"I need to absorb some of the culture of the Old World."

"You do have this thing about cathedrals, don't you?"

Shake threw down a young Scotch, motioned for another, and said, "Barb, old buddy, I'll be honest with you. There's no girl I'd rather be with than you. Never was, never will be. But I've got this weakness in my character, as we know. I can't be faithful to one woman. Great as you are in the sack, I'll always be looking for another Flying Wallenda."

"Eighty-eight," said Barb, putting her hand on Shake's shoulder and calling him by his football number, "I look ahead twenty years from now, and you know what I see? I see a lonely man eating dinner by himself in a Piccadilly Cafeteria somewhere in north Florida."

Shake said, "Not if there's a friendly bartender left in the civilized world. Besides, I'll always have you and Billy C."

Shake loafed around Europe for three months.

Researching life its ownself, he called it. He spent most of his time in London.

"They speak real good European in England," he reported in one of his letters.

We received a dozen letters and postcards from him. He dismissed the Riviera as France's revenge for the Battle of the Somme. Scotch was up to $10 a glass, and the beaches were so crowded that trying to find a patch of sand was like going to the Rose Bowl on New Year's Day. Madrid had a layer of smog that would choke a werewolf. Rome was falling apart. Ruins everywhere. The sidewalk cafés of Paris were no longer bristling with novelists. They had been taken over by Japanese tourists and guerrilla-theatre groups. Switzerland was extremely tall. London was the only city. People faithfully curbed their dogs, shepherd's pie was tasty. Everybody kept their brass polished. And you could even meet the friendly bar-maid who knew a supplier for monologue-inducing chemicals and the ever-popular paralysis weed.

One of his letters meant more to us than the others.

He wrote:

Hidy, gang—

By now, it has probably dawned on you goofy kids that you've always been in love, subconsciously anyhow. You belong together. Remember, Barb, you only started dating me instead of Billy Clyde in the first place because I won more medals in the junior high track meet.

You have strong physical attractions for each other's body parts. All of us know it. It's been very honorable of you not to ravish one another behind my back, but now it would be stupid.

Two people who think so highly of Home Ec
ought to get married. If you do, I promise to
be there, even though they're yelling at me to
finish the novel about Brett and Jake.

We have to keep Barbara Jane in the family,
B.C. Overaged preppies are lurking around
every corner, trying to grab her. I wasn't man
enough to make the sacrifice, but you are.
Running backs are tougher.

You will find going out together awkward at
first, I imagine. That's because of our history.
But there's a solution. Go to picture shows and
hold hands for a start. Then some evening when
you get back to the apartment, I find that, by
and large, it makes a difference in a relationship
if one of you will tie the other to a bedpost and
lick their whole body.

> Jesus used a Smith-Corona,
> *Old 88*

Shake had been right about the awkward part. I
mean, there we were living in the same apartment
and "dating."

It wasn't so much a case of dating. More accu-
rately, we were just a couple of old friends keeping
each other company as dinner companions and drinking buddies. Barb would go out with other guys, but
it was usually a business dinner of some kind. She'd
spring loose early and come and meet me.

One night we both got very drunk, likewise adven-
turous, and we did our best to make love. Barbara
Jane kicked me out of her bed before we got too far
along. It had something to do with my wisecracks
about Mopsy Newsome and Mary Alice Ramsey.

Everything changed one evening. We were staying
home to enjoy a pace night from the saloons. We
were sprawled out on opposite ends of the sofa in

the living room, watching the fire, drinking bottle-cap wine, listening to soft country music. Elroy Blunt was singing an old one.

I'll be feelin' better later,
Mr. Mood-Elevator.
Reach into my jeans
For more amphetamines.
Then I'll start to hum,
Me and Librium.
But soon I'll get my fill,
And I know one thing is true.
Ain't no druggist got a pill
To get me over you.

I didn't see Barb coming when she slid over next to me.

"I want to try an experiment," she said, putting her arms around my neck.

"I better call Nine-one-one," I said, being a wise guy. It was the police emergency number in New York, or as Burt Danby once said, a nickname for the Puerto Rican Day parade.

"Shut up," Barb said. "Don't laugh. Don't say anything about high school or college. Don't even grin. I mean it, Billy C. If you say one word right now, I'll tear your fucking throat out."

She then kissed me in a way I had often dreamed about.

I returned the kiss with what you might call a dedicated inventiveness. That kiss lasted a month. When our tongues came back from dry cleaning, we went to Fort Worth and got married.

The ceremony took place in a chapel of the University Christian Church, which was across the street from the TCU campus. It wasn't a formal wedding. We only rounded up some people who looked as if they had nothing better to do before going to lunch at Herb's Café.

Shake Tiller returned from Europe to be my best man and Barbara Jane's maid of honor. Big Ed was there to make sure the minister got tipped properly. Big Barb rearranged her shopping schedule to be present. Uncle Kenneth didn't have a baseball parlay working until that night. He was free to attend.

That was the guest list. Dr. Elwood Lindley blessed everybody at TCU and in most parts of Fort Worth. He blessed Big Ed's oil bidness, said young people were the hope of the world, acknowledged the talented tap-dance team of Jesus and Mary, forgave the Catholics and Jews, and pronounced us man and wife.

Then we went to Herb's Café.

Herb's had been our hangout on the South Side since before we were old enough to drink beer, but did. It was an old, lopsided, add-onto place with a bar on one side and a dining room on the other. If you could stand the smell of grease and cheap perfume, Herb's chicken-fried steak was probably the best in town.

At Herb's, we celebrated with extra cream gravy on our chicken-fried steaks and biscuits. We gathered around a table in the bar and listened to the jukebox and the chimes of the pinball machine. Big Barb reiterated her disappointment that Barbara Jane hadn't wanted a proper Fort Worth debutante wedding. Nonny Fulton's wedding dress had been fabulous, Big Barb said. Woody Herman's orchestra had played.

"Nonny Fulton's a pink balloon" Barb said to her mother. "She married an ice sculpture."

Big Ed expressed relief that his daughter had married one of us, me or Shake. "I was beginning to think you people had one of those ménage-la-twats going on," he said.

I've always found it impossible to explain good friends, old friends, to others. Most people don't have close friends, probably because they drive everyone away with their grinding small talk about small problems. Whatever it was that held Barb and I and Shake together might have seemed strange to Big Ed, but it was as natural to us as it must have been special.

We never thought there was anything odd about the fact that we loved, respected, understood, forgave, trusted, and looked out for each other. That was what good friends did—and did better than most families.

What happened over the next four years was that Barbara Jane and I made love like alligators eating marshmallows and still never missed a cocktail party or night out in New York to pay our respects to all of our cozy barstools.

Barb combined the roles of homemaker and famous model with an ease that everyone, myself included, found bewildering. How could that lovely cover girl have been such a good little cook and scrubwoman, too? I felt luckier than Cary Grant.

I continued to be regarded as an all-pro runner despite the nosedive of the New York Giants and the fact that I had to learn how to change light bulbs and carry out trash bags.

We invited Shake to keep living in the Park Avenue apartment after we were married. He said he would hold on to his co-op shares as an investment, but he really thought he should have his own place. Domestic serenity made him seasick. And he said he needed privacy for his clacker.

Clacker was what he called his typewriter.

He said, "Writers have to dwell a lot. They need

privacy for their clackers when they work on their dwells."

The Two Crazy Kids in Love were now Barb and me, not Barb and Shake. We kissed in public places, shared secret glances. We might as well have thrown snowballs, rode bicycles, and gone to street fairs.

We were the boy and girl in those movies that always have a sequence in which the lovers romp in a park or stroll past a river while leaves turn and dialogue is suspended long enough for a Marvin Hamlisch song to fall out of the sky.

If Barb and I would begin to act a little too cuddly, Shake would say, "Begin Central Park montage."

Shake by then had become the guy who occasionally found himself in the company of your killer-stud disco maven.

Barbara Jane reviewed Shake's girls just as she had once reviewed mine, but her reviews had no effect on Old 88.

"Some people call it spirituality; I call it a swallow," he said.

Barb often had difficulty finding something to discuss with Shake's fiancées.

There was this night when Shake was with another Shelly something-or-other, the usual twenty, the usual creamer, the usual six months removed from Hermosa Beach. The four of us were sitting in a booth at Runyon's.

We discussed a number of topics and Shelly listened patiently. She interrupted only once to ask if Nigeria was where Zulus came from.

Barbara Jane made an attempt to lure Shelly into a conversation. Leaning into the table, sipping a fresh young Scotch, she peered into Shelly's vapid eyes and said:

"Surf, ski, scuba, or skydive?"

Shelly's "huh?" was punctuated by a frown.

"What are you interested in, Shelly?"

Shelly wrestled with the question carefully; then with a bolstered smile, she said:

"I like shopping!"

That was when Barbara Jane spewed her drink on the table, and raced madly into the powder room. Barb's howling laughter could be heard at our table.

Those four years of marriage were the happiest of my life, football excluded. I rigidly believed that if you couldn't be the King of Morocco, the next-best thing was to be married to Barbara Jane Bookman.

Then came television.

Now it was that night in early September and I was lying in a hospital bed in New York with a knee that looked like condemned property, and the woman I loved was speaking to me from Los Angeles in a somewhat cheerier voice than I had wished.

After her opening line about Quasimodo, Barbara Jane said, "I didn't get to watch the game. We rehearsed all day. I looked in the control room to see if they had it on, but they were watching the Dodgers."

Barbara Jane was calling from her suite at the Westwood Marquis, a hotel to which Hollywood celebs were fleeing now that the Beverly Hills Hotel had been overrun by Midwest paving contractors and Long Island dentists.

"You missed one of the great two-yard runs," I said.

"How long will you be out?"

"It's the medial collateral."

"Not the medial collateral we know and love?"

She had heard me talk about football knees, about the medial collateral. She had seemed to understand that a football player would rather surrender a lung or an eye than a knee ligament. I wasn't one of those athletes who thought his body was a temple, but I'd keep myself in good condition the year round to avoid injuries.

"I'm out for the season, Barb."

There was a pause. Then she said:

"Aw, babe, I'm sorry. I know it must kill you, but, hey, all is not lost! You're a cinch to wind up on TV!"

"That makes three."

"Three what?"

"You're the third person tonight who's said I'm going to be on television."

"You'll be terrific. Just talk natural. Be you. Say all the things you say in bars, only leave out the fucks and shits."

"I'd rather play football."

"Babe, I know how much you love the game, but think about it. We're getting more mature, aren't we? This is a blessing! Now you have to find another career. You should go with CBS, even if the money's less than NBC's offer. CBS has higher ratings. ABC might be interested, but I doubt it. They've already got more announcers than events."

"Is this what mature people talk about? Television?"

Another pause.

"Do you hurt much?" she asked.

"Yeah."

"Poor babe."

"They're gonna cut on me tomorrow. Tie stuff back together. I'll be in a cast for four or five weeks, who the hell knows."

"I'll take the red-eye tomorrow night after rehearsal. I can spend a whole day with you. They won't mind me taking a day off. I mean, they will mind, but they'll understand."

"Don't bother to do that, Barb."

"I want to be with you."

"One day won't make any difference. I'm fine."

"Sweetheart, I'd stay longer—you know how much I want to be there—but an awful lot of people are counting on me out here. I can't let them down."

"Stay there, please."

"You mean it?"

The honest answer was no.

I said, "I wouldn't want to make a bunch of Hollywood guys so mad, they'd beat me to death with their pendants."

There had been a tenderness in Barbara Jane's voice but now it had vanished.

"Come on B.C., you're not being fair! We're talking about a football knee, not a heart transplant . . . a kidney removal!"

"Football knees are worse, if you play football for a living. I'm serious about you staying out there."

"I'm coming to New York."

"No!"

Not for only a day, I was thinking.

She said, "Okay, I know you feel rotten. You've blown the season. And I know you're worried. You're thinking it's curtains for Old Twenty-three if the knee doesn't mend. I know you're in pain. I'm sorry for all that, I really am, but, sweetheart, give this some thought: this show has a chance to make a big difference in our lives."

"How?"

"You mean aside from money, fame, and fortune?"

"We have that."

"Major money, B.C. If the show clicks, we can buy our own football team! What do you want to call them?"

"What about the Hollywood Pendants?"

"The new script came in yesterday," she said. "It's better than the others. It's not *Mary Tyler Moore, but* . . . it has charm. That's what everybody said today. Tomorrow they'll call it a piece of shit, but I have to hang in, don't I? Is it my fault the dippy network wants to spend a billion dollars to get a pilot they can fondle? Anyhow, I'm not a quitter."

Nobody was asking her to quit. I had only thought she would want to come back to New York and baby-sit me in my hour of need.

But just then, I only grunted, or sighed, whatever.

And she said, "If it were urgent, I'd be there and you know it! You're trying to make me feel guilty."

"You are guilty."

"I'll call you every hour. Well, every two or three hours. It depends on rehearsals."

"There must be more to showbiz than rehearsing. Don't you get to go to a lot of those 'in' restaurants where they invented trout pizza?"

"I love you," she said.

"Isn't there a lot of talk about heightening the dynamics of the storyline?"

"It'll be great to have you out here—even on crutches."

"Can I tour a studio?"

"I want you here as soon as you can travel. God knows how long I'll have to stay. If they like the pilot, we'll go right into episodes. You have to recuperate, anyhow. Do it with room service."

"I'll think about it."

"No, you won't think about it, you'll get on a fucking plane and you'll be here!"

Our conversation ended after I yawned—the pills were starting to kick in—and said, "Barb, I didn't mean to start an argument. You have too big an edge. Women can't remember pain."

THREE

Dreamer Tatum was the first person to autograph the cast on my knee the next afternoon, but his visit to the hospital was only partly social.

"We need you, Clyde," he worked up to saying. "We need you more than ever now. You can put your limp on the media, look real pained, and say, 'God, grant me the strength to march with my buddies.' We can do some shit with your ass, baby."

Dreamer was vice-president of the NFL Players Association, and what he wanted more than anything in the world, what he had always wanted, even more than another vintage Mercedes, was a strike.

He wanted football players to become auto workers, coal miners, teachers, machinists, garbage collectors, public-utility employees, and elevator operators.

For the fourth time in his career, Dreamer was trying to encourage all of the players on all of the teams in the National Football League—about 1,300 guys—to walk off the job. Quit. Not play football. And stay on a picket line for as long as it would take to force the twenty-eight owners to pay us more money and give us more freedom of movement, to put it in simple terms.

I had never been in favor of a strike. I had debated the issue at other times with Dreamer and

Puddin Patterson. In my judgment, a strike had no chance to succeed, and never would, for an excellent reason that I now put to Dreamer in the form of a question.

"How the fuck can you picket a yacht?"

"They got the tents but we got the dog acts, baby," Dreamer said. "We have the 'names.' You'd be a great spokesman for us, Clyde."

"You can't win, Dreamer. The owners have too much of that born-rich money behind them. They're members of the Lucky Sperm Club. You guys strike and they'll cancel the season, start over next year with new players."

"They need the 'names.' "

"You know how long it takes to make a 'name'? One headline."

"Sixty-five percent of the guys are ready to go out now. The rest will follow if we can get more people like you involved."

"How much have you got in the bank, Dreamer? Even if you sell all your cars, you can't live the rest of your life on it. A football team is just another toy to an owner. In the spring, they sail regattas around their off-shore drilling rigs. You strike and you're history. The Players Association will be the Window Cleaners Association. The dope dealers will be all right, but they're still the minority."

Dreamer said, "You don't understand about rich dudes. They hate to lose money worse than anybody. If we go out, they blow fifteen million apiece on their TV contract."

"Pocket change. A franchise is worth seventy, eighty million now."

"The common man's on our side, Clyde."

"The common man doesn't know shit about us or them. The common man thinks Vince Lombardi's still alive. All the common man cares about is some-

thing to bet on besides ice dancing. How do you bet
on that—which one has the tits?"

"Clyde, you could double your salary if you were a
free agent. Thought about that?"

"Not now, I couldn't," I said, glancing at the cast
on my leg.

"The thing we're trying to do, man, is get us a
salary scale that's determined by the players, not the
jive-ass owners."

"I know what you're trying to do," I said. "I read
in the paper where you said our demands are 'etched
in stone.' That's a great way to bargain."

"You talk tough in the papers. That's what newspapers are for."

The free-agent issue had been a nagging one in
pro football for years. Pro football was the only professional team sport that didn't have free agents. It
worked like this: if you played out your contract with
the team you belonged to—because they drafted you
out of college—you couldn't go to another club unless that club "compensated" the club you were with.
That was the kicker. Let's say I had wanted to leave
the Giants and play for the L.A. Rams because the
Rams offered me a higher salary. Fine, Burt Danby
would say. If the Rams pay the Giants ten million
dollars, they can have you. But the Rams wouldn't
do that, so I would be stuck with the Giants. Collu-
sion was what the players called it.

The owners argued that if it weren't for compensa-
tion, the best athletes would choose to play only in
the glamour cities, places like New York, L.A., San
Francisco. Nobody would want to play in Cleveland,
Buffalo, St. Louis, K.C., Detroit. The owners were
dead right about that in my case.

Dreamer now said, "If we don't strike, we're never
gonna get the free-market value for our services."

I couldn't hold back a laugh. "Dreamer, what would

your old daddy do if he heard you use a phrase like 'free-market value'? I thought we played the damn game because we loved it."

In that singular remark, I had hit upon the main reason I was opposed to a strike. Granted, the owners were richer than doctors, but they needed some deductions. We were paid better than sheetrockers. The average salary around the league was $130,000 last year, and that was for only working half a year playing a *game*. And guys like Dreamer and I probably made more money than the chairman of the board at Chrysler.

"Do me a favor, Dream Street," I said as he left. "Before you call a strike, give me the name of your broker."

Everyone had been right about television. That same day, an NBC executive called on the phone and offered me a lucrative contract to sit in a broadcast booth and babble.

Then the CBS executive came to see me in person.

Richard Marks was his name, and I decided he had been the head of CBS Sports for at least thirty minutes. He took a seat by my bed and began cleaning the lenses of his tinted glasses with a pocket spray and a Kleenex.

Richard Marks was a fit-looking thirty-five. He wore a black suit, a white shirt, and a regimental tie with a collar pin. He had an alarmingly short haircut, and his nails had been done. His face was boyish but humorless. It was a good guess he ran in marathons and had conquered wok cuisine.

He explained how it would be a major coup for him, being new in the job, if he could "bring Billy Clyde Puckett aboard." I would be his first notable acquisition.

Like the three men who had preceded him as the

president of CBS Sports, all of whom had come and gone within the year, stepping over corporate bodies to loftier jobs, Richard Marks had been unearthed from the Business Affairs division of the network. This meant he was a lawyer.

But now he knew everything about television production, live or tape, and he had a "vision" of what CBS Sports should be.

"We have to become more dimensional," Richard Marks was saying as I admired his nails and envisioned a pedicure. "We have to redefine our goals as broadcast journalists. The best announce teams have what I like to call an 'interplay,' *n'est-ce pas?* Do you like Summerall and Madden?"

I uttered an approving sound.

"I take a little credit for putting their act together," he said. "The idea was to marry Pat's infectious believability with John's scatalogical humor and informative expertise."

"Informative expertise is the best kind," I said.

Richard Marks said I had "potential" as an announcer because I was "natural." I was also "current." He considered it to be an inducement that I would work with Larry Hoage on NFL games.

"Excellent traffic director," Richard Marks said of Larry Hoage.

Larry Hoage was possibly the worst play-by-play announcer in the annals of television. He was a man who had successfully defended his Fluff Dry Award against all comers for a decade. More to the point, Larry Hoage had a way of making an off-tackle run for no-gain sound like a mid-air collision of 747's. But I didn't say any of this to the person who might want to pay me good money to go to several American cities and get drunk. What I said was:

"Larry Hoage has a familiar voice."

"Yes, he does," said Richard Marks, offering me a

fruit-flavored Cert. "Ideally, I would like for Larry to get fewer names wrong when he's calling a game, but he has a high recognition quotient, and you can't overlook this in television."

Richard Marks then outlined the future of CBS Sports for me.

"I want to enhance audience sympathy for the athletes as people," he said. "There are many instances during telecasts when we need to spend more time humanizing sports. You can help us do that. I plan to see to it that my network becomes the one that enriches the viewer. I want us to be frothy, keenly focused on issues; comedic at times, yes, but never pessimistic. Wary but not cynical. Aggressive but never inaccurate or chaotic. I see us as the network with texture, depth, spark, clear concepts, spontaneity, and above all, perhaps, the network with the inner conviction that a professional football game is very much a part of the human narrative."

I said, "Most of my friends seem to like announcers who just give you the score and the clock and otherwise shut the fuck up."

"That, too," Richard Marks said.

He asked if I was represented by IMG.

"Who?"

"Mark McCormack."

"No."

"The Hook?"

"Who?"

"Ed Hookstratten."

"No."

"Mike Trope?"

"No."

"Don't tell me you're with ICM! I didn't know they handled athletes."

"I'm not."

"Ron Konecky, of course. I'll give him a call and we'll bang the dents out of the fenders."

"Who's Ron Konecky?"

"Who's your agent?"

"I don't have an agent."

"How can you not have an agent? Everybody has an agent or a business manager. You don't have an agent?"

Richard Marks didn't seem to know whether to be flabbergasted or accuse me of an out-and-out lie.

"All I do is play football," I said. "My wife has an agent in L.A. Actually, he's a lawyer. She's never seen him, but he does her stuff. Barry somebody."

"Barry Sloan?"

"Could be. All I know is, some guy told her that in Hollywood, she'd better have her own Jew or they'd play racquetball with her liver."

"I'll give Barry Sloan a call."

"Why?"

"Why? You and I can't talk money, Billy Clyde. Things aren't done that way."

"Make me an offer. I'll probably accept it. What's the big deal?"

Richard Marks took a pocket calculator from his coat. He began pecking on it.

"Hmmm," he said. "Twelve games left in the regular season . . . playoff possibilities . . . these darn lashups are getting more and more expensive. Looks like our budget can stand to make you a . . . one-year deal for . . . well, let's round it off . . . a hundred thousand."

I cleared my throat. I wasn't balking. I honestly had to clear my throat.

So Richard Marks said, "Heck, I know you've talked to NBC. Make it one-fifty and we'll wrap it up."

NBC had only offered me $75,000. Richard Marks had already doubled it because I cleared my throat.

It made me wonder what a violent coughing spell would have done.

"NBC mentioned something about expenses," I said.

"Look," he said, "I hate this bargaining business. Of course you'll get expenses at CBS. We fly first class. Let's say two hundred thousand for the regular season, we'll negotiate the playoffs later—okay?"

I took the job with CBS. I would begin work the first week in October. A regional game. Me and Larry Hoage.

Some people might have thought that being paid $200,000 for going to twelve football games was sinful. Ordinarily, I would have agreed. But later on, when I thought about the fact that I would have to spend three hours at each of those games with Larry Hoage, and no telling how many dinners the night before, I decided I had sold out too cheaply.

Before he departed that day, Richard Marks said, "I don't think you need voice lessons. You still have your Texas accent. Good! It will create an aura of sincerity on the air when you're discussing the socioeconomic backgrounds and behavior characteristics of your fellow athletes."

Barbara Jane was delighted with the news that I had taken the color job with CBS.

"You'll like the grownup world," she said on the phone from California. "What did you think of the new head of CBS Sports? It's fantastic he came to see you personally. They usually send a drone."

"He's just another TV guy, as far as I can tell," I said. "Throw a Ping-Pong ball in a boxcar and you've got a Richard Marks."

FOUR

T. J. Lambert said he would fold me up like a taco
if I didn't stop in Fort Worth on my way out to
the Coast to join Barbara Jane.

He demanded I be on hand for TCU's home
opener against the feared Rice Owls. Rice was the
only school in the Southwest Conference with a worse
football record than TCU over the previous twenty
years.

A week had gone by and I was out of the hospital.

The cast on my right leg reached from mid-thigh
to the ankle and made my leg look like a parenthesis,
but I could get a pant leg over it. I was on crutches,
but I could hop around without them if I could grab
on to things. And I could drive a car.

I rented a Lincoln from Budget at the D/FW airport and pointed it west on a freeway. The skyline of
Fort Worth sprang up and loomed ahead of me,
taller and fatter than ever, and I marveled at how
my old hometown was beginning to resemble Phoenix, Denver, Atlanta, all of those cities that were
striving to become a bigger Dallas.

Certain cities would always have their own look,
their own feel. New York, Boston, San Francisco,
Washington, D.C., part of L.A., Chicago below the
skyscrapers, even a Jacksonville, Florida. But all other

cities in my mind were starting to look alike, think
alike, live alike.

Take the snow out of Minneapolis and you had
Phoenix. Take the cactus out of Phoenix and you
had Denver. Take the crab cakes out of Baltimore
and you had Kansas City. Dallas, Houston, and Atlanta were the worst examples of progress. They
were already Freeway Heaven, cities intent on link-
ing high-rise suburbs to new shopping villages to
new country clubs with condos. Cities where people
in the future were only going to communicate by
word processor or over strawberry Margaritas at
Happy Hour.

Now it was slowly happening to Fort Worth, once
the world headquarters for white socks, Western music, and TexMex food, an honest town where a man
wasn't considered drunk unless he was lying down in
a livestock pen and couldn't speak his native language.

Fort Worth was giving birth to clusters of those
steel-and-glass towers of its own, needles rising among
boxes of reflective glass, and its suburbs were starting to crawl with eateries overdosed in blond bentwood
furniture and imitation Tiffany lampshades.

For some, a rowdy night out in Fort Worth was
still a fistfight, a two-step, and a high school football
game. But for most guys it was an inane conversation with a racy receptionist while a hot stock tip was
passed across a platter of plastic nachos at Mommie's
Trust Fund, the newest singles bar in town.

Prairie geography was responsible, I was convinced.
Fort Worth was the same size and had the same lack
of pretension of a Jacksonville, but it didn't have an
Atlantic Ocean, a St. Johns River and an intracoastal
canal to keep the land developers from shredding
every outlying oak into mortgage paper.

Fort Worth seemed as determined as Atlanta to
imitate Dallas. One day soon, if the planners had

their way, everybody in Fort Worth could step gingerly into a restaurant specializing in fern salads and carrot boats.

Although I was surrounded by modern architectural wonders as I motored through downtown, one thing had yet to change. There weren't any people around. It wasn't a bomb scare, it was just Fort Worth. The rich folks were as cloistered as ever, and the people I did see were either bent over from age or had dents in their foreheads and prison haircuts.

I dropped off my bags at the Hyatt Regency and drove to the TCU campus for an audience with T.J.

"Your cast and them crutches is gonna help inspire my pissants," T.J. said. We were sitting in his office in the Daniel-Meyer Coliseum on a Friday in mid-September, the day before the Rice game.

T.J.'s office had a big window looking out on my old stadium. The office was almost entirely decorated in purple and white, TCU's fighting colors.

Each new head coach over the past two decades had added more purple decor to the coaching offices. He had then lost more football games than the coach he had replaced.

The carpet in the office was purple, T.J.'s desk was purple laminate, the walls were purple with white trim, and there were the mandatory messages on the walls that were intended to motivate the college athlete who could read.

One sign said:

MAKE SOMETHING HAPPEN!

Another said:

ANGRY PEOPLE WIN FOOTBALL GAMES!

My eyes lingered on the catchiest sign in his office. It said:

PRETTY COEDS DON'T SUCK LOSERS' COCKS!

"Has the chancellor seen that?" I asked T.J. innocently.

"He's a good old boy. Wants to win."

T.J. was probably right about the chancellor, Dr. Troy (Tex) Edgar, a man with an ever-present smile who wore purple, Western-cut suits and was more interested in raising funds for the university than anything else. Dr. Edgar could live with a T.J. Lambert who won football games. Like most chancellors, Dr. Edgar had no doubt been promised by his well-to-do alums that he could scare up more endowment in the end zone than he could at all of the Christian Fellowship dinners he attended.

One of the things T.J. had in mind for me while I was in town was an appearance in the TCU dressing room before the game. He wanted to introduce me to his players, whereupon I would say something to make their little hearts beat quicker.

"Tell 'em one of them bullshit Gipper things," he said.

"Like what?"

"Fuck, I don't know. Tell 'em how you went whistle to whistle against Rice one time when you had three broken ribs and a sore on your dick."

T.J. also instructed me to attend a reception for the coaching staff in the Lettermen's Lounge after the game. It was going to be a very nice function. I would see a lot of ex-teammates, probably, and several ex-TCU greats who had progressed from Honorable Mention to First Team All-America in the thirty years that had elapsed since they had worn the purple.

"Tonsillitis will be there, too. I want you to meet him," T.J. said.

"Who?"

"Tonsillitis Johnson."

"Is that his real name?"

T.J. looked at me sternly. "Tell you what, son.

Tonsillitis Johnson can turn our whole program around if we can get him."

Tonsillitis Johnson was something to behold, if I could believe T.J. He was a once-in-a-lifetime running back from Boakum, Texas, a little town in the central part of the state. He was 6 feet 3, 235, and so fast, he made Herschel Walker and Earl Campbell look like paraplegics.

Fast was only half of it. Tonsillitis had a 34-inch waist, a 52-inch chest, and could benchpress the King Ranch.

"He has a three-point grade average, right?" I said. "Over a thousand on his S.A.T.'s?"

T.J. blushed and looked away for a second. He opened a drawer of his desk and took out a document.

"I hadn't ought to show you this," he said, holding what looked like a questionnaire in his hand. "Lord knows, I wouldn't want no English professors to see it."

T.J. studied the questionnaire.

"They's a conference rule what says a high school athlete has to fill out one of these in the presence of the head coach. I asked Tonsillitis to fill it out this morning. He said he'd take it home and send it back to me. I said, naw, you got to do it here, hoss. It ain't hard, I said. Just put your name down there . . . your address . . . your high school. That kind of thing. Your momma and daddy's name. He started to fill it out. When he come to the place where he was supposed to put down his favorite sport, he looked at me and said, 'What we be doin' ratch ear?' I said, Put down your favorite sport. It's football, ain't it? He gimme a nod. I said, Write it down, hoss. So he did. Only . . . here's what he wrote."

T.J. handed me the questionnaire.

Tonsillitis Johnson had written down the word *"booley."*

"Booley?" I looked up at T.J.

"Something like that."

"Booleyball," I said, rolling the word around, unequipped to fend off a grin.

T.J. snatched the questionnaire away from me. He put it back in his desk, locking the drawer hastily.

"Booley," I said again, repeating the word to myself as I gazed out the window at the stadium, a fine old gray concrete edifice.

"He can make a difference around here, son," T.J. said firmly. "We get Tonsillitis Johnson wearin' that purple, we'll kick some serious ass."

Later in the afternoon I caught up with Uncle Kenneth at Sammie's Barbecue, a reliable emporium on a decaying side of town. No good barbecue joint ever flourished or even lasted in a swank neighborhood. Why would anybody eat in a place where they might encounter nouvelle brisket?

A platter of coal-black ribs sat in front of Uncle Kenneth. They reminded me of how much I hated Continental restaurants. I ordered two slabs of mesquite-smoked ribs, sauce on the side, with pintos, fries, cole slaw, and garlic bread. I then wallowed in all of it while Uncle Kenneth told me what was wrong with pro football.

Everything, he said.

The sixteen-game regular season was too long. Teams didn't try half the time, not until December. They held back, hoped to coast on through. The result was that every team was sloppy, undependable.

You shouldn't be allowed to lose seven games and reach the playoffs, much less the Super Bowl. The pros were the best thing that ever happened to college football.

In college, you had to tee it up every Saturday,

and you'd better not lose more than one game if you wanted a shot at No. 1.

The draft and the parity scheduling were making every NFL team ordinary. Why reward mediocrity? Make the weak sisters work their way back to the top.

The no-bump rule was a disgrace. Why were they making it harder and harder to play defense? So they could turn humdrum quarterbacks into heroes?

How come the pros had a way of taking a great ballcarrier out of college and teaching him how to fumble and slip down?

How come the pros had a way of turning great college pass receivers into split ends who dropped key passes?

How come most NFL teams had a head coach you never heard of?

Where did all of the 300-pound subhumans come from and why were they needed to fill gaps and paw each other?

When was everybody going to wise up to artificial turf? It made players bounce higher than the ball.

Who the hell watched Monday-Thursday-Sunday-Friday Night Football on TV? Gamblers were even tired of it.

Where were all the characters in the game, men like Bobby Layne, Sonny Jurgenson, Alex Hawkins, Bill Kilmer, Paul Hornung, Mean Joe Greene, Doak Walker, Jim Brown, Max McGee, Bubba Smith, Jake Scott, and Fred Dryer?

It had become the NRL, the National Robot League.

When did breathing on somebody get to be pass interference?

And did anybody really know what offensive holding was, other than the fact that it was something a zebra called when it was time to fuck you out of your bet but win him his?

"You left out dopeheads and guys who want to strike," I said.

"Billy, it's a shame. Your game's become a damned old bore. I'd almost just as soon watch pro basketball."

He sipped his Budweiser, and said, "No, I don't think I want to go that far."

"You still bet football," I reminded him.

"Over and under is all I'd fool with right now. Smart money don't bet teams the first ten or twelve weeks of the season. You don't know who's gonna have the rag on. When they start gettin' down to the playoffs, you can get some idea about form. Aw, I'll bet a zebra now and then."

Uncle Kenneth kept charts on game officials. Zebras. He was as certain there were notorious crooks among the zebras as I was certain they were only incompetent.

"Who's your favorite zebe these days?" I was gnawing on an exceptionally meaty rib.

"No contest. Charlie Teasdale."

Charlie Teasdale had been in the league for ten years. He was an experienced referee, lived in Dallas. He'd been involved in a number of controversial plays through the years, but I had chalked it up to his age—he was in his fifties—his blindness, and his stupidity. The replays had rarely proved Charlie right. When he had ruled no fumble, it had been a fumble. When he ruled in-bounds or out-of-bounds, it had always been the opposite. The fortunes of whole teams and individuals had often hung in the balance on Charlie Teasdale's first-down measurements and holding penalties. "King of The Call-back" was what Uncle Kenneth had nicknamed him.

"Last year the dogs covered fourteen out of the sixteen games Charlie Teasdale worked," Uncle Kenneth said. "He's a dandy. Man in Vegas told me he'd rather own Charlie Teasdale than Mobil Oil. Shake was asking about him the other day."

"Shake Tiller?"

"His ownself. He called me from somewhere."

"He called you about Charlie Teasdale?"

"He said he was trying to do some kind of magazine article. He said he wouldn't use my name or nothin'. He asked me about one thing and another. How the odds had moved on this game and that. He wanted to know what games I thought had been real funny over the past two or three years."

"Funny?"

"You know what I mean. All them games where they weren't supposed to do it but they did."

"Upsets."

"Prison offenses."

I didn't know anything about an article Shake was working on. He hadn't mentioned it to me.

"I guess he don't want to put you on the spot. You're still a player."

"That's debatable," I said. "I might be a broadcaster, but that's debatable, too."

"That's probably another reason Shake hasn't talked to you about his story. Broadcasters ain't journalists. They're Establishment. Ain't no NFL broadcaster gonna look down there on the field at old Charlie Teasdale and say, 'Welcome to Flag Day, sports fans. This one's for Charlie Teasdale and all of his close friends in Vegas.' "

"Vegas," I said with disgust, motioning to the waitress for the check. "Vegas doesn't know every Goddamn thing. Vegas says somebody went in the can every time there's an upset. Vegas thinks World War Two was fixed!"

"I reckon some of 'em did have Germany."

Outside Sammie's, my uncle helped me climb into the Lincoln.

I zipped down the window. "Let me ask you something, Kenneth. If Vegas is so fucking smart, how come it's in Nevada?"

I was obligated to have cocktails with Big Ed and Big Barb that evening, but I hadn't minded. They were sometimes more fun than whiskey. They had long ago secured their places among the most self-important people God had ever put on Texas soil.

I met them at River Crest Country Club, the oldest and most exclusive club in Fort Worth, a haven for local peerage and new WASP money. The club had a funky old golf course woven through well-shaded two-story homes. The homes would have been considered mansions in the Twenties and Thirties.

The clubhouse had once resembled one of those tasteful homes. Now it had been rebuilt into something that was either an architectural masterpiece or the Babylon Marriott. The design of the new clubhouse had been approved and the construction had begun while Big Ed was out of the country. When he returned, he had stomped into a board meeting and said, "Who's the silly bastard that thought the thief of Baghdad was a God-damn architect?" It was Big Barb's darkest secret that she had recommended the architect.

In character, every city had a River Crest, though in other places it might be called Brook Hollow, River Oaks, Timaquana, East Lake, or Burning Jew. It was a club in which you were likely to find more than one member who had yet to acknowledge the Supreme Court decision of 1954, and would strongly argue that *The New York Times* had exaggerated the death toll of the Holocaust by five and a half million people.

A high school kid took my car at the club's entrance. Monroe opened the front door of the building for me. Monroe was a congenial, elderly black man who looked no older to me now than he had when I was in Paschal and Shake and I had terrorized the club as guests of Barbara Jane.

As we shook hands, Monroe said, "I knew you wasn't gonna get up the minute you was hit, Billy Clyde. Ooo, that looked like it hurt."

"You ought to see Dreamer Tatum," I said. "My knee bent his mind out of shape. How are all the rich folks, Monroe?"

"Jes' fine."

"Jes' rich, you mean."

"That's it," he laughed. "Jes' rich, is all."

Big Ed and Big Barb were in the Mixed Grill.

They were at a table having drinks with a pale middle-aged fool, who stood up to leave as I arrived.

We were introduced. I didn't get his name—J. Thomas something—but I did get his Ivy League stutter and the tailend of a conversation.

"I q-quite agree with the older chaps," the Ivy Leaguer was saying to the Bookmans. "The toilet seats in the men's locker must be raised, hang the expense!"

"Sounds okay to me," I said, sitting down and saluting a bartender who recognized me and held aloft a bottle of J&B as if to ask if that was what I still drank.

The Ivy Leaguer's eyes were on Big Ed as he said, "Most of our older members have had hernia problems, you see. They simply can't sit on those toilets in the men's locker anymore without their balls dangling in the water when they make cah-cah."

Glancing at Big Barb, he said, "Excuse me, Barbara, but it's rather a s-serious problem."

"I should think so," said Big Barb, looking uncomfortable.

Big Ed said, "I'll vote with the majority of the board."

"That's all I ask," J. Thomas something replied. "Just w-wanted you to know I'm m-making it an agenda item for the spring meeting."

The Ivy Leaguer moved on to another group of members, all of whom were sinking deeper into drunken slumbers.

Other tables were occupied with men and women who sloshed their Martinis and stared at each other testily, except for those who stared at me, possibly wondering why a cripple had been allowed in the club.

My drink came while Big Ed and Big Barb devoted two full minutes to discussing my knee injury. Then Big Ed brought up a familiar topic.

"Here's to dinosaurs," he said, raising his glass of Stolichnaya on the rocks. "Had to remind the scamps at Bookman Oil and Gas today that we're in the bidness of finding dinosaurs, not dry holes! We're in the wine bidness, I said. Dinosaur wine!"

Big Ed smoked Sherman cigarettellos. As he lit one, he said, "You know where to find dinosaurs, don't you, Billy Clyde?"

I tried to look inquisitive.

"Well, they ain't in the God-damn Petroleum Club where my geologists hang out. Most dinosaurs either drowned in the ocean or they laid down and died of a happy old age in Texas and Arabia!"

"Makes sense," I said.

"See, what you got to do in my bidness is find you a big old cave under the ground where a bunch of dinosaurs have flopped down. When you find you a whole pile of 'em and they've fermented just right, you stick your straw in the ground and you drink that dinosaur wine."

He sipped his vodka and looked at Big Barb with a glint.

"Porosity—ain't that right?"

"Porosity," Big Barb said, noticing her hair in her reflection on the window glass.

"Big underground rock with enough pore space in it to store that wine for a million years," Big Ed said. "That's what I told my office today. I said you monkeys better get off your ass and grab me by the pores!"

"How is the oil business these days?" I asked, trying to be conversant. I was about as interested in the oil business as I was in computer science.

Big Ed sighed.

"We'll always have one problem. We got to deal with Dune Coons. More dinosaurs died in Arabia than anywhere else."

"Dune Coons?"

"Sand niggers," Big Ed said. "Your A-rabs cause the glut and they cause the gasoline lines. Whatever suits their ass. I was tryin' to deal with a Dune Coon the other day. I told him, I said, 'You know what would make this a better world to live in? It'd be a lot better world if all you OPEC sons-of-bitches didn't know nothin' about seismic instruments and infra-red satellite photographs and just went on to Mecca and hummed a bunch of shit!' "

Big Ed and Big Barb were physically attractive people. Big Ed had wavy gray hair. He wore finely tailored suits, kept an out-of-season tan. Acapulco was close if you owned a Lear. Big Barb was a regal brunette with the Rolls-Royce of face-lifts and butt-tucks. The worth of the diamonds and emeralds she might wear on a given night would feed West Virginia for a year.

We got around to talking about their daughter, my wife, and what Barbara Jane was up to in L.A., and were we having any marital problems that Big Ed and Big Barb could solve with money or phone calls to Senate subcommittees?

We were getting along fine for two people who seldom saw each other, I said.

"I just think it's absurd," Big Barb said. "Why in the world does Barbara Jane want to be an actress?"

I had wondered the same thing. All of the actors and actresses I had ever met, mostly through sports, had sooner or later exposed themselves as paranoid children.

They could give wonderful performances with the proper direction, cutting, and editing. They could appear to be perfectly natural and appealing on talk shows or at social gatherings. But they shouldn't be mistaken for human beings. They were aliens who were terrified and distrustful of anyone who didn't heap constant praise on them or didn't agree with every absurd thing they thought at all times. They measured artistic achievement in terms of fame and money. They had a cliché-clouded outlook of people outside their industry: smart businessmen were in a hurry, serious writers talked about the soil, the great athletes worked with kids, honest politicians looked concerned. Some performers could make me laugh or cry on the big screen, but that didn't mean I wanted to have dinner with them. It was a curious thing.

Barbara Jane had practically been dragged into the business. The hard-hitters who ran the entertainment division at ABC had tried before to get her to do a series. In her commercials, they thought she had "delectability," "likability," and "recognizability."

She had agreed to give it a try after she had been presented with an idea for a show in which she would play a young woman very much like herself, someone who would get to wise off regularly, who would be expected to look good, who would be supported by talented professionals.

So it was that the only answer I could give Big Barb for why her daughter wanted to be an actress was:

"It's a new challenge, I guess."

Big Barb then said, "She can't join Los Angeles Country Club."

I wasn't sure I heard that right.

"L.A. Country Club won't accept show-business people. Everybody knows that. We have friends who are members."

Big Ed confirmed this horrid fact.

He said, "They let Randolph Scott join, but only after he quit the movies. Hell, Bing Crosby lived across the street from the fourteenth fairway for twenty years, but they never let him in!"

I said I did not recall, in all honesty, Barbara Jane saying she had wanted to join Los Angeles Country Club.

Her mother said, "Not now, maybe, but what will happen if she changes her mind? If she's an actress, they simply won't have it. I think it's something you and Barbara Jane need to discuss."

Big Ed wondered who watched television, anyhow. News, sure. Sports. Space shots. But what else? All he ever saw when he turned it on at night was a bunch of faggots hopping around a living room being silly.

"Is Barbara Jane in one of those faggot shows?"

"She's making what they call a pilot," I said. "It's the first episode in what could be a comedy series if the network bosses like it. But that doesn't mean it will be any good—or even funny. Don't you want to see your daughter on Channel Eight every Tuesday night?"

"Not with faggots." Big Ed waved at a waiter.

The show was called *Rita's Limo Stop*. Barbara Jane played "Rita." The show was based on the premise that a pretty young divorcée who happened to be going blind would try to open a restaurant on the Upper East Side of Manhattan.

I had asked Barb the same question she had asked the producers. Why was "Rita" going blind?

"We had to think of something to make you more vulnerable," a producer had explained to Barbara Jane.

To the Bookmans, I said, "Rita has a partner in the restaurant. Amanda. It's kind of a Lib thing. Rita and Amanda cope with all these problems in the business world. The restaurant is a big load of trouble, and weird characters are supposed to come in and out."

"I hope one of them is an eye doctor," Big Ed said.

"I don't think Rita goes completely blind if the show gets good ratings," I said. "Maybe things will get a little dim now and then."

Big Barb didn't understand the name of the show. What did *Rita's Limo Stop* mean?

I said, "There are truck stops, right? The title's supposed to be a gag. New York? East Side? Rich people? Texas has truck stops, New York has limo stops."

"I always hire a limousine in New York," said Big Barb. "It's the only way you can shop and get anything done."

Big Ed asked what chance the show had to be funny.

None, I said, based on one of the scripts I had tried to read. But that didn't mean the show might not be a success. With few exceptions, sitcom humor catered to the intellect of a rooster.

I had saved the script I'd tried to read, thinking it would be invaluable evidence if Barbara Jane were ever called into a courtroom to explain why she had murdered Sheldon Gurtz and Kitty Feldman, the executive producers and lead writers of the show.

The first two pages alone would have ensured my wife's acquittal. A verbatim reproduction follows:

RITA'S LIMO STOP

COLD OPENING

FADE IN:

INT. CHIC RESTAURANT—NIGHT

(EAST SIDE MANHATTAN. PAN TO KITCHEN. RITA, A BEAUTIFUL GIRL, RUSHES OVER TO KO, A CHINESE CHEF.)

RITA

I'm starved!

(SHE GRABS A BITE OF FOOD OFF A PLATE.)

KO

No, you Rita! Velly good owner!

RITA

Thank you, Ko. I'm glad you agree. Now stop putting bean sprouts in the onion soup!

(RITA LEAVES KITCHEN, ENTERS RESTAURANT PROPER, BUMPS INTO AMANDA, HER PARTNER. THE RESTAURANT IS CROWDED, THE OWNERS FRANTIC.)

AMANDA

We've run out of lamb!

RITA

I wish we'd run out of bean sprouts.

AMANDA

This is serious, Rita. What are we going to serve?

RITA

Chili dogs.

AMANDA

Again? We're supposed to be a Continental
restaurant!

RITA

Our chili dogs are made with the best French
mustard! If we can serve bean sprouts in the
onion soup, we can serve chili dogs.

AMANDA

How did we get into this? We're getting our
brains beat out.

RITA

I've got that part down. It's all those days off I
can't get used to.

(AN ANGRY WOMAN INTERRUPTS THEM.)

ANGRY WOMAN

I wouldn't send a pornographic mugger to this
restaurant! The food stinks and the service is
rude!

RITA

I'm sorry but I've forgotten your name.

AMANDA

Trouble.

(RITA TURNS TO AMANDA.)

RITA

That was your husband's name, wasn't it?

ANGRY WOMAN

You won't see me in here again!

RITA

What have you got against grease?

(<u>ANGRY WOMAN</u> EXITS. RITA SUDDENLY
LEANS AGAINST A DOOR FACING, CLOSES
HER EYES, PRESSES ON HER TEMPLES.)

AMANDA

Rita, what's wrong?

RITA

Nothing.

AMANDA

Yes, there is!

RITA

I'll be fine, Amanda, as soon as the bean sprouts
go away.

AMANDA

Is it another one of those headaches?

RITA

Really, it's nothing a million dollars can't cure.

AMANDA

You must see a doctor.

RITA

He'd only find something wrong with an entree.

AMANDA

Do you ever wish we were still married—away
from all this?

RITA

It's the car pools I miss the most.

(A <u>CUSTOMER</u> RISES FROM A TABLE JUST

IN TIME TO HIT A TRAY BEING CARRIED
BY A <u>WAITER</u> WE HEAR A <u>CRASH</u>.)

AMANDA

Oh, no!

RITA

I wish they'd stop overtipping.

(NOW WE HEAR A <u>KITCHEN CRASH</u>.)

AMANDA

Oh, my God!

RITA

It's all right. That could be the last of the bean
sprouts!

(AMANDA CONTINUES STARING AT RITA
WITH A WORRIED LOOK.)

DISSOLVE TO:

"Can Barbara Jane act?" Big Ed was now asking.

"I don't think it matters, but I'll find out when I
get to L.A.," I said.

"When's it gonna be on TV?"

As I understood it, there was something in television called a "mid-season replacement" and something else called "a second season." The show had a
chance to go on the air in late October or late January. In October, the networks looked at the ratings
to see which car wrecks people were watching and
which car wrecks they weren't watching. They did
the same thing in January. The car wrecks nobody
watched got canceled and were generally replaced
with better car wrecks.

Big Ed said, "I never see car wrecks. All I see is
faggots in living rooms."

"Those are the hits. They never change."

"What network is it?"

"ABC."

"Which one's ABC?"

"The one without Dan Rather or Tom Brokaw," I said in an effort to be helpful.

Big Ed and Big Barb still seemed confused.

"Helicopter crashes *and* car wrecks?"

Still no clue.

"Olympics?" I said.

"Faggots," Big Ed scowled.

"Fags in the Olympics?" I couldn't avoid a look of astonishment.

"Hell, look how they dress when they compete in those silly events," he said. "Everything they wear crawls up their ass."

"ABC is the network with Howard Cosell," I said, taking a final stab at it.

"Oh, shit," said Big Ed, guzzling his vodka.

The plight of TCU's football program came up for discussion. Big Ed was an influential TCU alum, a major contributor to the athletic fund. Through the years, he had provided new lights for the stadium, artificial turf, a modernized weight room, four or five quarterbacks who excelled at throwing incompletions, a dozen or more ball-carriers who ran backwards, a bevy of linemen who never learned to block, and a vast amount of purple paint for the coaches' offices.

All Big Ed wanted for his untiring generosity was one more Southwest Conference championship. TCU had won championships regularly when he was a kid, but he hadn't enjoyed one since Shake and I had led the Horned Frogs to an 8–3 record in the early Seventies.

T.J. Lambert was the right man at the right time, Big Ed was convinced. He was the coach who could get the job done if the Frogs could only recruit a little more aggressively.

"I don't want any NCAA probations, but I can live with a few reprimands."

He was aware of Tonsillitis Johnson.

"Tonsillitis can do it all. He can take us to the Cotton Bowl straight as a Indian goes to shit."

"That's quick," I said.

Big Ed reached for another Sherman cigarettello. "T.J.'s worried we can't outbid Texas or Oklahoma for Tonsillitis. They'll give him a car, an apartment, a summer job that'll make him richer than two orthodontists. I said, Hell, I know how we can get that nigger. We'll give him his own 7—Eleven, tell him he can rob it any time he wants to!"

Big Barb shushed Big Ed with a look and a gentle tug on the sleeve of his coat.

I had never been able to shush Big Ed. Neither had Barbara Jane or Shake. Big Ed had been saying nigger for as long as we could remember.

We all said it as kids without realizing the hurt it caused. But if you have any feelings, you change when you get older and life drops some smart on you. You can even get pissed off when you hear it applied to a teammate who blocks his ass off for you and accepts you as *his* equal.

I don't know if Shake and me had become totally color-blind through sports, which is the best thing about sports. I hope so. We still said nigger in a joking way around black guys who acted like they understood there wasn't any hate in our hearts. Anyhow, the word wasn't going to disappear, no matter how loud your Eastern liberals hollered at your truck-stop Southerners.

I'd stopped worrying about the way people talked a long time ago. It was what a person was that mattered. And the truest thing of all was that I didn't have a black friend who wouldn't understand that you can't shush anybody worth $60 million.

At River Crest, all I did was seize the moment to excuse myself from Big Ed and Big Barb's company, telling the lie that my knee was starting to act up. What I really intended to do was go back to my hotel and get drunk alone.

It had become a pre-game ritual. After all, I had to help that other great liberal, T.J. Lambert, beat the Rice Owls the next day.

FIVE

Blue and gray crepe paper—Rice University's colors—cluttered the ceiling, crawled up the walls, and wrapped around benches in the TCU locker room. Over in a corner, a stereo blasted away with a scratchy recording of "Put On Your Old Gray Bonnet," the Rice fight song.

"It's inspired," I remarked to T.J. as we stood near a coffee urn, watching the gallant Horned Frogs lazily suiting up for the game.

"We've had it lookin' like this all week," T.J. said. "The equipment people done it. I've had 'em playin' that song all week, too. I figured it was a way to get our crowd sick to death of them Chinese cocksuckers."

"Chinese?"

"Yeah, fuck them rice-eatin' turds."

T.J. wheeled on his squad.

"Fuck Rice! Fuck ever grain in Uncle Ben's fuckin' box! Piss on China!"

T.J. was getting his game-face on. Two players responded with zeal.

"Rice eats shit!" somebody hollered.

"They eat owlshit!" came another cry.

I stirred the coffee in a paper cup. "Uh . . . T.J., what's China got to do with anything?"

"Chinks eat rice, don't they?"

103

I looked at the floor.

"Well?" he said.

"Well, what?"

"Well, I ain't gonna lose no football game to a fuckin' bunch of Chinks!"

I said, "T.J., they haven't moved Rice from Houston to Peking while my back was turned, have they?"

"Fuck Houston!" T.J. reminded the room.

I shook my head. "Coach, I guess I don't understand. Has Rice got a Chinese quarterback or something?"

"Naw, they got a nigger. Why?"

"No reason," I said. "I was just trying to pick up the thread of the plot."

T.J. bellowed at the Horned Frogs again.

"Who eats shit?"

"Chinamen!"

"What with?"

"Rice!" It was a group reply.

I refilled the coffee cup. "T.J., you *do* know where the name comes from, don't you? An old rich guy named William Marsh Rice founded the school. He was a person, like a Duke or a Vanderbilt or a Stanford."

"Them's schools," said T.J. He bit off a chunk of chewing tobacco.

"First, they were people," I said. "Leland Stanford was a robber baron. William Marsh Rice was a cotton-farmer robber baron."

"Billy Clyde," T.J. said to me with a sympathetic expression, "what the fuck's wrong with you? John Brodie and Jim Plunkett and them studs didn't play football for no sissy named Leland."

"You're right," I said.

He said, "Let me explain something to you. Rice pricks is engineers, ain't they? Scientists? Computer technology and all that shit? Well, who knows more about computers than anybody? Chinamen, that's who."

"It's the Japanese, isn't it?"

"Japs, Chinamen. God damn, Billy Clyde, gimme a fuckin' break!"

"I'm beginning to understand."

"Awright, then," T.J. said. "Fuck Rice!"

Out on the field during warmups, I met three of T.J.'s assistant coaches. Like the head coach himself, they were all dressed in purple knit shirts, knaki trousers, and purple baseball caps. They all had a mouthful of gum or tobacco.

It was a warm September afternoon. Being down on the field was a good feeling, a fanciful experience. I was looking around at the crowd that filled only half of the 46,000 seats in TCU's stadium when Mike Homer came up to me. He was the Frogs' offensive coordinator.

I asked Mike if TCU was ready to play a good game.

"You can't ever tell," he said, his eyes fixed on a cute TCU cheerleader who wore a white tank top and a short pleated purple skirt. She had frizzy blond hair and tanned, curvy legs. "Lots of high-class beaver up in New York, huh?"

"Yeah," I admitted, largely to please him. "We got a thrower?"

"Guess you get it lobbed at you from all directions."

"Pretty much. How good's our passer?"

"That there's old Sandi," he said.

Now I was staring at the cheerleader.

Mike Homer said, "Lord, I know she's somebody's daughter, but I'd wet her down."

The assistant coach then raced onto the field to slap a player on the side of his purple helmet for not throwing the ball with enough steam on it.

A few minutes later, I was shaking hands with Red Jeffers, the defensive coordinator.

"We ready?" I asked him.

"God damn, there's old Sandi," he said, feeling around on his crotch.

Sandi was in a huddle with the other TCU cheerleaders. While I wasn't all that fond of midgets, I said:

"Old Sandi's all right."

"You ain't shittin'," Red Jeffers said. " 'Course, I reckon she ain't nothin' to compare with New York whup."

"New York whup?"

"They got it up there, don't they?"

"Pretty much."

"Damn." he said, clawing at his balls again. "All them Wops and Jews with big titties. I'm gonna get my ass up there one of these days."

Red Jeffers then raced onto the field to slap a player on the side of his purple helmet for not digging out hard enough on a sprint.

The last assistant coach I met was Ronnie Bob Collins. He was in charge of the defensive secondary.

"Looks like we have some speed in the secondary," I said to Coach Collins. "Will they hit?"

"Not like that little shit over there," he said, looking at Sandi. "How'd you like to get hooked up with her? Tell you one thing. You wouldn't need no kickstarter on your tongue!"

The teams returned to their dressing rooms for last-minute instructions and nervous pisses before the opening kickoff. That was when T.J. formally introduced me to his valiants.

The introduction was moving enough. I was an All-American, an all-pro, a man who had once sneaked out of a hospital where I was recovering from three broken ribs to beat Notre Dame almost single-handedly on a Saturday very much like this one.

T. J. put his hand on my shoulders as he faced the Horned Frogs. "If Billy Clyde Puckett was eligible and I needed him today, he'd drag his butt out there—cast and all—and find some way to win!"

I didn't know what in the name of the Gipper I would say to the TCU players until I sat on the edge of a table and looked out at their farm-kid faces, their street-smart glances, at the white numerals on their purple jerseys.

Like most major college teams, and most NFL teams, T.J.'s current batch of Horned Frogs were predominantly white with certain positions reserved for black athletes.

T.J. went along with the thinking that had clouded the minds of other head coaches throughout the history of integrated football. A quarterback should be white, even if he was a lanky senior like Sonny Plummer, who knelt on the floor in front of me and whose arm reminded T.J. of a seal. A ball-carrier ought to be black, even if he was Webster Davis, a tailback T.J. hoped to replace next year with Tonsillitis Johnson, Davis being a runner T.J. described as having no right to be black because he was "too fuckin' slow." Elsewhere, tight ends were white, wide receivers were black; centers were white; offensive and defensive linemen were both—size was all that mattered; linebackers were white, cornerbacks were black. Safeties could be either shade if they were good outfielders.

There was more country-boy prejudice than scientific logic behind this thinking—the Hall of Fame is littered with exceptions. But nearly every coach is an ex-player who remembers the time some black athlete screwed up in a critical game situation. White players screw up, too, but a coach rationalized this by saying the white players are only trying too hard to win, whereas black players screw up because they aren't trying hard enough, seeing as how they're black, of course. A coach detests careless mistakes.

Coaches don't care if you understand their logic in the matter, and they don't give a shit whether you condemn it or not. All coaches are cautious and conservative by nature, mainly because their jobs often hang on the bounce of a fumble—and most of them spend their careers getting fired for not winning.

A coach creates his own mistakes at times, and he'll frequently do it by assigning his black athletes to the "hotdog" positions that he insists are best suited to the mind and body of the black athlete, positions in which the blacks themselves are the most "comfortable." These are the positions that require speed, skill, and strength, ideally all three, but don't necessarily require brainwork.

Coaches remind themselves and each other that a quarterback has to call plays or audibilize, a center has to pick up the blitz, a linebacker has to "read" before he reacts, and a tight end has to like the dirty work of blocking more than he likes to catch passes—and you want a coach to trust a *black guy* to do those things?

A coach in the 1980s had yet to be fooled by any of history's exceptions to his rules. Coaches had yielded to the changes in society but somewhat on their own terms. Coaches still hadn't seen a great black center—that must prove something.

But with the emergence of the black athlete had come another problem. Kids today, white or black, wanted to be told "why" before they jumped in the slop in the name of duty, honor, the old school colors—and that "why" was just too God-damn-much fucking trouble for most coaches to explain to a kid who was getting a free four-year education and all the pussy he could handle.

You jumped in the slop because a coach like T.J. Lambert said so or you got your ass benched or fired.

And now it was to a group of TCU athletes that T.J. wanted to fire—lazy, prideless losers—that I was expected to say something inspirational before they went out to challenge the Rice Owls.

I began by saying how fortunate they were to be playing football for a character-builder like Coach Lambert and his dedicated staff, men like Mike Homer, Red Jeffers, Ronnie Bob Collins.

Fear of losing an audience may have accounted for what I said next.

"Men, I saw something out on the field a while ago that reminded me of another Rice game," I said. "I saw one of your cheerleaders. Cute little girl named Sandi."

"Awwright," said Sonny Plummer, there on the floor in front of me. He and Webster Davis exchanged a high-five and pointed at their crotches.

I acknowledged them soberly and continued.

"My junior year we had a cheerleader who looked enough like Sandi to be her older sister—and it was. Her name was Tracy. I guess you could say Tracy was the most popular girl on the campus. Pretty little blond devil . . . vivacious, outgoing. Well . . . the Saturday of our game against Rice, right here on this field, she started walking over to the stadium from her room in the Tri-Delt dorm and a terrible thing happened. That great little girl . . . Sandi's older sister . . . she got run over and killed by a crazy, drunken Rice student in a sports car. Our team . . . we didn't find out about it till after the game—a game we lost."

I paused a minute, as if the thought of Tracy's

death had made me nauseous all over again; then I went on.

"Maybe you guys know what I'm gonna say next. Sandi's going to be out there yelling her heart out for you this afternoon. She'll be yelling for you to beat the Rice Owls the same way her sister would have cheered us on if she'd lived. So how 'bout it, gang? Let's even the score. Let's win this one for Sandi and her sister!"

T.J.'s voice boomed out. "Get them low-life fuckin' murderers!"

The Horned Frogs tore out of the locker room like maniacs, whooping, cursing, banging on locker doors, aching for the blood of the Rice Owls.

T.J. shook my hand.

"You did real good, son."

"Thanks, Coach."

"Was that a true story?"

"Part of it. We did have a cheerleader who looked a lot like Sandi."

"What'd she do?"

"The main thing she did was give Shake Tiller the clap."

The score was 12–3 at halftime in favor of Rice.

No touchdowns were scored. Rice recovered four fumbles inside TCU's 20-yard line and kicked four field goals to get its 12 points. The Frogs salvaged 3 points on a field goal in the last minute before the half. A 40-yard pass-interference penalty gave TCU the ball on Rice's 1-yard line. Three running plays lost 5 yards, and T.J. settled for the field goal.

In the locker room, T.J. was livid. He wasn't out-raged so much at the score, at the fact that his team was down by 9 points, as he was at the indifferent way the Frogs had performed.

They had shown no zip. They weren't hitting. They weren't alert. They didn't even look concerned.

"I'm takin' the blame for the way you puked up them two quarters," T.J. said to the team. "It ain't a question of no guts, it's a plain case of no energy, and it's my fault. Your problem is, you done left your blockin' and tacklin' in a bunch of that sorority whup!"

Girls were the enemy of football players, T.J. said. "If the truth was known, ever damn one of you got spermed out last night. Don't nobody look at me like I'm wrong!"

He spit tobacco juice on his pants leg, wiped off his chin, and said:

"I've give up on this game. Fuck it! You can let them slant-eyed sumbitches embarrass you if you want to, but next week things is gonna be different! The women on this campus is gonna get a lot less football cock on Friday night!

"When I was a young shitass, they said it was bad to mastrebate. Well, it took some time, but we put an end to that myth—and you're gonna do the same thing! Mastrebation is good for a football player! It's particularly good for a football player on the night before a game. Mastrebation takes the pressure off. Mastrebation has been the secret to more than one football team what kicked somebody's ass!

"You're gonna find out if you mastrebate instead of dippin' your wick, you'll conserve energy. It'll take the pubic hair off your brain. You fuckers done pubed me out in the first half. Embarrassed yourselves in front of Billy Clyde Puckett, a great All-American, and a good many of your mommas and daddys no doubt. If you'd mastrebated last night—right hand fast, left hand slow, don't make a shit—it wouldn't have happened, and it ain't gonna happen again to the Texas Christian University Horned Frogs, you can bust my ass if it does! Now get outta my sight! I ain't got no more time today to watch worms fuckin'."

The Frogs thoroughly dominated the second half. Sonny Plummer flapped his seal-like arm for two touchdown passes—they were end-over-end, but they worked—and Webster Davis plowed 12 yards for another touchdown, the longest run of his career. TCU won the game, 24 to 12. T.J. was triumphantly carried off the field on the shoulders of three beefy linemen.

I may have been the only observer who could appreciate the jubilant gestures the Frogs made with their left and right fists as they trotted past the south goal posts and disappeared into the tunnel leading to the Coliseum dressing room.

It may also have been true that others down on the field couldn't have understood what several of the Frogs were chanting as they pumped their fists up and down:

"Right hand, left hand, don't make a shit!"

Tonsillitis Johnson was a staggering sight.

There would have been no mistaking him as he stood in a corner of the Lettermen's Lounge after the game. Apart from the maroon satin warmup suit and yellow mirrored sunglasses he wore, he was the young man whose terrifying thighs threatened to burst out of his pants, whose chest, shoulders, and arms were carved from granite, and whose towering, rounded Afro looked capable of nesting a flock of tundra swans.

Before meeting him, I asked T.J. to refresh my memory about something. Wasn't it against the rules for a Southwest Conference school to bring in a prospective athlete to visit the campus before his high school football season was over?

T.J. answered with a suitably logical question of his own.

"Who the fuck's gonna tell anybody?"

Tonsillitis was accompanied by his older brother, Darnell, a confident-looking man of about twenty-seven. Darnell wore a beige polyester suit, a wool checkered tie, and he carried a valise. He was built as if he might have played football himself, but his physique was nothing to compare with that of Tonsillitis.

And it didn't take a person from Harvard Grad School to figure out that Darnell was his brother's agent and financial adviser. Come to think of it, a person from Harvard Grad School *wouldn't* have figured it out.

A high school athlete with an agent was nothing new. It was as old as a university's desire to win football games, as old as a sports-minded daddy who wanted to get the best deal for his kid. It was older than Knute Rockne—not that the discovery of it didn't constantly send a ghastly wave of shock through the minds of your beard-stroking educators and your naive sportswriters.

When Shake and I had been persuaded to become Horned Frogs, we'd had Uncle Kenneth for an agent, and Big Ed Bookman for a financial adviser. We joked later on that we had been undersold. I got a Pontiac Grand Prix and Shake got a Mercury Cougar. Uncle Kenneth got four tickets on the 50-yard line for all of TCU's home games. Big Ed got a couple of listless roughnecks on one of his drilling rigs in Scogie County during the summers.

These were small prices to pay for a couple of guys who became All-Americas and put some folks in the stands, but TCU was going to get our services anyway. We had planned to stay home. It had to do with Barbara Jane selecting TCU even though she'd had a choice of the finest institutions. She wanted to make her mother hot, I think. Big Barb's heart had been set on sending her daughter off to Holyoke, Sweet Briar, or Wellesley.

"Mom, I already know which fork to use for dessert," Barb had said.

Shake and I never regretted going to TCU, even after we'd heard tales about the real world.

In the real world, there was a thing called The Million Dollar Walk in Norman, Oklahoma.

The Million Dollar Walk at OU was a path that led from Owen Field to the dressing room. After an Oklahoma victory, the path would be lined with wealthy boosters eager to shake hands with those Sooners who had done the most to crush a Missouri Tiger or a Kansas Jayhawk.

A guy could shake hands, we heard, for as much as $5,000 on a good Saturday. Multiply that by five or six home games, it could keep a kid in beer and cigarette papers for a whole semester.

We understood that mail returned to the sender for postage due was a nice thing to receive if you happened to play for the Crimson Tide at Alabama. The player wouldn't be the actual sender, of course. Phony name. Which left everyone blameless: All the student-athlete had to do was count the crisp hundreds in the envelope, donor unknown, when Alabama was hovering around No. 1 in the polls.

The Designated Cigar Box in Athens, Georgia, was a receptacle for a recruiting fund, money used to entice bluechippers to learn how to say "How 'bout them Dawgs?" at the University of Georgia.

We were told the box would move around from

one motel to another each Saturday of the season in Athens. Generous Georgia alums would hear on the sly where the motel room was going to be—"210, Ramada"—and they would be expected to drop by before or after the game.

An off-duty redneck cop would guard the door and refuse admittance to anyone who looked like an NCAA investigator or a reporter. Inside the room, the Dawg supporter would find no people, no cocktail party, only a cigar box on a dresser with a slit in the top that was conveniently large enough for folding money.

Around the Southeastern Conference, it was suspicioned that when Georgia's slush fund fell below the $3.5-million level, there were desperately fewer Herschel Walkers on campus.

Dump McKinney had been a highly recruited quarterback from Daytona, Florida. All through his senior year of high school, every week, he would find a parcel of twelve prime New York strips on his doorstep. They were the gift of an anonymous University of Florida fan who hoped Dump would transport his gifted arm to Gainesville. The parcel of frozen steaks would include a note, something on the order of *"Go Gators, beat hell out of them Dawgs!"*

To this day, Florida fans rarely get to celebrate a victory over Georgia, even though the rivalry is bitterly intense and their annual clash in Jacksonville's Gator Bowl takes on the dimensions of Disneyland Meets Holy War.

But Dump liked New York strips. He did indeed seek his higher education at the University of Florida. And he kept on getting the prime cuts of beef until the middle of his junior year. They stopped coming after the Gators lost yet another close game to Georgia.

All Dump received after that game was the usual unsigned note, only this time it said:

"You heartbreakin choke-up motherfucker, I'm shippin your ass back to Oscar Mayer!"

Before the quest for Tonsillitis Johnson, T.J. had worn out a set of tires in the relentless pursuit of a most-wanted running back named Artis Toothis, a 188-pound speedster from Willow Neck, Texas.

T.J. made six illegal trips down to the Big Thicket, to Artis Toothis' home, a little shack which harbored the athlete's mother, father, aunt, and eight younger brothers and sisters, three of whom were squealing infants, not to mention six cats and four cur dogs.

On each visit, T.J. would sit for two and three hours with the family and animals, everyone watching soap operas on daytime TV. T.J. would smile politely as he bounced the babies on his knee and let the cur dogs hump his right leg.

As only T.J. Lambert could describe it, the house smelled like six hairy dykes playing anthill in a room with no ventilation.

On his last visit, Artis Toothis was not at home, but T.J. was promised the kid would be along any minute. Four hours went by. T.J. bounced the babies on his knee, gasped for fresh air, and watched the dogs hump his leg.

Artis Toothis finally stuck his head in the door, and said, "Be right back, Coach, I forgot somethin' at the library."

Seconds later, T.J. glanced out of a window. He saw Artis Toothis slide behind the wheel of a new white Jaguar in the company of an assistant coach from SMU.

Driving back to Fort Worth that night, the battle lost, T.J. almost turned his Ford Escort around three times.

"I wanted to go back and kick them fuckin' dogs," he said.

Coaches and faculty members will always insist

that recruiting violations are minimal and can usually be blamed on "overzealous alumni," who are
impossible to control. It helps their indigestion to
believe that.

Getting the best available athletes on your team is
one thing. Keeping them eligible is another. USC
raised this to an artform. Thirty-two Trojans on one
of USC's Rose Bowl teams were once discovered to
have passed a Communications course they didn't
know existed.

The cold, hard truth is this: no team that's ever
appeared in your Top Twenty over the past 100
years is guiltless of cheating in one way or another,
and this includes that pious campus with a golden
dome out there in South Bend, Indiana, the unin-
dicted Notre Dame. When USC and Notre Dame
collide every year in their big intersectional game,
they ought to call it the Transcript Bowl.

But if you stop to think about it, what's so criminal
about giving a kid a football scholarship, supple-
menting his income, or doing surgery on his grades?
College football takes a bunch of kids off the street
and exposes them to something besides car theft and
armed robbery.

And college football is big business. The money it
generates from endowment has built more wings on
libraries than all of the intimate friends of Beowulf.

College football has raised more than one chemis-
try professor's salary and bought more than one
computer on which some chinless wimp can get a
business degree by learning how to fuck up my bank
statements and credit references.

If you can get a free ride through college by playing
the oboe or repairing participles that dangle, why
can't you do it by putting 50,000 people in a football
stadium?

I didn't need to use those arguments on T.J., Tonsillitis, or Darnell. They were realists like me. And the four of us were now in a private confab discussing money while purple-blazered TCU immortals drank spiked punch in other nooks of the Lettermen's Lounge.

"Look here," Darnell said. "We can max out at Oklahoma at thirty thou a year. At Texas, we can max out at twenty-five a year, but Tonsillitis be startin' as a freshmens in Austin. Tonsillitis don't be needin' that E.O.S. shit, you dig?"

"E.O.S.?" said Coach Lambert. I was equally puzzled.

"End of sentence, baby. OU don't guarantee freshmens to start. Tonsillitis be winnin' the Heismans his first year."

"We'll start him as a freshman," T.J. said. "He can call plays if he wants to."

"Tonsillitis don't be callin' plays. Tonsillitis' brain be needin' to res' up for G.B.O.S."

"G.B. who?" I said.

"Get bad on Saturday."

Tonsillitis was also a person of character, Darnell said. When Feb. 8 came around, the national signing date, Tonsillitis would honor the L.O.I. he signed.

"Letter of intent?" I said.

"You cool."

I attempted to engage Tonsillitis in conversation by asking if he was worried about injuries this season, his senior year in high school.

"It could be expensive," I took pleasure in saying.

"Tonsillitis don't be gettin' hurt," Darnell said. "Tonsillitis be hurtin' other folks."

T.J. patted Tonsillitis on the back. "You're the best, hoss. Best I ever saw."

I kept looking at Tonsillitis for *his* answer. I would

liked to have seen his eyes, but I could only see my forehead in his yellow sunglasses.

Tonsillitis said, "You have ast me if I am worried about injurin' myself in my las' season. My answer to you is no. That would be undue worriation."

Darnell related a story about their childhood, the purpose of which was to convey to us that Tonsillitis had always been a tough competitor.

There was this night when the two boys had been taken to a double-feature by their father, a handyman. Tonsillitis was only seven years old at the time. The movies they had seen were *Blood Beach* and *My Bloody Valentine.*

"Kids is funny," Darnell said, smiling. "We came home and the first thing Tonsillitis said was 'Daddy, I'm gonna get a knife and cut you up.' "

Darnell and I laughed together, he at what Tonsillitis had said, me at the double-feature their daddy had chosen.

Tonsillitis' name had been intriguing me. I was compelled to ask Darnell where it came from.

"He was named for his uncle, Tonsorrell," Darnell said. "Everybody had trouble sayin' it right. We started callin' him Tonsillitis when he was little. Might as well be his real name."

The meeting adjourned with T.J. urging Tonsillitis to have a great year at Boakum High and not make any college decisions until he checked with the Horned Frogs.

TCU's head coach was asking for the right of last refusal.

"What number you want to wear on that purple jersey, hoss?" T.J. squeezed Tonsillitis' shoulder lovingly.

"Thirty grand," I said, answering for him.

"My man!" said Darnell, offering me his palm to slap.

Satisfied I had done all I could to help T.J.'s recruiting for the moment, I left to go meet an old newspaper buddy and see if Fort Worth nightlife had anything new to offer.

SIX

Mommie's Trust Fund was on the southwestern edge of the city in a half-finished shopping village bordered by half-finished condominium units. Beyond the condos lay infinity—and the dreams of other developers.

There was no room to park near Mommie's Trust Fund. I eased the Lincoln around a corner to another area of the shopping village and found a space by a Red Lobster, next door to an Arby's, pretty close to a Houlihan's, three doors from a TGI Friday's, just behind a Bennigan's, half a block from Chi Chi's, and directly in front of a topless-bottomless club called The Blessed Virgin.

I almost took a look inside the topless-bottomless club because of its marquee, which said:

Now appearing:
KIM COOZE
44—22—38
and
SIX ALL NUDE BABY SITTERS

Jim Tom Pinch was waiting for me at the horseshoe bar in Mommie's Trust Fund. The bar was already crowded with singles types. Rising young executives were deeply engrossed in conversation about commodities and tax-shelters with herpes carriers of all ages. They glowed beneath the imitation Tiffany lampshades.

I said hello to Jim Tom. He gave me a nod as he continued talking to the girl standing next to him, a retro gum-chewer in fishnet stockings and a pop-art minidress.

To the girl, Jim Tom said, "I'm lucky I inherited the same rod my daddy had. When he died, it took seven days to close the casket. That thing stuck straight up like this."

"I ain't heard that shit before, have I?" said the girl, sipping her strawberry Margarita and looking bored as she reached for a Vantage 100.

I demanded that Jim Tom and I take a table because of my leg, which we did. We quickly ordered three young Scotches apiece to save time and trouble for the ballet instructor moonlighting as a waiter.

"You wrote fast," I said to Jim Tom.

"Yeah, I just turned it over to Dexter and Vivian. Did the story on how good the Frogs looked, did the column on how bad Rice looked. Pure crap; don't bother to read it."

Jim Tom was the sports editor and columnist for *The Fort Worth Light & Shopper*, a man I had known since my playing days at TCU. He was the only sportscaster I trusted. Dexter and Vivian were Dexatrim and Vivarin, the caffeine bombs, Jim Tom's best friends in journalism.

"Saw you down on the field," Jim Tom said. "Why didn't you come up to the press box?"

"I figured Dexter and Vivian were having a spat."

Jim Tom was a twice-divorced man in his late forties. His hair was speckled with gray, he was developing a paunch, and he moved his right arm with difficulty. Arthritis was setting in. He was as mentally whipped as any newspaperman his age, just as underpaid, resigned to staying one jump ahead of the creditors.

He was the sportswriter who had helped me write the book that I called an autobiography and Shake called a diary. I dictated it into the tape-recorder, and Jim Tom typed. Jim Tom thought up the title: *Semi-Tough*. Then I decided not to have it published. It would have embarrassed too many of my teammates.

It wasn't the first time Jim Tom had blown a shot at literary fame. He'd once been offered a job with *Sports Illustrated*, but he passed it up because he hadn't wanted to change his by-line to James Thomas Pinch and bemoan the fate of the otter. Jim Tom had been sentenced to the newspaper business for life, but he said he could be reasonably happy if he didn't lose his mind and get married again.

As we settled in for a long night at Mommie's Trust Fund, Jim Tom admitted that his sleepovers were even becoming less frequent.

The pain was getting to be too much trouble to explain. He referred to the pain that would go shooting through his right arm and up into his shoulder just as his guest was about to pleasure herself.

I asked him if it was the arthritis that had driven away his two wives—the ambidextrous Earlene, who could hurl a clock-radio through a windowpane with either hand, and the incomparable Dottie, whose dress always seemed to get blown up around carpenters.

"No, it's the hours," he said. "A newspaperman shouldn't get married. All he cares about is his work. We go through life bitching at retarded editors . . .having heart attacks because of typographical errors in our stories, like what we wrote in the first God-damn place was *Farewell to Arms!* We go home wore out with nothin' left to give anybody. All a newspaperman needs is a bar where he can sign his name, some friendly conversation, and a typewriter with a ribbon that'll reverse. It takes a saint to be married to a journalist. Women ought to know better. Women ought to marry estate planners."

On napkins, spurred on by the steady flow of J&B, we made a list of morning-after lines, things a man had heard—or would hear—from a shapely adorable or a not-so-shapely adorable who had taken him up on his drunken invitation for a sleepover.

In the Top Ten were:

- "Hey, this is Saturday! I have the whole day free!"
- "Are these clean towels?"
- "That's a neat picture. Your wife is really pretty."
- "It's actually in remission."
- "You probably shouldn't drink so much. It would help."
- "Oh, don't worry, I would never pick up your phone."
- "What were you doing with that pinlight last night?"
- "Is it hard to get back on the freeway from here?"
- "Rich will answer if I'm not there, but it's cool, he's just a good friend."
- "In the bar, I thought you were the most cynical person I'd ever met."

Mommie's Trust Fund was about to max out at a hundred guys playing backgammon and two hundred girls wearing straw cowboy hats, tight T-shirts, designer jeans, and brass belt buckles that had "BULLSHIT" engraved on them.

"Why do you go to places like this?" I asked Jim Tom.

"It's my neighborhood pub."

As another tray of drinks arrived, Jim Tom said, "A couple of friends may join us in a minute. You care?"

"I'm not leaving with one of 'em," I said with alarm.

"That's all right. I might do a quickie in the forecourt, two on one. Not that I can get it up. You know what I yearn for, Billy Clyde? Old age. I won't have to do anything but lay on my back and bat clean-up."

"I didn't know you have to be old to do that."

"Maybe I'll grow a mustache, hit 'em with the whup-broom."

I drew Jim Tom into a conversation about sports. He was always good for a few lines I could use at banquets.

Twenty years of covering sports events had left him with an assortment of prejudices. He had never been in the cheerleader class of sportswriters, anyhow. It didn't take long for him to unload on his pet hates, which included almost every sport but college football.

The mention of ice hockey got him started.

"Who's ever seen a goal?" he said. "Forget a fucking *assist*. It's a bunch of guys named Jacques. Know what ice hockey needs? A five-thousand-pound puck. Two teams, East Coast, West Coast. They play one game. That's the season. Whatever ocean the puck winds up in, you've got a winner. You're gonna be a TV announcer. You could stand there in Omaha and say, 'Hello, everybody, I'm here in Nebraska where the puck will be arriving almost any day.' Fuck ice hockey."

"I heard you went to Wimbledon last summer."

"The linesmen were all wing commanders, squadron leaders, and group captains. McEnroe shot down six of 'em. He should have worn a swastika on his arm. I never could figure out which Swede had the dirtiest hair."

"Did you watch the girls?"

"I watched 'em double-fault and frown at their mothers."

"I saw Uncle Kenneth yesterday. He's still fond of pro basketball."

"Oh, me, too. The fucking season's ten months long, four thousand teams get in the playoffs, and all the armpits look alike. I'd rather watch cross-country skiing."

"I didn't know that was a sport."

"It's not. Cross-country skiing is how a Norwegian goes to the Safeway."

"You like college basketball," I said. "The Houston Cougars.

"Only when the cheerleaders turn it into a disco. You can watch tits bounce while they drag the coaches off to an asylum. You're right. I like the Coug-roes."

"Is there a copyright on that?"

"I called 'em the Houston Coug-roes in print," Jim Tom said. "When the hate mail came in, I pleaded typo."

I knew how much he despised baseball. I asked him how often he went to a Texas Rangers game.

"I like it when they change pitchers," he said. "You get to sleep an hour."

"Sounds like golf on television."

"Golf is a good game to play—if you don't have to keep score. Nobody can identify with those guys on the tour. They all drive the ball three hundred yards. Some blond guy makes a putt. Another blond guy misses a putt. Golf was fun when Arnold Palmer sweated through his shirt and chain-smoked. But you could see the same thing at a Tennessee Williams play and not get sunburned."

I tried boxing.

"¿Habla español?"

"Shake Tiller's working on some kind of pro football exposé," I said. "I don't know who he's writing it for."

"Playboy. Sounds like a hell of a piece."

"You know about it?"

"I've talked to him."

"Everybody's talked to him but me."

"He said he'll be in L.A. when you get there. He came through here on his book tour. We got drunk. I think he got laid. I mean, I don't see how he could have avoided it. You'll meet her. She's one of the debs I invited over."

I didn't like the playful look on his face.

"What have you got me into, Jim Tom?"

"It's just a family outing," he said. "I thought we'd go to Six Flags, put the kids on the log ride, stop off somewhere and bowl a few frames, pick up a barrel of Kentucky Fried, and call it a night."

We were both looking around the room for our ballet instructor when Jim Tom leaped to his feet.

He had seen the debs, his lady friends, coming up behind me.

He pulled two chairs over to our table. Not being an impolite person, I started to struggle up for proper introductions, but my shoulder gently bumped into Kim Cooze's awesome bosom.

"Oh, sweetie, do that again," said a husky female voice.

Exotic dancers did not have a track record of putting me into a state of euphoria, but I respected them as athletes. They were sometimes fun to talk to.

It was now after 2 A.M. We had moved our act to The Blessed Virgin, which was wholly disrespectful of closing times. Jim Tom and I each faced one of those medieval Scotches, the kind that looks more like rust than amber at that hour. We were sitting on barstools with the debs.

Kim Cooze was on my left and Brandy, a Baby Sitter, was on Jim Tom's right.

Jim Tom was in a dark lull, muttering that Vivian had let him down. Brandy, an eighteen-year-old ravager, was drinking straight shots of tequila and accusing the bartender of holding out on the dread.

"Ralph will be here in a minute," the bartender said.

"Yeah, he will," Brandy smirked. "Meanwhile, let's do some of yours."

"I'm empty."

"Uh-huh," said Brandy. "For somebody who's empty, you sure got a lot of snot on your sleeve."

Kim was an honest 44-22-38. She had short platinum hair done up in a Thirties look, large green eyes with false lashes that could have supported a string of Christmas lights, and makeup a half-inch thick. I estimated her age at somewhere between forty and Medicare.

Her awesomes were barely constrained by a scanty white halter. She wore black leather pants that fit like an oil-base paint. Her spiked-heel shoes had little pink bows on the instep.

I had caught her last performance of the evening, and couldn't resist complimenting her on originality. I had never seen an exotic dancer who opened her act with a brief sermon, and then dry-fucked a copy of the Bible.

"I'm an ordained Minister of Mystical Theology," she said. "I have a certificate."

Kim went on at some length about how we all reached God in different ways. I did it through football, she said. She did it by sharing her body and her beliefs with the world. Exposing your body was no sin, she said. She had analyzed her soul and concluded that she was mystically united with God. Her psychic dreams had told her to save the souls of others by reaching out with her extravagant body, which God had given her, and touching others.

I said, "Do you actually go so far as to fuck for God?"

"I don't like that kind of language."

I apologized.

"What's old Count Smirn up to?" Kim asked the bartender. "Better put two of him on the rocks for me."

The bartender slid her a double vodka.

Kim pressed her awesomes against my arm and rubbed her knee against my good left leg.

"When there's a bigger crowd I do a longer act," she said. "I left out the rosary tonight and a thing I do with a rhinestone cross. This jukebox isn't great, either. It's mostly country. I don't think God is opposed to country, but I seem to reach more souls through old-fashioned jazz and big-band sounds."

I asked Kim how she had gotten along with Shake Tiller.

"He's a very devout person," she said.

"Yes, I know."

"I cried when he told me the story about the crippled nuns. How they changed his life?"

"The who?"

"You were there, he said. The time you were little kids and skipped church to play touch football on the lawn by the convent? And it caught on fire?"

"Oh, yeah, that's right."

"That was so heroic," said Kim. "Not many kids would have gone in that burning building—and you weren't even Catholic!"

"Shake did it all. I just turned on the garden hose.

It's so long ago, I can't remember how many nuns he saved."

"Ten."

"Well, I'd have said six. The old memory sure plays tricks on you."

"Six were in wheelchairs." ·

"Right. It's all coming back to me. The flames were terrible. Some of those poor nuns were flying out of the windows like bats."

"God repaid you. He persuaded you it was all right to play football on Sunday. You see? Help others and God helps you."

"Shake spoke to God, I didn't. But I guess getting the word from a holy person like Shake is the same thing, isn't it?"

"It is!" said Kim, still rubbing her knee on my leg. "I transfer goodness and I receive goodness in return. My boyfriend in Dallas says he can sense the vibrations in the audience when I'm stripping for God."

Jim Tom backed off his barstool. He took Brandy by the arm.

"I'm outta here, Billy Clyde. I've had eight dozen Scotches and four million Winstons. I've had it."

"I didn't know you came in here to try to quit smokin'," said Brandy.

"See you next trip," I said to Jim Tom. "When Kim and I get settled in our mobile home in Bakersfield, you'll have to come out and visit."

Stretching his right arm and massaging his shoulder, Jim Tom wobbled behind Brandy and they went out the door. I turned to Kim with a yawn and patted her hand.

"It's not easy for me to confess this to a Minister of Mystical Theology, but I'm an atheist, Kim."

"That's not true."

"Also, I'm a happily married man," I said. "*And*

. . . I have an early flight in the morning. Today, I mean."

"Happily married men are the only kind I know. My boyfriend's married."

She ran her fingers up and down my thigh.

"It's been fun, Kim. You took my mind off the Middle East . . . Afghanistan . . . inflation . . . unemployment. Should I thank you or God?"

"Take Communion with me."

She put my hand on one of her 44s and held it there.

"God is good." She smiled sweetly.

"I don't see how I can take Communion with my leg in a cast."

"There's more than one kind of Communion, Bozo. Ever heard of Oral Roberts?"

"Uh . . . where do you generally hold Communion?"

She dumped her vodka into a plastic cup for the road. "I'm at the Holiday Inn on University. Pay up and let's blow this pop stand."

There were two versions of what happened next. There was mine, which was the truth, and there was Shake Tiller's cynical fantasy, which was guaranteed to get a laugh from the guys in the bars.

Kim's motel was on the way to the Hyatt Regency downtown. I did follow her car, a new Camaro, but I left her with a friendly honk as she turned into the Holiday Inn. Fifteen minutes later, I was tucked under my Hyatt Regency covers with nothing but three Anacin.

The way Shake liked to tell it, J&B had grabbed the steering wheel out of my hands. J&B had tracked Kim's turn signal like radar, parked the Lincoln with great haste, yanked me into her room, and made a $100 donation to her church.

Articles of clothing had then gone sailing in all directions, and I had quickly found myself pinned down on a motel bed listening to Kim's little exclamations of relish as something damp traveled toward my pelvis.

How a close friend could accuse a mature, responsible person like myself of such wretched behavior was beyond my comprehension, but of course I had learned to live with other vicious rumors about my character.

The next morning, curiously enough, I was surrounded by Shake Tiller as I limped into a gift shop in the D/FW airport. Shake's book, *The Art of Taking Heat*, was displayed everywhere.

I bought a copy to take on the plane to Los Angeles. I needed it for a prop.

I slumped into the seat I always requested—6B, aisle, smoking—and opened Shake's book to let the dry-wall salesman sitting next to me know in a pointed way that I would be unable to chat during the flight.

WHAT IS HEAT?

Heat is shit—and we all take it.

We take married heat, kid heat, boss heat, car heat, bank heat, credit heat, political heat, IRS heat, health heat, appliance heat, and every other kind of heat you can think of.

And all it ever does is make us grumpy and irritable.

But we can't talk about it until we start calling it what it is.

Shit. It's important that you get used to the word. It's more descriptive than heat.

It would have been in the title of this book if I hadn't taken some shit from the publisher.

The point is, the shit-givers of this world think that giving you shit helps you become a better person.

Well, we all know they're full of shit, don't we?

Shit givers come in two basic categories. There are those who don't know they're doing it, and there are those who give it to you on purpose.

The unknowing shit-giver is a person who goes along thinking it's his or her privilege to do it, like it's something you grow into as an adult.

This type can't seem to figure out why you're always mad at them. They're too busy giving somebody shit to understand that the people you genuinely like are the ones who don't do it.

Shit for your own good is the worst kind.

First of all, it means that somebody is giving it to you on purpose.

And of course you know what's good for you a hell of a lot better than anybody else—and you don't need that shit, right?

This is a book about how to turn it around on the people who bring all the heat into your life; who give you the shit, in other words.

I'm not a psychologist or a psychiatrist. You wouldn't have bought this book if you'd wanted to read *that* shit.

I'm just a person like yourself with one big difference. I got tired of taking it and decided to do something about it.

I don't have all the answers. For instance, I don't know how to handle death shit, particularly in a case where it happens to you.

What I mostly think you do is dress up real nice and go talk to that guy across the river.

But I do have some thoughts about the other stuff.

Let's start with a common example of the kind of everyday shit we run into.

A repairman comes to your home to fix your G.E. icemaker. He says it's fixed after he's been there a while and he leaves. But the minute he walks out the door, it doesn't work. Sound familiar?

Five times he comes to fix it, and five times he leaves and it still doesn't work even though by now you've paid him $1,657 for his labor.

Finally, on his next visit, he says it looks like you need a new icemaker.

That's when you give *him* the shit.

Here's how you do it.

You smile and say, "I need a new icemaker? Fine. I hope you have one with you."

He says he does.

"Great," you say. "Can you install it now if I make you a sandwich and give you a glass of iced tea?"

"Well, I don't know," he says.

"Aw, come on," you say. "There's a big tip in it for you, Guido."

"How big's the tip?"

"We're talking big. Do you really have a new icemaker in the truck?"

"Sure," he says.

"How much will it cost?"

"Two million dollars, plus tax."

You say, Terrific. Sounds fair enough. Oh, by the way, your office called before you got here. It was something about your wife."

"My wife?"

"Yeah, has she been ill?"

"No, not really."

You shrug and say, "I'm sorry I didn't get the whole message. I guess I was busy. It was something about a biopsy. The only word I remember is 'malignant.' "

The flight to Los Angeles was uneventful except for the manner in which an attentive stewardess—Dallas, killer bod—autographed the cast on my leg.

She wrote:

"Randi. 214 555-1488!"

"My wife will love it," I said to the girl.

"How long have you been married?"

"Almost five years."

"Perfect!" she sparkled. "You're about ready to bolt, Jack!"

The cab ride from the L.A. airport to the Westwood Marquis gave me sufficient time to dwell on the fact that foreigners who spoke no more than ten words of English were now driving as many cabs in Los Angeles as they were in New York City.

My driver acted as if he knew right where the hotel was, but instead of taking a northbound freeway to Wilshire or Sunset and hanging a right, he insisted on getting lost in a maze of side streets and then trying to recover by plodding his way along arteries peppered with stoplights. We passed all of the familiar places: shabby health spas, boarded-up karate schools, cut-rate camera shops, out-of-favor Italian restaurants, Trudy's Records, Tapes, Vitamins & Jogwear, Rusty's Bikes & Bagels, and several denim outlets for thinlegged pygmies.

I knew we had overrun the hotel when we cruised by the *Hello, Dolly!* set at Fox, but soon we crawled through the Beverly Hills flats and went by that house with the statue of the elephant in the yard. When we hit Sunset I shouted out the only thing I thought the driver might understand. "UCLA!" Happily, he turned left and we finally made it to the Marquis.

I didn't complain about the meter going $10 over what it should have been. The driver was of indefinable origin, but he obviously had an Iranian-Syrian connection, and I knew he would be dead in a matter of months. He would volunteer for a suicide mission on behalf of some insane cause and ram a truckload of TNT into an office building. With a bit of luck, he might choose a structure teeming with network programmers.

I checked into Barbara Jane's suite—our suite now—and called the number of the sound stage at the Sunset-Gower Studio to let her know I had arrived safely.

I had known she would be at rehearsal. Yet another try on the *Rita* pilot was coming up for a taping session before a live audience in a few days. It was touch and go for everyone, not a moment to relax.

"I'm here," I said after she was summoned to the phone.

"You're there. Good."

"You're busy."

"Yes."

"You're very busy."

"Yes."

"That comes as no surprise to this reporter. You also sound mad."

"Yes, but practicing genocide is improving my frame of mind. I'll be jolly tonight. Half the membership of the Writers' Guild will be dead by then. I'll see you at Enjolie's for dinner."

"Enjolie's?" I said with apprehension.

"Shake knows where the restaurant is. He's in our hotel."

I tuned in a pro football game on television to keep me company while I unpacked. The game was a lackluster affair in which the Washington Redskins were allowing the L.A. Rams to romp down the field like the Grambling band.

The Rams were ahead by 44 to 14 when I turned on the set. It was early in the fourth quarter. The picture on my screen came into focus as Dreamer

Tatum artfully stumbled and fell, letting a slow-footed Ram trudge by him on a 26-yard touchdown jaunt.

Dreamer was already on strike, I thought. He just hadn't walked off the job.

The sound that ricocheted around my room before I lowered it was Larry Hoage crying out to his viewers that he had just witnessed the reincarnation of Tom Harmon.

"Incredible!" screamed Larry Hoage. "Unbelievable! What a move he put on Dreamer Tatum!"

"Flag," said another voice, quietly. "They're bringing it back."

Undaunted, Larry Hoage yelled, "Talk about your O.J. Simpson! Talk about your Walter Payton! Talk about your Franco Harris!"

"Holding," the other voice said. It was the voice of the color man, Don Avery, a former linebacker for Miami.

Larry Hoage forged onward.

"That makes it fifty to fourteen, Rams, with the extra point to come! But we've still got a ball game, Don Avery! These Redskins are a fourth-quarter team, remember! We'll be right back!"

Larry Hoage was calmer when the telecast resumed after a commercial.

"Don, it's amazing how these Rams have overcome so many penalties today. That was their eighth holding call, their sixteenth infraction of the game! But you sure can't tell it's hurt them when you look at the old scoreboard!"

The color man said, "We've seen a lot of mistakes. Referee Charlie Teasdale and his crew have been pretty busy. The Rams haven't been smooth at all, but the Redskins haven't been able to take advantage of those mistakes. It's definitely an off day for Washington."

"Golly, Miss Moses, the Rams have put the old soo-prise on 'em today!" Larry Hoage chattered.

On the next play, the Rams ran the same sweep as before, this time from Washington's 41-yard line. As deftly as on the previous play, Dreamer Tatum let the Los Angeles ball-carrier brush past him. Two other Redskins tripped over themselves. And the Ram loped for a touchdown.

Larry Hoage was incoherent for ninety seconds, after which Don Avery mentioned the flag that had once again been thrown. This time it was clipping. No score.

Just then, my phone rang. It was Shake Tiller.

"Turn on the game," he said.

"It's on," I said.

"Great, isn't it? Dreamer bet the Over and Charlie Teasdale's got the Under. It's a hell of a contest."

"I think it's mostly a case of work stoppage where Dreamer's concerned."

"Could be," said Shake, "but it looks like he's trying to build up the strike fund while he's at it."

I went around to Shake's room and watched the rest of the game with him.

Due to a grotesque combination of penalties and Washington ineptitude, neither team scored again. In all, the Rams had four touchdowns called back in the fourth quarter.

Shake couldn't have been more delighted with the final result. Rams 44, Redskins 14. This put the total points scored in the game at 58. The over-and-under betting number had been 58 1/2, Shake said. Referee Charlie Teasdale had skillfully thrown enough flags to hold the Under.

"The guy's an artist," Shake said. "He doesn't usually have to resort to grand larceny, but fuck, he was up against the whole Redskin team!"

That was as good a time as any for me to ask Shake about the article he was working on.

"I'm gonna give the sport an enema," he said. "It's overdue."

"Why?"

"For its own good."

"That's the worst kind of shit. I read it in a book."

"Absolutely. That's why pro football deserves it. I'm gonna get even."

"For what? All the game did was make you rich and get you laid."

"You kidding? I made Burt Danby rich and got my ownself laid. It's a different game, man. It's a fucking bore. It's Wall Street football—a bunch of drones doing what a computer tells 'em to. Shit, B. C., you know how it was. We wanted to win every week. I might have acted casual, but I never played casual. We got after everybody's ass. We didn't take days off. Pride wouldn't let us. But I saw the poison coming. I didn't bitch about it? I didn't say they were using the rules and the zebras to make everybody equal? The competition's not on the field anymore. It's in the TV ratings. It's which owner has the best hors d'oeuvres in his luxury box. But you know what? They've tricked themselves. The greed's passed down. Now everybody's in on it. In a sixteen-game season, who'll remember those three or four games when the guys went south and bet the other side? The broadcasters will keep on saying how great they are—even when they hike their leg and call it a pass route. Don't be critical on the air, B. C. It won't sell. And I sure wouldn't want you to say a zebra can call holding on every play if he wants to, and isn't it curious how often it affects the game when he does call it? I've talked to receivers today, man. They come out of the huddle, they don't read defenses.

They read zebras. Try to figure out which way they've bet!"

Shake poured himself a cup of coffee from a room-service table.

"I think the public's wising up. TV ratings are starting to drop. There are more no-shows in the stadiums. It's NFL roulette. There's six cylinders in the gun, right? Used to be, you had five chances to catch a bullet when they pulled the trigger. There was always one lay-down artist. Now you've only got one chance out of six. One bullet in the gun. One guy who wants to win the game. On the Giants before you got hurt, that was you. You know what's in the other five cylinders? You have a coke-head . . . a gambler . . . a labor organizer . . . a millionaire who's too rich to care . . . and a zebra.

"Hey, we won a Super Bowl and it's great, man. Love my ring. I wouldn't take anything for it. But I gotta tell you something. Our last drive? We scratched and clawed and fought our ass off. You finally scored and the rockets went off, but I was a nervous wreck. I knew we had the best team. We deserved to win. That's what made it worse, especially when we got down close and could smell it. On every play from their thirty on in, I was thinking, Uh-oh, here it comes. Here's where Hose lays one up there for them instead of us. Turns out he bet the Giants."

"Hose Manning wasn't Dump McKinney."

"No, but I'm glad he never had a phone in the huddle."

"Uncle Kenneth said he talked to you."

"He confirmed some things."

"What are you trying to do to poor old Charlie Teasdale? He's worked some funny games, but so what?"

Shake did five minutes on Charlie Teasdale. Charlie was a housebuilder in Dallas in real life. High interest rates had almost buried him three years ago. He had been woefully in debt, but he had somehow worked his way out from under it although he hadn't sold any houses. Charlie Teasdale was also a degenerate old bastard who had whup stashed all over Dallas and Fort Worth. What did it add up to when you put all this together with the games he had officiated, games where the final scores had looked stranger than hieroglyphics?

"An unfortunate set of circumstances," I said.

"Try Charles Manson."

For the sake of argument, I said, "Some friends probably bailed him out of debt. Charlie's a dunce, Shake. He's inept. They ought to retire him. If you write what I think you're gonna write, you're liable to get your ass sued—and it'll be a hell of a lot easier for Charlie Teasdale to prove he's a fool than it will for you to prove he's a thief."

"He gave somebody a game," Shake said with calm satisfaction.

"To bet on?"

"Somebody we know."

"Who?"

"How was Fort Worth?"

Shake was savoring the moment.

"Not Uncle Kenneth," I said. "If Uncle Kenneth had hold of something that good, he wouldn't tell anybody, least of all you and me. He wouldn't trade it for a ticket to Heaven!"

"It wasn't Kenneth and it wasn't Jim Tom. It was a female acquaintance of ours."

Call me dense. I was stumped.

"She's a Minister of Mystical Theology."

"Kim Cooze told you Charlie Teasdale gave her a game?"

I didn't often sing soprano.

"She took it to the rack. Came back with a Camaro."

"Jesus Christ," I said, limply.

"Yep, tits finally got him," said Shake. "Now *I've* got him."

SEVEN

As a rule, I seldom created a disturbance in a restaurant when a waiter shattered me with the news that he was out of both the monkfish and the scallop mousse with dill and fennel.

But this was too much.

Rodney, our waiter at Enjolie's in Beverly Hills, was now apologizing to Shake and I because we were so late in ordering, he could no longer offer us the casserole with snails and chanterelles, or even the turbot with green peppercorns and hazelnuts.

"Rodney, you really know how to hurt a guy," I said.

We had been at the bar in Enjolie's for two hours. Barbara Jane, still at rehearsal, had got around to calling and telling us to go ahead and dine without her. She would be along as soon as she could, or, failing that, she would see me back at the hotel.

Enjolie's was the hottest new restaurant in Beverly Hills that month. It had blue Provençal wallpaper, dainty lace curtains framing impressionistic murals, Plexiglas dinnerware, and maybe not as many trees as the Black Forest but surely more shrubbery than the Everglades.

Shake and I had taken the precaution to wear conservative suits and ties. Experience had taught us to dress that way in Beverly Hills or else you ran the risk of being mistaken for someone in the entertainment industry.

Producers and directors wore sport coats with open-collared shirts unless they had come directly from a location, in which case they might feature a scruffy ensemble from Western Costume or a foul-weather sailing jacket and a cap with a braided bill.

Hollywood writers leaned toward windbreakers and fatigue jackets, occasionally an old crewneck sweater, although a writer had to be careful about the sweater and not have it thrust around the shoulders of his polo shirt like a junior studio executive.

Actors fell into the category of Formula One jackets, Dodger jackets, Laker jackets, Davis Cup jackets, anything sporting, with a two-day growth of fuzz on their jaws and sunglasses atop their heads. The idea was to look virile, athletic, and working.

An actress was less predictable. She didn't always find it necessary to rush into a bistro with a scrubbed face, looking as if she had just picked out any old raincoat and thrown it over her aerobic leotard and tights, and only had time for a squab salad and a little white wine because she had an early call tomorrow. An actress could look splashy, trendy, tempting, room-stoppingly beautiful, because it could always be assumed she had come from an exclusive party where she had mingled with the elite and powerful, men who had bravely put their artistic reputations on the line to produce such locomotives as *Porkula* and *Revolt of the Scumbags*.

Amid the shrubbery at Enjolie's, we were encompassed by three dozen of the most vibrant forces in the industry that week, but I had no way of being sure of it except to assume as much by the way they were dressed.

What I could be sure of was that I had no intention

of letting Rodney pawn off the *Trois Petites Merveilles* on me.

"Goose liver sautéed with what?" I asked the waiter, looking up from the menu he had wanted to snatch out of my hands.

"Xéres."

Shake and I exchanged looks over the tops of our menus.

Rodney said, "Goose liver sautéed in Xéres, delicately seasoned quail, and wonderfully flavored medallions of lobster. That *is* the *Trois Petites Merveilles.*"

Shake finished off a young Scotch as Rodney tapped his foot impatiently.

"I *do* have the lamb. We coat it in bread crumbs," said Rodney. "I *do* have the escargot wrapped in a chicken breast. I *can* get you the venison. It comes with pears and creamed spinach on a puff pastry with *poivrade* sauce."

"How's the duck?" Shake wanted to know.

"I'm afraid I *don't* have the duck, either. It's very popular. We smother it in papaya, blueberry, and kiwi sauce."

"Shit, Rodney, you're out of all my faves," said Shake.

"We've been extremely busy, as you can see."

"Tell you what," Shake said. "Just bring me two more J&Bs and a cup of coffee on the side."

"Me, too," I said.

Rodney performed an indignant pirouette and evaporated from our sight. But then Burrell came up to our table.

Enjolie's was one of those places that double-teamed you with Bad Witch, Good Witch.

"Has *anyone* taken your order?" Burrell said in a heartfelt tone with an apologetic look.

"Rodney's right on top of it," Shake said.

"Wonderful!"

"No joke intended," Shake said.

We drank another hour at Enjolie's. We might have left sooner if we hadn't become enthralled with the conversations at the tables around us.

Shake started writing on napkins when we heard a sport jacket say to a crewneck:

"Sidney's got the biggest balls in this town. *Becket*'s ripe for a re-make. He'll get Pryor and Murphy *both* in it."

We couldn't have missed the suede king who rushed in to join the starlet.

"Sorry I'm late, angel. My daughter got lost. My wife got pissed. Everything's okay now. You look terrific!"

Two deal-makers walked past our table, as one of them was saying:

"There's no downside. I wouldn't give you a downside. Did I ever give you a downside?"

They were followed by two secretaries, one of whom was greatly saddened because:

"They painted his name out of the parking space at noon. He was out of the building by five."

The historian pouring wine for the ingenue intrigued us. He said:

"You didn't know Hitler did coke? It's the entire explanation for World War Two. I can't believe no one's picked up on it."

Two screenwriters brought us up to date on their craft. First, one of them said, "It's in turnaround. Ned says grownups don't do foreign."

And a little later, one of them said: "Bob's the only writer who could have broken the spine of that script. You know how he did it? He made *him* the amnesia victim, *her* the skateboarder, and saved the reveal for the last page!"

Shake and I wrapped up the evening with dinner

at Fatburger. I found Barbara Jane asleep when I got back to the hotel.

I gave her a long hug and several kisses, but she was more or less in a coma. "Hi, honey," she stirred. "Glad you're here."

She was exhausted. Show biz was taking its toll on her. Further proof of it lay on the bed beside her in the form of a wadded-up memorandum.

It was the latest "inter-communication" that had come from the story department at ABC. It was for the eyes of everyone involved with *Rita's Limo Stop;* all of the people—performers, writers, directors, producers—who had been slaving on the pilot for weeks, never really knowing how many insecure, terror-stricken executives they were trying to please.

There had been blood spilled on every square foot of the set. One lead had been replaced. Supporting actors had been fired and re-hired. A guest star had been written out. Another guest star had been written in. The network had threatened the director with strangulation. The director had threatened the assistant director with expulsion from the business. The executive producers had filed complaints with every guild in town. The eighth team of writers had been brought in to "punch up" the script, and each page that flew out of a typewriter had made the show less humorous and less charming, if it ever was either of those things in the first place. All this to produce a half-hour of television comedy that would come up to the esthetic standards of *Three's Company.*

The cast would rehearse all day, and then somebody from the network who had once had a writing credit on a *Grizzly Adams* episode and was now a VP in charge of development would drop by and say, "Where are the jokes?"

The writers would pound their machines until dawn, the cast would rehearse all day again, and somebody else from the network who had once written questions for a game show and was now a VP in charge of deli orders would drop by and say, "It seems to lack charm."

And on and on.

All of the efforts to improve the script and turn the principal character into a more sympathetic, more vulnerable person had found "Rita"—Barbara Jane—being switched from a restaurant owner to the proprietor of an antique shop, then to the head of an adoption agency, and then back to a restaurant owner. At one session where everybody "went to the table," as they called it, "Rita's" eye problem had become a spot on the lung.

Hearing all of these reports periodically, I had been fearful that Barbara Jane would purchase a handgun and go prowling through the halls of the ABC building in Century City. Now I wondered how this "inter-communication" had affected her. I wouldn't know until she awakened.

The "inter-communication" had obviously been drafted by a recent graduate of a West Coast film school, but some faceless superior had initialed it, doubtless unread, and it had been circulated.

In its entirety, the memo said:

To: PRODUCTION STAFF & TALENT

From: STORY DEPT./ABC ENT.

Subject: "RITA'S LIMO STOP"

We are very excited about the potential of RITA'S LIMO STOP, and it is our feeling that we are well on our way toward creating a highly original and truly funny female buddy series. In an effort to make the best possible pilot, however, we have a few suggestions which we

think will improve the story. Since we are so
close to a blockbuster, it seems to us that it
would be a shame not to further strengthen and
delineate the characters so that the relationship
of our principals will be the main focus and
driving force of this unique comedy.

CHARACTERS:

First, we <u>must</u> deepen and enrich Rita and
Amanda so that their bond is more realistic
and substantial, so that we might attain the hot
mix we are all seeking, the magic you would
find, for example, if <u>Hud</u> were to have a head-on
collision with <u>Chinatown,</u> or, literarily, if certain
segments of <u>Crime and Punishment</u> were blended
into the fabric of <u>Death in Venice.</u> To make
this buddy relationship as dimensional as possible,
therefore, we might want to consider <u>not</u> having
Rita and Amanda be friends at the start. Perhaps
they don't know each other, or, for that matter,
even like each other throughout the 60-second
cold opening.

It might be that the street smart Rita regards Amanda
as dim-witted, and, conversely, Amanda might not
appreciate Rita's pessimistic approach and cynical
attitude toward life in general. It is our feeling that a
more antagonistic start between Rita and Amanda
would provide more texture to their burgeoning
friendship.

Second, as their uneasy bond grows into a symbiotic
relationship, they should grow and change. Rita
should drop her unyielding facade, and Amanda
should become more focused and directed as a result
of Rita's Pygmalion tutelage.

Third, we <u>must</u> emphasize their backstories and

personal histories even more. We should really get a sense of why life is so difficult for all of us. By establishing this, the audience will be rooting for them even more to succeed as career women. As in any classic buddy relationship, separately they would fail, but collectively they triumph, outlasting the troubled, rocky waters because they have each other as anchors.

Fourth, their vulnerabilities *must* be revealed at least five times in the pilot episode, but we shouldn't let this obscure their durability and self-discovery.

HUMOR:

We would like to eliminate the chaotic situation with the bean sprouts and reroute the humor more specifically toward our main characters and their enslavement in the restaurant. The best comedy comes out of real characters, and in line with that, we feel that some of the secondary and supporting players are too broad—the "Evita"-singing drag queen, for instance—and that, additionally, there are times when the dialogue goes too far in terms of bawdier humor. With regard to this, we recommend losing all references to "dykes" and "limp wrists," as well as Rita's quip—ad-libbed in the last rehearsal—about toxic waste being something the United States could export to Puerto Rico.

In short, we would like for the humor to explode from motivational rather than parenthetical origins.

SPECIFIC PAGE NOTES:

Page 1

Rita's power over Amanda <u>must</u> be clarified. And as of now, how well do we *know* Amanda really?

Page 2
We are concerned that Rita is depicted too brazenly when she reminds Ko, the Chinese chef, of his need for cosmetic dentistry.

Page 4
At present, our general feeling is that the relationship between Rita and her ex-husband might be extraneous to the storyline. His motives must be embellished. If he <u>does</u> want Rita back, why is he with the teenage fashion model? More backstory here.

Page 9
We like Ron, the 18-year old guru, and plan to build him up in future episodes, but as he now stands, he raises many plot points that are not fully explored. Rethink.

Page 12
The friendship that Rita strikes up with the Columbia professor seems forced. We think that by changing his character to an NBA basketball player, we can less inhibit the humor and achieve more of a <u>now</u> flavor overall.

Page 17
Rita cannot be this tough and cynical or the audience will view her as totally unsympathetic. <u>Why</u> does she hate the sales personnel at Bloomingdale's so much that she wishes a birth defect on all of their grandchildren? Here again, we are apparently dealing with an ad-lib.

Page 19
In order to explore the predicament of our

women more deeply, we should <u>hear</u> and <u>see</u>
the breaking of dishes more frequently. We are
<u>not</u> saying we want to stick to the structure of
farce exclusively, but we <u>are</u> suggesting that
there may be some very real opportunities for
double entendre, which, after all, is at the core of
all great comedy.

<u>Page 23</u>
It seems to make more sense to us for Rita,
rather than Amanda, to overpower the transvestite who bursts in with the automatic weapon
and insists on doing her recital of arias and folk
songs.

<u>Page 26</u>
While the 30-second epilogue is very well
crafted—an entree spilled in Rita's lap is quite
funny and the perfect ender—we would like to
suggest one tiny change. Isn't it more likely that
the entree would be a beef stew? All of us here
agree that curried lamb is rather oblique. Rethink.

GOOD LUCK, AND GOOD SHOW!

"They all have to die," Barbara Jane was saying
the next morning as we had breakfast in the room.

"Everybody?"

"Not the actors, they're okay. They don't hear what
they're saying, anyhow. It's just words to go with the
faces they make and the fists they beat against the
walls. You know how Carolyn . . . 'Amanda' . . . stud-
ies a script. She thumbs through it and says, 'Bullshit, bullshit, bullshit, my line. Bullshit, my line, my
line, bullshit, bullshit.' "

Barbara Jane was looking around on the room-
service table for something other than orange marmalade to spread on her rye toast.

"Has anyone ever eaten orange marmalade?" she asked. "Has anyone ever actually requested orange marmalade? Nobody in the whole world eats orange marmalade! So what happens? Every hotel serves it, every airline serves it, every place you go, there's nothing but orange marmalade! It's like chocolate-chip ice cream. Who eats that? You eat chocolate ice cream. You eat vanilla ice cream. But you don't eat chocolate-chip ice cream—and you don't eat orange fucking marmalade!"

"Here's some boysenberry," I said.

"Thanks!"

It was a tossup whether the director, the writers, or the executive producers should die first.

Barbara Jane said, "My first day on the set, the director seemed like a pretty shrewd guy. He said, 'We're all in this together and no matter what happens, remember one thing: the network is always wrong!' He says this, which I think is kind of neat; then he does every single thing every jerk from the network suggests! If somebody from ABC's mail room came by and mentioned pirates, the director would hand me an eyepatch!"

So far, there had been a total of sixteen writers assigned to the project, most of them working in pairs, none of them lasting more than two or three days, and none of them overburdened with originality.

Barb said, "Here's a sitcom writer's idea of humor. Say, 'I'm tired.'"

"I'm tired," I said.

" 'You're tired, what about me?' "

Barbara Jane looked at me vacantly.

"That's a laugh line," she said.

The other day, a new team of writers had come in to "punch up" the script. They had changed the line to "You're tired, what about *moi*?"

"I won't say *moi*," Barbara Jane had told the director, whose name was Jack Sullivan. "At gunpoint, I won't say *moi*."

The director had said, "It'll get a laugh, trust me."

Barb had said, "It's corny. It's dumb. It doesn't improve anything. Why can't I say something like 'You're tired, what about the plumbing?'"

The director had laughed. The writers hadn't laughed. The writers had only stared at Barbara Jane as if she had a deformity.

An argument over the line had lasted half a day. Barb had eventually won. She would say something besides *moi*. No one knew what it was going to be, but it wouldn't be *moi*. The writers never spoke to her again.

She said, "It's like they thought they'd written 'late in the summer of that year,' and I'd drawn a grease pencil through it."

"I've read about you temperamental stars."

"Oh, God, I know," she said. "That's the thing. I feel awful when we get into this crap. But it's not like I'm running around the set with a meat cleaver, threatening careers—which are more valuable than lives out here. I'm not Barbra Streisand. I'm not telling some director he'll never work in this town again unless he moves the Renaissance to a more recent century so I can costume it better! I just don't want to say dumb lines."

The show's executive producers, Sheldon Gurtz and Kitty Feldman, should be tortured first, then put to death.

Barb said, "As bad as the writers are, the executive producers are worse. They get to re-write the writers. Sheldon and Kitty couldn't write a bad check. Sheldon wears a ten-gallon cowboy hat. Kitty's about as big as a rodent."

Barbara Jane had asked Sheldon and Kitty why they were permitted to "polish" the scripts.

"Because we're the ones who have to deliver," Kitty had said.

And Sheldon had said, "We know what works, Barbara Jane. We wrote for *Fantasy Island.*"

It had been pretty hard to think of a comeback for that.

My wife was dashing around the suite now, gearing up for another day of show biz. She invited me to come along and observe the turmoil. I declined, opting for naps, magazines, movies on TV, and more room service.

"I'd better stay away until the taping," I said. "I don't like violence."

"Things should go smoother from now on," she said.

Tempers had peaked yesterday and the air had been cleared.

Barbara Jane had been rehearsing a scene in which she was supposed to walk across the room and answer the phone.

Sheldon had pushed the director aside and told Barbara Jane to grab a cracker off a table and eat the cracker as she walked toward the phone.

"Nope," Barb had said. "Sorry. No way. Dustin Hoffman eats a cracker when he walks across a room. Robert Redford eats a cracker when he walks across a room. Al Pacino eats a cracker when he walks across a room. I don't eat a cracker when I walk across a room, and neither would Rita."

Sheldon had said, "Please, don't be difficult. We know this character better than you do."

Barbara Jane had turned to the director for support, but Jack Sullivan had only shrugged and practiced his golf swing.

"I'm not going to eat the cracker, Sheldon," Barb had then said.

Kitty had stepped in.

"Barbara Jane, you haven't fleshed this out fully, and we have."

"Dadgumit, you know, I meant to, but I just got busy and forgot," Barbara Jane had laughed.

It was structured into the business that executive producers were given a good deal of authority on a pilot, as much as they could command when an empty suit from the network wasn't around. And they were needed. Somebody would have to "stay with the show" after it got on the air. Live with it, in other words. That would be the executive producers.

The performers would have it easy. They would only have to come in for a run-through, then the tape session. They would have the rest of the week free to play softball, change agents, and complain about Shirley MacLaine getting the part they had been up for in a feature film.

The director wouldn't be overworked, either. He could wander in off the golf course, do a take one and a take two, and leave word with an underling to make sure a cassette was sent to his home.

And the writers could go on to other things. They could grind out the same swill for other dreary pilots, punch up other mindless episodes, discuss burning issues within the Writers' Guild, and maybe complete a page or two on the outline of the novel they'd been working on for the past seventeen years.

But Sheldon Gurtz and Kitty Feldman were the people who would stay with *Rita's Limo Stop* if the network gave it a "go" and "ordered thirteen," which would mean the network had liked the pilot and wasn't going to "pass on it" or "burn it off in four."

It would not only become Sheldon and Kitty's baby, they would suddenly become mogulettes and might even be able to get a table in a Beverly Hills restaurant.

Barbara Jane said, "Can you imagine the mind it takes to want to do that—live with a sitcom? Execu-

tive producers aren't talented enough to create anything of their own. Rita was conceived by some poor,
starving writer whose name we'll never know . . . who's
probably kicking himself in the ass for ever mentioning the idea to Sheldon and Kitty in the first place.
Yesterday they punched up gags, today they're executive producers. As we speak, I assure you Kitty and
Sheldon think they're whipping *Hamlet* into shape."

"Do you eat the cracker when you answer the
phone?"

Barb's reaction to my question—a hearty laugh—assured me that Sheldon Gurtz and Kitty Feldman had
brought out the Texan in her.

Yesterday on the set, Kitty had said to my wife,
"Barbara Jane, we just can't have an impasse like this
every day. Eating the cracker may not seem important to you, but certain stage business can help develop a character, and in some circles, they call it
acting. You've heard of that? You might also try to
keep in mind that it is Sheldon and I—not you—who
happen to be responsible for making this show
homogenous."

"Aw, gee, I didn't know about the homogenous
part," Barbara Jane had said. "Homogenize *this*,
motherfucker!"

EIGHT

In the week that passed I saw Barbara Jane about as often as she saw the staff in our hotel lobby, but I did get updates on the wounded who were littering the alleys around the studio as the taping of the *Rita* pilot crept nearer. That event was now only twenty-four hours away.

I wasn't worried about the job my wife would do in the leading role. She could play Barbara Jane better than anybody.

And there were other matters to keep me occupied.

October had arrived and I had begun to get a little nervous about my own television career, a career that would be launched in a week's time.

I hadn't gone into television with the idea of winning an Emmy. It had just been something to do—something to keep me from playing in the streets. But like Barb, I didn't want to look foolish on the air, and yet I wasn't sure how I was going to avoid it working with Larry Hoage. Somehow, I had the horrible, sneaking suspicion I would be found guilty of stupidity through association. Was there life after stupidity? There was for Larry Hoage, but there might not be for me.

I was relieved of some of the worry after Richard Marks came to town. The head of CBS Sports called from the Bel Air Hotel to say he was on the Coast for a few days to "doll up an affiliate." He wanted to have a drink at my convenience. We discussed his crowded business calendar and worked out a time at his convenience.

He came by the Marquis late one afternoon. We sat in the lounge at one of those round tables where he could see into the lobby and not miss Willie Nelson, Mick Jagger, John Denver, Jack Nicklaus, or any other celeb who might arrive to check in.

In the first five minutes of our meeting, Richard Marks complained about the food he'd eaten at Chasen's the night before, the food he'd tried to eat at The Palm at lunch, and the fact that he had only been able to hire a stretched white limo. He had preferred something smaller.

He only stayed long enough to have a Perrier and lime, sign a few papers in his briefcase, and let drop the news that he had fired Don Avery, the color man who had been working with Larry Hoage.

"I had to cut him loose" was the way he put it.

For a disturbing moment, I was fearful Don Avery had been fired to make room for me, but that wasn't the case.

"He made two very tasteless comments on the air," said Richard Marks. "Did you catch the Redskins—Rams game a week ago?"

Only the fourth quarter, I said.

"You must have heard them, then."

Not that I recalled.

"First, he said there had been a lot of 'mistakes' in the game. Then he said it was an 'off day' for Washington. Larry Hoage's enthusiasm counterbalanced it. Larry has drawbacks, but he's a positive guy. He gave the Rams the credit they deserved. Bob Cameron called me at home before the telecast was even over. I can tell you the Commissioner wasn't very happy. He reminded me that NFL teams don't have off days, their opponents have *good* days. He wasn't pleased that the number of penalties was mentioned, either, but I reminded *him* that we're broadcast journalists. We have a job to do."

I was beginning to wonder if I would last fifteen minutes as a color man.

"Was it all that bad?" I asked. "What Don Avery said?"

"It's a question of credibility," Richard Marks revealed, checking the time of day on his 400-pound Rolex. "You, for instance, can say what you please."

"I can?"

"You're Billy Clyde Puckett. You've had a marvelous career. Viewers have been programmed to accept you as an authority. Who's Don Avery, anyhow? He was journeyman linebacker at best."

"I can say somebody fucked up? The zebras blew it?"

"If that's how you see the game. I'll back you up on your content every step of the way. I would hope you'll watch your language."

"I'm not Alistair Cooke."

"Clean is all I meant."

"I can do clean."

My first game would be in Green Bay. The Packers against the Redskins. Richard Marks had assigned me to a Washington game on purpose. He wanted me to conduct a thoughtful, incisive interview with Dreamer Tatum, the man who had put me in television.

"It'll make a fantastic insert," he said. "Now, that is broadcast journalism!"

An insert was one of those pre-recorded interviews a network liked to put on the air in the middle of a touchdown drive. Instead of getting to see a 30-yard pass completion, you got to watch Phyllis

George talk to a rotund lineman about his off-season interest in needlepoint.

Shake wandered down to the Marquis lounge after Richard Marks left. For a week, Shake had hardly been out of his room. He was finishing up his *Playboy* piece on the wonderful sport of pro football. He was nearing his deadline. The magazine wanted to publish the article in its January issue, which would be on the newsstands in December when the NFL playoffs would be starting.

Perfect timing. The public's interest in pro football would be at a fever pitch while Shake would be telling America the game was a fraud.

I passed along elements of my conversation with Richard Marks to Shake as we turned our backs to others in the room, mostly agents watching their clients have sneezing fits.

"You've got it made," Shake said. "You know why he fired Don Avery? Because he didn't *hire* Don Avery. His predecessor did. He has to back you up on everything you say on the air or admit he's made a tragic error in judgment. You know the likelihood of a network mogul admitting a mistake? You're golden, man."

T.J. Lambert put us on a conference call. It was later that night and T.J. wanted to speak to Shake and me at the same time. We picked up separate phones in Shake's room and heard the joyous news. TCU was going to win a national championship next season. Not the conference championship, the national championship, the one that puts a coach in a class with "all them Darrell Royals." The Horned Frogs were going to be No. 1 in so many polls, the mascot might have to be changed to a Trojan or a Cornhusker.

T.J. was a little drunk, but he said he had good

reason to be. And he just wanted to share this happy moment with a couple of old friends and stalwart Horned Frogs.

He said, "It looks like I'm gonna have me a Tonsillitis Johnson and a Artis Toothis in the same backfield!"

T.J. coughed, then belched. We heard him holler at Donna, his wife, "Damn, honey, I done cheated my ass out of a fart!"

Now he came back to us on the phone to explain how this recruiting miracle was going to happen.

"I got Tonsillitis in my pocket," he said. "Ain't no question about that. Big Ed Bookman gimme a blank check and said, 'Here, T.J., throw a net over that nigger and haul him in.' I done laid a Datsun 280 on his ass, and six charge cards. My coaches has talked to our sororities. Tonsillitis has got so much white pussy waitin' for him in Fort Worth, he's gonna have to get Riddell to make him a wooden dick!"

Artis Toothis was another story, a bit more complicated. Artis Toothis, the speedster from the Big Thicket, last year's most-wanted blue-chipper, had wound up at SMU all right, but he had dropped out of school. His explanation to the press was that he had been lonely and unhappy in Dallas, which was to say that he had been forced to enroll in a freshman English class, and he had heard a rumor that his meal allowance of $3,000 a month was far below the figure a running back at the University of Texas was getting.

Artis had gone home to Willow Neck in the sleek white Jaguar he had decided to keep. He was mostly just lolling around the house now, playing with the cur dogs and watching one of the 240 TV channels he could pick up from the satellite dish an SMU alum had had installed in the yard.

SMU's coaches couldn't very well complain about

Artis' keeping the Jaguar. It would be an admission that he had received an under-the-table gift in the first place.

But the vital thing was that Artis Toothis hadn't played a single down of football for the SMU Mustangs. From the start of two-a-days, he had complained of a pinched ankle, thereby giving himself time to shop around for better opportunities. Under the rules, therefore, he could lay out a season—this one—and be eligible to play for another school next year. And the other school was going to be TCU.

I asked T.J. why he was so certain of it.

Big Ed Bookman was arranging it, the coach said. Big Ed had come to the conclusion that looking for chaparrals was more challenging than looking for dinosaurs. Big Ed had already proved himself in the oil bidness. Big Ed had realized that if he could bring the No. 1 college team to Fort Worth, it would be the crowning accomplishment of his life. They would probably re-name River Crest Country Club after him.

Any project this big had to have a solid foundation. Big Ed had begun laying the groundwork for it by hiring Tonsillitis' brother, Darnell, as his personal assistant at Bookman Oil & Gas. He was paying Darnell a whopping salary and he had given him a big office next door to his own. Darnell's job had nothing to do with oil or gas, of course. Darnell's job was to put Tonsillitis Johnson and Artis Toothis in TCU's backfield.

Only today, T.J. reported, Darnell had visited with Artis Toothis down in Willow Neck and it looked like they weren't that far apart in the negotiations. It was nothing Big Ed couldn't handle with Grovers. Grover Clevelands. Thousand-dollar bills.

"You know Big Ed," T.J. said. "Ain't nobody

gonna out-Grover Big Ed when he gets that look in his eye."

T.J. let out a delirious hoot. Then he said:

"Can you imagine what it's gonna be like to have them two burners in my backfield? Good God a-mighty! I won't have to do nothin' but get out of their way and mastrebate!"

The head coach of the Horned Frogs couldn't wait for the present season to be over so he could start putting in his two-back offense for next year. Since the victory I had witnessed over Rice, the Frogs had beaten only one other foe, UT-Arlington. They were 2-and-4, and they still had to face Ohio State in an intersectional game along with the strongest teams in the conference, Houston, Baylor, Texas, and Texas A&M.

It looked like another 2–9 record for T.J.

"I done writ this sumbitch off," he said.

Of the gloomy prospect of having to go to Columbus, Ohio, T.J. said, "I don't know what pea-brain scheduled that cocksucker!"

Shake and I congratulated T.J. on his re-building job. We had never dreamed the day would come when TCU would start to operate like a big-league school. Now it was upon us.

"This thing could snowball," said the coach. "Big Ed wants Darnell to keep representin' athletes as a sideline."

"Sideline to what?" I said, laughing.

T.J. said, "Darnell is a geologist, in case anybody wants to know. We got a fuckin' scroll hangin' on his wall."

Shake said, "Coach, it looks like we could be good for years to come if we don't go to jail."

"I ain't worried about them NCAA phonies," said T.J. "They can come down here and sniff around

all they want to. We'll strap some perjury on they ass
and send 'em home!"

I owned up to T.J. that a thought was making me
dizzy but giving me considerable pleasure at the same
time. I said it was not easy for me to envision a black
man—Darnell Johnson—sitting in an office in Big
Ed Bookman's oil-and-gas building, not far from River
Crest Country Club, right there on the fashionable
West Side of Fort Worth, Texas, USA.

"Big Ed don't give a shit if he's polka-dot. All Big
Ed wants is a winner."

Barbara Jane was a little edgy the following morning, but she had good reasons. The grand final *Rita*
taping was set for that night at eight o'clock, and
even before the cameras would roll, she faced a busy
day. Something had to be done about her hair. Decisions had to be made about her costumes. Two dress
rehearsals were scheduled during the day. And why
had it turned into a Broadway opening?

No longer was the show going to be taped before
an ordinary TV audience, the usual vagrants and
loons they swept up off the sidewalks in front of the
studio. I would be there. Shake would be there. A
throng of bicoastal network executives would be there.
Big Ed and Big Barb were flying out for it in their
Lear. Burt Danby and Veronica were flying out for
it in *their* Lear. And who could say how many real
actors and actresses might be in the audience?

Barbara Jane had known it was going to be like
this, but she had put it out of her mind until now.
Other things had been more urgent, like stamping
out the hated *moi*, and letting Sheldon Gurtz and
Kitty Feldman know who had the fastest gun.

Now she was thinking about it as she changed the
contents of a purse into another purse, and had
cigarettes going in three different ashtrays.

"I'm not sure I could get through it without Jack," she said.

"Nicholson?" I was looking up from the sports section of the Los Angeles *Herald-Examiner*.

"Sullivan, Biff. My director."

Biff was an old joke between us. Biff was how Barbara Jane addressed me on those occasions when I would get something wrong, say something dumb, or do something forgetful, like not stub a check or lose a dinner receipt.

By calling me Biff, it kept her from getting angry, but it also reminded me that I had been semi-negligent in some way.

Her use of Biff dated back to college days when we had only been friends.

The origin of it was a Jim Tom Pinch column in *The Fort Worth Light & Shopper*. My name had appeared in the opening paragraph of Jim Tom's column as "Biffy Clyde Puckett."

I was slightly surprised by the change in her attitude about the director, Jack Sullivan.

"I thought the director had to die?" I said to Barb as she snuffed out one of the three cigarettes.

"He did, but now he doesn't. He's been wonderful. He has taste . . . a great sense of timing. He's terrific."

"Why was he keeping it hidden?"

"It's his style," she said. "He was getting to know the people. He likes me—and he likes Carolyn Barnes. He knows how to work around all the crap, make it seem more intelligent."

"What's he ever done?"

"A ton of things. Features in England. He's directed on the stage. TV movies. All kinds of stuff."

"Why is he fooling around with a sitcom?"

"Money, Biff." A look sometimes went with Biff, too. "Mondo scratcho, as Burt Danby would say."

I saw Barb to the door.

"What does Jack Sullivan look like?"

"Oh, nothing special."

"I guess his crooked arm and clubbed foot only make him more sensitive, huh?"

Barbara Jane said, "He's handsomer than you, as a matter of fact. He's far more thoughtful, much better educated, and dynamite in bed!"

She kissed me and left.

That afternoon I kept an appointment with a bone specialist in Beverly Hills. It was time to see how my knee was getting along.

Dr. Tim Hayes was supposed to be the top bone guy on the Coast. Burt Danby couldn't have recommended him more strongly. "Hell of a guy," Burt had said over the phone. "Member at Bel Air . . . ranch in Santa Barbara. Married to a juicy broad I'd love to nail. Jesus, is she something! She used to pull the curtain on one of those giveaway shows. All legs and teeth. Tim'll take care of you, ace. He did Jimmy Caan's shoulder and I think he did Lee Majors' elbow."

I went to see Dr. Hayes anyhow.

His office was in the heart of the Beverly Hills shopping district. It was on the second floor of a narrow space in a block where the discerning ornament seeker could buy a silver-plated tennis ball for only $1,700, where the anorexic wife of a studio boss could find the $8,000 jumpsuit she had been trying to buy, and where ardent music lovers could spend up to $32,000 to correct the sound on their stereos.

In Dr. Hayes's wood-paneled anteroom I announced myself to Joan Collins, the receptionist. She was whispering into a phone as she pointed me toward a glass partition, behind which sat two nurses, the Linda Evans twins. They were both snickering into phones. One of the Linda Evans twins pressed a buzzer, a door opened, and I was met by Victoria Principal, another nurse. She led me around a corner, where I exchanged a hello with the Dyan Cannon nurse. Victoria Principal then rapped on a door, turned the knob, and I entered a room in which Tom Selleck held an old Tommy Armour putter and was stroking golf balls across the carpet.

"Billy Clyde!" the man smiled. "You are some kind of football player, fellow!"

"Dr. Hayes?"

We talked about the par-4s at Bel Air for a while, then about the Rams, Dodgers, and Lakers. He finally got around to giving me an examination.

The doddering old clowns in New York had done a pretty fair job on my operation, he said. My cast could be removed in about ten more days. I could stow the crutches. Just don't overexert myself. Too bad it hadn't been a cartilage. These days, they could zap a cartilage back into shape like magic. Put you right back in the lineup. Ligaments were different. Ligaments took time—and rehabilitation.

The doctor said, "Billy Clyde, it's a damn shame, but I wouldn't even consider playing football again, if I were you. Another bad blow on that knee and you'll be a mess."

"I'll just have to see how it goes."

"I'm quite serious," he said. "You want to ride on a rim the rest of your life? You don't need that. I know what I would do. If I were Billy Clyde Puckett? A guy your age? With your reputation? I'd rest on my laurels and ball myself into a stupor! I guess you have to beat 'em off with a machete, right?"

"I was thinking the same thing about you," I said. "I noticed one or two distractions when I came in here."

Dr. Hayes reacted with a look of pain. "The staff? Not hardly. I only keep those bitches around to dress up the office. No, sir. I learned my lesson about war babies a long time ago."

"War babies?"

Dr. Hayes explained that war babies were the storm troopers of the feminine population. It must have had something to do with being army brats. Their fathers had never been home and they'd watched their mothers get fucked over by guys with ducktails and long key chains. War babies ranged in age from, oh, 38 to 44, and their main thing was to get even with men.

"War babies can look terrific," he said. "But don't let that fool you. They're meaner than wild dogs, pal, and they can *slam-dunk* Rodeo Drive!"

Dr. Hayes's advice was to stick with the "smooth babies."

In fact, he knew of a smooth baby who could help with my rehabilitation. She was a bonafide therapist. Her office was in the next block.

"I know how to exercise," I said.

"Don't say no till you've seen her," he winked. "We're talking redhead, twenties, great tits . . . mouth like a crocodile."

"I have a knee," I said. "I don't need a prostate to go with it."

I left the bone specialist's office that afternoon thinking the world was badly in need of a treatment center for whup victims. But then the more I thought about it, the more I realized the world already had a treatment center for whup victims. It was called Beverly Hills, wasn't it?

NINE

Big Ed Bookman poured himself another glass of vodka and said he knew for a by-God fact that Lucille Ball was dead.

"Lucille Ball's not dead," said Shake, dealing with a convulsion.

"Damn sure is," Big Ed said, plunging his hand into the bucket of ice.

We were in our suite at the hotel. Big Ed and Big Barb, Burt Danby and Veronica, Shake and myself. I had ordered up some whiskey so that we might prepare ourselves properly for the *Rita* taping.

I, for one, was not about to go into that studio and watch my wife perform before a "live" audience of 500 people without getting keenly, not so prudently—and yet cunningly—shit-faced.

From what I could gather, Shake, Big Ed, and Burt had the same idea in mind.

Big Ed, Burt, Shake, and I were standing in the middle of the living room of the suite. Big Barb and Veronica were on a sofa, deploring the rising cost of Hermès handbags.

Big Ed now said, "You know so God-damn much, Shake Tiller, tell me why Lucille Ball's not dead."

"She just isn't," Shake said.

"You eat dinner with her last night or something?"

Shake laughed a no.

"That's because she's dead," Big Ed said. "I forget when it was ... four or five years ago. She died about the same time as that old fat boy. There's another son-of-a-bitch who wasn't funny. What's his name? I can't remember. Don't matter. Show biz was all over for Ed Bookman when Gary Cooper died."

"Gary Cooper died?" I glanced at Shake.

Big Ed gave me an explicit look. "I'll guarantee you Gary Cooper is dead. Gary Cooper is deader than soccer!"

"When did it happen?"

"I don't know," said Big Ed, "but he hauled off and died, just like Lucille Ball."

I turned to Burt Danby.

"Lucille Ball's not dead, is she?"

"Blanko," said Burt with a shrug.

To Shake Tiller, Big Ed said, "All right, answer *this!* If Lucille Ball ain't dead, what's her God-damn show doin' on television in black-and-white?"

Big Barb and Veronica meandered over to our conversation group.

"What's this about Lucille Ball?" Big Barb wondered.

I said, "We're trying to decide whether she's alive."

"Why?"

Shake tumbled onto a couch.

"That's right," he said, starting to wheeze from laughter. "Why is it important? *I* don't need to know. Do you need to know, Billy C.?"

"I'd sort of like to know," Burt said.

Shake came up from the couch, gave Big Barb a hug, and said, "You just asked the greatest question I've ever heard."

Big Ed held an unlit Sherman in his teeth as he said, "I got one! Jimmy Stewart!"

He turned down the flame on his Dunhill, and

said, "No, wait! It's Gregory Peck! It's either Jimmy Stewart or Gregory Peck, by God!"

Shake said, "If it's Gregory Peck, we can say good-bye to the screenplay as we know it."

"Why's that?" I said, reaching for the young Scotch.

"I know a guy out here who told me how to write screenplays," said Shake. "On page forty-two, Gregory Peck stands up in his trenchcoat and tells everybody what the movie's all about. On page eighty-four, Gregory Peck stands up in his trenchcoat and tells everybody what the movie's all about again. On page a hundred and fifteen, the movie's over. Gregory Peck slings the trenchcoat over his shoulder and gazes into a spiritual dawn."

"That was a God-damn-good movie, too," Big Ed said. "Gary Cooper wasn't in it, but I liked it."

"They can't make movies like that anymore," said Burt Danby, looking depressed. "What are they gonna do, put a trenchcoat on one of those Italian gnomes, let him go up in the B-17 and teach the crew how to breakdance? Jesus . . . this fucking town."

Big Ed wanted to know what the names of those "silly newspapers" were.

"Barbara Jane refers to 'em," he said.

"The trades?" Burt volunteered. *"Daily Variety* and *The Hollywood Reporter*?"

"That's them," said Big Ed. "They could provide a hell of a public service. They ought to print a list every day. Who hadn't died yet."

Shake said, "I'm with you, Ed. I say if Lucille Ball's not dead, let's tell people."

"Don't have to be a big story or anything. Just a list. Jimmy Stewart . . . Gregory Peck . . . Lucille Ball—if they're sure of it."

Shake clinked his glass of J&B against Big Ed's glass of Stolichnaya. "You got it, Ed. It's time to eliminate all this damn guesswork."

I was cornered by Veronica Danby down on the street before our limo parade left for the studio.

"We have something in common," she said.

"We do?"

"You're going to be exercising your leg. I study with this amazing woman who used to be a soloist with the Ballet Russe. Her grasp of body alignment is not to be believed! I have learned how to isolate *so* well! Most people don't know there's a correct way to use your feet when you exercise. Are you aware of the feet?"

"I think so."

"Feet are *so* critical."

"Feet are right there."

"Of course, I know my body will have to be re-shaped eventually, even with all of the aerobics I'm doing now, but I hope to prolong it through proper exercise for ten years or more. What I wanted to say to you is that the right kind of exercise is every bit as important as skin care and diet, it rrreally is!"

"Thanks for the tip," I said.

Shake insisted on riding in the limo with Big Ed. He wasn't going to let a good thing get away.

"You're tired, what about Poland?"

The show was in progress, and Barbara Jane (Rita) got her first ample laugh from the audience with that line. She now moved away from Carolyn (Amanda) to see about a table of "customers" who were dining at Rita's Limo Stop.

The next thing we heard was the muffled voice of the director as it came over the loudspeaker from the control room.

"That's a better ender for Scene One than what we have," the director's voice said. "Let's set up in the living room, please."

All of us were sitting on the second row of an

elevated grandstand in the studio. We looked down on the television set, at the cameramen, technicians, lights, and cables.

The set consisted of the restaurant as a large centerpiece, the kitchen of the restaurant to our right, and the living room of Rita's apartment to our left.

To one side of us in the bleachers, as part of the audience, were the bicoastal network executives, a blend of dark-suited men and tailored women, all looking morbid. Their drones were seated around them, earnest young people who were filling up pages of yellow legal pad with production notes.

Directly across the aisle from us were two harlequins who couldn't have been mistaken for anybody other than Sheldon Gurtz and Kitty Feldman.

Sheldon Gurtz was a chubby man of medium height, about fifty. He had a beard and wore thick glasses, a denim suit, a string tie, his white 10-gallon cowboy hat, and sneakers. When he crossed his leg, I definitely noticed an Argyle sock.

Kitty Feldman wore a beret, dark glasses, Cossack boots, a sack dress, and smoked with a cigarette holder. Kitty Feldman wasn't actually as small as a rodent, but she would fit in your carry-on luggage.

I pointed out Sheldon and Kitty to our group. Sheldon and Kitty were enemies of the people, I said.

Big Ed studied the executive producers for a moment that dragged on. His eyes were still on them as he said to himself:

"Big Silly and Little Silly."

The cameras rolled again after a man held aloft a sign that said, "QUIET, PLEASE, and another man adjusted his headset and signaled to Barbara Jane.

Barbara Jane, who was standing in the living room of the set with Carolyn, had changed from something smashing and casual by some kind of Adolfo into something more smashing and more casual by some kind of Gianni.

As the action began, Barb walked across the living room but stopped to pick up something off of a coffee table.

"Robert Redford's been in my apartment!" She wheeled on Carolyn.

Nobody laughed but Shake and me—and Carolyn.

"Is that a cracker?" said Carolyn (Amanda), fighting to stay in character.

"Yes!" said Barbara Jane (Rita). "And there are only three people in the world who leave a half-eaten cracker lying around in your home! Dustin Hoffman, Al Pacino, and Robert Redford!"

Carolyn said, "How do you know it wasn't Dustin Hoffman or Al Pacino?"

"They're too short to reach the table!"

I surveyed the audience. Sheldon and Kitty weren't laughing.

Buoyed by the audience's response, Barbara Jane and Carolyn set a land-speed record for ad-libs.

Carolyn said, "Rita, Dustin Hoffman's a wonderful actor. Didn't you like *Kramer versus Kramer?*"

"I didn't see it."

"Why not?"

"I know how to make French toast!"

I reached behind Big Ed and tapped Shake on the shoulder.

"She's going down in her own flames," I said.

"That's our girl," said Shake.

Back on the set, Carolyn lit a cigarette—stage business—and said, "I've been thinking about the restaurant, Rita. Maybe we ought to take toxic waste off the menu."

"Too expensive?"

"Well, that, and . . . we've never been able to get the seasoning right. Jerry called you today."

"My ex-husband?"

"He's still your husband. The divorce isn't final yet."

"His personality is."

"Jerry thinks you're being tough with the lawyer because he's going out with a younger woman."

"You call that girl young? Just because she hasn't been potty-trained?"

Sheldon Gurtz and Kitty Feldman left their seats and started up the aisle, still unamused. Perhaps it wasn't pleasant to see a show kidnapped before your very eyes.

In the final scene, a network-ordered script change had turned the transvestite with an automatic weapon into a punk rocker who had come into the restaurant for dinner, the logic being that a young musician was more of a now character.

Barbara Jane hadn't liked the change. I was wondering how she might handle it.

The young musician's hair was orange and purple, he wore a peeling T-shirt, and there were four safety pins stuck in his cheeks.

Barbara Jane measured him momentarily, and said:

"Are you here to dine or would you just like to sit and bleed awhile?"

Looking at the menu, the kid said, "What have you got in the Top Forty?"

"The lamb curry is nice. But you probably aren't into New Wave. It's too Rock Perennial, I suppose."

"Huh?"

Barbara Jane said, "It doesn't bother me if a group can express alienation with a beat I can feel—a rudimentary, garage-band rock-and-roll, so to speak, but you probably like to break furniture, don't you?"

Barbara Jane lifted a plate of curried lamb off the tray of a passing waiter.

"Uh . . . like . . . far-out," said the punker.

"Can you describe your music?"

"Right!" he said, overjoyed to hear a familiar cue. "We have a technocratic, mystical quality combined with the hostility of Heavy Metal, you know?"

"That's what I thought," Barbara Jane said. "Here's how Duke Ellington and I deal with that!"

She shoved the plate of curried lamb in his face.

This of course got a huge laugh from the audience. The crew broke up. Carolyn stumbled across the set and collapsed in a chair.

"That's it, gang," said the muffled voice of the director over the loudspeaker. "They call it a wrap."

The audience shifted from laughter into prolonged applause as Barbara Jane, with gestures of acute apology, began helping the stunned young actor wipe the food off his face and neck.

The reviews from our group were all good.

Shake and I had always said that if we were ever going to watch a sitcom again, it had better have a good friend or a close relative in it.

Big Ed said, "That was enjoyable. By God, old Barbara Jane knew how to handle that faggot."

Big Barb and Veronica were certain that Barbara Jane's smashing and casual outfit in the second act had been a Versace.

"Isn't Gianni wonderful?" said Veronica. "He combines Calvin's understatements with Oscar's flamboyance."

Big Barb said, "We met him last month in Palm Beach. We flew down for Klaus and Mimi's horticulture party at The Breakers. He designed Mimi's coveralls. Everyone dressed like a gardener and carried a hoe. It was a delight."

Burt Danby remembered Carolyn Barnes from another period in his life. "Jesus," he said, "I didn't know Carolyn was still around. I could have sworn she ate six miles of cock and lived in Holmby Hills now."

The Bookmans and Danbys went on to the Polo Lounge so they would feel like they had been to Los Angeles. Shake and I waited for Barbara Jane. I also wanted to congratulate the director.

Jack Sullivan was a nice-looking guy in his late thirties. He had an effeminate way of running his hand through his hair when he talked, and I detected the hint of a British accent, but he must have been straight or my wife wouldn't have embraced him so enthusiastically.

Shake and I were down on the set. The studio had emptied, the director had emerged from the control room when Barbara Jane, having already received our plaudits, lurched from my arms into his.

"You beauty!" said Jack Sullivan, giving Barb a hungry kiss.

Other husbands might have read more into their behavior than friendship and relief, but I didn't. I knew show-biz people hugged and kissed often, even when they detested each other.

"She was great," I said to Jack Sullivan.

And Shake said, "Not since Carole Lombard have we seen—"

But Shake was interrupted by Jack Sullivan, who said, "Great? She's beyond category!"

Almost before any of us knew it, we were being encircled by the network bicoastals and their drones along with Sheldon and Kitty. Everyone was assembling for the post-mortem.

Two of the bicoastals bothered to introduce themselves to Shake and me. We weren't intruding on anything, they said. Stick around. One of the bicoastals said the New York Giants were his team. He asked what the odds were on the Giants' making the playoffs.

"They're a mortal lock to lose twelve games," Shake said.

The bicoastal didn't seem to grasp the fact that I was out of the Giants' lineup. I would never know what he thought my cast and crutches were for.

The troops congregated in the living room of the *Rita* set, some sitting, some standing, some pacing. Sheldon and Kitty, afraid to go near a dark suit or a tailored woman, huddled in a corner with an earnest drone and looked as if they were explaining to him that what he had seen had nothing whatsoever to do with their ingenuity.

No one seemed to want to speak at first, and I never did figure out which dark suit and tailored woman had the most authority. None of them had an overabundance of it. Even I knew that the phantom decision-makers were somewhere back in New York.

The silence was broken when Jack Sullivan said, "Well, I liked it!"

This got the bicoastals talking.

"It has a chance," said a dark suit.

"I think it has a chance," a tailored woman agreed.

A second dark suit said, "Are you saying it has a chance-chance or just a chance?"

"It has a very good chance," the first dark suit said. "I'd liked to have heard more jokes."

"I'd liked to have seen a little more charm," said the tailored woman.

Another dark suit said, "I don't see how we can give it a go yet."

"We could give it a limited go," said a different tailored woman.

"Yes.. we could," the second dark suit spoke up again. "Or . . . not."

"What about a tentative go?" the first dark suit asked the group.

Bicoastals shook their heads affirmatively.

"We'll get more jokes in the episodes," someone said.

"And build up the charm."

The second tailored woman said, "It certainly has a better chance than it did."

The first dark suit turned to Jack Sullivan.

"Jack, I need to know this before I go back to New York. If we give it a tentative go . . . or a limited go . . . or even a full go . . . how long can you stay with it? Can you stay thirteen?"

"It depends," Jack Sullivan said. "I can stay with it for six. Thirteen? Hard to say. I've been talking to Paramount about a feature. They have Brooke Shields committed, but I'm not sure they're going to get the cooperation they'll need from the Politburo."

The director came back to the hotel with us for a nightcap in the lounge.

That was where we learned that *Rita's Limo Stop* was a cinch for a full go of thirteen episodes. Jack Sullivan was more aware of what was going on in the entertainment division of the network than any of the dark suits and tailored women. One of the phantom decision-makers in New York was an old buddy. They had shot commercials together. The network was desperate for *Rita* and planned to throw it into the prime-time lineup in late January as a mid-season replacement.

Had the pilot been the worst piece of shit anyone had ever seen, it wouldn't have mattered. But the pilot wasn't that awful, Jack Sullivan said. The pilot was well into the upper half of mediocre—and Barbara Jane was fetching, a potentially fine actress. With her looks, her spark, and her built-in familiarity as a model, she might just hit the old demographics in the heart.

Rita was practically the same thing as on the air, he said.

ABC was going to cancel two shows for certain, *Car Wrecks* and *Jerome. Rita's Limo Stop* was going to get one of the slots and *Celebrity Car Wrecks* the other.

The network's whole schedule was being juggled. *Just Up The Street* was shifting from Friday night to Thursday night. *Buffed Up,* the comedy-adventure series about a group of daredevils from Redondo Beach, was taking over the eight-o'clock spot on Sunday night.

The network hoped to blow everybody away on Saturday night with a powerhouse lineup. ABC intended to throw *Kindergarten Disco* into the hammock between *Don't You Love it?* and *Cruds!* That would give the network three big winners in a row.

Rita would fall into the nine-o'clock Sunday-night slot. It looked like a rating-getter. *Buffed Up* would be the leadin, and *Return of the Humans* had been rock-solid at nine-thirty for more than two years.

Jack Sullivan smiled at Barbara Jane and said, "I didn't want to tell you this before. We couldn't afford to let up. Looks like you and I are in for some steady employment."

Barb said, "I'd feel a lot better about it if they'd put us behind *Cruds!* on Saturday. We'd be a mortal lock."

She rattled the ice in her empty glass at the bartender.

Shake said to Barbara Jane, "Let me see if I understand this. You're an actress?"

"Uh-huh," she said.

Shake turned to me. "Billy C., I don't know what we're gonna do with Barbara Jane Bookman."

I said, "She always had a missing gene. I knew it when she quit the Pi Phis."

The three of us laughed together. Barbara Jane leaned over and gave Shake a kiss; then she leaned over and gave me a kiss.

And the more we exchanged looks, the more we laughed—as we had so many times in the past about so many things that other people hadn't understood.

Jack Sullivan was observing us with a faint, puzzled grin.

Barb finally said to the director, "Jack, you'll have to excuse us old boys from Texas if we think all this shit is pretty funny."

Part Two

GOING DIXIE

TEN

As a place to visit, Green Bay, Wisconsin, had never meant much more to me than a night in a motel room, three hours of football on an Arctic grassland, and a chartered jet making a getaway in a blizzard.

Therefore, in any discussion of Green Bay, I had always been at a disadvantage when sportswriters I knew had compared it to having a villa in Sorrento or taking a cruise around the Greek islands.

But I no sooner hobbled inside the terminal of the Green Bay airport when I was given reason to wonder if this trip—my first announcing job for CBS— might have something more interesting in store for me.

Kathy Montgomery met my plane.

My leather overnight bag was swinging from my shoulder and a crutch was under each of my arms when she stopped me in the airport lobby.

"Hi," she said. "Welcome to Leningrad."

She introduced herself as a member of the CBS crew and said she was going to be my "stage manager."

She took the bag from me. Easier on the hobble.

"I'm not supposed to meet people at airports," she said, "but, golly, Billy Clyde Puckett! How could I turn that down?"

In the beginning, I said I would be talking about

events that happened a year ago. The drinking man's memory becomes all the more clouded in a year's time, so I wouldn't want to exaggerate my first impression of Kathy that day.

She was just your average, friendly, likable young girl of twenty-four who happened to be outrageously fucking gorgeous.

As Kathy Montgomery drove me to the motel where the CBS crew was staying, I learned some things about my stage manager.

She was a graduate of Berkeley, but she was ingrained with the sanity of a South Dakota childhood. She had grown up in Sioux Falls. She had been with CBS for three years, having gone to work for the network as a secretary just out of college "to get in the door." She had just been promoted to stage manager from "broadcast associate," which used to be called "production assistant," or "PA," or, more to the point, "go-fer." Stage manager was another step toward becoming a producer or director of "live" events, news or sports. That was her goal in life, to work "behind the camera."

"When it's live, I'm spun," she said.

I took that to mean she was enthusiastic about live telecasts.

She would be up in the broadcast booth during the game with Larry Hoage and me. Her job was to keep us coordinated with the producer, give us cues, hand us promo cards, alert us to improvisations— and see that we didn't run out of coffee. She had been assigned to our "announce team" for the rest of the football season.

"Like it or not, you got me," she bubbled. "I'm your trusty sidekick."

I didn't do the old line about what's not to like, but I'd be less than candid if I said it hadn't entered my mind.

This was a gray, misty Saturday in Green Bay. A bite was already in the wind although the date was only Oct. 9. The work clothes on the sidewalks would soon be blooming into mackinaws.

"When did you get to town?" I asked Kathy.

"A month ago yesterday."

By the time we reached the motel, I had found out from Kathy that my appointments for the afternoon and evening were plentiful.

Wade Hogg, the Green Bay coach, was expecting me to drop by his office. Ray Hogan, the Washington coach, was expecting me to drop by his motel room. It was customary for the TV color man to visit with both head coaches before a game. The color man needed to know what surprises, if any, to anticipate. The Redskins were headquartered at our motel. That would make it easy for me to knock off the all-important insert with Dreamer Tatum.

Kathy said, "I spoke to Dreamer Tatum. He's real happy you're going to be here."

"He's a friend."

"Dreamer's the guy who whaled on your knee, right?"

"He didn't mean to."

"That's how it was for us in college. At Cal, you're supposed to hate Stanford. But everybody I knew liked Stanford. Everybody I knew at Stanford liked Cal. I think the hate's more for the Old Blues and the Down-on-the-Farms. Stanford has a neat band. 'White Punks on Dope' is one of their fight songs. Ever heard it?"

"It missed the charts, I guess."

It was Kathy's information that Larry Hoage would be arriving in the early evening on somebody's corporate jet—one of those Tennecos, Nabiscos, or Fritos. Some rich guy was making sure the celebrity announcer reached his broadcast assignment from a speaking engagement.

"You know Larry Hoage?" Kathy asked.

"I've only loved him from afar."

"He'll complain about his room. That's always first."

A dinner reservation had been made in the motel's "gourmet" restaurant for me, Larry Hoage, Mike Rash, the telecast director, and Teddy Cole, the telecast producer. Rash and Cole were bright young guys, really good at their jobs, Kathy said.

"What about you?" I said to the stage manager, who could have retired the Miss South Dakota Trophy if she had ever entered the contest.

Kathy was an exquisitely built 5-8, a golden-haired beauty with mischievous, sea-blue eyes and what you call your radiant complexion.

"Dinner's just for the big guys," she said.

"Used to be. If you're gonna be my trusty sidekick, dinner's part of the deal."

"Really?"

"I've always had a weakness for the Nordic combined."

Body. Eyes. Hair.

"The what?"

"Nothing. You're coming to dinner."

"Great! I brought a clean pair of sneaks."

Inviting Kathy Montgomery to come along to dinner was a harmless enough thing to do, I thought. There was no point in letting our professional relationship begin on an awkward social footing.

Contrary to what Shake Tiller would say about it in the months to come, I'm certain I would have extended the same invitation to my stage manager if she had been a sawed-off little bilingual, erudite beefo-dyke from an Eastern girls' school instead of the winner of the Nordic combined.

Here again, I knew how to deal with the unfounded accusations of those who questioned my moral fiber.

A man simply told the truth.

Or lied.

Before America had been brain-washed by television, a professional football coach had never been called brilliant. A coach was wily, crafty, shrewd, inventive, determined, cagey, respected, innovative, sometimes even lovable, but never brilliant. He wasn't called a brilliant organizer, administrator, delegator, thinker, or teacher because he didn't know anything about self-promotion. He kicked a player in the butt and told him to win games.

Every coach in the National Football League is brilliant now. He's perceived as brilliant for many reasons. One, he speaks a foreign language: "Zone, gap, flex, crease." Two, he has a loyal staff. Three, he has an energetic organization. Four, his owner stands behind him. Five, his computerized scouting system has revolutionized the game. Six, the whole community's on his side. Seven, he has an unselfish family. Eight, he's earned the respect of every player on his team. Nine, he never panics during a game. And ten, he has a vague past in which he learned some kind of secret from either Paul Brown, Vince Lombardi, or Bear Bryant.

But the main reason he's brilliant is because television says so.

Meanwhile, there are things about the brilliant coaches that puzzle me. If they're so brilliant, why do they all use the same offense and defense? Why do they all say, "We like to establish our running game, then throw"? Why do they then say, "You win with defense"? And why can't they answer a simple question about what happened in a game until they've seen the films?

Players always know what happened in a game. If it's a game you lost, it's because some dumbass missed a block or dropped a pass. If it's a game you won, it was because the quarterback ignored the brilliant coach's "game plan" and threw a pass on a busted play and a leaper went up and outwrestled somebody for the ball.

If the Pittsburgh Steelers of the Seventies had stuck with Chuck Noll's game plans, they would have lost three of their four Super Bowls. They'd still be running Franco Harris on trap plays. But Terry Bradshaw, the quarterback, happened to notice that he needed to get some points. So he chunked the ball a mile into the twilight, and Lynn Swann jumped 10 feet off the ground and caught it, and this made Chuck Noll brilliant.

Shoat Cooper had been brilliant when Hose Manning would throw the ball away and Shake Tiller would go catch it.

Shoat could explain it to the sportswriters with brilliance. He would say, "Our reference was Red all the way. They showed us Blue but they jumped into Yellow. Naturally, we had to switch from Odd to Even. Against a Concealed Zone, you have to go underneath. We knew the Crease was there."

Shoat often talked like this to the players, but when his terminology overdosed the alphabet, we would only pretend to listen.

Nobody on our team would have understood the play if Hose Manning or Dump McKinney had come into the huddle and said, "Brown left, eighty-nine flex, overload K, Y-sideline, Z-trap motion on two."

We would have had to call time-out until the laughter stopped.

That was the kind of thing they said in the Dallas huddle, which was why the Cowboys, despite their enviable record all these years, had never beaten a team that was physically worth a shit.

What Hose or Dump was more likely to have said in our huddle was "Their right corner looks a little stoned to me. I'm gonna throw it over the fucker's head. Y'all try to block somebody."

Much of this was going through my mind as I now sat in the presence of Wade Hogg, Green Bay's brilliant new coach.

The contrast between the offices of Wade Hogg and T.J. Lambert would have gone a long way toward reinforcing Uncle Kenneth's argument about the college game being more fun. In Wade Hogg's office, I felt at first like applying for a personal loan, but then it became a problem to maintain a dignified posture as I studied the signs on *his* walls.

Wade Hogg's most prominent sign was framed and hung on the wall over his Portabubble. The sign said:

FORCE + WORK − CONFUSION = SUCCESS!

Given enough time and thought, I decided Green Bay's defensive unit could probably understand the wisdom of that, but I would have defied anyone other than Wade Hogg to explain the sign that said:

$W = \frac{1}{2}$ MVT. $+ \frac{1}{2}$ INSP.

"Simple," said Wade Hogg. "Winning equals one-half motivation plus one-half inspiration."

I studied the sign another moment as the coach said:

"One of the things I've introduced to the Packers—it's new in the league, by the way—is the correct use of energy. We're pretty sold on it around here. What we tell our people is this: the *energy* of an object will *grow* as its speed increases. We want our energy to grow! If you're a football team and your energy doesn't *grow*, you've got a kinetic problem. What we believe is that *work* transformed into energy exerts *force*. There's no question about that. And a growing force is a football team to contend with!"

I wished Wade Hogg luck and said I hoped he didn't run into too many teams that stressed blocking and tackling.

"Oh, I think fundamentals will always be a part of the game," he said. "Where we've taken the lead is in the way we've learned how to transfer our kinetic energy from a gravitational to an elastic object. How's the knee coming along?"

"Okay," I said.

"Those damn gravitational injuries," he said, shaking his head. "Wouldn't have happened if you'd been in our elastic program."

I had tried to picture Wade Hogg as the prehistoric interior lineman he'd been when he played for the Detroit Lions. It was easier than picturing him as the head coach of the Packers, but it was my guess he wouldn't have the job much longer if he didn't stop reading that fucking book, whatever it was.

Later, I was up in Ray Hogan's room at the motel with my head swimming in X's and O's.

The Redskins' coach was more of the old, traditional taskmaster, the kind who drew diagrams as he talked—and talked in a language that only a football coach could decipher.

"We don't care what they do tomorrow," said Ray Hogan, scribbling on sheets of motel stationery. "If they show us this, we're here. If they're here, we're right here. You can't do this to us. We'll do this. Let's say they're in a three. Hell, that gives us this! They go to a four, we do this. Or this. If they bring in the nickel, this is open. We'll take what they give us. I'm not worried about our offense. They'll play Redskin football."

"Like they did against the Rams?" I didn't think it would hurt to give old Ray a jab.

"Aw, that was just one of those given Sundays," he said. "All teams have 'em. Your people have 'em. We had this open all day. Never could hit it. We could have run here till Christmas. Put this guy out here, they have to do this. Look what that leaves? Hell, it's a landing strip! Of course, we kept trying to do this—and they wouldn't give us that."

"Zebras tried to help you out."

"They dropped a few, didn't they? Well, they get a lot of criticism, but they do a pretty good job overall."

"You think all of them are honest?"

"In the *National Football League*? Our game officials? Goodness, Billy Clyde, that's the craziest question I ever heard! Of course they're honest! They're wrong half the time but they're honest! It's those dang judgment calls! Did he or didn't he? Was he or wasn't he? All coaches die of a judgment call sooner or later."

"Charlie Teasdale makes his share of them," I said.

"Charlie will drop a flag for you. Old Quick Flag, we call him. He likes to drop one early, let you know who's boss out there. I've accused him of wanting to get on television too much."

"What does he say?"

"You can't talk to an official. You can talk to a Pope or a king or a president, but you can't talk to an official. Charlie's a real bad official, but he's not dishonest."

Ray Hogan said you had to know how to use the officials to your advantage.

"They almost never call the same penalty twice in a row. So if we get a holding call, we tell our people to grab anything that moves on the next play. In other words, you hold after a hold, don't you? If we get a pass-interference call, we tell our people to undress the scoundrels on the next play! But this isn't anything new, Billy Clyde. Hell, I bet they taught you this in high school in Texas, didn't they?"

Yes, they had.

I pressed the other point one more time.

"Coach, you don't think there's even a remote chance an official would do some business?"

"Not a chance," said Ray Hogan. "For one thing, they're too stupid."

I asked the Washington coach if there was anything I needed to know about his defense.

"We'll be in this most of the time," he said, returning to his diagrams. "It's been good to us. We may show 'em this now and then, try to get 'em to come here. Right here's where we'd like to keep 'em. You're not going anywhere here. We'll come if they do this. We'll come if they do that. We love for 'em to try this! It's all up to Dreamer tomorrow. If Dreamer decides he wants to come to the dance, our defense will be all right. They'll play Redskin football."

Was Dreamer Tatum coming to the dance?

I asked Dreamer the blunt question as the two of us had a drink in the motel bar. We were waiting for Kathy and a camera crew so we could do the insert.

Dreamer gave me a look when I put the question to him.

"Between you and me, Clyde?"

He could trust me, I assured him.

"I'm Dixie," he said.

I told Dreamer I had assumed as much when I saw the Rams–Redskins game on television.

"You changed the future of pro football," Dreamer said. "Our conversation when you were in the hospital? I got to thinking about it later. You were right. We couldn't win a strike. I'm leading the Players Association in a new direction."

The problems were the same, he said. The players didn't have collective bargaining. The owners had

completely undermined the free-agency system. A
football player was less able to get a fair-market
value for his services than a steelworker. A player's
salary was still determined by the "whim" of the
owner.

"We threatened a strike," he said. "We made a big
noise about wanting a percentage of the TV reve-
nue, trying to force a wage scale on 'em. They only
called us Commies. They don't realize it's only another form of profit-sharing. Profit-sharing is a hundred years old in this country, man! The owners'
grandfathers invented profit-sharing! Looks like the
grandfathers were smarter people, doesn't it?"

We were alone in the bar. Dreamer lowered his
voice anyhow and had a gleam in his eye as he said,
"We're going to Plan B, Clyde. Operation Dixie.
That's the code name. It came out of our board-of-
directors meeting."

"Play bad on purpose?"

"We're *all* goin' Dixie," he said.

"What do you think you'll accomplish?"

With satisfaction, Dreamer said, "An inferior
product!"

"And?"

He said, "The big turn-off is coming, man. The
public will wake up one day and say, 'What's this shit
coming down?' We keep our jobs, but the game
becomes a joke. TV ratings drop. This hits the owner
in his pocketbook. Stadiums are empty. Coaches get
fired by the dozens. Players get traded frantically.
Every team is a bag of garbage. A seven–nine record gets you to the playoffs! The press gets hot.
Ball clubs are an embarrassment to their communi-
ties. Owners commit suicide. We figure in less than
two seasons, we can create mass hysteria."

"How many players are going along with you on
this?"

"In a strike action, we were never going to get more than sixty-five percent. That became apparent. Too many Republicans in the league. Operation Dixie takes it out of the realm of politics. We think we have ninety-five percent right now. Among other things, there's less risk of injury."

"Sorry you didn't think of it sooner," I said. "I'd still be in a uniform."

"You could play on crutches now and you wouldn't get tackled!"

Dreamer said the Players Association had appointed a Script Committee.

Members of the Script Committee were in charge of thinking up ways to break the hearts of the owners and fans. Missed field goals from close in, fumbles on key downs, dropped passes for touchdowns. These were only a few. The possibilities were limitless.

Everybody was looking forward to the hilarity of it, Dreamer said. "A team drives all the way down the field. A field goal will win it. They're on the five-yard line. The owner's up in his box celebrating, but—"

"It's blocked?"

"Bad snap," Dreamer's grin was what you'd call sinister.

How was it all going to be resolved in the master plan? I inquired.

Dreamer said, "The owners will figure out what's going on and ask for a meeting. We'll get a wage scale and free agents with bargaining power. In return, we play football again."

"If it goes on too long, you won't regain the public's confidence."

"That's true, but it's a problem of the owners', not ours. What's the worst thing that'll happen? The NFL dies, right? So what? Somebody starts a new league. Rich guys will always want to own football teams and they'll always need athletes. We've got 'em, Clyde. We've got 'em right here."

Kathy and a two man camera crew came into the bar. There was a nice spot where we could do the insert, she said. It was over in a corner of plastic flowers near the indoor swimming pool.

On our way to set up for the interview, I said to Kathy, "Dreamer was just telling me how the Redskins are ready to get after 'em tomorrow."

She looked at Dreamer, and said, "Pumped up, huh?"

"I've never seen a team as well prepared," he said.

Kathy positioned Dreamer and I on a small brick wall that separated the indoor swimming pool from the motel's Pong games, vending machines, and Astro-Turf putting green. She handed me a microphone.

"Just chat informally for about ten minutes," she said. "Try to look relaxed. It'll help with the editing if you can keep your questions and answers as short as possible."

"How much of this will they use?" I asked.

"About sixty seconds," said Kathy. "Maybe ninety."

"That much?"

"Go!" Kathy said, as a hand-held cameraman moved in closer to us.

Our faces—Dreamer's and mine—grew solemn. Holding the mike, I turned to the Redskins' corner-back and said, "What about this Washington team, Dreamer?"

"They're the most dedicated athletes I've ever been associated with, Clyde. Our workouts have been the most intense I've ever seen—and you know the old saying: if you practice well, you play well."

"You're a vice-president of the Players Association. There's been a lot of strike talk, as we know. Has this had an effect on the football we're seeing this year?"

"I'm glad you ask that question," Dreamer said.

"We have our differences with the owners, of course, but I look for a settlement in the near future because the players and the owners have a big thing in common: love of the game. From the players' point of view, we would never let our negotiations interfere with the competition on the field. We're football players first. To answer your question, I've never seen the quality of play on a higher level."

"The injury," said Kathy, intruding. "Talk about the injury."

"My injury?" I said.

"Keep going, we're rolling!"

To Dreamer again, I said, "Uh . . . let me ask you about a rumor, Dreamer. Is it true you've been seeing a psychiatrist since you caused the injury that put me out of pro football?"

Dreamer was alert.

"Uh . . . I haven't actually sought professional help, but I've discussed it at length with a good friend who studied psychology in school."

"At Ohio State?"

"Yes. He reminded me I'd played football for Woody Hayes and I couldn't be held responsible for my violent actions in an adult society."

"I would agree with that. And I'd like to take this opportunity to tell America I don't hold a grudge. You had a job to do, Dreamer. I respect that."

We shook hands with sincerity—on camera.

And Dreamer said, "It's a tendency I haven't been able to bring under complete control. I see a ball-carrier and there's this crazy, animal urge that takes over my body. It's like I'm possessed and the only emotional release I have is to hurt somebody. Quite frankly, I wouldn't want to be in a Green Bay uniform tomorrow."

"Great!" Kathy said, stepping in to take the mike. "That's incredible! Richard Marks will go bonkers."

"All a man knows is what people tell him," I said.

Kathy said, "It's fantastic! We have the scoop on the strike! We have the inner feelings of the man who injured you! We have—"

"Kathy," I said, cutting her off. "We'll chat later, okay?"

I led Dreamer off to the side for a moment. In a half-whisper, I asked him if he was aware of the magazine piece Shake Tiller had been working on.

"We helped him on it," Dreamer said. "He's not gonna come out and say Operation Dixie is an official position of the Players Association. He's gonna lay it out as his own theory—a rumor. This'll get their attention, baby."

"Who, the FBI?"

"The owners, man."

I hadn't known exactly what would be in Shake's story, other than a libelous condemnation of the zebras. Shake hadn't wanted me to read the article before he sent it off to *Playboy*. What I didn't know wouldn't hurt me.

"We laid it all out for him," Dreamer said. "We wanted it in print, like a trial balloon, you understand what I'm sayin'? There's a better-than-even chance the owners are idiots and they can't figure out what's going on. Shake's story will tell 'em. We'll deny there's an Operation Dixie, but the idea will be planted. It'll fester in their minds. The more it festers, the quicker they'll come to the bargaining table."

"I'm trying not to be troubled by the logic," I said.

In parting, Dreamer said, "If you'd been more active in the association, Clyde, you'd know this is what's called creative use of the media. It's just another way for us to tell the owners how it is. We're saying if you fuck with *us*, Jack, you're fuckin' with your heartbeat!"

*   *   *

Larry Hoage's firmly held layers of streaky gray hair somehow looked heavier to me in person than they had on television.

He had come to dinner that night in a cashmere hounds'-tooth jacket over a white cashmere turtleneck, and—it was more than a hunch—makeup.

The color of his face was in that area between an orange golf ball and coffee with cream. The face had undergone a couple of lifts, and his teeth had been painted. Larry's face also told you that the mind which controlled it had never, in all his forty-odd years, given a thought to anything more complicated than his own personal appearance.

Larry Hoage was not the Talking Head on which all other television personalities had been patterned, but he was the perfect example of a man who had made a fortune out of radio and TV through the sheer lunacy of his profession, and had mistakenly attributed this accident to his intelligence.

Like so many others in his business, Larry Hoage had become a personality on looks and voice alone. He was everything wrong with broadcasting, but you couldn't convince anyone in broadcasting of it. Larry had become a recognizable face, therefore he was a star.

He had come up the usual way. He had done it all for a TV station in Los Angeles—news reader, weather reader, editorial reader. One evening he had filled in for the sports reader, and somebody had liked his enthusiasm, his delivery. Sports was fun and Larry's ho, ho, ho's made it even more fun, somebody thought.

The network began to call on him in emergencies to do play-by-play on college football and basketball games. Another fool thought he had talent. One of Richard Marks's predecessors. Larry was thus assigned to the NFL. That's when Larry got serious.

The NFL wasn't sport, it was patriotism. A new NFL
shill was born. The league liked shills, hence the
network liked Larry.

All this started fifteen years ago. Larry had since
become established, a big name. He knew how to
shake hands with affiliates, tell jokes to sponsors. He
never refused an assignment, never complained about
being overworked. If you needed a guy to fly all
night and host a surfing show or interview a Bulgar-
ian weightlifter, Larry was your man.

The network publicity department promoted him
as hardworking, studious, reliable. He was a "good
family man," it was said, because he had a dopey
wife and two dopey kids and lived in a dopey house
in Orange County. I had no doubt that on the walls
of his den you would find photos of Larry lounging
in golf carts in Palm Springs with Gerald Ford, Gene
Autry, and Bob Hope.

Perhaps worse than anything, Larry believed that
the endless clichés in which he spoke were his own
original thoughts.

I stood up to greet Larry when he arrived at our
dinner table. "Number Twenty-Three," he said.
"Shake Tiller, Eighty-Eight; T. J. Lambert, Fifty-
One; Hose Manning, Seventeen—one of the great
New York Giant teams!"

"Hose was Number Nine," I said.

"Pablo Patterson, Sixty-Seven," said Larry.

"Puddin Patterson?"

"How 'bout that game in the snow? Everybody on
their feet at Yankee Stadium, the field a virtual quag-
mire, the wind whipping through the bleachers. I
thought the Eagles were home free, but old Eighty-
Eight showed 'em! Whatta catch!"

"I caught it."

"Glad to have you aboard, Billy Clyde! At ease,
sport, we'll carve out a niche for you!"

Larry shifted us around so that he could sit at the head of the table. This way, he could face the room; rather, the room could face him. Kathy and I were on his left. Kathy looked more grownup in a skirt, sweater, and heels. Mike Rash and Teddy Cole were across from us. Mike and Teddy could have passed as twins in their jeans, fatigue jackets, uncombed hair, and laid-back attitudes.

Every time I looked at Larry during dinner I remembered an old Texas expression. In a convenient moment, I'd murmured it to Kathy Montgomery: "If Larry had a brain, he'd be outdoors playing with it."

Only Larry had complained about the frozen lobster tails, the lukewarm baked potato, and the salad bar in the motel's gourmet restaurant.

The others were finishing off the remains of a good Michigan wine, and I was finishing off the remains of a young Scotch, as Larry said, "Well, chilluns, I think we're in for a real old-fashioned, gut-bustin' sidewinder tomorrow! This is going to be some kind of football game!"

Nods and hums greeted Larry's statement.

He turned to Kathy and said, "Before I forget, tell the front desk to put me in another room. These walls are so darn thin. The guy next door to me has a bladder problem. I don't want to listen to *that* all night!"

"No problem, be right back," said Kathy, bolting out of the dining room.

A waiter brought the dinner check while Kathy was away. Larry Hoage was handed the check, an act that startled him. But he quickly looked relieved as Teddy Cole reached over, picked up the check, and casually signed it.

"Can't argue with the producer," Larry said to me. "Producers have the big pencil!"

My colleague held out his wineglass to Mike Rash.

"How 'bout it, El Directo? Any *vino* left?"

Mike Rash emptied the last of the wine into Larry's glass as Kathy returned to the table. Larry was being moved to a suite.

"I gave the bell captain five dollars to make sure he does it now," she said.

"Now, you put that on your expense account, young lady!" said Larry.

"She's not allowed," Teddy Cole said, digging lazily into his pocket. He tossed a $5 bill to Kathy.

"It's no big deal," Kathy said, hesitant to pick up the money.

I took out my moneyclip and pulled off a $100 bill. Offering it to Kathy, I said, "Here, I'll put you on *my* expense account."

Kathy poked me on the arm.

I put the hundred away, having had my little joke. Mike Rash mentioned to Larry that I had done a "very good" insert with Dreamer Tatum that afternoon.

"Excellent job," Teddy Cole said.

"Really neat," said Kathy.

"Dreamer Tatum!" Larry Hoage blustered. "Number Thirty-Two! You don't run the football at *him*, boy! You'll come up a day late and a dollar short!"

"He's a good one," I said.

"Yes, sir, chilluns, you don't stick your hand in the cookie jar when Dreamer Tatum's around! He'll snatch you bald-headed!"

"Billy Clyde interviewed him today," Teddy Cole said.

"Dreamer Tatum is one of the all-time greats!" Larry Hoage guaranteed us. "He'll come after you like a hookin' bull!"

"We're not on the air yet, Larry," said Mike Rash.

Larry stood up.

"Okay, chilluns, I've enjoyed it, but it's time for the Old Professor to do his homework!"

He looked down at Kathy.

"Press guide in my room?"

"Yes."

"Flip card?"

"Right."

"Today's papers?"

"Check."

"Gate pass?"

"Done."

Now he looked at me.

"Glad to have you on the flight deck, Billy Clyde. Don't worry about a thing. Any problems, I'll get you down out of the fog, no sweat!"

"Thanks, Larry."

"Who do you like in this melee?"

"Well . . ."

"I'll tell you who *I* like. When you've been around this sport as long as I have, you kind of get an inkling, you know? I've got a feeling the Redskins are going to cut the old wolf loose when they ring that bell tomorrow! Yes, sir, I think Washington's gonna put the big britches on 'em!"

On his way out of the restaurant, Larry paused to sign autographs for people at two different tables. I thought of getting their names and turning them over to the proper authorities. With such lunatics on the prowl, I figured no one in Green Bay was safe that night.

Kathy, Mike, Teddy, and I walked into the lobby. I presented the option of a nightcap in the motel bar before bedtime. Everyone passed.

Mike and Teddy said goodnight. They shuffled away down separate hallways.

"Sure you don't want a drink?" I said to Kathy.

"No, thanks. I have to be up at dawn."

"Why?"

"There's a lot of stuff to take care of."

"The kickoff's not till one o'clock."

"It's sleaze work, but that's what trusty sidekicks do."

She offered me a handshake.

"Hey, listen, it's really neat to know you. This is gonna be fun, having you around," she said.

Unexpectedly, then, she gave me a quick kiss on the cheek.

"See you up in the booth!" And she walked away.

I watched her all the way down the hall. When she had disappeared around a corner, I hobbled toward my own room to call the missus.

ELEVEN

Things were certainly hopping at Enjolie's in Beverly Hills, which was where the long-distance operator had managed to locate Barbara Jane Bookman, star of *Rita's Limo Stop*.

It was official. Word had come in that afternoon. *Rita* was a full go for thirteen episodes. It was slotted into ABC's prime-time lineup in January.

Naturally, everybody had to celebrate. Barbara Jane had gone over to Enjolie's to meet Carolyn Barnes and Jack Sullivan. And the old Dom Perignon corks were flying all over the room, soaring into the bucketed trees and bouncing off the threadbare sweaters of screenwriters who were discussing the use of the CUT TO as Dickens would have applied it.

"I'm afraid we're making a scene," Barb said.

"How are the witches taking it?"

"The good witches think we're somebody important. They aren't sure who, but they're smiling. The bad witches are watering the flowers."

"You did good," I said. "I guess now I'd better find out where Sheldon Gurtz has his suits made."

Only half the war was won, Barb said. Now the show had to get the ratings. It had to make the Top Twenty—like Notre Dame every season, even with 5 losses—or it wouldn't be renewed for next year. This made it all the more important for the scripts to be good, and all the more necessary for Sheldon Gurtz and Kitty Feldman to die.

"You didn't invite them tonight?"

"They're having their own party in the Valley."

"Hardly as festive as where you are."

"Might be better. They'll have Hula Hoops."

"So Barb, what does it all mean—in terms of life its ownself?"

What it meant was, Barbara Jane was going to stay at the Westwood Marquis for another three months for sure. I would try to be there as often as possible. If the show was successful in the ratings, she would stay on even longer because the network would want to start shooting episodes for next fall.

The prospect of becoming a bicoastal myself did not thrill me, but I didn't want to bring up a selfish point at the moment, not in the midst of a gala occasion.

"All we can do is root for good scripts," I said.

"Jack's going to write some of them."

"Jack?"

"Jack Sullivan, Biff."

"Oh, right."

"I think—I hope—Jack can take over as executive producer. It could make the whole difference in whether the show takes off."

"Seems like a good guy," I said. " Shouldn't I congratulate Carolyn Barnes? Put her on a minute."

"Uh . . . she's in the ladies' room. I'll tell her for you. How's it going out there? Ready for the big debut?"

Other than Larry Hoage, I said I had only met the director, producer, and stage manager. They were all good people.

"Who are they?"

"Mike Rash is the director. Teddy Cole produces. They're a couple of young hotshots."

"Did you say stage manager?"

"It's a person in the booth who helps coordinate everything. The stage manager's sort of a step above a go-fer, your own trusty sidekick. The stage manager met my plane."

"Good guy?"

"I like him okay. His names's . . . Ken Montgomery."

"I have to get off the phone, babe. Three adorables are waiting to call their service. Be yourself tomorrow. Have fun. Enjoy it. I'm going to tape the game."

"Did you get a Betamax for the room?"

"Jack has one. We're going to watch it at his house."

There was more than one reason why I had trouble getting to sleep that night. I was hyped-up about the telecast, of course. I was also beginning to feel a growing concern over my wife's fondness for her director, Jack Sullivan. But I wouldn't want guilt to slip away without a share of the credit.

I had lied about my stage manager and it had been a cowardly thing to do. Why had I lied? I hadn't laid a glove on Kathy Montgomery. Why the guilt?

Well, I knew why. I had flirted with Kathy. And why had I flirted with Kathy? Because she was a good-looking rascal and I was a man—and all men have that one-eighth of a gangster in them.

As Connie had once said to Uncle Kenneth, "They couldn't any more get the sorry out of you than they could scrape the shit off a Navajo blanket!" That was it. Men were one-eighth gangsters, but women were one-eighth bitches. Jump ball. It was called life its ownself, and you had to learn to laugh at it, live with it.

But I still hadn't been able to go to sleep that night until I'd read the chapter of Shake's book that had been inspired by his childhood.

MARRIED HEAT

Most married people are unhappy.

The main reason they're unhappy is because they can't go to movies as often as they once did.

This breeds a restlessness that spreads poison all through the relationship.

They start to expect too much from each other, to make unreasonable demands, and look for things to give each other shit about.

Married people give each other more shit about money than anything else.

That's because money is what it takes to eat, buy clothes, go to movies, and take vacations.

The big difference between married men and married women is their outlook on money. Women like to spend all the money on wallpaper and drapes but always have the same amount of money in the bank in case of an emergency. Men like to spend all the money there is on good times, then make some more when they run out, or maybe not buy new wallpaper.

One of the reasons married men like to talk to single women is because single women almost never talk about wallpaper or drapes. Single women mostly talk about dope.

A few years ago, single women liked to talk about hard-ons, which was still better than wallpaper. And married women hardly ever talked about hard-ons.

That's changed. Today, married women probably talk more about hard-ons than single women because they know more deckhands. Married women meet the deckhands on cruises their husbands shouldn't have taken them on because the money should have stayed in the bank where it belonged.

Loretta Lynn, the singer, once said the truest thing in the world: "Love don't grow old; people do."

The result of that truth is a tired marriage. And big trouble. The shit starts to fly.

First thing a man knows, he's told he can't have a Labrador retriever. So to get back at his wife, the man says if she wants to go to a movie, she can go hire a fag to take her.

Then they start to argue about everything that happened twenty years ago—and naturally it all comes down to where'd the money go that was here the other day?

There ought to be a marriage boutique that sells a certificate for the husband to keep around the house to show his wife when she gives him heat about money.

He can whip out the certificate when she looks at the bank statement, sees they're broke, and starts to raise blood-curdling hell.

He can show her the certificate and say, "Heck, Matilda, I thought it would earn more if I took it out of savings and put it in the Corporate Income Fund."

"How much do we have?"

"Gee, I don't know, but I'll ask the broker Monday. I'm sure it'll be worth more after he rolls it over."

This will relieve her mind. She can go look at wallpaper and the man can relax and watch the Texas—OU game in peace.

I have long advocated government-subsidized marriage. Without married people, our society would collapse. Married people are the only ones who vote, and somebody has to elect the vermin who call themselves servants of the people and appoint the bureaucrats who fuck up our lives.

Thus, if married people are going to be the backbone of our nation—and if these same married people are going to suffer the most abuse from each other—they should be paid by the government to do it. This would take the heat off love and put the heat on hard work, which is what a lasting marriage requires.

Social diseases have caused a fair amount of shit in marriage.

Husbands and wives alike tried unsuccessfully for years to sell their partners on the toilet seat, drinking glass, bedsheet explanation for social diseases.

Recently, I have noted a trend toward more creative thinking.

Wives who initially contract the dose from a deckhand have now learned to blame their husbands for passing it on to them. Since all husbands are guilty of cheating anyhow, they believe it, accept their time in the penalty box, and buy presents to make up for their sins.

What of the man who catches the dose and is certain he's transmitted it to his wife and can't afford to buy presents? In the old days, a man threw himself on the mercy of the court, but the gutters became littered with divorced men who were financially ruined because they threw themselves on the mercy of the court.

A pro football player named Dump McKinney once gave his wife the clap and saved the marriage for a year with one of the most inspired schemes I've ever heard of. The trick was to get his wife to take a penicillin shot for a reason other than the clap. One night they were paying bills together when an idea came to him.

He hit her in the hand with a staple gun.

"Honey, you better get a penicillin shot," he said. "You can't be too careful with tetanus."

Pride of ownership is the biggest reason married people take shit from each other. People feel they have a right to give their mates excess heat because they married them in the first place. They could easily have married the other people they were fucking, but they didn't. They married who they married, which means their partners became "property."

This one is easy.

All marriages should have a loan-out clause. A couple would agree beforehand on how many loan-outs they were going to need, per week, per month, per year.

If the husband wants to loan himself out to a ball game for a night, it would be his privilege. And if the wife wants to loan herself out to a deckhand, it would be her privilege.

People being only human, of course, any system might be taken advantage of by the self-indulgent personality.

There would be those husbands and wives who would claim they had lost count of their loan-outs and had gone over the limit.

Oops, sorry.

Well, there's a very good way to put an end to that kind of married shit.

Divorce.

"Holy Roman smokin' candles, Billy Clyde Puckett! You know what they say about that kind of football player, don't you?"

"No, Larry, what do they say?"

"They say he may have a small belt buckle but it's what he's got in the *gut* that counts!"

Larry Hoage referred to the Green Bay fullback, Edgar Morris, who had just gained two yards on a draw play at mid-field in the second quarter of a football game in which neither team had scored.

It hadn't been the fault of Charlie Teasdale that no points were on the scoreboard. The referee had marched both teams into scoring range with his penalty flags, but luck didn't seem to be going anybody's way.

Bad snaps had cost the Redskins two field goals from inside Green Bay's 10-yard line.

Green Bay had driven to Washington's 1-inch line, first down. But the Packers' quarterback, Beaner Todd, had fumbled on first down, Edgar Morris had lost yardage back to the 7 on second down, a third-down pass had been dropped in the end zone by Elbert Sweeney, Green Bay's tight end, and a 17-yard field-goal attempt had failed because of a strange mixup.

The Packers' soccer-style placekicker, Gerhard Munger, an East German, was right-footed. But Loren Doss, the holder, had positioned the ball for a left-footed kicker. Because of his deep concentration before the snap, the East German hadn't noticed this. When he swung his leg, he had caught the holder in the rib cage.

It had been a small price for the holder to pay for his union, but I hadn't betrayed Dreamer Tatum's confidence by saying this on the air. I had only said:

"That's how Gerhard got out of Berlin. He went through the wall instead of over it."

Now it was almost halftime and Larry Hoage was barking at the microphone again.

"It's first down, Packers. They look like they're ready to take somebody to the woodshed, Billy Clyde

Puckett! You had an in-depth look at these two teams before today's kickoff. What'd you find out about the way they prepared for this donnybrook?"

"They practiced offense and defense."

"And what a great football team they are!" Larry shouted.

He hadn't heard me at all. The whole game. He had never heard anything but his own voice from the moment he went into broadcasting.

"Don't go 'way, chilluns. We've got a real old-fashioned, gut-bustin' sidewinder going for you out here in meat-packin' country! We'll be right back!"

Larry whirled around in his swivel chair and glared at Kathy Montgomery, who wore a headset and stood behind us.

"This coffee's cold!" Larry snarled. "What the devil's going on up here? It's pretty darned unprofessional, if you ask me!"

Like the superb stage manager she was, Kathy magically produced a backup thermos of hot coffee, a jar of CoffeeMate, a box of sugar cubes, and some plastic spoons.

She poured a fresh mug for Larry, who didn't leave his chair; for the cameraman at the end of the booth; for the color man—I was broadcasting from a standing position on Larry's right—and for Hoyt Nester, a man who took his job quite seriously.

Hoyt was seated on Larry's left. He was the play-by-play man's spotter and statistician, a man I judged to be in his seventies. Hoyt's beard was a white Vandyke, his tam was dark green, his Eisenhower jacket a lighter shade of green. Hoyt Nester lived next door to Larry Hoage in Orange County. A bigtime announcer like Larry could choose his own assistant. The network paid Hoyt some loose change and picked up his expenses.

Earlier in the day, I had pointed at Hoyt and said to Kathy:

"There's an oldtimer with some stories to tell. What's it cost not to hear any of them?"

Now, I thanked her for the coffee. Which wasn't the only thing she had produced for us before, and during, the telecast. She had provided hotdogs, soup, notepads, ballpoint pens, well-sharpened pencils, paper clips, rubber bands, statistical summaries from the league, magazine and newspaper tearsheets, media guides, a tub of ice, a pitcher of water, cold drinks, a trash basket, all of the promo cards in perfect order, and a little flask of J&B as a welcoming gift for me. She had even recruited Vivian and Dexter, in case the need might arise.

While we were in this commercial break, she said, "You're doing great. How do you like it?"

"You can see more up here."

"That's it?"

"Smells better, too."

"Is there much talking down on the field? To the other team?"

"Oh, sure."

"What kind of things do you say?"

"It depends."

"On what?"

"I don't know. How the game's going. If it's a close game you'd both like to win, there's not much talking. Lot of cussing. But if it's pretty well decided one way or the other, a guy might ask you if you've seen old What's-his-name, or how's old So-and-so doing? He might tell you he's got some good Colombian, if you want to meet him outside the dressing room after the whistle."

"What do you say when you cuss each other?"

We each had one ear off of our headsets.

"You really want to know?"

"Sure, it's fascinating."

"Well, let's say we're down on the goal line. I might wink at a couple of linebackers and say, 'Here I come, girls, y'all ready?' "

"Good. What would they say?"

"Oh, one of them would probably say something like, 'You ain't got enough shit in your pants to come this way, motherfucker!' "

Kathy shrieked.

Over the one ear of our headsets, we both heard Teddy Cole's voice.

"It's okay, Billy Clyde. Your mike was off."

There wasn't much to do during the halftime but eat another hotdog, drink more coffee, and go to the john. Not until the last two minutes before the second-half kickoff. That's when Kathy told me to put on the headset and watch the monitor.

On the headset I heard the voice of Brent Musburger, who was back in New York in a studio. He seemed to be saying that CBS's newest color man— me—had raised the flag on Iwo Jima, invented the cure for cancer, and in my spare time had taught crippled children how to walk again. And on the monitor I watched as Old 23, wearing a TCU uniform, broke loose for several long gains against the Arkansas Razorbacks, Texas Aggies, and Baylor Bears. Old 23 then appeared in a New York Giants uniform and broke loose for several long gains against the Minnesota Vikings, Dallas Cowboys, and Philadelphia Eagles. Next, Old 23 was in slow motion, scaling up the ass of Puddin Patterson and diving into the end zone to score the winning touchdown against the dogass Jets in the Super Bowl. Finally, Old 23, in a clip from a home movie, was out on the terrace of his Manhattan apartment, hugging, kissing, and having a laugh with a windblown Barbara Jane Bookman.

"You're live with Brent," said Kathy, as the cameraman in the booth wheeled the lens toward me.

Looking away from the camera, I said, "Hello, Brent. We've got a gut-bustin' sidewinder out here in Green Bay."

There was static on the headset. I couldn't hear the reply. I shrugged at Kathy. She shrugged back.

"Just vamp," she said.

I frowned.

"Say something . . . anything!"

"Brent?" I said into my equipment mike. "I appreciate the insert. Sorry they left out the stuff about the Viet Namese refugees I've adopted and all the civil rights legislation I've passed, but tell everybody thank you."

The third quarter of the Redskins—Green Bay game was highlighted by Dreamer Tatum's defensive play.

Dreamer managed to be tying his shoelace when Tommy Maples, a Green Bay receiver, caught a flat pass and scored from 35 yards out. In his own end zone, Dreamer juggled a sure interception into the hands of the Packers' tight end. Touchdown, Green Bay. The fastest Dreamer ran was when he and a teammate, Jamie Brock, took off in pursuit of Green Bay's Edgar Morris, who broke clear on a dive play and went 75 yards for a touchdown. Dreamer didn't catch the Green Bay runner, but he did catch Jamie Brock, tripping him just as the Packer was about to be overtaken.

In between these awesome maneuvers, Dreamer acted like a man in a frenzy. Before the ball would be snapped, he would hop around in a nervous fit, looking as if he had never been so eager to hit somebody.

This moved Larry Hoage to a higher decibel level.

"What a competitor!" he raved. "You don't close the barn door on that fella, no, sir! Dreamer Tatum is some kind of football player!"

Charlie Teasdale kept trying to put the Redskins back in the game, but Washington couldn't take advantage of the penalty flags he threw at the Green Bay defense.

From the control truck, Mike Rash asked if I wanted to make a comment on the officiating.

I waited for the right moment. It came when Charlie resorted to an obscure call, defensive holding. He called it against Green Bay when Washington had tried a quarterback sneak for a first down. Who would a defense hold on a play like that—and why—even if it had time?

On the air, I said, "If Charlie Teasdale's flag stays on the ground much longer, they're gonna have to send out for plant food."

Kathy Montgomery tapped me on the shoulder. I looked around to see her thumbs-up sign.

The last two minutes of the game took an eternity, as usual. More often than not, this is because the zebras call extra time-outs so the networks can get all of their commercials in.

Green Bay was going to win the game, 21 to 0. Hoyt Nester was packing up his statistics and reference material as he said, "Looks like the hay's in the barn."

Hoyt yawned and unwrapped a homemade tunafish sandwich.

I heard Teddy Cole tell Larry Hoage to surrender the air to me. The producer wanted me to deliver some expertise on why Green Bay had dominated the second half.

"Throw it to Billy Clyde, Larry. We may have to go with a panic close," Teddy said.

"Right you are, Ted," Larry Hoage said over the air, leaving what viewers we had left to wonder who "Ted" might have been.

Larry then said, "Well, Billy Clyde Puckett, the old Green Bay Packers lived high on the hog today—Wade Hogg, that is! Yes sir, it looks like the Pack is back! They came out of the chute with fire in their eyes and a tiger in their tank and turned this old-fashioned, gut-bustin' sidewinder into a cakewalk! They'll be singing and dancing in the streets of Green Bay, Wisconsin, tonight! The pesky Washington Redskins came in here to play a good football game, but they got crawled on, climbed on, and laughed at by a bunch of angry Green Bay Packers who look like Super Bowl contenders if I know a thing or two."

Hoyt held up an index card to Larry. The card said: "TEETH AND CLAWS." Larry acknowledged it as he kept talking.

Still at the mike, Larry said, "The Redskins were lucky to get outta here today with their teeth and claws. That's how it looked to me. So, Billy Clyde Puckett, you're a man who knows what it's like down there in the trenches where the mayhem is, where it's muscle on muscle, what's the story behind the story of this Green Bay verdict? How'd the Pack tie a knot in 'em today?"

"Larry, it all came down to one thing. Green Bay scored more points."

TWELVE

Clandestine activity was a course I had flunked as far back as high school. You could drop me behind enemy lines and the first farmer who came at me with a pitchfork could find out the location of our airfields and all the schedules of our troop trains. No man ever caved in to torture any quicker than I did. I would confess to things I hadn't even thought of if it would prevent an argument.

Normally, Barbara Jane only had to look at me suspiciously when I would come home from a road trip with the Giants, and I would blurt out the names of everybody I had been with in every bar, even if some of the names were Micki, Misty, and Trixie and I hadn't gone anywhere near the little dumplings.

It was astonishing, then, that I handled the Kathy Montgomery problem as craftily as I did over the next two months. To the West Coast delegation, my stage manager's name was still "Ken Montgomery," if the name came up at all, which it rarely did.

In the meantime, and by necessity, I lived the life of an airline pilot. I was Barbara Jane's bicoastal husband on Monday, Tuesday, and Wednesday every week, lounging around the suite at the Westwood Marquis, whereupon I would leave for my next TV assignment on Thursday. This meant that on Thursday, Friday, Saturday, and Sunday, or for most of those days and nights, I would be with Kathy Montgomery, my trusty sidekick.

But if I was with Kathy more than I was with my wife, my wife was with her director more than she was with her husband. The only way we could have changed this would have been for one of us to give up what we were doing, but we both liked what we were doing, and it would have been foolish to turn down the money on top of that. So I didn't know who, or what, to blame for the situation we had worked ourselves into, other than life its ownself.

Modern living is what some people call it.

After my first telecast in Green Bay, I had received relatively high grades from everyone at the network. Mike Rash and Teddy Cole said I ought to be nominated for an Emmy simply for not talking too much. About a thousand letters came into CBS in New York that said the same thing. Comments in newspapers around the country were generally favorable. Jim Tom Pinch's column was naturally a rave.

Jim Tom wrote:

Billy Clyde Puckett is living proof that action speaks louder than words, even when the action is as rancid as it was in the Green Bay—Washington game. The proper words to describe that game could never win the approval of Standards and Practices. Much to the pleasure of any intelligent viewer, Billy Clyde shut the hell up as often as he could, save for his shrewd line about Referee Charlie Teasdale's flag, which must have made everyone wince in the Commissioner's office.

Two days after my debut, the head of CBS Sports called to give me his professional opinion of it.

"I thought you brought a lot to the dance, old man," said Richard Marks. "Not to be picky, but in my view, you ought to speak up more. People want to hear what Billy Clyde Puckett thinks. I'm sure you were being cautious your first time out, but don't be afraid to jump in. You have an open mike."

"Larry doesn't let you in much," I said.

"I don't have the same negative feelings about cross-talk that some of my predecessors did. Cross-talk often adds to the excitement of a telecast."

"Cross-talk?"

"When you both talk at once. For instance, if you jump in, but Larry keeps spinning a yarn. I say let it play."

"Mike and Teddy want me to avoid that."

"Mike and Teddy work for me."

"More cross-talk. Got it."

"I'm not saying it's something you should plan. I'm only suggesting you address yourself to the audience more often. Look, Larry Hoage isn't the best announcer in the business, but he's far from the worst, and he brings an enthusiasm to a broadcast the sponsors like."

"They do?"

His statement shouldn't have surprised me. I'd known a few agency guys in my day. They could derail an elevator.

Richard Marks said, "Oh, yes, Billy Clyde. With our friends who buy time, Larry Hoage ranks right up there. Larry doesn't give you much dead air, you see."

Like none, I thought.

"That's why sponsors love him," Richard Marks said. "Don't place too much importance on what Larry says. Keep in mind that his words are only a bridge from the last commercial to the next."

I said, "You guys know more about it than I do,

Richard, but I wonder if there aren't some people out there who might like a quiet stroll from one commercial to another?"

"No such animal," he said. "Our surveys would have turned them up by now."

My talk with Richard Marks convinced me of only one thing: I had to get as much money out of the networks as I could before they were doomed to oblivion by their own surveys—and movies on cable.

My cast came off that week, which was the same week Dr. Tim Hayes's right foot was in a bandage.

I didn't notice his foot at first. I was in such a good mood at the prospect of being released from prison, I was busy dropping witticisms on the Dyan Cannon nurse who assisted the bone specialist in removing my cast.

"You're from Texas, aren't you?" the Dyan Cannon nurse had asked.

"Yep."

"What part?"

"Just about all of me."

Dr. Hayes said my leg looked pretty good, by gosh, considering those decrepit New York butchers had worked on it. I should start exercising slowly, he said. Walk whenever possible. Climb stairs.

"It'll be a while before you can break into a dead run," he said.

"I'd better not run into a war baby, then."

"Not the one who chased me out of the house," he said.

That's when I saw him limp across the office on his bandaged foot.

"What happened to you?" I said.

"Oh, it's just a little strain on the metatarsal-cuneiform ligament," said Dr. Hayes. "Unfortunately, it's the ligament that connects the first metatarsal to the mid-foot area. It's the, uh . . . ligament you use to push off on . . . to walk or run."

"Sorry," I said. "You were running from a war baby?"

"My wife, actually. Phyllis."

"You're *married* to a war baby?"

"Why do you think I know so much about them?"

"He married three war babies," said the Dyan Cannon nurse.

The nurse looked at Dr. Hayes.

"Tell him how you hurt your foot," she said.

"I'm sure he's not interested," the doctor said.

"I am now," I said.

"They got in an argument," the nurse said. "He called her a war baby. Phyllis went after him with a steak knife. He strained the ligament trying to keep from falling in the pool."

Dr. Hayes said, "You can't joke with war babies. That's another thing, Billy Clyde. I kidded Phyllis about the plastic sandwich. I said it was the only thing she liked to eat."

In the doctor's terminology, a plastic sandwich was an American Express card between a *VISA* and a MasterCard.

"Is everything okay now?" I asked.

"It will be, as soon as I get my things out of the house," Dr. Hayes said. "It'll probably take a week or two. War babies don't simmer down too quickly."

"I'm glad they never had a team in the NFL," I said as I left that day.

By the end of October, Barbara Jane had done two more episodes of *Rita,* neither of which was satisfactory as far as she was concerned. Sheldon Gurtz and Kitty Feldman were still the executive producers. They had written both of the episodes themselves. Between Barb and Jack Sullivan, nearly every line of dialogue had been changed, but there hadn't been enough time to re-work the storylines.

In one episode, Barbara Jane had been expected to become romantically entwined with a foreign race-car driver, a handsome dumbbell with a French accent.

"If I'm going to have a love interest, why does it have to be a jerk?" Barbara Jane had said to Kitty.

"Paul is attractive," Kitty had said. "Women are intrigued with men like Paul."

Barb had said, "Beverly Hills women, maybe. Rita lives in New York. Rita wouldn't let Paul sell her a pair of shoes."

Sheldon had stepped forward and said, "Barbara Jane, you haven't studied the great films. Paul always gets the girl."

"Paul doesn't get the fucking girl." Barb had raised her voice. "Paul gets the luggage!"

The character of "Paul" stayed in the script, and "Rita" did act somewhat taken with him, but through the efforts of Barbara Jane and the director, it became clear that "Rita" had only acted interested in "Paul" because she wanted to hire him as a waiter for Rita's Limo Stop.

In the other episode, Sheldon and Kitty had scripted a story in which "Rita" was talked into seeing "Amanda's" shrink and ended up almost having an affair with him.

"Rita hates shrinks," Barbara Jane had argued.

"Why does Rita hate shrinks?" asked Kitty.

"Because *I* hate shrinks," Barb said. "There's never been a shrink that somebody didn't go to high school with!"

The shrink had stayed in the script—and so had that line of Barbara Jane's. "Rita" used it on the shrink after telling him that her parents weren't responsible for the time she broke her Susie Homemaker oven.

* * *

One morning in the Marquis suite in late October before I had to leave on another assignment, I asked Barbara Jane some questions about Jack Sullivan. I found out he was separated from his wife and two kids, who were in London. He was, in fact, British, but he had lived in California for a number of years, long enough to have become de-cricketed.

"Does he date anybody besides you?" I said to Barb.

She gave me a hard look.

"That's a funny choice of words," she said. "We call it work."

"All those dinners?"

People in show biz often have to eat, she said.

She then asked me why I had found it necessary to leave town on a Thursday for a Sunday broadcast.

"Moi?"

I explained to Barb that Thursday was only a travel day, and it took all of Friday and Saturday to familiarize myself with the personnel on the ball clubs, and to do all of the inserts, to spend enough time with the coaches to feel confident about the things I would be saying or not saying when we did the game on Sunday.

I said, "In broadcast journalism, we don't do a lot of playing around like you people in the entertainment division. We're live."

I didn't say I got spun when we were live.

She said, "Well, I don't suppose there's anything wrong with our marriage that a faith healer can't fix."

"We have a good marriage, Barb—if you look at the total universe."

She had smiled, then, and we had been drawn into an embrace. We had kissed with a warmth and passion that had been missing lately because of our lifestyle.

In that moment, we were reaffirming something besides love. A devotion of some kind that reached far back in the past.

As I left her in the hotel that day, she had said, "See you next trip, Biff."

The absurd thing about the deal with Kathy Montgomery was that nothing had developed between us but friendship.

I considered myself a grizzled veteran at spotting indicators. But while Kathy had littered the countryside with adoration for me as a human being, and while she knew how to make a man feel like he was the nicest, wittiest, most charming and talented person who had ever entered her life—I had even been saddled with the responsibility of becoming her "best friend"—she had not given me the slightest hint that she wanted her body molested.

So we had settled into a friendship that was fun but, well—let's be honest—frustrating. I mean, two months of lunches, dinners, relaxing, work sessions, of constant companionship, with one of the most delicious creatures I had ever been around was getting to be a strain. Like all lookers, Kathy had some temptress in her.

What I really wanted to do, as I told Shake Tiller, was make the discovery that Kathy had this disgusting birthmark on her hip; then I could put her in perspective.

Shake had met Kathy by now. We had spent a couple of Sunday nights with him in New York when we had bailed out early after a telecast in Philadelphia and another in Atlanta.

"Face mask," Shake had said when he was introduced to her.

We drank away those evenings showing Kathy our Manhattan, the old trudge up and down Second and Third Avenues—the quest for the perfect jukebox.

Shake recognized right off that Kathy, aside from her stunning looks, had other things in common with Barbara Jane. Like Barb, Kathy knew how to sit around, she could hold her whiskey—drank Scotch, of course—didn't fancy dope, and laughed infectiously at all the right things.

Kathy lived in a Manhattan that was unfamiliar to Shake and me. It was the Manhattan of inexpensive restaurants, of neighborhood taverns where the biggest celebrity to walk in the door was the bar owner from across the street, the Manhattan of tiny apartments in which the top of the dinner table had to be lifted off before the occupant could bathe.

I had taken Kathy's word for these things. I hadn't been invited to her apartment, and I hadn't asked her over to see mine.

On those Sunday nights when we had been with Shake, we had done nothing but laugh at life its ownself and damage our brains with alcohol.

Kathy had never broken through and stayed with us until dawn. She had gone home at the reasonably sane hour of 2 A.M.

It was on the second of those evenings, after Kathy had left us in a back booth at Runyon's, that Shake alerted me to what he called a neon indicator.

Earlier that night, we had spent five or six hours at a table by a plate-glass window in T.J. Tucker's. Kathy had monopolized the conversation with a discourse about the splendors of Barbara Jane.

"She's my idol, really," Kathy had said more than twice. "I can't wait to meet her."

Shake had looked amused by this, a fact that wasn't lost on me. Kathy had gone on to pronounce Barbara Jane the most beautiful girl she had ever seen in a magazine or a TV commercial. And she was certain Barb had to be the most incredible person in

the world, marvelous in all ways, or, I, Billy Clyde
Puckett, wouldn't have married her.

"It's so neat," Kathy had said. "You three guys
all growing up together and being so close and
everything."

She said she still had some good friends back in
Sioux Falls, but they were nothing like us. They
hadn't "been anywhere," or "done anything." The
Zip Feed Mill was their favorite skyscraper. And as
for her chums at Berkeley, well, who could say what
they were up to now. Melissa had gone pre-med,
Christina had gone punk, and Eric had been locked
in his bedroom since his junior year with a buffalo
head, black window shades, and blue light bulbs.

"I wouldn't want to be anywhere near South America when Eric busts out of there," Shake had said.

Now it was only Shake and me at Runyon's. We
were welcoming a serious last-call for youngster as
Shake was telling me I'd blown the indicator.

"What do you think all that shit about Barbara
Jane was?" he said. "You think Kathy doesn't want to
fuck the guy who's married to the most beautiful
woman in the world? Forget the fact you've got some
dough . . . that you're an 'older man,' but not that
old . . . that you're a famous athlete . . . and you're
on TV. She wants to make it with Barbara Jane
Bookman's husband, man."

"Why?"

"To prove she can," said Shake. "She's a woman,
Billy C. She knows God-damn well she's every bit as
good-looking as Barb, and she knows something else,
too, you better believe it. She knows she's got ten
years on her!"

What, I wondered, had Kathy been waiting for?

"What are *you* waiting for? It's there, man."

I liked her, I said. I genuinely liked her as a
walkaround pal, a trusty sidekick. Kathy was fun to

be on the road with. What was I going to do on the road, talk about the advances in hairspray formula with Larry Hoage?

"If you fuck her, does that mean you can't like her anymore?"

"It means I'd get involved," I said. "I need an affair like I need to take a shit and fall backwards."

"Why do you think Kathy wants to have an affair? She's probably got a boyfriend with a guitar full of dread."

"I don't think so. She's not a chemist. She seems older . . . more career-minded than most girls her age."

Shake said, "She acts older around you, sure."

"Why don't you fuck her?" I laughed. "That'll solve everything."

"I feel like I already have."

Shake couldn't have thought Kathy was that ordinary. The winner of the Nordic combined?

"You don't think she's better-looking than your average homewrecker?" I said.

"Yeah, she's a killer, but there's a lot of that going around."

An Elroy Blunt song came up on the jukebox. We stopped talking to listen, to pay homage to our old friend.

Life don't owe me a living
But a Lear and a limo ain't bad.
I could do without dope and women
But Beverly Hills would be sad.
I stole this song from Willie.
I guess I've made him mad:
He said Life don't owe me a living
But a Lear and a limo ain't bad.

Elroy had been dead three years. He was a high-rolling friend of ours who had once played ball with us and had then made it big as a country-and-Western singer and songwriter.

The world had been a safer place without Elroy in it. The year we went to the Super Bowl in Los Angeles, Elroy rented an estate in Beverly Hills and threw a party that lasted a week and almost cost us the game. He didn't invite anyone who wasn't from Peru, Nashville, Austin, or didn't have tits.

Elroy was anti-sleep. I don't think chemicals let him sleep the last five years of his life.

He had said, "What's the good of havin' a wet dream if you're not awake to enjoy it?"

Elroy was only thirty-one when he spun out, which means he out-lived his hero, Hank Williams, by four years. Elroy and all five members of his band were killed when their bus hurtled off a bridge and dropped into a valley about two miles below Aspen. Apparently, the groupies on the bus had been giving everyone a blowjob at the same time and unfortunately this had included the driver.

Life don't owe me a living
But a Lear and a limo ain't bad.
They've sure made it easy
To have all the fun I've had.
If I can't find Willie to thank him
I guess I'll take out an ad.
He said Life don't owe me a living
But a Lear and a limo ain't bad.

When the song was over, I said to Shake, "Maybe everything's okay like it is. If Kathy throws me down in the back seat of a rent car some night, fine. It'll be self-defense. If she doesn't . . . on with television."

Shake said, "Stop being a starry-eyed 'good friend.' If you don't, she'll drive you nuts and break up your home, man. Then she won't even respect you. Do one of those Jim Tom lines on her and fuck her, get it over with."

"What kind of Jim Tom line?"

Shake said, "Some night when you're with her in a bar, make a confession. Tell her you always have to sit down when you take a piss, the doctor doesn't want you to lift anything heavy."

THIRTEEN

The distressing news from Fort Worth in early December was that Tonsillitis Johnson's mind had been warped by an East Indian swami—and T.J. Lambert's whole future was heaving in a sea of disaster.

Just when T.J. and Big Ed Bookman had been so sure that everything was under control, that Tonsillitis was as good as theirs—TCU's, actually—Darnell Johnson had brought them word of this sudden and unforeseen complication.

Tonsillitis, it seems, had fallen under the spell of Swami Mukamananda, and the blue-chipper was seriously thinking about giving up football. Swami Muktamananda, also known as Haba, had all but convinced Tonsillitis that he should move to New Delhi, live in a ditch, and seek life's fulfillment by washing down elephants.

"Mooka banana who?"

I had asked the question sleepily because T.J.'s phone call had awakened me in the dead of night at the Westwood Marquis.

"I don't know how you say it," T.J. said, "but the sumbitch is about to ruin my life."

The point of T.J.'s call was to beg me to come to Fort Worth as soon as possible. Shake Tiller was already on the way. There would be a meeting between me, Shake, T.J., Big Ed, and Darnell to try to figure out what to do about reclaiming Tonsillitis' mind.

Going to Fort Worth wasn't all that much of an inconvenience for me, as it happened. My last telecast of the regular NFL season was scheduled for Dec. 12 in Dallas—Cowboys against the Giants, my old team. All it meant was going to Texas a few days early.

On the phone that night, T.J. told me some of the sordid details of what had happened to Tonsillitis.

Because of the swami, Tonsillitis had refused to play in his last high school football game, Boakum's annual bloodbath against archrival Eula. Swami Muktamananda had passed through town and had given a lecture at Boakum High. Tonsillitis, being president of the student body, had met the swami. They had talked about "the value of life." And the next thing anyone knew, Tonsillitis had been in a trance before the Eula game and wouldn't move from the bench.

Boakum's coach, Mutt Turnbull, had pleaded with his star to go out on the field and defend the honor of Boakum. Tonsillitis had only mumbled, "What I be wearin' a helmet for? What I be doin' on this planet?"

Darnell, Tonsillitis' older brother, was more frustrated than anybody. Darnell had been at the game and he had reminded the running back that big money was at stake, never mind the natural hatred that one had been born with for Eula.

Tonsillitis had said to Darnell, "Folks be hittin' one another for no reason. I wants to quit football and grow my own food."

Darnell had said, "Hey, baby, we're talkin' gusto here, you understand? Mucho Dolores."

"Swami say life don't be measured by numbers,"

Tonsillitis said. "Swami say happiness don't be livin' in no end zone."

Darnell had almost lost his temper.

He had said, "Yeah, well, swamis be fuckin' with incense and shit. Get your ass off that bench!"

Nothing had worked. Tonsillitis hadn't played in the game, and, as of now, he wasn't planning to play for TCU or any other college. He was meditating and eating rice and lentils.

Neither T.J. nor Big Ed had seen Swami Muktamananda. Darnell had been in contact with him, however, and was trying to work out an economic solution.

For enough money, Swami Muktamananda might be tempted to persuade Tonsillitis to play football again.

"I ain't sure you can buy swamis," T.J. said.

T.J. sounded very low on the phone.

He said, "It's a hell of a thing, ain't it, son? Here I got me the greatest football player in captivity and somebody's done jacked with his brain. What does that tell you about our God-damn educational system?"

I asked if there was anything new on the Artis Toothis front.

"Looks like we're okay there," T.J. said. "Artis Toothis is an ambitious young man with a good business head on his shoulders. He's the kind of person America can be proud of."

Artis Toothis was ready to wear the purple-and-white and look after his real estate investments. Only the nuts and bolts of his contract were yet to be worked out. For example, he was insisting on a guarantee that he would play the same number of minutes and carry the ball the same number of times as Tonsillitis.

T.J. returned to the mournful subject of Tonsillitis by saying, "Can you believe TCU's luck? I just wish somebody would tell me how a robe-wearin', meditatin' cocksucker can get a nigger worried about the value of life!"

T.J. was badly in need of friends around him.

He said, "I'll tell you the truth, Billy Clyde. I feel like I been eat by a coyote and shit off a cliff!"

With one week of regular-season games left in the NFL, everything was working out splendidly for Dreamer Tatum and the Players Association. There wasn't a team in the league with a record you could sell to a junk dealer.

The best won–lost record in pro football was 8–7.

This record was shared by twelve teams. San Francisco, Los Angeles, and New Orleans were tied at 8–7 in the National West. Green Bay, Minnesota, and Detroit were tied at 8–7 in the National Central. Miami and Buffalo were tied at 8–7 in the American East. Seattle and Denver were tied at 8–7 in the American West. And Pittsburgh, Cleveland, and Cincinnati were tied at 8–7 in the American Central.

As for my old division, the National East, the standings were funnier than a society column.

NATIONAL EAST	W	L	T
Dallas Cowboys	7	8	0
Philadelphia Eagles	7	8	0
St. Louis Cardinals	7	8	0
Washington Redskins	5	10	0
New York Giants	0	15	0

Two things about the standings were unique. The winner of the division, Dallas in all likelihood, would be going into the playoffs with no better than a .500 record, and the Giants were having their worst season ever.

Washington's season had been a big disappointment, but not to Dreamer Tatum. He said the Players' Association could be justly proud of its Redskin members. Having begun the year as favorites in the division, the Redskins had crushed the hearts of fans all over D.C.

Dreamer had boasted to me that the union had never been in a stronger position. Mediocrity was rampant throughout the league.

Against the brunt of this mediocrity, the Commissioner's office was strenuously trying to sell the myth that parity was a blessing. Through the TV and radio broadcasters and the few journalists they controlled, the Commissioner and his staff peddled the propaganda that America's fans were excited about the closeness of the divisional races, that the country was ecstatic over the fact that 21 out of the 28 teams still had a mathematical chance to make the playoffs after 15 long weeks.

Most sportswriters knew better and said so. They were attacking the league for killing a great sport.

As of late November, nobody had dropped more napalm on the NFL than Jim Tom Pinch, but of course Shake's article in *Playboy* had yet to appear. It was due out the week we would be in Texas.

One of Jim Tom's columns hit harder than most.

Pinchs Palaver
by Jim Tom Pinch

Here is a list of things I would rather do than watch a football game in the NFL:

1. Buy a condo in Lebanon.
2. Go to a rock concert.
3. See a movie with special effects in it.
4. Join a religious cult.
5. Sit in the no-smoking area of a restaurant.

   6. Discuss wine.
   7. Watch a marathon.
   8. Talk to a swimmer.
   9. Eat a fishhead.
 10. Get married again.

Here is a list of people I would rather spend an evening with than any coach, general manager or owner in the NFL:

   1. Bert Parks.
   2. Minnie Pearl.
   3. Renée Richards.
   4. Boy George.
   5. Jerry Lewis.
   6. Michael Jackson.
   7. Liberace.
   8. Andy Warhol.
   9. Sonny Bono.
 10. The Dukes of Hazzard.

Here is a list of franchise moves that would improve the quality of play in the NFL:

   1. Dallas to Bogotá.
   2. Giants to New York.
   3. The Raiders to Vegas.
   4. Miami to Cuba.
   5. Rams to Warner Brothers.
   6. Green Bay to Tahiti.
   7. Houston to the Bermuda Triangle.
   8. Jets off the board.
   9. Natchez to Mobile.
 10. Memphis to St. Joe.

Wake me up when the Super Bowl's over, but don't bother to tell me who won. I already know.
   CBS.

The Script Committee of the Players Association had been composed of six players, one of whom was

Dreamer Tatum. The others were Tom Buckner, a center for the 49ers; Randy Hall, a quarterback for the Eagles; J.D. Sealy, a linebacker for the Raiders; Harold Coleclaw, a defensive end for the Dolphins; and Tommy Crouch, a wide receiver for the Patriots.

The scripts for all of the games had been placed in the hands of trustworthy union members. The scripts couldn't always be followed precisely because of the zebra factor, but Dreamer said the Players Association had been more than satisfied with the results.

Personally, I thought the Script Committee paid too much attention to plot.

In a San Diego—Seattle game, the Chargers blew a 39-point lead and lost a close one to the Seahawks. The Chargers couldn't have pulled it off without the artistry of their quarterback, Scott Thirsk. A loyal union man, Thirsk threw seven interceptions in the second half.

A punter for the Cleveland Browns, Parker Knowles, lost a game to the Steelers in the final minute by missing the ball with his foot.

The old Statue of Liberty play was resurrected in a Buffalo—Chicago game. Al Donahue, the Buffalo quarterback, held the ball long enough for Willie Hughes, a Chicago Bear linebacker, to pluck it out of his hand and gallop 57 yards for a decisive touchdown.

On a field-goal effort from Atlanta's 5-yard line, the 49ers' Tom Buckner snapped the ball 40 yards over the placekicker's head, which in turn led to a game-winning touchdown for the Falcons.

Harold Coleclaw and Tommy Crouch made a real show of it in a Miami—New England game. Coleclaw intercepted a pass and rumbled 50 yards for what looked like a touchdown, but he absent-mindedly spiked the ball before he crossed the goal. Tommy Crouch picked up the ball and ran it out to mid-field before he fumbled it back to the Dolphins, who then drove to a winning field goal.

This was the Cowboys' first season under John Smith, the longtime assistant who had replaced the retired Tom Landry, but Dallas still sent in the plays from the sideline. Temple Stark, the Cowboys' tight end and a staunch union man, shuttled in the wrong plays all day in a game against the Eagles. Nothing came of it because no one with the Cowboys, including the new head coach, knew the difference. And in any case, the Cowboys couldn't outfumble the Eagles' Randy Hall.

"We have some dedicated people," Dreamer said.

Now it was December and I had gone to Fort Worth.

I checked into the Hyatt Regency again. Later in the week, after Kathy and the CBS gang came in for the Cowboys–Giants game, I would move to the Adolphus Hotel in Dallas. TV crews needed to stay together.

Shake had left word at the Hyatt for me to meet him at Mommie's Trust Fund. Jim Tom and the Junior League would be there.

Before slipping into my combat clothes for the evening—jeans, sport coat, golf shirt, loafers—I called Barbara Jane, as I always did, to let her know the plane hadn't been hijacked to Cameroon.

Someone at the studio gave me a number where she could be reached.

I put through a call to that number and an Oriental answered.

"Who's this?" I said.

"Ying."

"Could I speak to Mrs. Puckett, please?"

"No Miz Pluckett."

"Is Barbara Jane Bookman there?"

"Babla Blookman?"

"Yes. Very pretty lady."

"She here, no can talk."

"Why?"

"Miz Blookman on tennis court."

"Is this Mr. Sullivan's residence?"

"Yes, Mr. Sullivan house. No can talk. Velly busy on tennis court."

I left a message for Barbara Jane: "We'll always have Paris."

"Who message flom?" Ying asked.

"Martina," I said.

Mommie's Trust Fund was packed with the predictable array of debutantes and entrepreneurs.

I pushed my way up to the bar, where Shake and Jim Tom had staked out some turf. Shake greeted me by saying, "Order us another drink, Billy Clyde. I'll go ask those girls what color cars they want."

Jim Tom was already trying to break up an argument between Vivian and Dexter.

I was hardly there long enough to order my first youngster when Jim Tom made a recruiting move on a blonde adorable with a fearsome set of homegrowns inside a T-shirt that said: ORDER A LA CARTE.

"Hold it!" Jim Tom said, as he grabbed the girl's arm. "You from a foreign country?"

"If you count Hurst-Euless," said the girl. "Who wants to know?"

"I'm Jim Tom Dexter. Who're you?"

"Somebody who ain't got time for your bullshit."

The adorable tried to remove his hand from her arm.

Jim said, "What's that say on your shirt, darlin'? I had to drop out of school to fight a war."

"It says you can't afford the full-course dinner."

"Want a drink?"

"I have a drink on the other side of the bar, thank you."

Jim Tom said, "I want you to meet my celebrity friends." He nodded toward Shake and me.

"Hi," the girl said.

Shake and I both stuck out our hands.

"Hello," I said. "My name's Fat Chance."

"I'm Raw Deal," Shake said.

"We got some dope," Jim Tom said to the girl.

"You don't have *enough*," she sneered.

"Seriously, darlin', what's your name?"

"Flo."

"Cash Flo?"

"You got it!" The girl sprang free and dissolved into the crowd.

"I love these places," I said to Shake.

"It's the most fun I've ever had," he smiled.

Two hours later the three of us were standing outside The Blessed Virgin, admiring the marquee, which now said:

Appearing Nightly:
KIM COOZE
44-22-38
and
SIX ALL NUDE CAMPFIRE GIRLS!

Our wrists were stamped at the door by a 6-5, 250-pound psycho. We moved into the darkness of The Blessed Virgin.

From the jukebox came the sound of an old Dixieland rendition of "Baby, Won't You Please Come Home?" Kim Cooze was performing on the stage.

As we edged toward the bar, we watched Kim slip out of her nun's habit and get down to her G-string and pasties. She then began to co-exist erotically with a religious cross that was covered in rhinestones.

"The Medicis never got enough credit," Shake said. "Where would art be today?"

We ordered enough Scotch to see us through a gloomy winter. Kim continued to save souls in the audience. When our eyes adjusted to the light, Shake was the first to spot Charlie Teasdale. The zebra was sitting at a table with three other men.

"I'll be damned," I said, as Shake pointed him out.

Seeing the zebra in The Blessed Virgin relieved my mind about the elegy to pro football that Shake had coming out in *Playboy*.

Until that moment, I hadn't been a hundred percent convinced that Kim Cooze had told him the truth about Charlie Teasdale.

There was enough youngster in my veins to make me want to wander over and say hello to the zebra.

"Go ahead," Shake said. "I'm curious to know what he says."

I carried a fresh Scotch with me and pulled up a chair at Charlie's table.

"What do you say, Charlie?" I smiled. "I didn't know you were a fan of the ballet."

Charlie looked surprised to see me, but he didn't seem overly embarrassed to be caught in The Blessed Virgin.

"Why, Billy Clyde Puckett," he said, "how in the world are you? How's your knee?"

He introduced me to his companions, Roy, Wayne, and Hank. There was a homebuilders' convention going on in Dallas, Charlie let me know quickly. He had thought his friends, Roy, Wayne, and Hank, should get a taste of Fort Worth nightlife, too. Fort Worth was more fun than Dallas in some ways, he said. They were going to leave in a minute. Maybe they'd go cut to the stockyards area and hear some Western music at the White Elephant or Billy Bob's.

"You're doing real good on TV, Billy Clyde," Charlie said. "I don't get to see you, of course. I'm always working, but people tell me you're not a bad announcer. Don't talk too much."

Roy wanted me to autograph a napkin for him. I did. Then Wayne decided he better have an autograph for his eight-year-old boy.

"What's his name?" I asked.

"Wayne."

"Wayne junior?"

"Naw, just Wayne."

Roy directed our attention to the stage, where Kim Cooze writhed on the floor and tantalized her tummy with rosary beads. The jukebox had progressed to a Dixieland version of "Who's Sorry Now?"

At an opportune moment, I said to Charlie, "I know you guys don't like to talk to journalists, but can I ask you a question?"

He said, "Hell, Billy Clyde, I don't mind talking to anybody, but the league has these rules."

"I kind of thought since I was Establishment, it wouldn't hurt."

"Go ahead," Charlie said, taking a drink of his draft beer.

"Why do you throw so fucking many flags in a game, Charlie?"

"I knew you were going to ask me that," he cackled.

Roy, Wayne, and Hank weren't listening to us, preoccupied as they were with the entertainer on the stage.

Charlie said, "I want to tell you something, Billy Clyde. You don't have any idea what a hard job we have. Nobody does. You can't have a thin skin and wear a whistle around your neck in the National Football League. I'm a purist, I suppose. I don't like to see a player get away with anything. Our job is to see that a team doesn't get an unfair advantage over another team. There's too much at stake. Shoot, I'm just like everybody else. I like to see the best team win because of the skills of their players and coaches, not because of a judgment call. But I'm not going to let a team win because they're getting away with something, not if I can help it."

Charlie had gone into officiating like most zebras — as a hobby, a sideline. And like most zebras, he had come out of the ranks of collegiate officials. He had refereed in the Southwest Conference before he had joined the NFL.

The way it worked was, a college zebra would apply for a job in the NFL on the sly. He wouldn't want his conference to know he was thinking about going into the pros. The NFL would watch him for a couple of seasons. If the league liked his work, he would be accepted, pending a physical, an eye test, and a rules test.

The zebras in the NFL were required to take these tests regularly. I often wondered how Charlie passed the eye test every year.

The referee was the boss zebra in a football game. He could overrule the field judge, the back judge, the umpire, or the head linesman. They all made the same amount of money, but the referee had power. No zebra had ever used his power like Charlie Teasdale, according to Shake Tiller.

Zebras worked as teams in the NFL. In other words, Charlie always officiated a game with the same field judge, back judge, umpire, and head linesman. The league wanted it this way. If the zebras knew each other's mannerisms, tendencies to be in or out of position on certain plays, thought processes, prejudices, strengths, drawbacks, physical stamina, they could function better. It was supposed to make for a better game.

Shake had uncovered no evidence that anyone on Charlie's crew was guilty of "doing business." Charlie had been working all year with Bob Stewart, an experienced field judge from Chicago; Ben Kincaid, a good back judge from Terre Haute, Indiana; Sam Pugh, a veteran umpire out of Birmingham; and Raymond (Rat) Farmer, an ex–pass receiver for the Lions who had become a head linesman.

The fact that Shake had no proof of wrongdoing on the part of Charlie's crew members didn't get them off the hook with him. NFL crews got their game assignments ten days ahead of time and Shake said this left them with plenty of opportunity to tell their friends or business associates which game to put a circle around.

The league instructed—and trusted—the zebras to keep their assignments a deep, dark secret, even from their families, right up until the opening kickoff. The NFL saw it as a way of safeguarding the officials from the influence of gamblers, death threats, mobsters, and so forth.

But as Shake said, if the zebras were so good at keeping secrets, how come everybody from Uncle Kenneth to the valet parking guys in Vegas always knew what game Charlie Teasdale and his crew would be working?

Now in The Blessed Virgin, after Charlie had made his noble speech, I said, "Charlie, you do know you've made more controversial calls than any zebra who ever lived, don't you?"

"Camera angles," he said.

"Camera angles? That's where the losers go to file their complaints?"

He said, "Billy Clyde, television is the worst thing that ever happened to officiating. Oh, I've blown some. I've been out of position. But at the time, I thought I was right—and most of the time, I was. Our league cameras have different angles from the networks. On most of those calls you're thinking about—the Miami fumble, the Cleveland out-of-bounds, the 49er end zone—our league cameras proved I was right."

"My first broadcast, the Green Bay–Washington game? You had a defensive holding call that was a beauty."

"They held up the tight end."

"It was a God-damn quarterback sneak!"

"Could have been a quick-out."

I finished my drink.

"Charlie, how come every bettor I've ever known thinks the zebras do business?"

"Well, they have to blame somebody when they lose. The dumb guys have been robbing the smart guys for years, Billy Clyde."

"I'm a little drunk, Charlie, or I wouldn't say this to you, but the fucking zebras sure turn a lot of games around."

He said, "You've got it wrong. We don't turn the games around. Players turn the games around by trying to take advantage of the rules. All we do is catch'em."

I stood up.

"Good to meet you," I said to Roy, Wayne, and Hank.

They glanced at me hastily. Their eyes then returned to the stage, where Kim Cooze was now totally nude. She had discarded her G-string and pasties and was sensually rubbing her whup against a lifesize cardboard statue of Jesus.

Charlie Teasdale had seen the act before, I presumed. He kept facing me.

He said, "Billy Clyde, I'm willing to lay my knowledge and my judgment on the line every time I go out on the field. If I know I'm right, they can burn the stadium down and I won't care. *Part* of the pleasure of officiating is being able to walk off the field knowing you were right."

Back at the bar, I reported to Shake that Charlie had made a good case for his integrity.

"So does Kim," Shake said.

Kim's routine ended as she faked an orgasm with the statue. Charlie and the homebuilders left.

It was a good hour before Kim, wearing a peasant blouse, jeans, and boots, came walking past the bar and discovered Shake and me standing there. Jim Tom was still with us, but then again, he wasn't. He was whispering sincerities to a Campfire Girl named Kelly Ann.

Kim squealed when she saw us. She smothered us with hugs and kisses and demanded that we remain silent for a moment while she said a prayer, thanking God for sending us back to The Blessed Virgin.

"Have you heard what's happened to me?" Kim said to Shake excitedly. "*Playboy* took my picture! It's going to be in the magazine with your story!"

"I saw Charlie here," Shake said.

"Every other night," Kim said. "I was just talking to him outside in the car. He won't say what game he's working next week. Claims he doesn't know yet. I said, Well, when you find out, there's an apartment over on Hulen I sure would like to buy. One more game might do it."

"Thinking about settling down in Fort Worth, are you?" I said.

"The Lord wouldn't want me to leave at a time like this."

Shake asked if there was anything new happening to her show-biz career.

"Yes!" she chimed. "The photographer who took

my picture for *Playboy?* He said after the issue came
out, he bet he could sell a whole layout on me to
Hustler."

"The literary quarterly," said Shake. "I've heard of
it."

"I can work here as long as I want to," said Kim.
"After the joint gets all that publicity, they'll pay
anything to keep me. Listen, I've got two more gigs
tonight. What do y'all want to do later?"

Shake and I traded looks.

I said, "We have a business meeting in the morning, Kim. I'm going Dixie."

"So am I," said Shake.

"We could have a nice party," Kim said.

"Another time," Shake said.

"I can get Brandy to go with us," Kim suggested.
"You remember Brandy, don't you, Billy Clyde? She
went with your friend?"

"Brandy's a great American," I said.

Kim said, "She's a wise-mouth little thing, but I
pray for her, and I've never heard any complaints
about her athletic ability."

Shake said we really had to leave. Kim wouldn't let
us pay the bar check. She hugged and kissed us
again, and did something with each of our hands to
remind us of her 44s, not that it had been necessary.

I interrupted Jim Tom to see if he was interested
in going with us. He wasn't.

"This here's Kelly Ann," Jim Tom said, introducing
us to the Campfire Girl, who was about eighteen, a
sleaze-style lookalike for Sandi, the TCU cheerleader.

Kelly Ann fished around in her handbag, came up
with a black capsule, and chased it down with a shot
of tequila.

Jim Tom grinned at us. "Kelly Ann's twelve but
she's got the body of a nine-year-old."

"Why don't you swallow my farts?" Kelly Ann said to him.

Jim Tom fell against the bar rail. "Zing went the strings of my heart," he said.

Shake and I said goodnight to the lovebirds and went to get some eggs and talk about a swami.

FOURTEEN

Through the two glass walls of Big Ed's office on the eighth floor of the Bookman Oil & Gas building, you could almost see every stump, scorpion, and mesquite tree in West Texas.

On the two wood-paneled walls of the office, you could see a dozen oil paintings of the drilling rigs and producing pumps that had brought immense wealth to Big Ed.

Some of those holes had been dug by the grandfather Barbara Jane had never known—except through legend. "Deep Salt" Bookman was a rowdy old West Texas wildcatter who earned his nickname by drilling deeper and hitting more saltwater than just about anybody before he finally got lucky and hit oil.

"Deep Salt" Bookman wasn't in the same league with the greats of the Texas oil bidness. He had never been as revered as Cap Lucas, who hit Spindletop, or Mike Benedum, who brought in the Pecos pool, or Dad Joiner, who discovered the East Texas field when he drilled the Daisy Bradford No. 3. But "Deep Salt" had made and lost three fortunes in the Twenties before anyone had ever heard of Haroldson Lafayette Hunt or Sid Richardson.

Barb's granddaddy had given Big Ed a leg up in the bidness, which was enough production to see

him through college and buy him a '36 Ford road-
ster. But it was to Big Ed's credit that he had taken
big rich on his own.

Big Ed Bookman, who had lettered as an end at
TCU—he was 6-2 and that was considered big in
those days—actually amounted to more than a big
voice and a drawl he liked to exaggerate when he
was in the company of pretentious Easterners. He
held a degree in geology from TCU and he had
gone through law school at the University of Texas.

And he had fought a war. Big Ed had flown P-38's
in the Fifth Air Force during World War II. He had
been a highly decorated fighter pilot who had come
out of the Air Corps as a twenty-four-year-old combat major. He had been in the air battle over the
Philippines in January of '45 when his friend Tommy
McGuire, America's second top ace, had been shot
down and killed. Big Ed's war experiences alone
would have made him a superpatriot.

Big Ed had come home from the war and started
looking for oil. He had found Big Barb first—Barbara
Jane Bender, a pretty girl from a nice, middle-income
family in Fort Worth.

Barbara Jane's mother had not been called Big
Barb until little Barb, their only child, had come
along in the early Fifties.

The early Fifties was when Big Ed had made the
strike in Scogie County. Scogie wasn't any Pecos or
East Texas field, but it had been almost as big as the
Sprayberry discovery out around Midland and Odessa.

Since then, Big Ed had found more oil and gas in
Erath County, Palo Pinto County, in Wyoming, Canada, and Florida. He had also found time to stalk big
game in Kenya and Rhodesia—he still called it Rhodesia, none of that Zimbabwe nonsense—to sail the
rough waters off the coast of Australia, to play killer

tennis, shoot golf in the high 70's, and pilot his own Lear.

He was a man who loved his country, his state, his city, his family, his friends, and his bidness, and he wouldn't give you a dime for anybody who didn't feel the same way.

Big Ed said what he damn well thought, did what he damn well pleased.

"That's what fuck-you money is all about," he took satisfaction in saying.

The Ed Bookmans were as close to Texas royalty as you could be—Big Ed through birth and performance, Big Barb through marriage. But their daughter and I and Shake still thought they were kind of funny.

And now in Big Ed's office that morning, I could see on his face the look of a man who wanted to have Swami Muktamananda measured for a cement robe.

Big Ed, T.J., Darnell, Shake, and myself were all sitting around a conference table, warming up each other's coffee cups, as Big Ed said:

"You think I can't get it done? I'll call Vegas! I can get it done quicker than that swami can say shish-ka-bob! It won't cost me a wink of sleep, either! Foreign sons-of-bitches are bad enough when they wear their black suits and their mirrored sunglasses and try to tell me how to run the oil bidness! Now I got me a Hindu lunatic who's fucking around with college football! God damn, I wish I had my own hydrogen bomb!"

"India ain't good for shit," said T.J. "What they got over there? A bunch of fuckers in bedsheets makin' mudpies, is all."

Shake made the valid point that murder wasn't the answer to the problem. He said that Swami Muktamananda, or Haba, might be the only person through which we could reach Tonsillitis Johnson and get his mind straightened out.

Darnell said, "Swami's a tough dude. I've had three meetings with him. Mr. Bookman gimme the authority to offer him three hundred thou, but he just sit there cross-legged."

The number impressed me. So did Darnell. Darnell talked that jive shit that he thought white people expected of him, but his face told me he was no dummy. You know how some guys have a smart look? Darnell had it. I'd found out he'd not only played ball at Texas Southern, he had graduated with a business degree. Until now—until he had become Big Ed's "geologist"—he'd been a bookkeeper for Big Rufus, a fast-food chain that specialized in barbecue, headquarters in Houston.

Darnell had been determined to get out of Boakum, not to wind up like his daddy—be a handyman the rest of his life. Football had got him out. And football was going to get him somewhere else, you could tell. Football and Tonsillitis.

All I knew about the mother of Darnell and Tonsillitis was that she still cooked the chicken and dumplings—"C's and D's," Darnell said—for the Boakum High cafeteria.

"Would you really pay three thundred thousand for Tonsillitis?" I said to my father-in-law.

"For a national championship?" said Big Ed. "I'd go a lot higher. That's all it'd be. Tonsillitis and that Toothis kid can take us straight to Number One."

"Where would you max out?"

While Big Ed was making up his mind about it, Darnell said, "Swami don't care about money. Swami be talkin' about America—how Americans confuse *style* with *substance*."

"Hear that?" T.J. said, a little wild-eyed. "Try *that* shit on!"

Shake said it sounded like Big Ed hadn't come up with enough "substance" yet.

"Half a million," said Big Ed, arriving at a figure. "But I'd damn well want the assurance that Tonsillitis was back to normal and wasn't hangin' upside-down in his bedroom."

"Upside-down?" I looked at Darnell.

Darnell said, "Tonsillitis be hangin' upside-down thirty minutes ever day before lunch."

Tonsillitis was also into incense, meditation, exercises. He was staying in shape—that was one good thing. Darnell didn't know what you called it when Tonsillitis placed his hands on the brick magnets and hummed for an hour.

"He's chanting," Shake said.

"Rrr-i-g-h-t," said Darnell. "You know about that shit, baby."

"What the fuck difference does it make, hummin' or chantin'?" T.J. said. "All I know is, the best football player in America is sittin' down there in Boakum, Texas, with his head out of whack, and I'm sittin' up here at TCU tryin' to pull a string out of a duck's ass."

Big Ed came up with a plan. He wanted Shake and me to go to Boakum, make an effort to talk some sense into Tonsillitis. There was a chance he would listen to a couple of famous football players. If we had no luck with Tonsillitis, we were to meet with Swami Muktamananda.

We were to offer the swami $500,000 to convince Tonsillitis that the only way to purify his soul was to play football for TCU. The swami could take the money all at once or in deferred payments; whatever his tax man suggested. This was Big Ed's final offer. The swami could take it or leave it.

Darnell said he might need twenty-four hours to

set up the meeting with the swami. The swami didn't live in Boakum. He was commuting from Austin.

"It's all I know to do," Big Ed sighed. "If this don't work, we'll just have to find us another nigger. Excuse me, Darnell."

Darnell had a good feeling about the plan. Five hundred thousand dollars was "mucho Dolores." Big Ed might have bought himself a swami, he said.

Shake's article on pro football hit the newsstands that afternoon. We bought two copies of *Playboy* in the hotel gift shop and barricaded ourselves in the Hyatt Regency suite. We gave the hotel operator a list of the only people we would take calls from. We ordered two quarts of youngster, a gross of BLT's and French fries, and a vat of coffee from room service. We kicked off our shoes, pulled out our shirttails, turned on TV, and settled in for the night.

The list of people who tried to reach us and left plaintive messages were Bob Cameron, the NFL Commissioner, Burt Danby, Shoat Cooper, Richard Marks, Kim Cooze, somebody from *The Today Show,* somebody from *20/20,* representatives of *The New York Times,* the *New York Daily News, The Washington Post, The Boston Globe, The Los Angeles Times, The Dallas Morning News,* the *San Francisco Chronicle,* and *The Miami Herald.*

Plus a man named Mort from the Coast who left word that he was an independent producer who knew a rich Arab.

Barbara Jane's call was the first one the operator put through to us.

Barb said she liked Shake's story. It had all the elements of a good movie. Boy meets flag, boy loses flag, boy gets flag.

I asked how her backhand was coming along.

Jack Sullivan's house in the Hollywood hills was

marvelous, she said. He had a lovely pool near the tennis court. Everything in the house worked, as opposed to the continual problems of a New York apartment. Houses like Jack Sullivan's were so nifty, they almost made you think Los Angeles wasn't a penal colony.

Progress was being made on *Rita,* so much so that everyone was beginning to feel good about the show. And this was making everybody nervous. What if they had a hit? What if she were to win an Emmy?

"What if *I* win an Emmy?" I said. "They're talking about nominating me."

"Dueling Emmys."

Barbara Jane said the episodes were going more smoothly. Sheldon Gurtz and Kitty Feldman were easier to work with. The hours weren't as long anymore. There had been time to rest and relax, catch your breath.

Strange, but these changes had taken place in the last forty-eight hours. Show biz was like that, Jack Sullivan had said. Somewhere, sometime, on every project that had any merit something clicked, visibility improved, and everybody started to "cook."

Jack Sullivan's house had become a country-club hangout for the cast.

"Are you talking to me from poolside?" I said.

"Of course."

"You're in a lounge chair with a cordless phone, right?"

"Yes," she said. "And I have a plate of fried wonton beside me."

"There's something I'll never understand about cordless phones," I said.

"What?"

"When they ring, how'd they know where you were?"

Barbara Jane said to congratulate Shake on his

article and ask him what country he planned to move to.

I mentioned to Barb that I couldn't hear a lot of gaiety coming from Jack Sullivan's pool or the thump of any tennis balls, but perhaps it was the less-than-ideal connection on the cordless phone.

"Carolyn's here but she's in the sauna," Barb said. "The others are on their way over."

Barb said she was sorry I wasn't going to be there over the weekend. It looked like they weren't going to be working on *Rita*. We could have spent some time together, darn it.

It was too bad, I said. She would just have to work on her serves and suntan without me, but she could think of me toiling away in a broadcast booth, trying to score a completed sentence against Larry Hoage's prevent defense.

Shake took a congratulatory call from Dreamer Tatum, and another from Jim Tom.

Dreamer predicted the Players Association would vote Shake its Man of the Year.

Jim Tom said the photo of Kim Cooze had sold the story. *Playboy* had only used a two-column "accent" picture of Kim on the lower lefthand corner of a page, but the photographer had captured her bare 44s from a very flattering angle.

Jim Tom also said the picture of Kim was going to turn Charlie Teasdale into a folk hero.

He said, "The only thing a reader's going to wonder is why Charlie didn't give her *two* games—one to go with each of those things!"

When Kathy called, she sounded like she was in a near-panic. "We have to find Shake Tiller," she said. "Richard Marks wants you to do an exclusive insert with him. We'll use it at the top of the show Sunday. Richard says we'll fly Shake to Dallas, pay all his expenses. We'll send a company plane for him! Do

you know where I can reach him? I've tried everywhere. Billy Clyde, this is really important. Richard's
going crazy. He can't get you on the phone. He's
calling me every fifteen minutes to see if I've found
you or Shake. If I don't set this up, he may fire me.
If I *do* set it up, he may promote me! Where's Shake?
Can you talk him into coming to Dallas?"

Holding the receiver where Kathy could hear my
voice, I said, "Shake, you want to go on TV with me
Sunday?"

He said, "I thought you'd never ask."

"Oh, my God!" said Kathy. "He's there? Shake's in
the room with you?"

Yes, I said, but don't tell Richard Marks.

Career-wise, I said, it would be better if Richard
Marks thought it was going to take her three days
of intense cloak-and-dagger work to arrange the
interview.

I said, "Tell Richard you have reason to believe
Shake's on a sampan in Hong Kong harbor, but he'll
come to Dallas as a personal favor to you because
you're a friend of mine."

She said, "I love you, Billy Clyde! I do!"

"See you Friday."

"I've never been to Texas. I'm excited."

After I'd spoken to Kathy, I said to Shake, "Part of
the joy of being a grownup is seeing young people
get ahead in life."

Shake was mixing us a cocktail as he said, "B.C., if
you don't fuck her now, I'm going to."

Shake's *Playboy* article was illustrated on the two
opening pages by a wide-angle photo of a zebra
reaching for his flag as an L.A. Ram carried a football into an end zone.

I re-read parts of the story in bed that night.

A Not So Fond Farewell to the NFL
by Marvin (Shake) Tiller

Once upon a time there was a great sport in America that brought pleasure and excitement to millions every week of every autumn.

It was called pro football. I played the game in those days. Now I no longer play and it's just as well. The sport has turned to shit.

Today you can't find anybody around the power structure of the NFL who doesn't look like they suck blood.

The owners ought to walk with a goose step. The general managers should wear black cloaks. The coaches need to be locked up in rubber rooms. And the zebras—the game officials—belong in correctional institutions.

Don't worry about the players. They've all gone Dixie, anyhow—which is where the fans are headed.

It's about time for the playoffs to start this season, and I can't wait to see how the zebras are going to make a bundle on those games.

Offensive holding is their old reliable. They can always lean on that. You can be sure they'll rely on it if a team looks like it's going to turn the game into a runaway.

That's because the zebras who aren't crooks have been instructed by the league to keep the contests close for the TV audience.

My favorite crook in the league is Charlie Teasdale, a referee whose bimbo is pictured on this page.

For the past three or four years I've suspected Charlie of doing business in the games he worked because he could toss flags like a frycook tossed eggs.

Charlie picked his spots, although he had a

tendency to like underdogs. Not to win, just to "cover."

I ran a check. Three years ago, 10 out of 12 dogs covered in the games he worked. Two years ago, 11 out of 14 dogs covered in the games he worked. Last year, 14 out of 16 dogs covered in the games he worked.

To the sharp guys who could get a bet down before the kickoff in a game Charlie officiated, he was more fun than stock dividends.

This season, back in late September, Charlie made a mistake. He gave a game to somebody I know, the lady whose homegrowns are dressing up this article. Her name is Kim Cooze. She's an exotic dancer at The Blessed Virgin, a strip joint in Fort Worth, Texas.

I found out what Charlie was up to by accident. Kim told me. I have to confess that she told me after we had been intimate.

Kim didn't know I was a writer at the time. She only told me about the fix because she thought I might want to get in on a good thing.

She bet the game and won a new Camaro. As this was written, she was expecting to get other tips from Charlie. I'm sure she did. This is the only one I can prove, but one's enough. Or too many.

Remember the Miami–Jets game on Sept. 28? Miami was favored by 6½ points. The Dolphins only won by 6, so if you bet the Jets you won your money.

That day, the Dolphins should have beaten the Jets by 30. But Charlie Teasdale called back three Miami touchdowns because of offensive holding— and he made that controversial call on the Miami fumble in the last minute. That fumble cost the

Dolphins a field goal, 3 points that would have covered the 6½.

Kim had bet the Jets. Lucky girl. Good old Charlie had told her how much he liked the Jets with the points.

I have Kim Cooze's sworn affidavit to this fact. I also have her voice on tape.

Why would Kim go public with this information? Well, let's be honest. It wasn't out of love for the game.

She wants the national publicity. She hopes it will help her career. She bills herself as a "mystical theologian who strips for God."

Here's a tip from me. If you're ever in Fort Worth, Kim's act beats going to the Pancake House.

Why would Charlie Teasdale, an established referee in the National Football League, a family man, give a game to a woman like Kim Cooze?

Jesus Christ, man, have you looked at those tits?

Shake went on to say in the article that he could predict how Charlie Teasdale would respond to his charge. Charlie would see no need to defend his holding calls in the Miami–Jets game. You can always call holding, he would say. He had only penalized the Dolphins in those instances where they had been guilty of "flagrant" holding.

The Miami fumble, he would say, was strictly a judgment thing. It's possible he had blown it. If so, he was sorry. But he had seen the ball "come out" before Dwayne Arrick, the Miami runner, was down. And from his angle, it had looked like Lewis Shoop, the Jet linebacker, had gained "possession" of the ball before it wound up under a mound of Dolphins. Charlie would insist his whistle had stopped the action when the Jet had been on the ball.

In the article, Shake said he had looked at films of

the game carefully and you couldn't see the fumble. Charlie would say that Shake had seen the play from poor camera angles. The league would support Charlie rather than stoke the fire of a controversy.

Charlie—and the league—would also wonder who would take the word of a publicity-seeking stripper for anything? And the league would let it get around that Shake Tiller, the ex-player who wrote the story, had experimented with "drugs."

The Commissioner, Bob Cameron, would issue a statement reminding America that NFL officials, like the CIA, are "fair game" for writers. Writers know they can say whatever they please about the zebras because, like the CIA, zebras never dignify "malicious rumor" by commenting on it.

The article had made *Playboy's* editors very nervous. The magazine's lawyers had nibbled on it like chipmunks, gnawed at it like wolves, hopped around on it like Siamese cats.

In the days leading up to publication, Shake had been forced to sign a paper taking full responsibility for the content of the exposé. In exchange for this, Silvia Mercer, his agent, had managed to have his fee doubled. Shake was getting a record $47,500 for the piece.

"Milan Kundera wouldn't get that kind of money," Silvia Mercer had bragged to Shake.

"He would if he worked without a net," Shake had said.

Playboy's editors finally decided to run the story over the protest of their lawyers because Shake convinced them his documentation was unassailable.

"Your documentation is a stripper," one of the lawyers had argued with Shake.

"That's right," Shake had said. "Who wouldn't believe a stripper before they'd believe a fucking lawyer?"

The NFL fan was further captivated by these excerpts:

The players are my friends. For this reason I'm not going to use any names or quotes to verify the fact that the players have had a plan in effect this season that's designed to bring the owners to the bargaining table over the wage-scale and free-agent issues. You'll have to take my word for it.

You, the fan, have known it simply as boring, sloppy, emotionless football, which is what the National Football League has come to stand for.

Boredom began with overexposure on television. It reached its zenith with parity—and it looks like the only thing that will cure all of it is another Great Depression. That would bring everything back to reality.

This season, the players are in a rebellion, quietly, underground. They may as well be on strike for all of the effort they're putting into the games.

They know they could never win a strike against the wealthy owners, so they're trying to win their demands their way. They're giving the league total parity. No team is worth a damn.

If you say you've watched the games and you don't believe me, that's your problem. Keep watching. You must like sick humor.

As bad as things seem in the NFL, we aren't without remedies. Here are some ways to pump life back in the game:

• Award bonus points for teams that recover their own spikes in end zones.

• Award bonus points for all white guys who score touchdowns.

• Eliminate the extra-point kick. It's a yawn. Make teams run or throw for their conversions.

• Allow only one field-goal try per game—and if the kicker misses, he has to go back to Rumania.

• No more holding calls. Let the weight lifters fight it out in the line.

• Outlaw the quarterback sneak, the draw play, the prevent defense, and the kill-the-clock incompletion.

• Do away with the fair catch.

• Take up the artificial turf. Tear the roofs off stadiums.

• Find out what "encroachment" is and get rid of it.

• Move the two-minute warning to the start of the game.

• Shorten the regular season to 12 games.

• Cut back to 16 teams in the league. When did Buffalo, San Diego, Denver, Atlanta, Tampa, Kansas City, Seattle, New Orleans, Foxboro, Indianapolis, Houston, and Minneapolis ever get the idea they were major-league in the first place?

• Take periodic urine samples from the league's investigators.

• Make all owners live in the cities where they own teams.

• Shoot down the Goodyear blimp. Show more closeups of cheerleaders on television.

• A team forfeits one game for every Hollywood celebrity who turns up in an owner's luxury box.

A last word about Charlie Teasdale and his family.

Not that it would have stood in the way of journalism, but one fact made this exposé easier for me to write. Mrs. Teasdale is legally blind.

I am told that Mrs. Teasdale will think the pic-

ture of Kim Cooze is an architectural illustration
of the twin domes on a new stadium complex.

I hope Mrs. Teasdale's friends, out of sympathy
for her feelings, will use good judgment in what
they tell her about the contents of this article.

Finally, the reader is entitled to have the following question answered: why would a former NFL
player like myself write these things about his
sport?

Because I used to love pro football and I want
my game back.

Shake's story was all over the newspapers. Ex-
PLAYER ACCUSES GAME OFFICIAL OF 'FIX.' EX-PLAYER
SAYS NFL GAMES ARE 'JOKE.' NFL SHRUGS OFF EX-
PLAYER'S ACCUSATIONS.

It was front-page news in most of the league cities.
The Fort Worth Light & Shopper even gave it banner
play over the prominent state legislator who had
confessed to operating a child-pornography ring in
Austin.

The story in Jim Tom's paper was compiled from
wire reports. It pretty much covered all of the reper-
cussions to Shake's piece.

Charlie Teasdale was quoted as saying, "We don't
allow magazines like *Playboy* in our home, therefore I
can't comment on the story. I can tell you that the
name 'Kim Cooze' means nothing to me."

To which Kim Cooze said, "He never heard of me,
huh? Ask him how Old George is. That's the name of
his whatyoucallit. The story is absolutely true."

Tom Buckner of the 49ers, the president of the
Players' Association, said, "In a free society, Shake
Tiller is entitled to his views, and the First Amend-
ment guarantees a magazine the right to publish
those views. The leadership of the Players Association has no knowledge of a specific plan to destroy

the game, but we can't speak for every individual member."

Dreamer Tatum said, "There are so many intangibles in football, it's impossible to say whether Shake Tiller is right or wrong in his theories. If I were a fan, I can only say I would be intrigued."

Commissioner Bob Cameron said, "Pro football has never been healthier. Commercials for the Super Bowl are selling for nine hundred thousand dollars a minute. I rest my case."

Pete Rozelle, the ex-Commissioner, now a U.S. senator, released a statement through his office. It said:

"There are forces at work in this country that would like to change our way of life. We must oppose these forces with all of our vigor."

The reaction of all of the NFL owners was the same. In a matter of words, they said: "Consider the source."

Burt Danby said it more colorfully.

"Mondo whacko," said Burt. "I've known Shake Tiller a long time. The guy's a complainer. He'd turn down Ali MacGraw if he knew she had a cavity."

When I came out of my bedroom the next morning at the Hyatt Regency, Shake was hanging up the phone in the living room of our suite. He was laughing.

"That was Bob Cameron," he said.

"You took the Commissioner's call?"

"He liked it."

"He *liked* your story?"

The Commissioner had told Shake he naturally wouldn't be able to say so publicly, but everything in the article was accurate. The Commissioner said he had guessed the players were up to something. He was going to urge the owners to give in on the wage-scale and free-agent issues.

Bob Cameron wasn't a bad guy. We had known him well, even hung out with him, when he had been an assistant under Rozelle. He had once worked in Network Sales for CBS, and in the days when we chased whup with him around New York, he was the liaison between the Commissioner and TV. It was because of his expertise in knowing how to heist the networks on television packages that he became the logical successor to Rozelle. The owners elected him Commissioner by a unanimous vote after Rozelle resigned to run for public office.

Shake was still grinning with amazement from the phone call as he said, "Charlie Teasdale's through after this season. So are eight other zebras. Bob says they'll be allowed to retire for 'personal reasons.' That way, it'll save the league embarrassment. He says he's been trying to think of a way to get rid of those guys without a scandal. Now he has the ammunition. My story. If they don't go quietly, he'll put 'em in the joint."

"You kicked ass," I said.

Shake said, "The Commissioner said me and him ought to get drunk together some night—like the old days. He said if I'd keep it off the record, he'd tell me some real horror stories about the zebras."

"What else did he say about the players and owners?"

"He says his sympathy is with the players, but the owners approve his expense accounts."

"Life its ownself," I said, somewhat relieved, somewhat bewildered. "You never know what that old boy will think up next."

"No, you don't," said Shake. "He's got a bag of tricks, doesn't he?"

FIFTEEN

We took the farm roads to Boakum. It turned the journey into a three-hour drive in my rented Lincoln, but Shake and I agreed it would be fun to look at the knobby hills and pastures and live oaks and Herefords and goats of Central Texas. We weren't in as big a hurry as the heavy haulers that stormed past you on the freeways and tried to beat you to the next place to stop for a Lone Star and a hot link.

We drove slowly and sometimes lingered for a minute or two in a lot of little towns that brought back memories of Friday-night high school football games, of car chases in which we all should have been killed, of punchouts and cussfights, of brassieres and panties that had been left in the back seats of Buicks and Dodges, of terminated pregnancies, of good greasy cheeseburgers you couldn't find anywhere anymore.

We wondered if our old high school coach, E. A. (Honk) Wooten, was happy in retirement, now that he couldn't greet all the pretty girls as "Gizzard Lip," beat everybody's ass with his paddle, and lift his leg to make a clever noise like T. J. Lambert and blame it on "them damn cafeteria beans."

We talked about all of the girls we had known,

about the ones we'd liked to have known better, the ones who had undoubtedly gained too much weight by now, the ones who had kept their looks, and the ones who were raising hell because the dentists they'd married hadn't filled enough teeth to buy them a house in River Crest.

Shake might have married Barbara Jane at one time, though he says not. Since then, he had not even been close to marrying anyone, although he spent more time under the covers than a chronic invalid.

Now he guessed he might never marry—not until he was fifty, or so he was saying in the car.

He said, "I'm pretty selfish of my time, B.C."

"No shit."

"I don't know how you do it. I couldn't deal with the crap that married guys have to take. If I was married to Barb and she put one minute of rage on me, I'd drive a stake through her heart."

"Barb doesn't do rage," I said. "She does lip."

"You know what I mean."

What he meant was the heat his mother, Matilda, had strapped on his father, Marvin senior, when he was growing up.

Marvin senior owned an electrical-supply store. Marvin senior and Matilda both worked there. So had Shake when he wasn't at football practice. Tiller Electric made them a nice living, but that didn't mean they were country-club rich. Shake had suspected this was one reason why his mother was mad all the time.

Barbara Jane and I had never thought of Matilda as an angry person. We knew her as demanding, a perfectionist, but she had never been anything but charming around us.

Shake said we didn't know the real Matilda. Nobody did but him and his dad, an easygoing guy with a fixed smile on his face. If Shake was right about Matilda, you had to wonder why Marvin senior ever smiled. In the privacy of their spotless, ranchstyle home, Matilda would turn into Magda Goebbels.

Matilda had a penchant for telling Shake and his dad how to dress, what to eat, what to say, where to sit, what to watch on TV, how much money to spend on anything, where to keep the thermostat, how many logs to put on the fire, why they couldn't have a pet, where they should go on vacation, which movies to avoid, what vitamins to take, who their friends should be, how to balance a checkbook, why a certain posture was bad for you, when it was going to rain, and why crisp vegetables were healthy.

If Shake and Marvin senior ever disagreed with any of this, they had the Third Reich to deal with.

We were seniors in high school when Shake's mother died. She never recovered from an operation after an automobile accident. Shake had lived at All Saints Hospital while the doctors struggled with Matilda's internal complications. He had watched her fail slowly.

Matilda had still enjoyed periods of consciousness in which she would tell everybody where to sit, what not to eat, and why smoking and drinking was bad for you. Knowing the hour was near, she even found the strength to dictate her own funeral arrangements. She wanted to be buried in her light blue summer dress by Geoffrey Beene. Felipe from Neiman's should do her hair. She requested mood music from a Gordon Jenkins album, no organ, please. Matilda's funeral demands weren't unreasonable if you measured them against those of Lucy Wood, a Pi Phi we had known in college. Lucy was the daughter of a wealthy rancher in the Panhandle. She was also a diabetic who did herself in on Dr Peppers. She had left a note asking that her father see to it she was buried in an evening gown sitting up behind the wheel of her red Ferrari with a carton of Dr Peppers beside her.

Matilda had been partly to blame for her own demise. She had insisted that Marvin senior turn the wrong way up a one-way street. Rather than argue about it, Marvin senior had taken the turn, and their car had collided head on with a drunken priest in a Chevrolet. Marvin senior had only suffered a broken arm.

Four months after Matilda died, Marvin senior had married Holly McFaddin, a woman who kept books for him at Tiller Electric. Two years later, after all of us were in TCU, Shake's dad sold the business and made eough on the sale to retire in modest comfort.

Marvin senior and Holly, a woman Shake had always liked, bought a home in Ponte Vedra, Florida, and they were living there today. Shake would visit them on occasion and stay until he was overgolfed by their conversation.

Shake could now look back on his youth, at the home in which he was raised, with humor. His most vivid memory of Matilda was the time she had unleashed a weeklong reign of terror followed by another week of smoldering silence because of a careless remark his dad had made.

One evening at the dinner table, Marvin senior had said, "My momma used to cook with lard. That's why everything tasted so good."

On our way to Boakum, we were passing through another peaceful-looking, tree-lined town when Shake said, "Looks pretty, doesn't it? You know what's going on behind these closed doors?"

"Rage?"

"Fucking right. I guess I'll never understand why it's necessary."

"It's a people deal," I explained.

Shake confessed that for the first time in his life he had been feeling a little lonely, even when he was being held hostage by a shapely adorable, but it hadn't made him want to get married.

The only thing it had done was make him want to start on a novel again. He might hire a thirty-year-old Swedish housekeeper who could double as a masscusc.

"To live in?"

"If she looks like Kathy Montgomery and doesn't speak English," he said.

I wondered how the language barrier was going to solve the loneliness problem.

"I don't want her for a friend," he said. "My friends will be the characters in my book."

By appointment, we met Tonsillitis Johnson and Mutt Turnbull, his coach, at K's Restaurant in downtown Boakum.

Downtown Boakum was a courthouse surrounded by four blocks of deserted storefronts with head-in parking for the only other vehicles we could see, which were four pickup trucks and a Datsun 280Z. Tonsillitis' car, courtesy of Big Ed.

K's Restaurant looked like a place I had spent half my life in. It was a rural Herb's Café.

Leatherette stools along a serving counter. Linoleum-top tables. Tile floor. A black-and-white TV on a shelf playing a Gunsmoke re-run. A blue-and-orange Boakum Bobcats pennant on the wall above a squad picture of last year's Class AA state champions, the Boakum Bobcats. Antique brass cash register. George Jones on the jukebox. Meatloaf special on the menu. Tired K cooking in the kitchen and tired Marvene behind the counter. And two fence-menders trying to beat the pinball machine.

"Finesse that fucker, Dace!" said one of the fence-menders as the machine clanged and flickered.

Tonsillitis and Mutt were seated at a table in the rear of the place. We sat down with them as Marvene brought us coffee we hadn't asked for and put another cup of tea in front of Tonsillitis.

Tonsillitis was wearing a Levi jacket over a T-shirt and his yellow reflective glasses.

Mutt Turnbull was exactly what I had expected to find. He was a squat little guy in his forties who was getting bald, the kind of man of whom his friends would say: "Mutt, you ain't gettin' any smarter, you're just gettin' wider."

"I reckon you boys is the biggest names what's ever been in here," Mutt said. "You don't care if Marvene takes some Polaroids, do you?"

Marvene came to the table with the Polaroid camera.

"We're flattered," I said. "Will we be on K's wall?"

"Honey, y'all are the Red Cross!" Marvene said. She snapped the pictures and brought us a slice of homemade chocolate pie.

"Sorry about the Eula game," Shake said to Mutt.

"Broke my heart is all it did," the Boakum coach said. "We'd have gone all the way again, but I hadn't ought to complain. Tonsillitis has give me more to brag about than anything else I'll have in this life."

I asked Tonsillitis if he felt the same about football—was he still confused?

"Haba say to probe for the inner truth," he said.

"You can probe in college and still play football," Shake said.

"College be havin' material value. Haba say material value is the road to evil."

Mutt Turnbull said, "You ain't gonna get nowhere with him. The swami's got him up to his ass in clean air, clean water, pure food, and pure spirit."

"Is that all you want?" I said to Tonsillitis.

"Haba say it's the way to inner peace."

Shake said, "Tonsillitis, would you play football again if Haba said it was all right?"

"Haba don't like football."

"Haba might change his mind."

"Who gonna change Haba?"

"Grover."

"Grover who?"

"Grover's the boss swami."

"I never heard of Grover."

"Haba has."

Tonsillitis said he would follow Haba's teachings, even if they led to playing football again.

That was all we needed to know.

"Where can we find Haba?" I asked.

Tonsillitis said Swami Muktamananda was waiting for us across the street in the square. The swami refused to patronize K's because the restaurant served carbonated sodas.

We left Tonsillitis and Mutt in K's and walked over to the square, where we found Swami Muktamananda sitting cross-legged under a hackberry tree.

The swami was a black man in a beard and dark glasses. He was wrapped in a bedsheet, wore a baseball cap that said "BLUE SOX" and a pair of high-top tennis shoes. There was no other swami in the square. It had to be him.

Shake and I plopped down on the grass with him, introduced ourselves.

"You are men of sweetness, I have a way of knowing," said Haba.

I came right to the point.

"Haba," I said, "we've got a gentleman in Fort Worth who's reached his E.O.R."

"I do not understand," said the swami.

"End of rope," I said. "The gentleman wants Tonsillitis to play football for TCU so bad, he's willing to increase his contribution to your cause."

"I have no cause, I only have my teachings."

"My man thinks your lectures would be greatly improved if you had five hundred thousand dollars in the bank."

"Oh, my," said Haba.

I said, "The man's name is Ed Bookman. He's extremely wealthy and a man of God. Although he's a Christian, he respects your beliefs. He says he's convinced you will have many more visions come to you out of the pitch blackness if a half a million is deposited in your account at the United Bank of Austin."

Shake said, "I've lived a cloistered life myself, Haba, and I've learned something about bucolic. He don't pay the lights, gas, and water."

"You have spoken a truth," Haba said.

I said, "Mr. Bookman says he will make half of the contribution now and the other half when your disciple signs his letter of intent on Feb. 8. This is assuming we have a deal."

Swami Muktamananda saw the need to meditate for a moment, to ask his divinity for guidance in the matter. He tilted his head back, put his palms together.

Coming out of it, he said, "These funds would be taxfree?"

We drove back to Fort Worth on the interstate. I put the Lincoln on cruise control, stuck an Elroy Blunt tape in the cassette deck.

We were a few miles outside of Boakum before I asked Shake the question of the hour:

"Do you think Big Ed knows Darnell is the swami?"

Shake said, "I don't think Big Ed cares as long as he gets Tonsillitis wearin' that purple."

SIXTEEN

Kathy looked prettier than I had ever seen her. She sat across from me at dinner on Friday night of that week. I was introducing her to good Tex-Mex food at Casa Dominguez, a restaurant and sports salon near downtown Dallas where my picture hung on the wall in a gallery of other desperadoes.

"It's interesting," Kathy said of the corn tortillas that were stuffed with orange cheese and chopped onion and covered with a delicate brown chili gravy.

"You can't get this in New York," I said. "In New York, you get swill—cottage cheese inside pita bread with tomato sauce on top, or something worse. There's a place in Midtown that claims to serve chicken-fried steak. I asked a waiter one night if the gravy was any good. 'It's wonderful' he said. 'We make it with mushrooms and sherry.' He should have had his tongue cut out. The chef should have had his hands cut off."

"Is this chicken-fried steak?"

"No, it's enchiladas. Tex-Mex. Chicken-fried steak is something else. Chicken-fried steak is just . . . food."

"I like steak and I like chicken," Kathy said. "I'm not sure I'd like them together."

She misunderstood, I said. A chicken-fried steak was a cheap piece of beef that had been tenderized—

had the shit beat out of it. Then it was cooked in a batter like fried chicken. "You pour cream gravy over it."

"Gravy made with cream?"

"If it's done right, it looks like scrapbook paste, but it tastes better. The chicken-fried steak was invented in 1911 in Lamesa, Texas, by a man named Jimmy Don Perkins. He was cooking in a café and got his orders mixed up. They can talk about Davy Crockett all they want to. Jimmy Don Perkins is my hero."

"Is that what they teach in school down here?"

"They should," I said. "I wish a guy from Fort Worth had invented the chicken-fried steak, but all we can claim are the ice cream drumstick and the washateria."

Kathy looked at me with concern.

"Historical facts," I said. "God bless I. C. Parker and J. F. Cantrell. In 1931, I. C. Parker was working for Pangburn's Ice Cream Company. He accidentally dropped an ice cream cone covered with peanuts into a pot of liquid chocolate. The world took it from there. The saga of the washateria goes back to 1934. All J. F. Cantrell was trying to do was survive the Depression. His cleaning business was going broke. He put in four washing machines, let people do their own, and called it a washateria. The place is near where I grew up. It's a landmark."

"I could have gone my whole life without knowing these things," Kathy said.

"I come from a pretty famous high school," I said. "You know who went to Paschal? Ginger Rogers. Ben Hogan, the golfer. Alan Bean. We had the third man on the moon. Who went to your high school?"

"Ona Schulenberg."

"Who's that?"

"She was the first woman to walk three thousand miles backwards. I had her for English grammar."

Kathy had arrived from New York that afternoon. She had checked into a room on the same hall as Shake and I at the Adolphus in Dallas. We had moved to another suite that was 35 miles east.

Years ago, the Adolphus had been one of the swell hotels in Texas, like the Menger in San Antonio and the Driskill in Austin. It had a nightclub with an ice rink and a restaurant where Bonnie and Clyde used to go to dinner. It was in the heart of downtown Dallas, only a block or so from the original Neiman-Marcus. The Adolphus had fallen into a period of despair but it had been remodeled and furnished with fine antiques and it was a swell place again. Its elegance recalled a better time in our lives than the modern glitter of America's suburban hotels.

Before going to dinner that night, I had spoken to Barbara Jane in California. I had filled her in on the Tonsillitis—Darnell—T.J.—Big Ed drama. She had screamed with laughter at her daddy buying a fake swami.

"That's half a million out of your inheritance," I had reminded her.

"The joke's worth it," she had said.

Considering all the millions Big Ed had left, she may have been right.

Barbara Jane had confirmed the fact that she was going to have the weekend free. She had been tempted to fly down to Dallas.

I had talked her out of it. She wasn't going to miss anything but a lousy football game and dinner with Teddy, Mike, and Ken, I'd said.

"Ken?"

"My stage manager."

"That's right. You still like him?"

"He's okay," I'd said.

Kathy and I had invited Shake to come to dinner with us at Casa Dominguez, but he had other plans. His plans had included a tour of the bars out by SMU and the hope of finding a Tri-Delt of loose morals who had been stood up by a Kappa Sig.

Kathy was into her third frozen Margarita at dinner when I said, "Did you know the Margarita was invented in El Paso, Texas, in 1942?"

"Stop it," she said.

"It's true. The bartender's name was Pancho Morales. He was looking for a way to tame the tequila one night . . . to keep his customers from breaking so much furniture. That's when he came up with the idea of adding Triple Sec and lime juice."

I was impressed with how adultly Kathy handled the Margaritas I ordered for her so quickly.

All they did was give her a friendly glow.

I had learned through experience that there was a fertile hour with Margarita drinkers. Smart money had to be alert.

If you missed that hour, you were no longer with the lascivious harlot of a porno film, you were with an unidentified body that had been dredged up from the Hudson River.

Kathy drank her Margaritas without salt around the rim of the glass, which was how salt crept into the conversation.

She never ate salt, she said.

I didn't accept that.

"Everybody eats salt on *something*," I said.

"Not me," Kathy said, tossing her golden hair and sipping her unsalted Margarita. "If food is cooked properly, you don't need salt."

"Eggs," I said. "You can't eat eggs without salt."

"I can."

"I don't believe you."

"Why not?"

"How often do you eat eggs?"

"I don't eat eggs every morning, but I eat them sometimes."

"Fried or scrambled?"

"Both."

"Soft-boiled, too?"

"Yes."

"Without salt?"

"Why do you find it so peculiar?"

"Don't get me wrong," I said. "I love eggs. I'm an egg guy. But if I had to eat an egg without salt and pepper, you'd have to rush me to a hospital."

"It must be how you were raised."

"Yeah, I'm normal. I was raised on salt and pepper."

She smiled at me.

I said, "I'm gonna think of something you can't eat without salt."

"You can't."

"Give me a minute," I said, taking the challenge seriously.

I inhaled a young Scotch and did the same thing to a Winston.

"Honestly," she said, "You can't name anything I would put salt on."

"I've got it," I said, believing I had it. "Popcorn."

"I don't eat popcorn," she said with a look of apology.

Back at the hotel, I steered Kathy to the lobby bar for a nightcap.

We took stools at the service bar rather than sit in the cushiony sofas and chairs. A serious drinker never sits in cushiony sofas and chairs. If they don't put you to sleep, they make it impossible to stand up without tearing your coat.

Except for the bartender and a waitress who were discussing auto repairs, we were the only people in the lobby bar.

Our stools were close. We were almost touching shoulders. Kathy switched to Scotch when we ordered a drink.

I said, "I tried to get you drunk on Margaritas, but I think I got myself drunk on Scotch. Seeing as how I'm drunk, I have an excuse for letting you kiss me right now."

"You're lonely," she said—and startled me with a wet kiss.

My response led to a longer kiss—and some clutching. In the history of moist kisses, these didn't deserve to be enshrined in a movie library, but they were interesting enough to make me motion to the bartender for the check.

"Shall we go meet our destiny?" I said.

In a whisper, she said, "Billy Clyde, I'm not going to bed with you. It's not like I haven't thought about it. I have. But . . .we can't do it."

I suggested we talk about it upstairs.

She said, "Your friendship means too much to me, it really does. I want to be friends with Barbara Jane, too. You guys are special."

Where were the Jim Tom lines?

I said, "What's a friend for if you can't count on 'em? You do know we're going to wind up in bed someday, don't you?"

"Not if we don't let it happen."

She initiated another kiss, but this one fell into the sister category.

"There's something else," she said, softly. "I've been wanting to talk to you about it, but I could see you were getting interested in me—and I couldn't help but like that. You're Billy Clyde Puckett. I'm nobody."

"We owe it to sports," I said. "We're not talking about a lifetime commitment here."

"I'm in love with somebody," Kathy said. "I want the two of you to meet. I want all of us to be friends."

"Tomorrow," I said. "Tomorrow, he'll be the best fucking friend I ever had."

She laughed as I signed the bar tab.

Kathy was aloof in the elevator. It was obvious that she had no intention of raping me.

In the hall outside the door to her room, she gave me a long hug but only a kiss on the cheek, and she said:

"You mean so much to me, Billy Clyde. You have no idea. See you in the morning, huh?"

"I learned something tonight," I said.

"That I have a lover?"

"No, that doesn't surprise me. How the hell can a girl who looks like you not have somebody? I learned something about Barbara Jane."

"What?"

"She does mental telepathy."

Feeling an indescribable sense of relief, even an odd pinge of pride at not having made a complete fool of myself, I walked to the door of the suite. I looked back down the hall. Kathy had waited to enter her room until she could wave goodnight to me.

I smiled at her like a sophisticate, went into the suite, turned on the movie channel, and watched an idiotic romance I'd already seen three times on airplanes.

At mid-morning on Saturday, we set up the Shake Tiller interview in the Adolphus suite. Lights, two cameras, lapel mikes, Kathy directing.

Kathy had to caution Priscilla not to walk in front of the cameras or make any noise at the bar once the cameras started to purr.

Priscilla Handler, an SMU co-ed, was Shake's holdover houseguest from the previous evening. She was a willowy, olive-skinned, sleepy-eyed beauty of about twenty. She was wearing one of Shake's dress shirts as a bathrobe, and nothing more that I could tell. She had made a face when told to turn off the TV so that we might conduct the interview, but generally speaking, Priscilla seemed to approve of our suite. She also approved of Shake Tiller's stash. Priscilla looked like someone who intended to practice hedonism for the next thirty-five or forty years.

"When will this be on TV?" Priscilla asked anyone who cared to answer.

"Tomorrow before the game," I said.

"Here in the room?"

"Yes," said Kathy. "We aren't blacked out."

"Dilly!" Priscilla said. She opened a can of beer, lit a joint, and made herself comfortable in an easy chair where she could watch us do the interview.

Priscilla's shirttail scrooched up as she wriggled in the chair. Her bare legs and hips were exposed. There was even a glimpse of the whup thrown in. This didn't bother Priscilla, but one of the hand-held cameramen was distracted.

"You want to go to the game?" the cameraman said to Priscilla. "I have an extra ticket."

"I hate the Cowboys," Priscilla said. "Talk about stuck-up people!"

She drew on the joint.

"Y'all go ahead and do your deal," she said. "I'll keep still."

Kathy had been staring at Priscilla. I couldn't have guessed whether Kathy thought she was looking at a reptile or just your average Tri-Delt.

On camera, I introduced Shake Tiller by saying I had known him since the third grade when he had driven Old Lady Hedderman half-crazy with ventriloquism. I had known then he was destined for fame.

I said he had the mementos to prove he had been a great football player—a Super Bowl ring, a wall full of plaques, an assortment of game balls. He had since become a successful writer—a noted author, I said—but the NFL wasn't too happy about this fact right now.

Grinning as I faced him, I said, "I guess the first thing anybody wants to know is why you wrote that story and embarrassed everybody in pro football."

"Had to," he said. "It got to where I couldn't sleep at night. I'd close my eyes and see zebras jumping over safety-deposit vaults."

"One in particular," I said. "Charlie Teasdale, the referee."

"No, I'd always see Charlie in Switzerland," Shake said. "He'd be opening numbered accounts."

"Your story says Charlie Teasdale tried to manipulate the scores of games."

"He didn't *try*, he did it," said Shake.

"Your main source is an exotic dancer."

"I have other sources I can't name."

"What about the rest of the zebras? Any crooks?"

"I don't have proof, but if you want an opinion, I'd vote guilty on some others. Too many games have looked like science fiction."

"Aren't you relying on the word of gamblers and bookmakers?"

"In part," Shake said. "Who's a better judge of reality?"

"Your story says the players have been having a little fun of their own this season, like not putting forth their best effort. Why are they doing this, if it's true?"

"It's true. Look at the records of the teams. Nobody's going to get to the Super Bowl with better than a 10–8 record. The winner of the Super Bowl will have an 11–8 record and call itself the 'world champion of pro football.' Are you kidding me? Contrast this to the 17–0 record that Don Shula's Dolphins had back in '72 . . . to Lombardi's great Packer teams . . . to our 15–2 the year the Giants did it all. The pros have become the biggest boost to college football since Grantland Rice named the Four Horsemen. In college, it takes a 12–0 or an 11–1 to be a national champion. What's happened is this. The players want a say in determining their wage scale and they want the right to become free agents. The owners won't give 'em these things, and meanwhile, the owners want parity. They're getting it, man. The players have gone Dixie."

"What you're saying is, the players are intentionally giving America an inferior brand of football, and they're going to keep doing it until the owners realize what's going on and come to the bargaining table?"

"Right," said Shake. "The players have the ability to turn every game into a comedy. I say they're already doing it. The owners ought to be worried."

"I fail to see what good it will do to kill the sport," I said.

"They won't kill the sport. They'll just kill the NFL. Some rich guys will start a new league and the players will be back at work."

"There are thousands of fans who must not agree with you. . . . They're excited about the season."

"That's their problem," Shake said. "But I don't think there are enough fools out there to keep the league alive."

"With all this in mind, what do you look for in the playoffs?"

"I'd like to buy some pharmaceutical stock," Shake said. "There's no telling how much speed it'll take to keep America awake."

"Who do you think's going to the Super Bowl, and who'll win?"

"I like boredom over tedium by a fumble."

Shake thought it better not to go to the Cowboys–Giants game Sunday. Too many people in Texas Stadium would want to ask him about the *Playboy* article—or assassinate him.

He stayed in the Adolphus suite with Priscilla, a girl he liked in a curious way. Priscilla might be what he had been searching for his whole life, he said. She was certainly good-looking and had no shame whatsoever about the fact that she was only interested in eating, sleeping, fucking and doing dope.

They had discussed the possibility of Priscilla going back to New York with him. She could keep him company while he worked on the novel. There would be no unreasonable demands on her. All she would have to do was eat, sleep, fuck, and do dope.

Leaving SMU would be no problem for Priscilla. She would deal with the spring term the way most of her friends did.

"Drop City" was the academic phrase she had used.

"You know what's great about Priscilla?" Shake had said. "Nothing's complicated."

Kathy Montgomery had never seen Texas Stadium, so I gave her a guided tour Sunday morning.

We started in the big private club above the west end zone that was for drinking, dining, socializing, dancing to live country music, or even watching the game for those who were still sober when it came time for the kickoff. In many ways, the Cowboy Club was like being back at Mommie's Trust Fund.

I led Kathy on a tour of the private suites in the stadium. Most of the doors to the suites were standing open, enabling us to glance inside at the decor and the revelers. An owner of one of these suites could decorate it as he or his wife saw fit.

Kathy was fascinated with everything she saw, which included cocktail parties in progress in a French Provincial living room, an *Art* Deco patio, an Early American library, a harem, an aquarium, an exercise gym, an oyster bar, a bird sanctuary, and an unfurnished room in which we found six airline stewardesses drinking champagne.

We stopped by the visiting owner's box for a drink with Burt Danby and Veronica. I no longer felt any guilt about having Kathy with me. She belonged to somebody else. She was my trusty sidekick and stage manager, that's all.

Needless to say, Burt was taken with Kathy.

"Jesus," he said, gaping at her from hair to ankle, "I knew broadcasting was a grimy, thankless business, but I didn't know it was fucking gutter work!"

Kathy accepted Burt's unique flattery with a smile.

"You're Billy Clyde's 'assistant'?" Veronica said to Kathy.

"I'm the stage manager," Kathy said.

"Hmmm," Veronica said, not believing it for a second.

The Danbys were with two couples who had flown to Texas with them on the team plane. Their names weren't worth remembering. They looked as if they could tell you nothing more than where to shop for floral trousers or hand-knitted sweaters in the vicinity of Greenwich, Connecticut.

Burt said to me, "You're good on TV, ace. You don't drill a hole in me like that fucking Larry Hoage. Jesus, can he talk? He can say less in more words than six guys running for governor!"

"I've been thinking about football," I said. "The doctors say I'd be crazy to try to play again. I like television. You were right, it's a soufflé. Maybe my playing days are over, is what I'm getting at."

"You want the truth, Billy Clyde? Once a knee, always a knee. You'd never be the same again."

"What about the Gucci knee you promised?"

"I'm an owner," he said. "I lie!"

I asked Burt what he thought about Shake's exposé.

"Loved the broad," he said.

"That's it?"

"What else is there? It's print journalism, Billy Clyde. A week from now, it's history. And you know what? Our TV ratings will go up. Who's not going to watch pro football now? Jesus, it's like we've got our own game show. Joe Bob and Martha sit there with their Miller Lites and their Velveeta sandwiches and try to guess who the crooks are. 'There's one!' 'No, it's not!' 'Yes, it is, he dropped a flag!' It's dynamite. When you see Shake, tell him kiss on the lips from the big guy."

"Do the other owners agree with you?"

"We've got some assholes who worry about integrity," Burt said. "I was on a conference call with the Competition Committee. I said relax, guys, how many times have you seen integrity going to the bank?"

"The quality of football doesn't bother you?"

"With my team?" said Burt. "If we'd *tried* this year, we'd still be oh-for-fifteen!"

"So you think the players are laying down—like Shake says?"

"A few pinkos, big deal. It's nothing we can't cure with a checkbook."

Kathy astutely asked Burt who was going to replace Billy Clyde Puckett on the Giants. They surely weren't going to stay with Amos Hixon, the rookie from Prairie View who had been filling in for me.

"He's gone," Burt said. "I'll take any white guy I can get. We'll have the first draft choice. I'd like to get the kid from Illinois, but he's got Count Dracula for an agent. I may trade for the guy at Tampa Bay."

"Ron Tooler?" I said. "He's slow."

"Yeah, but he's white. You want to know the real trouble with pro football, Billy Clyde? Forget the zebras. Too many spookolas, that's our problem."

"Too many what?" said Kathy.

"Mola gomba," Burt said. "We're getting too many. Pal of mine at Y-and-R's been a season-ticket holder for twenty years. He doesn't go to the games anymore. He says, 'Fuck it, I already take *National Geographic*.' I argue with the networks about it. I told 'em one of these days if we aren't careful, we'll be right in the shitter. They say I'm wrong, look at ice hockey. They say ice hockey's an all-white sport but nobody watches ice hockey on TV. You can't give it away. Jesus, I know why nobody watches ice hockey. It's got nothing to do with color. They don't watch ice hockey because it's played on fucking ice! We're gonna be in trouble if we don't cut back on the mogambo, I'm serious. That'll be some great Super Bowl one of these days—Swaziland and Mozambique in the fucking Rose Bowl!"

Before the game started, Kathy went to the broadcast booth to prepare her picnic, and I wandered down on the field to visit with Shoat Cooper and some of the Giants.

The old coacher said, "I sure wish I had you with us today, Billy Clyde."

"Looks like you need more than me," I said.

Shoat said, "This season ain't exactly been my idea of high times. I'm gonna have to get me some lumber and nails and start over, is all I can do."

Where did he intend to start?

"Not a bad place right there," said Shoat. He looked at Dump McKinney, who was flipping passes to receivers. "That withered-arm sumbitch can't spiral it from me to you."

"You need help in the offensive line," I said.

"Tell me about it," the coach said. "Powell there

can't spit over his chin. Brooks ain't been off his belly since October. Jackson's so slow, he has to make two trips to haul ass. Burris swapped his brain for a tree stump. I ain't been around so many jewels since the last time I was in Woolworth's."

I spent a moment with Dump McKinney.

I asked the quarterback what the Giants might try to do against the Cowboys today.

"Get out of their way," Dump said.

Larry Hoage welcomed our TV audience to a "broncobustin', calf-ropin', steer-wrestlin' wingding of a ro-day-o" that was coming from "deep in the heart of Dallas, Texas, where the deer and the antelope roam."

Larry glanced at me for a comment on the game before the kickoff. I said it had been a while since I had seen an antelope in Dallas, but I'd bet Neiman-Marcus had one in stock.

The Cowboys secured a spot in the playoffs by rolling to a 24-to-0 lead over the Giants in the first quarter. They scored on two intercepted passes for touchdowns, two field goals by their placekicker from Kuwait, and two safeties, which were the result of Dump McKinney slipping down in his own end zone while looking for a receiver.

Larry Hoage gave full credit to Dallas' "Doomsday Defense," which hadn't existed for years.

There was a moment during the first half when we watched a cut-in from the New York studio on our monitor. That day Charlie Teasdale was refereeing a game in San Francisco, and when he had taken the field at Candlestick Park, he had received a standing ovation.

Larry Hoage hadn't read Shake's story, I gathered, or read anything about the exposé in the newspapers, or even listened to Brent Musburger on the cut-in, because when New York came back to us, Larry said over the air:

"What a great tribute to a great guy! We don't give the officials enough credit, by golly! Kind of thing you like to see!"

I was standing up, my broadcast habit now—and looking down on the field in the third quarter, when I heard Kathy's voice on my headset.

"Wow—Barbara Jane Bookman, it's you!"

My wife was in the broadcast booth.

I took off my headset and started over to give Barb a kiss.

"Nice surprise," I said.

"So is she," said Barb, retreating coldly, telling me with a look that Kathy Montgomery was never going to be her best friend.

I knew there was something I didn't like about Learjets. If your father-in-law owned one, and it happened to be sitting around in Los Angeles on business, and his daughter happened to get on it, she could be in Dallas in two hours, and surprise you in a broadcast booth, and get the wrong impression about your stage manager. Because of the Learjet, a guy could get separated, even divorced, and be miserable the rest of his life. The Learjet had its drawbacks.

Now in the broadcast booth, Barb turned to Kathy, and said:

"Hi, Ken. How's it going?"

"Ken?" Kathy frowned.

I said, "Her name's Kathy, Barb. Kathy Montgomery. She's a good girl and a good friend."

Barbara Jane said, "I see why you leave on Thursdays for a Sunday game. Good luck with your life, asshole!"

With that, Barb whirled out of the booth.

I went after her. Not in a panic, but hurriedly.

Out in the stadium corridor, as Barb was getting on the press elevator, I said, "Come on, honey, it's not what you think—and I'm on the air, damn it!"

"Wrong," she said. "You're on the street."

SEVENTEEN

Leukemia was a butterscotch pie compared to marital discord. My dad had been right all those years ago. Marital discord drove a toothpick up your ass with a sledgehammer and dragged you backwards through a sewer drain. Marital discord could turn you into a knee-crawling, dog-puking drunk, a dope-sick, no-count, sorrier-than-white-trash, store-bought son-of-a-bitch whose ass wasn't worth wiping with notebook paper. Marital discord made you so God-damn tired, you couldn't eat spaghetti.

Marital discord didn't necessarily make you a bad broadcaster, though. I was nominated for an Emmy in December, as the playoffs got underway.

I would have been prouder of it if almost every broadcaster in sports television hadn't been nominated, either as the Outstanding Sports Personality—Host or Outstanding Sports Personality—Analyst.

It wasn't until after the news of the nomination had come in the mail at the New York apartment that I found out the three networks had nominated their own people. The imbecile Larry Hoage was even nominated by Richard Marks, so it wasn't as if we'd been selected by a panel of Walter Cronkites.

I only felt like I deserved an Emmy if you compared me to Larry Hoage, but being separated from

Barbara Jane, I kind of wanted to win the thing out of some feeling of vengeance.

None of our friends could believe Barb and I were separated, and neither could I. And none of our friends could do anything about it. Everybody made a plea to Barb in my behalf—Shake, T.J., her parents, Burt Danby, Dreamer, even Kathy, which must have been the briefest conversation of them all, knowing Barb. Shake was as good a friend of Barb's as he was mine, except that when it came to domestic matters, men stuck together. He went out to the Coast, a mercy trip, to try to patch us up. Came back with a bruise.

I had tried once. Pride wouldn't let me go any further.

In a conflict between men and women, pride becomes the adversary of both.

The day after Barbara Jane had turned up in the broadcast booth in Dallas, I had returned to the Westwood Marquis and we'd had one of those debates that never get you anywhere and only infect you with an anger that's hard to get rid of because it burns the lining of your soul.

I began by saying, "Barb, this is the first real problem we've ever had. We've got a chance to show what we're made of here."

"You've done that," she said.

"You're wrong about me and Kathy Montgomery," I said. "I know why you think what you do. I should have told you about her from the start. I was an idiot. I can't really explain it, except that good-looking women don't like to hear about other good-looking women . . . do they?"

"Good-looking?" said Barb. "She's fucking immortal! You do have good taste."

"Kathy's a kid," I said. "She's a young girl out of Berkeley . . .a television junkie. She's ambitious. She thinks I'm a big deal. Girls her age are always into hero-worship, I can't help it."

"Is this going to be the tenor of our conversation?" Barb said, lighting a second cigarette to go wih the one in the ashtray. "Are you going to remind me every two minutes that she's younger than I am?"

"Nothing happened between us, that's the point," I said.

"Bullshit."

"It didn't."

"Bullshit!"

"You're wrong," I said. "Why do you think it did?"

"Because I've seen her and I know *you*. Two months with Ken! How dare you?"

"What the fuck have I done?"

"You lied to me . . .took advantage of me. How many Kathys have there been? I know you, Billy C.! I've known you all your life! You've got about as much willpower with women as you do with barbe-cue ribs!"

"Why'd you marry me?"

"I loved you. I thought you had become a grownup."

"Did I hear a past tense?"

"Yes!"

"You don't mean it."

"The hell I don't!"

"You're just hot, Barb. I admit you have a right to be. I misled you—it wasn't really a lie—for some dumb reason I can't explain, but you don't stop loving somebody because of that."

I tried to go near her. She stopped me with a look of "territorial ferocity," as Shake described it in a book. Women were better at it than leopards.

"You'd like Kathy if you knew her," I said.

"Ha!"

Somehow, I had known that was the wrong thing to say, even as the words came out of my mouth.

"She looks up to you," I said, making it worse.

"Good!" said Barbara Jane. "I'll send her an eight-by-ten!"

"While we're on the subject of friends," I said, "what about the suave Jack Sullivan?"

"What about him?"

"What's going on there?"

"Oh, no," said Barb. "Uh-uh, you're not going to turn this around. You're the asshole here, not me. And I want you out of here—now!"

"Jack Sullivan's just a good friend . . . a director, right?"

"That's right."

"Well, that's all Kathy is—a good friend and a stage manager.

"Did you hear what I said? I want you out of here."

"What the hell will it take to convince you, damn it?"

Barb said, "A couple of snaggled teeth and a case of acne would help."

I smoked one of Barbara Jane's cigarettes.

"Marriage is a full-time job, Barb. Happiness is a state of mind. I'm ready to work on it if you are."

Barbara Jane looked around the hotel suite, mystified.

"Who am I talking to? When did Joyce Brothers come in the fucking room?"

"What do you expect me to do?" I said.

"Leave."

"Just walk out? Walk out that door?"

"Yeah. You put one foot here, the other foot there, and pretty soon . . ."

"I think I will."

"Fine."

"I think I won't be back."

"Better."

"You don't have a good enough reason to give me all this shit, Barb."

"Oh, really? I've got five years to look back and wonder how many chicks you made it with and I don't have a good reason?"

"None," I said. "Starting with Kathy."

I didn't think it would serve any useful purpose in our discussion if I confessed that making it with Kathy had crossed my mind. Deep down, I felt I would never have gone the distance with Kathy that night in Dallas. I would have pulled up lame somewhere. With Kathy, it had been a question of trying to get to the bottom of a puzzle. Once the puzzle was solved, the game was over. I didn't know how many people would ever believe this, but I knew it was true. Christ, it wasn't as though I'd never scored a pretty girl before.

"Goodbye, Twenty-three. I know how lonely it is on the road, but you'll manage," Barb said.

"You're gonna be God-damn sorry if I walk out that door."

"Life is full of gambles."

I went to the door.

"You don't want any of your clothes?" she said.

"Fuck clothes," I said. "I got clothes and broads stashed all over the country!"

I doubt if T.J. Lambert could have slammed the door any harder than I did. As an old inanimate object kicker, I gave it my best effort.

Shake Tiller's pro football exposé had created some havoc in the television industry, of course. Because of the cloud that hovered over the quality of the competition one might expect in the playoffs, CBS's leading announcers, Pat Summerall and John Madden, were advised by their agents and business man-

agers to withdraw from broadcasting any of the
playoff games or the Super Bowl.

Their advisers felt that their reputations would be
damaged if they lent credibility to what might well
be a noncompetition. Only the players knew how
seriously the playoff games were going to be contested.

Richard Marks tried to quadruple their fees, but
Summerall and Madden rejected the offer, which
was how Larry Hoage and I wound up doing those
games. I didn't have a broadcast reputation to worry
about. It didn't matter. And Larry Hoage would
have thrown a side-body block on Mother Teresa to
get at a microphone.

The pro football scandal had finally overtaken
Larry, although he and his friend Hoyt didn't discuss it as often as they discussed topsoil, garden
tools, and Orange County zoning quirks.

I had become good friends with Teddy Cole, the
producer, and Mike Rash, the director, partly because we had a common dislike for Larry Hoage.

Teddy and Mike were in their late twenties. They
had come out of the University of Miami. They were
quicker than laser beams at their jobs. They saw life
through the monitors in their control unit, never
missed the right picture, knew when to go close,
when to pull back. They were young pros, the type
of electronic journalists who could witness a live as-
sassination and instinctively know to alert the tape
operator, bring up the audio, point cameras at everything that moved. They had given me some good
tips. Things like keep your sentences short, you can't
mention the score of a game too often, and always
try to think of the one characteristic that will describe a ballplayer—Dreamer Tatum has the suede
market cornered, Dump McKinney's got a 6.2 voice
on the Richter scale, Point Spread Powell tapes his
ankles up to his neck.

Teddy and Mike both did fine imitations of Larry Hoage behind his back. At a dinner table or around a hotel bar, their routines kept all of us loose.

Teddy might say:

"This is Larry Hoage comin' at you today with a wingding of a bell-ringer from Hiroshima, Japan, friends! Here comes the *Enola Gay* now. She's up there in the sky looking like a fat old hen that's ready for roastin', but I've got an idea she's cooking up a soo-prise of her own. Yep! It's bombs away, as I like to say. The old egg's heading for the heart of the city! We'll be here to bring you all of the action, but right now, let's go back to Brent for an update on the race at Daytona!"

And Mike might say:

"This is Larry Hoage comin' at you from Auschwitz, Poland, friends, and have we got a barn-burner for you today! These rough-and-tumble Nazis are rarin' to go. They've got the coaching, the desire, and like they've said all season, this is the one they want! Be that as it may, Billy Clyde Puckett, I've got a hunch about these pesky Jews. I think they just might take it!"

Christmas deal.

It hadn't meant much to me since the Christmas morning I had awakened to discover I'd made that mysterious transition from cap pistols to sleeveless sweaters.

Now it had even less meaning because Barbara Jane and I were estranged. It was just as well that the holiday fell between two playoff games.

Christmas Day found me in a motel on the outskirts of Detroit. I endured a turkey dinner in the company of Kathy, Mike, Teddy, Larry, and Hoyt Nester, who kept us entertained with zany tales of his fun-filled years as a CPA.

Teddy, Mike, Larry, and Hoyt all exchanged funny gifts that came from adult bookstores. Kathy gave me an engraved cigarette lighter to go with the other three I had. I gave her a tricky sweater that a sales-lady at Henri Bendel's had picked out for me.

I tried to call Barbara Jane on Christmas Day. She was unfindable. Ying, the houseboy at Jack Sullivan's, informed me that Barb and Jack were spending the weekend in Del Mar with friends of the director. Ying wouldn't give me the Del Mar number even though I threatened to crawl through the phone and dust his chop suey ass.

I wouldn't have minded knowing if Barb had liked the emerald ring. It wasn't a ring her mother would have been dazzled by, but I thought it was a decent present to give someone who no longer spoke to me.

Barb had sent my present to the apartment in New York. It was a Porsche wristwatch, one of those multi-gadgeted things that nobody can tell time on but an extraterrestrial visitor.

Coincidentally, we both quoted lines from Elroy Blunt songs in our cards to each other.

My card to Barb had said:

> *I can't taste the gravy*
> *When there's heartache on my plate.*

And her line to me was:

> *He leased a high-price body*
> *For his low-rent mind.*

Okay, she topped me. There was nothing to do but fall back on my old philosophy and remember that laughter is the only thing that'll cut trouble down to a size where you can talk to it.

* * *

The playoff games thrilled Dreamer Tatum and the Players' Association more than they thrilled the fans.

Larry Hoage and I worked the wild card game between the Cardinals and Vikings on Dec. 19 before we went to Detroit. That game set an NFL record of twenty-two turnovers before the Vikings came away with a nine-to-six victory.

In the game between Minnesota and the Lions on Dec. 26 in the Silverdome, the Christmas spirit carried over an extra day. The Vikings gave away six fumbles. The Lions gave up the ball five times on interceptions. Half the time, I thought I was watching volleyball or soccer.

When I said as much over the air, Larry Hoage only caught the word "soccer."

"There's an interesting game," he said to our audience. "From what I hear, soccer's really starting to take off in Europe."

The Lions defeated the Vikings in Detroit by the score of 10 to 3. They broke the 3–3 tie in the third quarter with an 80-yard drive that featured three pass-interference penalties. Detroit's quarterback, Kelvin Thorpe, sneaked across for the winning touchdown on his fourth try from the 1-foot line.

The fourth quarter offered little more in the way of excitement than incomplete passes and offsides penalties.

We were in Dallas, back at Texas Stadium, for the NFC championship game on Jan. 2, a memorable contest between the Cowboys and Lions. Kelvin Thorpe of the Lions scored two quick touchdowns for Dallas in the game's first five minutes by throwing interceptions to Len Ikard, a Cowboy linebacker. Dallas held on to the 14-to-0 lead for the rest of the game.

In the last three quarters in Dallas, neither team advanced the ball past mid-field. There was so little action on the field that Teddy Cole and Mike Rash threw every insert into the telecast they could muster up, most of them having to do with the off-season hobbies of NFL players.

Those viewers who stayed with us saw film clips of Hudson Stone, a defensive tackle for Dallas, building model trains; of Dallas quarterback Alvar Nunez cooking beef *fajitas;* of the Lions' Oran Rippy, a strong safety, boarding a plane with his pet goldfish; and of Gregg Glasscock, a Dallas running back, being handcuffed by federal narcotics agents.

Brent Musburger did the voiceover on all of the inserts. He explained that Gregg Glasscock had been cleared of trafficking in drugs. The 5-pound sack of Gold Medal flour he had been seen to purchase from a fishing-boat operator in Key West had later tested out to be a 5-pound sack of Gold Medal flour.

Earlier that same day, the AFC championship game was played in Miami. The Seattle Seahawks had beaten the Dolphins 2 to 0 on the last play of the game. What happened was, Jackie Barnett, the Miami punter, inadvertently stepped out of his own end zone for the safety that gave the victory to Seattle.

It was a humiliating way for Miami to lose the game. A near-riot had erupted in the Orange Bowl. Barnett had been placed in the protective custody of police.

Jim Tom Pinch defended Barnett in print. He wrote that Barnett's blunder—if that's what it was— had prevented the most boring game in the history of football from going into an overtime period, an overtime that would have caused turmoil with every sportswriter's airline reservation. It was a mercy killing, Jim Tom said, and Jackie Barnett was a hero.

Dallas and Seattle were thus going to the Super

Bowl on Jan. 16. And Larry Hoage said on the air that he, personally, had never looked forward to a Super Bowl with such nerve-tingling anticipation. He said it was clear to him from the playoffs that the NFL had brought "rip-snortin', rockribbed defense" back to football.

The TV ratings for the playoffs were drastically off from previous seasons, and at the same time, the college game dealt its own blow to the sagging image of the NFL.

In the Cotton Bowl on New Year's Day, twenty-four hours before those so-called championship games in the NFC and AFC, the Auburn Tigers (10–0–1) and Texas A&M Aggies (11–0) played for the shouting rights to who's No. 1.

Pat Summerall and John Madden did a first-rate job of broadcasting the game for CBS. Richard Marks had shown good judgment in assigning his best announce team to an event of such magnitude, even though it seemed likely the network would be sued for having breached the contracts of Terry Culver and Roxanne Lark, the popular boy and girl who were CBS's regular college football announcers.

"I'd like to see 'em try to bounce Larry off a broadcast," Hoyt Nester said.

We all watched the Cotton Bowl game on TV in Teddy Cole's suite at the Adolphus—Kathy, Teddy, Mike, Larry, Hoyt, and me. Kathy and I rooted for the Aggies, me because of the Southwest Conference, Kathy because of the Aggie fight song. Teddy and Mike rooted for Auburn. Larry rooted for Summerall and Madden to make mistakes. Hoyt kept stats from force of habit.

The lead changed hands eight times in the game. Three touchdowns were scored in the last seven minutes before Auburn made a goal-line stand and slipped by with a 38-to-35 victory in one of the greatest poll bowls anyone had ever seen.

Only seconds after the game ended, I got a call from T.J. Lambert. He wanted to tell me that Auburn would have every starter coming back and remind me that, sadly enough, Auburn was the first opponent on TCU's schedule next season.

He said, "Here I am tryin' to bring us back from the dead and I got to play me a national champion the first pop out of the box. The game was signed up five years ago when Auburn wasn't worth a shit; now they'll be comin' in here with their dicks hard."

"You'll have Tonsillitis and Artis," I said.

"They won't have played no college game."

"Maybe it'll rain. Hold the score down."

"It could rain fish fuckin' rooftops and it wouldn't help me none against them sumbitches. How's Barbara Jane?"

In very good health, I said, as far as I knew. Her show was going to premiere in two weeks—the night of Super Bowl Sunday, in fact.

"You ought to have your head examined," T.J. said.

"Why? ABC made the decision. They think it'll get a big rating that night."

"I ain't talkin' about TV, asshole."

"What are you talking about . . .?"

T.J. said, "You're married to the greatest woman in the world and you can't keep Leroy's helmet on."

"I haven't done anything, T.J."

"No need to lie to me, son."

"I'm not lying. Barbara Jane's overreacting."

"You got that blonde with you right now, don't you?"

"We work together."

"You're in big trouble, son. You better straighten yourself out."

"You want to meet Kathy? I'll bring her over."

"I don't allow no whore lady in my home."

"She's not a hooker, for Christ's sake. She's a good girl. She's a pal."

"She must be somethin' else for you to shit on Barbara Jane."

I tried to convince T.J. that I wasn't having an affair with anybody but J&B at the moment, that Kathy was a decent human being, a victim of circumstances who felt awful because of Barbara Jane's opinion of her and even worse about what had happened to my marriage. Kathy would like nothing better than to think of a way to undo the damage if it were within her power, I said. But the problem was in Barbara Jane's mind.

"The problem's got nothing to do with whup," I said.

"It don't, huh?" said T.J., who then whistled into the phone—a long, low, rippling noise.

"What's that?"

"Face mask," he said.

There had been no way to reason with Coach Lambert that day.

EIGHTEEN

I guess going to a Super Bowl would be fun if you were a person who's just escaped from a mental ward or a maximum-security prison. The National Football League likes to promote Super Bowl Week as one of the grand experiences on the sporting landscape, but anybody who's ever been to one will tell you it's basically a six-day cocktail party followed by a frivolous, over-hyped football game that every poor, hungover bastard in town has come to loathe before it's even been played.

I thought this after I went to the game as a player, and I thought it even more after I went as a broadcaster. You can't get over the suspicion that you're there for reasons other than to let two teams decide a championship. It's as if your primary purposes are to celebrate the mere existence of the NFL, to rejoice in the Commissioner's good health, and to drink a thousand toasts to the $900,000 commercial minutes that have been sold for television.

When the Super Bowl goes to New Orleans every so often, as it did for the Dallas–Seattle game, you can multiply the dementia by 10. That's because the French Quarter, which never closes anyhow, becomes a combination of spring break and Tet offensive.

Going to the Super Bowl as a broadcaster made it a little more bearable, but not much.

CBS took over an entire hotel in the French Quarter that week, the Saint Louis. We had our own courtyard, our own bars, our own dining facilities. We could hide. We could avoid the insanity.

The insanity was out there on Bourbon Street if you wanted to wade into it, but you could escape quickly. Nobody could get at you but the invited guests of the network, and since there were only 5,000 of those, we were protected better than most visitors to the city.

I got two extra rooms in the hotel for Shake Tiller and Jim Tom Pinch and their guests. Shake brought Priscilla and Jim Tom brought Kelly Ann. Unnecessary baggage, as I saw it. One look inside The Old Absinthe House in the French Quarter was proof enough that the city was jammed with Priscillas and Kelly Anns of every size and accent. As Uncle Kenneth would say, you always bet the Under on wives at a Super Bowl.

Shake had come to New Orleans reluctantly. As he had said, "I try to avoid eighty thousand people whenever possible."

But having a room in the CBS stockade appealed to him. He would be close enough to life its ownself to stand on his balcony and holler at it, but it couldn't climb up and get to him.

The days of Super Bowl Week were filled with organized interviews at which the press swarmed around a Dallas Cowboy or a Seattle Seahawk and tried to get him to talk at length about the case of chicken pox he had suffered as a three-year-old.

Kathy Montgomery arranged for me to do inserts with every starter on the two teams and both head coaches, John Smith of the Cowboys and Turk Kreck of the Seahawks. Richard Marks wanted coverage on everything.

"We don't want to miss an angle," he had said.

The angles we got from the player interviews ranked right up there with most player interviews at most Super Bowls.

Alvar Nunez, the Dallas quarterback, said, "I have a lot of respect for our opponent."

Gary (Gun Mount) Gittings, the Seattle quarterback, said, "It's going to be one of the great games."

Marshall Hammond, the Cowboys' top pass receiver, said, "I see it as a collision between two brilliant coaches and two brilliant systems."

Borden (Swinging) Vine, the Seahawks' fleet pass receiver, said, "I just hope it's not decided by an injury and nobody gets seriously hurt."

In private and off-camera, none of the players admitted to me that they had ever heard of Operation Dixie or a Script Committee.

John Smith, the coach who had taken over from Tom Landry at Dallas, was a tall, handsome man who dressed like a banker. In the middle of our interview, he reached inside his breast pocket and handed me a small, leatherbound copy of the New Testament.

"What's this?" I said.

"Well," he smiled, "you might say it's our secret weapon."

"There you have it," I said to the camera. "John Smith's gonna isolate on Leviticus and hit 'em in the Proverbs."

The interview with Turk Kreck, Seattle's coach, was enhanced by his candy-striped leisure suit. I hadn't seen a leisure suit in years.

Turk was a barrel-chested former guard with the Browns who couldn't help spitting on you when he talked. Jim Tom once wrote that Turk Kreck was the only man who could spit inside your glasses.

"Some people think this is a party," said Turk, "but the Seahawks are here to play football."

I asked Turk what he thought was going to decide the outcome of the game.

"It better not be a zebra," he said, splashing me with the z.

"We're in luck," I said. "Charlie Teasdale won't be working the game."

"He could be the halftime entertainment," Turk said. "Let the cocksucker run out on the field naked and everybody who catches him gets to stick a flag up his ass! Are we live?"

We went to all of the parties. Kathy and I, Shake and Priscilla, Jim Tom and Kelly Ann.

All three network parties, those of CBS, NBC, and ABC, were on the same riverboat. They had the same seafood buffet, the same jazz band, and the same guests. The riverboat was overcrowded with ad-agency people, team owners, movie stars, and select members of the press.

Jim Tom looked around the first night and said, "I have a new motto. Life is hard—then you die."

Shake was grilled by some of the owners at the parties. They wanted to know if he actually believed what he had written in *Playboy*, if the players had been trying to sabotage the game.

Shake never mentioned Operation Dixie or the Script Committee, but he said the playoff games had made it clear to him that the players had not packaged their best product, as it would have been clear to anyone but a lamebrain owner.

Acacia Kirby, the rich widow from Tyler and Cuernavaca who now owned the Dallas Cowboys, suggested that Shake move to Russia.

"You've done our nation a terrible disservice," said

Acacia. She was a bony woman in her fifties, a third-generation oil heiress. Her face looked as if it had been drained of blood and glued onto a neck and shoulders that were excavated from parched land. Acacia's late husband, Polk, had talked her into buying the Cowboys from Clint Murchison for $100 million, after which he, Polk, had choked to death on a bite of *cabrito*.

"I know about your husband," Shake said to Acacia. "What year did you die?"

The owner of the Seattle Seahawks, Karl Lutcher, a man from La Jolla, California, who had amassed a fortune selling arms to Arabs, was more concerned about the motives of the players than Acacia Kirby.

"There may be some truth to what you wrote," Karl Lutcher said to Shake. "I haven't liked the way some of our fumbles have looked. But I expect both teams to give us their best in the Super Bowl, don't you?"

"No question," said Shake. "You're going to see an exhibition you'll never forget."

The Seattle owner could have taken that two ways. He chose the wrong one.

"It's a relief to hear that from you," he said. "I know you're close to some of the players."

Looking at Shake and me both, he said, "How 'bout a prediction? I think we've got 'em outcoached. You can't give Turk Kreck two weeks to get ready for somebody."

Shake said, "There are things you have to keep in mind when you're talking about a football game. Each team will have eleven men on the field."

Karl Lutcher nodded.

"And there's only one ball," I said.

He nodded again.

"Think about it," said Shake.

"I hear you," the owner said.

"The field's a hundred yards long," I said. "Not ninety-nine."

"And there's sixty minutes on the clock," Shake said. "Not fifty-nine."

"Another thing," I said. "That one ball? It's got air inside."

"It's not round, either," said Shake.

"Good point," I said. "It's damn near shaped like a football."

"Put it all together and what have you got?" Shake said to the owner. "It's why we're all here."

Jim Tom and the girls had been listening to us. As we walked away from the Seattle owner that night, Jim Tom said, "I've learned how to handle Super Bowl parties. Every time I yawn, I put a drink in my mouth."

We saw Burt Danby at all of the functions. Most of the time, he would be working his way through the crowd, trying to give Veronica the slip.

The first time we ran into Burt on the riverboat, he glanced at Shake and said, "Holy shit, it's Sherlock Holmes!"

He then pumped Shake's hand in friendly fashion and got around to noticing Priscilla and Kelly Ann.

"Hi, girls," said Burt. "Ever been on a Lear?"

Shake introduced Priscilla Handler and Kelly Ann Robbins by saying, "Burt, I'd like you to meet Sonny Jurgenson and Bill Kilmer."

"I'm exhausted," said Burt. "Fucking Super Bowls will kill you. Last night I kidnapped the Lindbergh baby, robbed a liquor store, threw up on my wife at Moran's, caught syphilis from a hooker, stole a police car, and set fire to an orphanage."

"That'll win," said Kelly Ann.

Traditionally, the Commissioner tossed the biggest party of the week. This time, it was on Friday night at the River Gate, a convention hall. Bars, buffet tables, and Dixieland bands seemed to be everywhere, along with 10,000 people you had never seen before in your life.

The Commissioner and the owners and their wives were segregated from the rest of the party. Their tables were behind velvet ropes and a ring of uniformed guards.

We assigned Priscilla to talk her way past the guards and get Bob Cameron's attention, which she did with ease. The Commissioner came outside the ropes to visit with us. Priscilla came back with a heaping platter of barbecue shrimp and raw oysters.

"You worried about the game?" Shake asked the Commissioner.

"More than the owners," he said.

"What do you expect?"

"I'm afraid to think about it."

I said, "Bob, I know you've checked it out. How many guys in the game are strong union men?"

"Too many," Bob Cameron laughed. "Food poisoning won't work. That's off the record, Jim Tom."

"I wasn't even listening," said Jim Tom, wearily. He then took out a spiral notebook and pretended to write something in it. "Commissioner poisons Super Bowl," he said.

Back at our hotel that evening, Kathy and I sat in the courtyard after Shake and Priscilla and Jim Tom and Kelly Ann went up to their rooms. This was the night Kathy opened up about her lovelife. She said she wouldn't dream of discussing it with anyone but me—her best friend—but she needed to talk about it with somebody who would be sympathetic and understanding. The relationship was getting complicated. She could see it leading to a crisis, a choice, something that could affect her work, her career, her whole life.

It had all started three years ago when she had

first moved to New York. She had met this older man in a restaurant on the East Side, Gino's, over by Bloomingdale's, and she had let herself get involved with him.

He had taken a liking to her, pursued her, practically adopted her. She had always been attracted to older men. They were more interesting than people her age. The man was in his early fifties and quite wealthy, but very married. That part had always bothered her, but every girl she knew at CBS was also "dating" a married man. Why was it so hard for a girl to meet a single guy in New York who was interested in something besides stock options and his mother?

"I won't tell you my friend's name," Kathy said. "It wouldn't mean anything to you. He's a lawyer."

The thing that had further complicated the relationship was that Kathy had accidentally, through a chance meeting at a party, become friends with the man's daughter, Denise.

I was told I would like Denise. Denise wasn't a raving beauty, but she was intelligent, artistic, "deep," a wonderful, unselfish person.

Denise's father didn't know about his daughter's friendship with Kathy—and he could never know. It would cause too many family problems.

I said, "I can see where he wouldn't want his daughter to know he's fooling around, but how long can you go on like this, Kathy? Are you in love with him? If he loves you, he'll get a divorce."

"That's what he wants to do," Kathy said, "but I have to stop him. It'll be terrible."

"Why?" I said. "It solves everything. People your age make things too God-damn complex. You love the guy, he loves you, you get married. He'll be happy you and Denise are friends, believe me."

Kathy took my hand. She looked at me soulfully.

"I'm not in love with *him,* Billy Clyde. It's . . . Denise."

I had never been on a jetliner that lost 10,000 feet in altitude, but in that instant, I thought I could appreciate the sensation.

"You're in love with *Denise?*"

I didn't awaken anybody in the hotel. No one came out on the balcony to look down at us in the courtyard.

Kathy was calm. She said, "Denise and I have something together that's truly inexpressible."

I doubt that any man ever made a quicker decision. To prevent the possibility of my becoming the butt of some longstanding gag, I knew then and there that I'd never tell Shake Tiller or any other guy about Kathy Montgomery's sexual preference.

Maybe someday when the statute of limitations was over, Shake and I would have a good laugh about the time I'd been mentally seduced by a dyke.

Once again, I didn't sleep well. The bereaved person seldom does. Kathy would continue to be my friend, my trusty sidekick, but as I lay in bed that night, I couldn't help thinking about the tragic waste of that Nordic combined.

Denise was a lucky girl.

Whitey Duhon, the famous Cajun comedian-singer, sang his own special version of our National Anthem in the Louisiana Superdome. Four thousand school children dressed like Jean Lafite formed a circle around Whitey Duhon, who stood on the 50-yard line with his fiddle.

Mike Rash went in tight on the entertainer, ignoring the balloons, doves, and giant mechanical crayfish, as the beloved Whitey sang:

Oh, say you gonna see, boy,
by dat old dawn's early light, what you think?
You gonna proudly hail dat thing, boy,
and the LSU Tigers,
they be gleaming, too, I tell you dat!

And those rockets red glare,
filet gumbo, hey?
The catfish swimmin' in air
give proof to you guys
in your Mardi Gras hats,
our flag is still there
in the French Quarter night,
you better believe it, Al Hirt!

Oh, say does dat music wail, boy,
o'er dat land by the coonie's Bayou.
What you think of dat,
Kawliga me-oh?

The Super Bowl game itself was of less interest to
me than the fact that the spectacle didn't start until
six o'clock in the evening. This was by design of the
NFL and CBS, a ploy to hog the prime-time TV
audience. And what this did was put the game up
against the premiere of *Rita's Limo Stop*—for thirty
minutes, at least.

For those thirty minutes, my wife and I were on
rival networks. Me live, her on tape.

Of course, by nine o'clock that night Barbara Jane's
show on ABC was getting a bigger break from the
Super Bowl than she and her co-workers could ever
have imagined possible. I should say Barb's show was
getting a bigger break from the Script Committee of
the Players' Association.

When *Rita* came on the air, it was late in the third
quarter at New Orleans and the Seattle Seahawks
were leading the Dallas Cowboys by 49 to 14. By

then, nobody could have been watching CBS or listening to Larry Hoage and me but those among the nation's infirm who didn't have remote clickers.

On the first play of the game, Seattle's Gary (Gun Mount) Gittings had thrown a bomb to Borden (Swinging) Vine, and the Seahawks had scored on a 75-yard touchdown pass.

Describing the re-play, I said, "You can see the Dallas defense is confused here. Nobody's going with Vine, the man in motion. I don't know why Dallas only has nine men on the field."

Dallas took the kickoff after that touchdown and made two first downs. But then Alvar Nunez, the Dallas quarterback, came under a heavy pass rush, retreated 30 yards, and threw the ball straight up the air. The ball floated down and into the arms of D. H. Peeler, a defensive end for Seattle. D.H. Peeler never broke stride and scored with the interception.

Those two touchdowns had set a trend for the game. Gary (Gun Mount) Gittings kept throwing passes for touchdowns. Alvar Nunez kept throwing interceptions, except when he was throwing away pitchouts.

We had Spivey Haws, a former defensive back with Buffalo, doing interviews on the sideline for us. Teddy Cole and Mike Rash went to him every chance they got as Seattle built its lead.

When the score was 35 to 0 in the first half, Spivey Haws was lucky enough to steal a moment with John Smith, the Dallas coach.

Spivey Haws said, "Coach, you're down by thirty-five points. Any chance you can get back in the game?"

"We'll be all right," said John Smith. "We just have to turn up the volume a little."

In the middle of the third quarter, with Seattle

leading by 42 to 7, Spivey Haws cornered Turk Kreck, the coach of the Seahawks.

"Coach, did you have any idea you'd get this kind of effort out of your team today?"

"Football!" shouted Turk Kreck, spraying the interviewer in the eye with the *f*. "We came to play a game called football!"

Spivey Haws had ducked the second *f*.

The zebras weren't a factor in the game. They would have been helpless against the Cowboys, anyhow. Dallas' ineffectiveness was complete.

But at Hoyt Nester's urging, by way of an index card on which he had printed "GAME OFFICIALS NOW," Larry Hoage felt the time had come for him to comment on the zebra scandal.

"Chilluns," Larry said on the air as the last seconds of the third quarter ticked away, "I've been hesitant to say anything before now, but I'd be remiss not to put in my two cents about the officiating in the National Football League. It's too darn bad we have some striped-shirt brethren who let their flags ruin the whole rhythm of a ball game! Look! By drat, they're doing it right this minute! They're stepping off another penalty against the hapless Cowboys!"

"Uh, Larry?" I said, hoping to interrupt.

"They're taking it back to the thirty, the thirty-five . . . the forty! It's a long one. Looks like half the length of the field!"

"It's the end of the quarter, Larry."

"Downright disgraceful how these whistle-happy dictators tamper with the flow of a game!"

"The quarter's over, Larry. They're changing ends."

"As if the Cowboys haven't been hog-tied enough today! We'll be back with more leather-poppin' Super Bowl action after this."

Larry turned to Hoyt. "How was it?"

"A-okay," said Hoyt.

"On the button?"

"Wilco."

"Rrrr . . . oger," said Larry.

The idea to break new ground in broadcasting occurred to me spontaneously. First, Teddy Cole suggested I try to liven things up as the fourth quarter began. Teddy said he could hear clicks all over the country because of Seattle's big lead. That's when I said to the audience:

"If I were watching TV at home, I know what I'd be doing, folks. I'd switch over to that new comedy on ABC. I hear *Rita's Limo Stop* is semi-funny."

From the control truck, Mike Rash said, "That's a no-no, Billy Clyde. Can't plug another network. Better disclaim it with a joke or something."

"Why?" said the voice of Teddy Cole.

"You don't pop the opposition, Teddy."

"Screw it, Mike. Let him go with it."

"Screw us, you mean."

"Nobody wants to watch this bag of shit, Mike. Go, Billy Clyde. It's your wife's show. That gives you license."

A noise came from the truck.

"What's that?" I asked.

"Mike did a headset," Teddy sighed. "So far, it's a one-headset show. We normally do a three-headset show."

Mike Rash had done that thing a director or a producer would sometimes do in the course of a live telecast. He had removed his headset and slung it against the control board, which was a way of saying, "Okay, fuck it, *you* do the show."

Seattle had scored another touchdown during all this. The Seahawks were now ahead by 56 to 14.

On the air, then, I said, "Larry, I can only think of fifty-six reasons why I'd like to be watching *Rita's*

Limo Stop instead of this game. Wonder if we can get it on our monitor?"

"Right you are, Billy Clyde Puckett," said Larry. "These Cowboys have flown apart like a two-dollar suitcase!"

The phone rang in the broadcast booth. Kathy handed me the receiver. It was Richard Marks calling from the Hospitality Room back at the New Orleans hotel. He was watching the game from there in the company of clients, who were more interested in their commercials than anything.

"Fantastic!" said Richard Marks. "Keep it up."

"Keep what up?"

"Plug *Rita*."

"I was just trying to be funny," I said. "There wasn't much going on here."

"Two of our sponsors bought time on *Rita*. They think it's great."

"Mike Rash doesn't."

"Mike Rash works for me."

"He needs a new headset."

Richard Marks said the clients in the Hospitality Room were watching *Rita's Limo Stop* on a separate TV set.

"How is it?" I asked.

"Quite amusing," said Richard Marks. "Barbara Jane is appealing. I think it has a chance."

"Does it have a chance-chance, or just a chance?"

"It has a very good chance."

Teddy Cole demanded that Larry Hoage give me the mike. Larry Hoage did so by saying:

"Well, Billy Clyde Puckett, what are your thoughts *now* on that Cowboy pick you made last night?"

"Larry, I have an update on *Rita's Limo Stop*. With ten minutes to go in the second half, Barbara Jane Bookman has a two-touchdown lead on Kitty Feldman."

"Absolutely! Some days, you just can't drive a train up a dirt road. But you gotta give these Seahawks all the credit in the world. They came in here loaded for bear!"

"Right you are, Larry Hoage. I want to congratulate our friends at ABC for having the guts to put a comedy up against a serious event like this. Hi, Barb. If you're listening, good luck in the ratings."

The Script Committee drew heavily on cynicism to account for Seattle's last touchdown in the Super Bowl's final minute.

Sam Galey, Seattle's punter, booted a high one to Dallas' twin safeties, Kyle Lease and Doboy Mims. Lease and Mims took turns fumbling the ball until it wound up back in their end zone. Lease and Mims then got into a shoving match with each other, and Seattle's D.H. Peeler had no recourse but to recover the ball for the touchdown that made the final score 63 to 14 in favor of the Seahawks.

As Larry Hoage went into his wrap-up on the game, I got another phone call in the booth.

An exultant Dreamer Tatum was on the line.

"Was it beautiful?" he said.

"It was beautiful, Dreamer."

"You can't say enough about the Cowboys," he said. "They didn't miss a single opportunity. Nunez was incredible, but he had a lot of help. It's bound to be the lowest-rated Super Bowl ever. Hell of a day for the union, man."

"Never have so few done so much for so many," I said.

Dreamer said, "You couldn't tell on TV. How many people left in the fourth quarter?"

"About sixty thousand."

"Great!" Dreamer was calling from Washington, D.C., from the Players Association headquarters in the Machinists & Lathe Workers Building.

"Clyde, I want to let you in on a scoop. I just talked to the Commissioner. Some of the owners had a meeting in the second half down there. The Commissioner says they're ready to give in on free agents, the wage scale, everything we want. We beat 'em, baby."

"It's a done deal?"

"Pro football's alive and well again."

"Congratulations," I said.

"You, too."

"I didn't do anything."

"Moral support, man."

"Won't it be dull next year without a cause?"

"Oh, we'll have a cause," Dreamer said. "I've got some thoughts on revenue-sharing the owners aren't going to like."

"You can always go Dixie."

"I'm hip, but you didn't hear it from me, Clyde."

I handed the receiver back to Kathy and listened to Larry Hoage sign off for us. He was saying:

"So for all of us here at CBS Sports, this is the Old Professor saying so long from Mardi Gras Land, where the Seattle Seahawks are the champeens of pro football. The Cowboys stood tall in the saddle, fought their hearts out, but the Seahawks put the big lasso on 'em. That's the story of the best Super Bowl *I've* ever seen."

Kathy put a promo card in front of Larry.

"Now," said Larry, "coming up next over most of these CBS stations ... *Scuzzo!* More hijinks and hilarity as three pockmarked teenagers find their own way to deal with the outdated value systems of their parents and teachers. In tonight's episode, Ross, Debbie, and Phillip set fire to their high school gymnasium, and ..."

"We're off," said Teddy Cole from the truck. "Good show, everybody."

* * *

Rita's Limo Stop got a 26 share. In TV talk, that's a raging hit. Anything between a 26 and a 32 share of the viewing audience is cause for every bicoastal to claim as much personal credit as he or she can. It put the show among the ten most-watched programs of the week—which isn't as important as the share. Carving out a share of the night, the hour, the half-hour, is everything where television ratings are concerned.

When the figures came in two days after the Super Bowl I was back in New York, awaiting word on my own TV future. Richard Marks had at one time mentioned that the network might use me on other sports during the winter and spring. The only other work I had planned was some banquet appearances. If CBS wanted me to hang around some other sports events, I was willing. Another town, another cocktail.

While I was in New York waiting for Richard Marks to make up his mind, I trapped Barb on the phone at the Westwood Marquis.

"Nice going on the share," I said.

"Thanks."

To say my wife's voice was cool would be like saying Alaska has polar bears.

"How are you?" I asked.

"Fine."

She didn't ask how I was, so I said:

"I'm fine, too."

She didn't respond to that either. I said, "I popped your show on the air. Pretty funny, huh?"

"I suppose."

"Did you hear it?"

"We were out."

"We?"

Nothing.

I then said, "The apartment looks fine. A cleaning lady comes in."

"Is her name Ken?"

"Are you ever going to *not* be mad?"

"I have to go now."

"I miss you, Barb. I love you."

"Good."

And she hung up.

A few days later I was summoned to Richard Marks's office in the CBS building on 52nd and Sixth. There, I was informed that I would be used on a spot basis as a regular sports broadcaster. I still didn't have an agent, but we agreed on a ridiculous, six-figure salary.

Richard Marks said, "I wish you would get an agent before we negotiate your contract for football next season."

"I'm doing okay without one," I said.

My assignment for the spring and summer was to go to some golf tournaments, sit on a tower behind the 15th green, and say things like "Let's go to Sixteen."

I thought I should be honest with my boss and tell him I didn't know anything about professional golf.

"It doesn't matter," Richard Marks said. "You can't see golf on TV. The ball's too small. We don't expect ratings. It's a prestige buy."

Richard Marks shook my hand. "You're a full-time announcer now, Billy Clyde. How does it feel?"

"Words can't describe it," I said.

Three words could have described it. Guilty as shit.

The head of CBS Sports asked about my travel plans over the coming weeks. There were some speaking engagements, I said; otherwise, I'd be on a New York barstool.

"I'll want my people with me at the Emmy Awards

dinner in March," he said. "It's an industry night. Good occasion to show your strength."

I said I would be more than happy to attend, thinking it would be an opportunity to see Barbara Jane. Her show had been on the air only two weeks, but it had already nominated itself—or ABC had— for several Emmys: Barb for Outstanding Actress in a Comedy Series, Carolyn Barnes for Outstanding Supporting Actress in a Comedy Series, Jack Sullivan for Outstanding Director of a Comedy Series, and Sheldon Gurtz and Kitty Feldman for Outstanding Writers of a Comedy Series.

It had always seemed to me that they gave away Emmys as often as they gave away Grammys. Like once a month. Daytime Emmys, nighttime Emmys, local Emmys, News Emmys, Sports Emmys, technological Emmys. Like most people, I never knew when a year started or ended for television, exactly how and why anybody got nominated for an Emmy, who voted, or who won, except that every channel I ever watched in every city I was ever in had an "Emmy Award–winning Eyewitness News team."

But this was a year in which all of the Emmys were to be given out on one big, black-tie evening in the grand ballroom of the Waldorf, an awards telecast on which three comics would fight over the microphone while a parade of rock stars eagerly opened the envelopes, hopeful of finding dread inside.

"Do we have a chance to win anything?" I asked my boss.

"I hope not," said Richard Marks. "The industry tends to vote mediocrity."

Shake Tiller tore himself away from Priscilla and his novel, which was tentatively titled *The Past*. He flew down to Fort Worth with me for what T.J. Lambert called The Big Signing.

We arrived in Texas on Feb. 7, the day before Tonsillitis Johnson was supposed to sign his letter of intent, the document that would deliver him to T.J. and the Horned Frogs for the next four years.

That evening, we went to dinner at Herb's Café with T.J. and his wife, Donna. It became a night to celebrate because T.J. let us in on the news that Tonsillitis had already signed his letter of intent with TCU.

The ceremony the next day would only be for the media, for the publicity splash.

"It's not legal, is it?" I said to T.J. "It doesn't bind him to anything if he signs before Feb. 8."

"It binds him to Big Ed's ass," said the coach.

I found out about the alumni award that night. T.J. couldn't keep the secret. His good friends Barbara Jane Bookman and Billy Clyde Puckett had been named co-winners of the first annual Horny Toad trophy, an honor to be cherished as the years go by.

"The what?"

TCU's trustees had been wanting to find a way to honor old grads who had distinguished themselves in life its ownself. They had come up with the Horny Toad Award—toad being a frog, as in Horned Frog, and horny being a toad with horns, as opposed to the other kind, a toad with a hard-on.

T.J. said, "The committee voted you and Barbara Jane the co-recipients because they couldn't decide between the two."

"Who's on the committee?"

"The chancellor and the trustees. Big Ed and them."

"It's a classy name."

"You're the first Horny Toad, son."

"I'm deeply moved."

Donna Lambert said, "You should be proud, Billy

Clyde. They could have given it to some poetry freak."

While the announcement of the award would be forthcoming in the spring, the presentation wouldn't be made until the fall. Barbara Jane and I would receive our plaques at halftime of the opening game against Auburn in early September.

"Maybe we'll be speaking by then," I said.

T.J. apologized to Shake Tiller.

He said, "They wanted to honor you, too, hoss, but I guess they's folks around here who think you hadn't ought to have put so many shits in your book."

"I still have my art," said Shake.

"How's art doing?" I smiled.

"He's been tired lately," Shake said.

"Still play the sax?"

"Piano."

Donna Lambert said, "What are y'all talkin' about?"

We were talking about Shake's new novel, I said. *The Past.*

"What's it about?" T.J. didn't really care. He was being polite. The only book T.J. Lambert had ever read was *Darrell Royal Talks Football.*

Shake answered the question by saying, "It's about everything that's happened."

"To people?" Donna wondered.

"That's part of it."

"I like James Michener," she said.

Shake said, "Well, this is kind of what Michener would write if he'd gone to Paschal."

I put another youngster down my neck and made a suggestion. "I'd like to go around the table and ask everybody how to get my God-damn wife back," I said.

"Stop fuckin' that blonde," said T.J.

"I haven't fucked her."

"Sad but true," Shake said.

Donna said, "Billy Clyde, if you were smart, you'd go to Barbara Jane on bended knees."

"She wouldn't respect me."

"She would, too. If you open up your heart to her, she'll take you back in a redhot minute."

"Not till he stops fuckin' that blonde," T.J. said.

"I'm not fucking her," I said, forcefully.

Shake said, "People ought to get married on water skis. You wouldn't hear all the vows. You'd never know you fucked up."

This was a softer line on marriage. Shake had once said people should only get married in burning buildings. With luck, a guy could catch on fire and never have to go to a school carnival.

I looked squarely at T.J. and said, "I haven't fucked Kathy Montgomery, okay? Maybe I thought for one stupid night I wanted to fuck her, but I didn't, and now I don't, and I won't, and we're just friends, and that's all the fuck there is to it—and it's not worth breaking up my fucking home!"

Donna Lambert said, "Y'all feel free to say fuck any time you want to. It don't make a shit there's a lady present."

Tonsillitis Johnson signed his letter of intent at noon on Feb. 8.

The ceremony was held in the Lettermen's Lounge at TCU. It was attended by Jim Tom and two dozen writers and radio and TV reporters, who formed a half-circle around a table at which all of us were seated: me, Shake, T.J., Big Ed.

At a given signal from Big Ed, Tonsillitis was led into the room by Darnell, and the two of them were accompanied by Artis Toothis.

As they entered, flash attachments popped on Nikons, and hand-held TV cameramen scurried about.

Darnell Johnson looked extremely prosperous and dignified in his gray three-piece suit and horn-rimmed glasses, almost as prosperous and dignified as Artis Toothis in his three-piece suit and horn-rimmed glasses.

Tonsillitis again wore his maroon satin warmups and yellow mirrored sunglasses, but he had added a white headband.

T.J. stood up at the table and introduced Darnell. Addressing the media, Darnell said:

"This is a great day for TCU. As you know, Artis Toothis has announced his plans to be playin' football here. Today, we are deliverin' to this university the other bes' football player in humanity."

Big Ed handed Darnell a gold pen. Darnell handed the gold pen to Tonsillitis.

"Sign your name, baby," Darnell said to his brother.

"Ratch ear?"

"Right there where it say."

I watched as Tonsillitis signed his name on the letter of intent, just on the odd chance that he might spell it "booley." No, he spelled it clearly and correctly. *Tonsorrell Baines Johnson.*

Everybody shook Tonsillitis' hand, Darnell's hand, T.J.'s hand, Big Ed's hand, Artis Toothis' hand. Pictures were taken of Tonsillitis with everyone, in twos, in threes, in groups.

T.J. then spoke to the press.

"Men, I don't need to tell you what this means to me. A coach wins football games with them horny old boys who want to eat the crotch out of a end zone. I got me two of 'em now. TCU's on the way back! Around this conference, they been sayin' you couldn't melt us down and pour us into a fight, but were gonna show 'em next fall! With Tonsillitis and Artis wearin' that purple, were gonna be jacked-off like a housecat."

In the press conference that followed, Tonsillitis was asked what he planned to study in college.

"Joggaphy," he said. "Joggaphy be tellin' you what's Eas' and Wes'. I like to look at pictures and maps and shit."

T.J. was asked if he would allow Tonsillitis to wear his headband at TCU. The reporter pointed out to T.J. that many black athletes wear headbands. It gave them a sense of pride in their ancestry.

"I got no problem with that," said T.J. "He can wear his headband . . . or his helmet."

When the proceedings were over, Big Ed took me aside.

"What are you going to do about my daughter?" he said.

The answer was that I would wait and hope she came to her senses, realize she was still in love with me, and make some overture about getting back together.

"She says you're having an affair. You say you're not. Who do I believe?"

"Ask Shake."

Big Ed chuckled. "Shake Tiller hasn't answered a question seriously since he was ten!"

"I'm not having an affair, Ed. The girl's good-looking, that's the problem. That's why nobody believes me. We're just friends."

"Some friend. She broke up your home."

"Kathy didn't break up my home. Barbara Jane broke up my home. What about that director your daughter's always with: does he bother you?"

"The faggot?"

"Jack Sullivan's not a fag. I wish he was."

"He could fool me at a costume party."

"Does Barb talk about him?"

"She says he's considerate."

"That's trouble."

"I know," said Big Ed. "Between you and me, Billy Clyde, that's the worst God-damn word women ever learned the meaning of."

"I've got supportive up there."

Big Ed lit a Sherman. "The director's a faggot whether he knows it or not. At least you been going around with a normal person."

"There is that," I said, looking away. "What do you hear from the swami, Ed?"

It was more than an effort to change the subject. I wondered if Big Ed realized, or cared to admit, that Darnell and Tonsillitis had worked a scam on him.

"Gone," he said. "If I had to guess, I'd say the Hindu son-of-a-bitch has moved on to the Big Eight or the Pac-10."

So Big Ed didn't know. Maybe I'd tell him someday after Tonsillitis made All-America, or won the conference for him, or scored so many touchdowns he turned white.

"By the way, thanks for the Horny Toad," I said. "T.J. told me."

"It's a real fine award. The trustees wanted to give it to me. I said naw, they didn't. They wanted to *trade* it to me for some more of my dinosaur wine. Go on and build your new library, I said. I'll pay for the damn thing."

"Tell your daughter I love her," I said.

On the way to the airport, Shake and I stopped off for a drink with Jim Tom Pinch at Herb's. Jim Tom wanted us to stay over another night so he could take us to Honey Bun's, Fort Worth's newest tit joint.

"Can't do it," Shake said. "Fun's about worn my ass out."

On the flight back to New York, Shake made literary notes to himself. I listened to tapes on my

Aiwa recorder and thought about crawling to Los Angeles on my elbows and knees. Happily for my wardrobe, I had rejected the idea by the time the plane landed.

NINETEEN

A simple smile from Barbara Jane and my whole life was a highlight film. For a moment, I was nine years old and we were back in elementary school together. Then I was joking with her in a hallway at Paschal. In another instant, we were sitting under a tree outside a dorm at TCU. Finally it was that night in New York when we had kissed like sex-starved teenagers and fallen into love its ownself.

All this happened because our eyes met in the grand ballroom of the Waldorf before the Emmy Awards began.

Kathy and I had walked in and were looking for our CBS friends and suddenly there was Barb. She was sitting at the *Rita* table with Jack Sullivan, Carolyn Barnes, Sheldon Gurtz, Kitty Feldman, and a handful of bicoastals.

Because there had been a sweetness in Barbara Jane's smile, I ushered Kathy over to my wife's table. Barb stood up and gave me a hug and a friendly kiss. Just the touch and smell of her would have shattered me if I hadn't been an allpro.

"You're handsome in a tux," Barb said.

"I had to go for the slick."

"You should wear it more often."

"Well," I said, "the band doesn't play that many formal dances."

Barbara Jane and Kathy were both wearing plunging gowns. They looked sensational. Standing between them, I felt like the emcee of the Miss Universe contest.

"Hello, Kathy," Barb said, nicely.

"Hi," Kathy replied. "God, you look neat!"

Kathy smiled at me and said, "There's our table. I'll go on."

Kathy walked away to the CBS table where Richard Marks was seated with Larry Hoage, Teddy Cole, Mike Rash, Brent Musburger, others.

Feeling the stares of the gang at the *Rita* table, I nodded a hello at everyone.

Jack Sullivan said, "Billy Clyde, you're excellent on the air. Don't let them change your style."

I thanked him.

"Are you going to win an Emmy?" I said to Barbara Jane.

"No," she said. "We hear Shirley Foster's a mortal lock for best actress."

"Who's Shirley Foster?"

"The star of *Cruds!*"

"Call me Biff," I said.

I lit a cigarette for Barbara Jane and said, "I'm not with Kathy, Barb. I mean, we came together tonight, but . . . she's involved with someone."

"A lawyer," Barb said. "Shake told me."

"I would have told you but I never get to talk to anybody but Ying."

"We'd better take our seats."

"I want you back, Barb. We can work it out. Can I see you tomorrow?"

"We're going back to L.A. in the morning. I'll be busy all summer. I'm renting a house in Santa Monica. Our ratings are through the roof. They've ordered twenty-six shows for next year. And . . . there's some movie talk."

"My wife, the movie star. Who would have thought in the fifth grade that—"

"Ex-wife."

"We're still married."

"It's a state of mind, isn't it?"

I let that slide and said, "They want me to do golf tournaments."

"That'll be fun for you."

"I don't know anything about golf."

"Your stage manager can research it for you."

"You don't know how to let up, do you?"

She said, "I've been hurt, Billy C. I don't know how long I'll feel this way."

"Well, if you ever get over it, I'm findable," I said, and went to the CBS table.

Which was where I got intolerably drunk.

The awards dinner lasted four hours. The middle two hours constituted the telecast when all of the important Emmys were presented.

I bribed a waiter to bring me youngsters by the threes and fours while everyone else at our table drank champagne or wine and poked around on their plates at the green peas and slivers of mystery meat.

During the two-hour telecast, I watched an endless procession of actors and actresses and producers accept Emmys for an endless list of shows I had never heard of.

Barb had guessed right. She didn't win the Outstanding Actress in a Comedy Series Emmy. But neither did Shirley Foster for *Cruds*! The award went to an actress named Diane Connors for a show called *Goose and Bomber*.

Rita was honored in another category. Sheldon Gurtz and Kitty Feldman won for best writing of a comedy series— for a script in which every line had been changed by Barb and Jack Sullivan.

When they made their acceptance speeches, Kitty spoke first, although she had trouble reaching the mike.

"I accept this award on behalf of the entire cast and crew," she said. "It's a great team."

"We're a family," said Sheldon. "It's the happiest show I've ever been a part of."

The sports awards came after the telecast was off the air, very late in the evening.

My category, Outstanding Analyst, which should have gone to John Madden, was taken by Laird Rinker, the twentytwo-year-old ex–surfing champion who did water sports for ABC.

At first, I wasn't sure why Larry Hoage had leaped up at our table and hollered, "Yippy-ty-yi-yee," but then I realized he had won the Emmy as the Outstanding Sports Host.

As Larry Hoage walked up to the stage and the mike, I tried to comfort Kathy Montgomery, who was in shock.

"This is the profession I've chosen," she said with sorrow in her voice.

"Only in America," I said to her. "It's a great country."

Larry Hoage's acceptance speech ran to such length that it practically cleared the grand ballroom. I only recall the beginning of it.

"Back in Orange County, California," he said, "the year was 1937 and a baby boy was born to the humble, hardworking couple of Bertha and Fred Hoage. This country was slowly digging its way out of a wingding of a financial depression. It was a hopeful year. Nobody could have known we were on the brink of another calamity—a gut-bustin' sidewinder of a shootin' war. Well, sir, that little curly-haired boy . . ."

From April through August I went to so many golf tournaments I felt like an alligator on a shirt pocket. CBS did tournaments in Augusta, Georgia; Hilton Head, South Carolina; Memphis; Columbus, Ohio; Washington, D.C.; Atlanta; Chicago; Philadelphia; Hartford; and Akron.

They were all the same event to me. Our cameras would point at the clouds because somebody said a golf ball was up there, and then our cameras would point at something rolling across the ground and going off the screen.

I learned to recognize a dramatic moment. That was when a golfer punched the air with his fist.

My job on the telecasts was relatively easy. I would sit up on a tower behind a green and try to guess which sets of tits in the gallery were following which golfers.

Every so often, the producer, a guy named Frank, would talk to me on the headset. He would say something like "Billy Clyde, holler down at the one in the green shorts. Tell her to turn around."

Occasionally, he would even tell me to say something on the air.

All I would have time to say was

"Here's Ben Crenshaw. There are some other guys with him. They're all gonna walk around on the green a while. Let's go to Sixteen."

Kathy Montgomery was promoted to associate producer at the first of the summer. She was assigned to golf, which pleased her because it was live.

She worked in the main control truck with the producer and director. Her responsibility was to cuss out the graphics person for getting scores wrong and to count everyone down to commercials.

At times by accident I would hear Kathy over my headset. She would be spun. "Thirty seconds till

Ideal commercial!" she would sing out. "Twenty-five
. . .twenty . . .fifteen!" That was before I heard Frank
say to her, "Kathy, if you want to stay in this business, take a Demerol."

Kathy was just another one of the guys now. She
was still a good friend, somebody to drink with, eat
dinner with, loaf around with on the road. She still
looked great. But all I saw when I looked at her was
another eager electronic journalist in faded jeans
and a sweatshirt.

One evening in July we were in Chicago and Kathy
asked if the two of us could go out to dinner, somewhere quaint and expensive, and talk about life its
ownself the way we used to.

She took us to a restaurant where there was nothing on the menu for me to eat but the ice in my
Scotch glass—Chicago's version of Enjolie's. That was
the night she confessed that it was all over with
Denise.

She said Denise had verbally attacked her for not
being committed to their way of life. Denise had
always been insanely jealous of me. And Denise had
broken it off and moved to Eugene, Oregon, with a
middle-distance runner named Janet.

"Denise was right," Kathy said. "I wasn't committed. I don't know why I got into that life. I'm a *girl*,
Billy Clyde. I really am! I can't tell you what a relief
it is to know it, to have a good feeling about it. You
know what? I've never stopped thinking about you.
You're probably the reason I'm back to normal."

"What are you saying, Kathy?" I couldn't avoid a
grin. "Does this mean you want to have an affair
with me now? I'm therapy?"

She said, "I just want to tell you how much I love
you. You're about the most important person in the
world to me."

"Kathy, I love Barbara Jane," I said. "One of these days I intend to get her back."

"You will. You two belong together. I can't imagine you and Barbara Jane with anyone but each other. All I want to be is your friend."

"You are."

"You mean it?"

"Of course."

"Can we be close like this after you and Barbara Jane are back together?"

"We'll be friends."

"Could we be sitting here like this?"

"Similar, I suppose."

"Promise we'll stay good friends, Billy Clyde."

"I promise."

"That's why I think it would be okay."

"What would?"

"If we made love tonight. Want to?"

I dare say most men in my position that evening would have had Kathy in bed as quickly as they could have hurled their bodies in front of a taxi. Even if they hadn't been aroused, they would have done it for research: to study all the tricks Kathy would surely have learned from Denise.

I, however, could only sit there and drink for another hour and giggle at the irony—and miss Barbara Jane more than ever.

On an August evening in New York, between a Hartford and an Akron, I dropped by Shake Tiller's apartment to see if I could tempt him to leave his clacker and go look for the perfect jukebox.

Priscilla answered the door with a joint in her hand. She was wearing a sleeveless blouse tucked inside a pair of old jeans that had been cut off at the pubes.

"There's a great horror movie on," she said. "Want to watch?"

"No thanks," I said. "Where's Tolstoy?"

"In his office. I gotta go. Something really weird's getting ready to climb out of a black hole."

Priscilla hurried back to her pile of pillows on the carpet in front of the 26-inch color Sony.

Shake's office was the spare bedroom in his apartment. It was a room with three walls of books, a manual clacker, a desk, a leather swivel chair, a coffeepot, eight cartons of cigarettes, six ashtrays, twelve bottles of correction fluid, a three-hole punch, a stack of white paper, and a big three-ring notebook in which there were 200 pages of *The Past*.

He didn't care to go out drinking. "I can't make any money on Third Avenue," he said. "I can make some here."

Our trip to Fort Worth for TCU's opening football game against Auburn was coming up. Tonsillitis Johnson and Artis Toothis were going to be unveiled to the world on the night of Sept. 5.

The word from T.J. was that Tonsillitis and Artis were looking good in two-a-days. Darnell Johnson had brought in four 280-pound junior college transfers to block for them. He had brought in a junior college quarterback, Jimmy Sibley, whose only job was to hand the ball off to them.

Tonsillitis and Artis appeared to be happy at TCU, principally because classes hadn't started yet and they had traded in their Datsun and Jaguar for turbo Porsches.

"I've done some math," Shake said in his office. "Big Ed's paying twenty-three thousand dollars apiece for Tonsillitis' fumbles. Every time Artis fumbles, Big Ed'll pay seventeen thousand. That's based on the current value of Artis' real estate holdings. Incidentally, Barbara Jane's coming down for the award."

That was more than I had known about it. I had spoken to Barb off and on during the summer. Her attitude about me hadn't changed that I could tell. She had seemed to be living a contented life in her Santa Monica beach house, playing tennis, going out with Jack Sullivan, and getting ready to appear on the cover of *People* magazine when the much-improved *Rita* series exploded on the new television season.

Shake divulged that Barbara Jane had been in New York for a week while I was away at a golf tournament. Shake had seen her often. Dinners and stuff.

"She misses you," he said.

"She knows where she used to live."

Before I let Shake get back to his clacker, I looked at his manuscript to give it the old first-paragraph test.

"Do you mind?" I said as I opened the notebook.

"Nope," he said. "It needs some lipstick and eye shadow."

I turned to the first page of *The Past,* and what I read was:

> Of all the things Karen could have told him about herself that night, the last thing he had expected to hear was that she had fallen in love with Diana.

"You know!" I said.

"Yeah."

"How?"

"I kept wondering why Kathy never fucked you. It finally dawned on me she had to be a lesbo princess."

"Who have you told?"

"Nobody."

"I don't believe you. It's too good to keep."

"I haven't told anybody," Shake insisted.

Despite the denial, the odds were heavily in favor of Shake telling Barb about Kathy.

There would have been two reasons. One, the joke on me was irresistible. Since the three of us were kids, Shake and Barb and I had never let the other two get away with anything. This wasn't making fun of somebody drinking a piña colada, but it might as well have been to Shake. People foolish enough to get married ought to know there would be your basic rage problems like Barb and I were having, and if you had any intelligence, you laughed at it and went on with your mortgages and casseroles.

And that reason tied in with the second. Shake would misread it as an opportunity to help me win back Barbara Jane—a woman, after all; a *wife*. It would prove that I couldn't have been having an affair. All I'd done was let myself get infatuated with a dyke, and that was funny, man—the kind of thing your clacker enjoyed putting into a novel.

But Shake would have been mistaken if he thought that it would help Barbara Jane overcome her disappointment in me. Sometimes, Shake wasn't the smartest guy he knew, especially when it came to marriage.

As much as anything, Barbara Jane's ego had been bruised. In a sense, it was immaterial whether I'd gone the distance with Kathy. The damage to my marriage had been done when I had been distracted by Kathy in the first place.

Barb would never know for sure if Kathy and I had screwed, just as I would never know for sure if Barbara Jane and Jack Sullivan had screwed, but I was willing to call it a dead heat and blame those adventures on our lifestyle. What was important now was that we stop punishing each other for those adventures.

Barb and I were both so strong-willed, so eaten up

with pride, that we ran the risk of staying apart forever just to prove we could.

My hope was that Barbara Jane would come to understand, as I think I had, that those relationships we stumbled into with Kathy Montgomery and Jack Sullivan could never have lasted.

I didn't see how Barb and I could ever outrun Paschal High, and that's what I thought would bring us back together eventually.

Some people might call it an affliction. I called it love.

All this being the case, there was just enough macho bullshit in my cells for me to prefer that Barbara Jane not learn the truth about the lesbo princess.

Which was why I asked Shake in his apartment that day to swear on a stack of Russian novels that he hadn't told Barb about Kathy.

"Hey, come on, B.C.," he said. "I've done some shitty things in my life, but I couldn't do that to a guy."

TWENTY

It was a clear night, not indecently hot for Texas in early September, and the stars that swept across the sky above the stadium made it look like the Skipper had called in a decorator.

TCU Stadium throbbed with an overflow crowd of 50,000 people, largely due to the 20,000 fanatics who had followed the Auburn Tigers to Fort Worth. A third of the stadium was a mosaic of Auburn blue-and-orange.

Shake and I were down on the field during the pre-game drills. We were taken with the fact that TCU's players weren't as nervous as TCU's coaches, but we didn't know what to make of it.

While T.J. and his assistants constantly slapped their hands together, whistled, yelled, and raced about, the TCU players limped around, stretched, tampered with their equipment.

In particular, Tonsillitis Johnson and Artis Toothis blundered through their warmups like men with sore muscles.

I kept looking at Big Ed's box on the 50-yard line in the West Side stands, twenty rows up from the TCU bench. I was watching for Barbara Jane, who had yet to arrive.

She was flying in for the game—and her alumni

award—on the Bookman Lear. Uncle Kenneth had volunteered to meet her at the airport and bring her to the stadium.

Big Ed and Big Barb were visions of purple. Big Ed wore a purple blazer, a purple tie with a white shirt, and a white Stetson. Big Barb was resplendent in a purple suit and white Garbo hat.

In the box with Big Ed and Big Barb was Darnell Johnson, the assistant to the president of Bookman Oil & Gas. Darnell had neglected to wear anything purple, but he looked as prosperous as ever in his suit, vest, and tie.

Now the TCU band and cheerleaders, led by Sandi, formed a corridor through which the Horned Frogs retreated to the dressing room for T.J. Lambert's final words of encouragement and advice.

Shake and I went into the dressing room behind the team.

T.J. faced the squad and hung his head, waiting for everyone to quiet down before he spoke. The moment came, and in a somber tone, he said:

"Men, I don't have to tell you what you're up against tonight. They're the national champions. They're as good a team as I ever saw. They're waitin' for you out there like pallbearers. TCU don't mean dookie to Aubrin. But you know what I think's gonna happen? I think we're goin' out there and strap so much quick on 'em, they'll have to get their ass sewed up wih barbed wire! Now let's do it! Fuck Aubrin!"

There were no whoops from the players. They left the dressing room laughing and joking.

Standing at the dressing-room door, I felt a little rush of purple as I said to Artis Toothis:

"Go get 'em, Artis."

"I got the claim check, baby," he said. "We pickin' up baggage tonight!"

To Tonsillitis Johnson, I said, "Have a good one, hoss."

"Ain't nothin' to it," he said. "We gonna hit 'em with a pocketful of flash."

Shake and I were back on the field behind the TCU bench as the two squads knelt for a prayer before the opening kickoff. Auburn may have been praying, but there was little doubt in my mind that T.J. was reminding his lads that it was more blessed to die at birth than fumble a football.

The teams took the field for the kickoff. That was when I saw Barbara Jane and Uncle Kenneth come down the aisle to join Big Ed and Big Barb and Darnell in the box.

Barbara Jane waved at us. She also waved, smiled, shrugged, and gestured at people she knew in the stands—and signed a couple of autographs before she reached the box.

"I know that girl from somewhere," Shake said.

Auburn kicked off to TCU and the ball sailed out of the end zone. The offensive unit of the Horned Frogs trotted out to their own 20-yard line in their dark purple jerseys and purple helmets, Tonsillitis wearing No. 1 and Artis wearing No. 99.

On TCU's first play from scrimmage, Tonsillitis took a pitchout from Jimmy Sibley, the transfer quarterback. All Tonsillitis did on his first carry as a collegian was break five tackles and rumble 80 yards for a touchdown.

"God damn," said Shake, "he hit that cornerback so hard, the sumbitch'll be left-handed the rest of his life!"

I looked up at the box in time to see Big Ed and Darnell swap high-fives.

The Frogs kicked off to Auburn. The Tigers couldn't make a first down and punted out of bounds on TCU's 37-yard line. On the first play from there,

Artis Toothis took a pitchout from Jimmy Sibley, sped around a corner, and nobody touched him as he went 63 yards for another touchdown.

Now, up in the box, Big Ed Bookman and Darnell Johnson, a white man and a black man—in public, in an old Texas cowtown—embraced and kissed each other on the cheek.

That was a sight I wish I could have shared with all the semi-holy reformers who want to fuck with college football.

The score was 42 to 3 at the half. Tonsillitis Johnson carried the ball nine times for 249 yards and three touchdowns. Artis Toothis carried the ball 12 times for 187 yards and two touchdowns.

Before the half ended, and just after Tonsillitis had plowed 16 yards for his third touchdown, I had worked my way over to T.J. on the sideline and said, "Like we've always known, coaching makes the difference."

T.J. had looked like a man who was half-spellbound, half-brainsick.

He had said, "I ain't sure my heart can take it, son. Them two fuckers is gonna scatter everybody like monkey shit!"

Barbara Jane and Uncle Kenneth came down out of the stands and onto the field as the TCU band performed at halftime. Chancellor Troy (Tex) Edgar and a gentleman from the alumni association appeared. They were waiting to escort Barb and me to the center of the field to give us our awards. Shake Tiller went to the dressing room to relieve himself—to "shake hands with the unemployed," an expression he had picked up in England.

As Barb and I kissed politely, I said, "You've done a lot for this university. I want you to know we appreciate it."

"How are you?" said Barb.

"Overwhelmed with gratitude. Filled with renewed devotion to the campus that expanded my intellectual horizons."

"Other than that?"

"Not worth a shit." I said. "You?"

Uncle Kenneth said, "If I'd made a bet on marital discord, you kids would have brought me in crisp. How long you been separated, eight months? I'd have gone with the Under, sure as the world."

"Dumb guys have been robbing smart guys for years," I said. "A crooked zebra told me that."

"I've been a dumb guy," said Barbara Jane. "I've been robbing myself."

Barbara Jane's look was the one I'd been waiting for.

I hate to put it like this, but her look made my poor heart swell up.

I said, "Would a guy assume from your demeanor that he's happily married again?"

"A guy could assume that."

I glanced at Uncle Kenneth. He had the confident smile of a man who had shoved it all in on a mortal lock.

"Does your director approve of you being here?" I asked.

"He didn't get a vote."

"I've been thinking about the bicoastal life," I said. "It might not be so bad. I like Fatburger."

"I miss football," said Barb. "Can I go to some of the games with you? Would there be room for me in the booth?"

"I love you, Barb," I said with as much persuasion as I ever had.

"I love you," she said. "I never stopped, you know."

Before I could grab her up in my arms, we were suddenly marched onto the field by the chancellor and the gentleman from the alumni association.

The voice on the P.A. system said something about the awards. We were handed plaques. There were handshakes. I don't know that either of us heard any of the words that were spoken. We just kept looking at each other.

And now we walked away, slowly, over to the sideline, and then toward the south end zone where we could see Shake Tiller in the distance. Shake was leaning against the goal post.

"So Biff," said Barb. "Did you make it with that time bandit from Berkeley?"

Time bandit.

Barbara Jane's review of Kathy Montgomery had finally come in.

I gave the question some serious thought.

"Barb, I know you don't want me to lie to you again," I said. "I . . .yes, I did."

"Ha!"

Barbara Jane threw her head back and laughed raucously. It was honest laughter, a sound that was so much a part of her—and our past.

"You macho bastard," she said, still smiling, "you *would* say that, wouldn't you?"

"Do you like Shake's book? I hate it."

"He told me about Kathy, but that's not why I'm back, Biff."

"Who do you want to play in the movie? I'd like to play me.

"Kathy's a neat role."

I pulled Barbara Jane to me. We kissed as if we were all alone on the field. And then we kept walking. And in the stadium where I'd heard so many cheers, where the scent of winning was in the air again, it occurred to me that I'd scored the greatest victory of my life. Barbara Jane had come back.

We met Shake Tiller at the south end of the field. Nobody said anything. We just looked around in the stadium, and back at each other, and the three of us started to laugh.

I guess you could say we were laughing at life its ownself as we stood there in an old familiar huddle under a spray of Texas stars.

About the Author

Life Its Ownself is Dan Jenkins' fifth novel, his eighth book. His published fiction includes *Semi-Tough* (1972), which is also available from Signet, plus *Dead Solid Perfect* (1974), *Limo* (1976), and *Baja Oklahoma* (1981). Mr. Jenkins is a native of Fort Worth, Texas, who has lived in New York City for the past 23 years. As a Senior Writer for *Sports Illustrated*, he has written more than 500 articles on the subjects of football and golf.

Mr. Jenkins is married to the former June Burrage of Fort Worth, the co-owner of two highly acclaimed restaurants in Manhattan (*Juanita's* and *Summerhouse*). Their daughter, Sally, is a sportswriter for the *The Washington Post*, and their sons, Marty and Danny, are working in television and photography in Texas and New York.

Super Sports Books from SIGNET

(0451)

☐ **THE ILLUSTRATED SPORTS RECORD BOOK by Zander Hollander and David Schulz.** Here, in a single book are 350 records with stories and photos so vivid they'll make you feel that "you are there." Once and for all you'll be able to settle your sports debates on who holds what records and how he, or she, did it. (111818—$2.50)*

☐ **THE COMPLETE HANDBOOK OF BASEBALL, 1984 Season, edited by Zander Hollander.** The essential guide for every baseball fan including: the greatest thieves in baseball history; all time award winners, from Cy Young to MVP; Batting and Home Run Champions from 1900; and four decades of World Series Results. With 250 profiles, 250 photos, career records, rosters, schedules, statistics—the most comprehensive handbook available, from spring training to the World Series! (128311—$3.95)*

☐ **THE LEGEND OF DR. J: The Story of Julius Erving by Marty Bell.** An electrifying action-profile of the fabulous multi-millionaire superstar. "Graceful and admirable!"—*Dick Schaap* (121791—$2.95)

☐ **EVERYTHING YOU ALWAYS WANTED TO KNOW ABOUT SPORTS*** *and didn't know where to ask by Mickey Herskowitz and Steve Perkins.** Here is the book that answers every question a sports fan ever had in the back of his mind and tells the truth about all the whispered rumors of the sports world. (124715—$2.75)

*Prices slightly higher in Canada

Thrilling Reading from SIGNET